THE PAINTER'S DAUGHTERS

Emily Howes

Simon & Schuster
New York   London   Toronto   Sydney   New Delhi

Simon & Schuster
1230 Avenue of the Americas
New York, NY 10020

First Simon & Schuster hardcover edition February 2024

SIMON & SCHUSTER and colophon are registered trademarks of Simon & Schuster, LLC

Simon & Schuster: Celebrating 100 Years of Publishing in 2024

For information about special discounts for bulk purchases, please contact Simon & Schuster Special Sales at 1-866-506-1949 or business@simonandschuster.com.

The Simon & Schuster Speakers Bureau can bring authors to your live event. For more information or to book an event, contact the Simon & Schuster Speakers Bureau at 1-866-248-3049 or visit our website at www.simonspeakers.com.

Manufactured in the United States of America

1   3   5   7   9   10   8   6   4   2

Library of Congress Cataloging-in-Publication Data is available on file.

ISBN 978-1-6680-2138-5
ISBN 978-1-6680-2140-8 (ebook)

For my mother

And as for sweet Peggy Gainsborough, she lived her own unselfish life, and found her full complement of happiness in the love of those so dear to her, and never regretted the position and title which had been, as it were, almost forced upon her.

Emily Baker, from *Peggy Gainsborough:*
The Famous Painter's Daughter, 1909

If you have no dreams, you will live within them.

Robert Burton, from
An Anatomy of Melancholy, 1628

PART ONE

PEGGY

Patina

First, the canvas.

Not one, but many. Great oblongs carried in and out, wrapped carefully in shrouds. Like bodies, we always thought as we watched them from the window. Like great stiff bodies, short, tall, thin, and wide, one for each of them as they came in their carriages and swept away again. And underneath the shroud, stripped back in privacy, the sheer blank expanse of it, the bareness of it, like naked skin.

The tools in his studio are meticulously arranged, like instruments in an orchestra; easel, palette, smudge pan, straining frame, primed cloth, maulstick, pencils as sharp as a pin or as fat as a finger, Dutch quills and swan quills, jeweling pencils and bristle pencils; a brush for every fleck in your eye, to smooth every coarse hair. Devices to conjure life, and then soften it back into perfection.

It is Saturday afternoon. Late August, the air hot and still in the shuttered house. And my father is beginning something, beginning someone.

The door of the studio is ajar. All is quiet. We loiter, Molly and I, hoping to be seen.

He is standing with his back to us, his fingers rubbing his cheek where the afternoon whiskers are beginning to grow. The canvas in front of him, waiting. In one hand he is holding something small and white. He dips it into a shallow bowl and raises it, dripping.

A muffled giggle, a creaking floorboard. He half turns.

"Now, who might that be?"

We try for silence, but Molly steps on my foot.

"Reveal yourselves this moment or be tipped into the paste water!"

He knows it is us.

"Hello," I say. My voice is too loud in the afternoon silence.

He sees us in the doorway and stretches out his hand. He looks hot and weary.

"Come in, you vagabonds, and let me see you for a moment before I work."

And then he adds, as we push the door too eagerly and it bangs against the wall, "But I have a dreadful head on me, so absolutely no singing, dancing, shrieking, disagreeing, and most particularly, no dangling from my neck."

Molly is fond of dangling from his neck although she is older than me, and heavier.

"What are you doing?" I ask him.

"He is washing the canvas," Molly says. "I've seen him before."

"Not washing it, Moll, but getting it ready. Come here and I will show you."

The studio smells of paint and soap and stale beer and some other smell I do not know, but that rests on my father's hands and hair and on the sleeves of his jacket.

"Now then," he says, "the Captain first, as she is the smallest. Hold out your hand, Peg."

4

I stretch out my upturned palm, and into it he puts a stone, rough and white like bone. And then he wraps his own large hand around it, guiding, dipping the pumice down into the bowl of water and bringing it out. Together we move it over the canvas, smoothing, working away at the knots and bumps. His hand is red and lined, a working hand, and mine is a shell inside it.

"That's it, my Captain," he says. "Gently now."

We dip the stone again, and there is no sound but our breathing and the water sloshing gently in the bowl, and then the rasp of the stone against the skin of the canvas.

Molly hangs beside me, watching.

"When is it my turn?" she says. "When is my turn? Is it my turn now?"

"Wait a moment, my Molly."

"It isn't your turn, Moll," I say. "It's still mine."

Water trickles down my arm, tracking its way toward the sleeve of my dress, and I want to stop it tickling, but I do not want it ever to stop being my turn.

Molly leans in, brown curls falling over her face, and she is reaching out to tap our father's arm, to ask again, but sharp footsteps cut across the floor. It is our mother, fat beads of sweat on her upper lip, coming at us in a flurry of words.

Lady Astor is coming, she is saying, to see about a portrait, and we must leave at once, and Peggy, go and change your dress immediately, it has splashes and drips all down the front of it, and what are we doing in here anyway, tormenting our father, who has plenty to do that is not taking care of little girls, and dear God, Thomas, must it always smell of beer in here, and out, out and find something else to do. Out, out, out!

And so we are banished, and hurry from the room, my hands still dripping. Together we slip back through the hallway, past the carefully hung portraits that say, *Look what happens here, look who you can be*—two small girls vanishing like twin ghosts up the stairs off to find another game, another way to pass the time. We are invited in together, we are conspirators together; welcomed, banished, summoned, always together. And when Molly forgets, I remember for her.

Later, when the canvas is smooth and dry, unmarred and unmarked and ready, he will show us how to paint the first layer, a rich ochre red, the color of earth and blood all mixed up together. Because the earth color will not kill the other colors, he tells us, and we think it is funny, the red letting all the other colors live. Red for justice, virtue, and defense; green for hope; carnation for subtlety and deceit; popinjay for wantonness. Hidden messages to warn, to praise, to flatter. Each one blended into the edge of a ribbon or the fall of the light from the sun. It is a form of magic that only he knows.

Ever since those early days I have thought of colors as having their own life, their own agency, as if they are characters in a story, clamoring to be heard. Now I am the kind of green you get in shadows, terre verte, perhaps, the muted underpaint. That is what secrets do. But as a child in our Ipswich days I was pink, the tender pink of flesh, pale and iridescent against the dark Suffolk earth. And Molly too. We were the same color then.

Frame

Our house is broad and made of white stone, and it sits right in the middle of Ipswich, on Foundation Street. Inside it is always dark, from winter to summer, with stairs leading down to the hall where the walls are covered in face after face, red-hatted admirals and beady-eyed clergymen who stare back at you from their dusty rectangles. Our mother in her fancy bonnet is there. Our grandfather in his bob wig. On our father's side, for we must not mention our mother's. And there, in the center, high above our own heads, we too hang, twinned, in a vast frame. We aren't for sale, exactly. We are selling.

Look up and see what my father can make you, for the right price. That is what we are saying. He can stop time. He can hold you inside the knots and flourishes of the gilded wood, caught in movement, caught on an in-breath. The shadowy greens merge and fold over one another in layers of paint: umber, burnt sienna, caledonite. I am reaching out for a butterfly, a cabbage white, the kind we find in the Ipswich hedges. My fingers hover over its creamy wings. It is my hand, I always think, and it is not. The hand in front of me has cat scratches on the back, and something sticky from lunch on the thumb, and dirt under the fingernails. The hand on the wall glows. It is perfect. We step through the shadows, our dresses gleaming lead white and Naples yellow. I

7

look up at my painted self and wonder what happens next. What I would do if I caught it.

We must stay out of sight when customers come, but we watch them looking at our painted faces, safe in our hiding spot behind the banister. Molly puts her arm round my shoulder, and we crouch, as the silk slippers and brown leathers of the Ipswich gentry shuffle in and out like small creatures, wearing away the polish on the floorboards. When a particularly important person comes, a squire perhaps, or his small, stiff, powdered wife, my mother stands in the hallway and fans the door for half an hour beforehand, because when the wind blows the right way, you can smell the warm, sharp scent of the hops from the brewery in our house. This, says my mother, is inelegant. Molly whispers to me that she thinks it is quite inelegant to stand flapping the door about for all that time like a chicken trying to take flight, which I think is the funniest thing I have ever heard. For a while we pretend to be chickens, leaping over the herb beds in the kitchen garden, clucking and beating our wings, until Molly trips and bangs her nose on one of the sticks that divide the plants, and there is blood, and crying, and our mother comes out to tell us off.

In the rest of the house the walls are not covered in faces, not yet. They are a patchwork of countryside views, of brooks and fields and peasants and carts, and of trees that billow out as if the wind is moving the paint. That is what my father loves, and when there are no faces left to finish, he will take his easel and some bread and cheese in a napkin and come back late, red from the sun. Sometimes, if we are lucky, we are given brush boxes and water cans to carry, and trail after him all the way across the fields like the wise men bearing gifts. When his eyes begin to narrow and don't see us anymore, we race off to play, on the hunt for tiny river creatures or broken treasures washed up in the Orwell mud.

And then we hear our mother's voice, as we always do, fretful, raised. "Thomas, I cannot allow it. They are running about

Ipswich like wildcats. It will do us no good." And our father will say, "It is how I grew up, Margaret, and it did me no harm," and, "I will not have my daughters packaged up in silk before their time," and, "Let them have their freedom, for now, Margaret." And on she will rail, but on this one, single point, she cannot dominate him.

When she is petulant and defeated, he will put his arm round her waist and say, "Come now, Margaret," and she will say, "Do not kiss me, Thomas, for your breath is extremely beery," but he will pull her toward him and she will lean back and twist her round, reluctant head to let his lips meet hers.

As well as his yellow fields and his carts in brown rivers, he paints the two of us, over and over again. Our arms wrapped round each other; a closeness so thick you can feel it, our gaze always steady. In brown dresses as gleaners in the field, which we hate, and in our silks, reaching up to fix each other's hair, which makes our arms ache. But when he calls, "Moll! Captain! Come and be daubed," then whatever we are doing, even if it is something absorbing and wonderful, we leave it without looking back and run.

When you stand in the muted light of his studio, it is the quietest place you will ever be. It is not a clunking, echoing silence, the kind you get in church. It is a contained quiet, a silence so thick that your every move, even the rise of your chest as you breathe, is magnified. It is as if he is casting a spell, and he must take a part of you for his magic to work.

The last time before we grow up, he paints us with a cat. We are rather fond of the cat, who is called Barnstaple, and who slides in through open windows to find the warmth of our bed. He is fat and ginger and cross at being immortalized in oil. He wriggles out of our arms so persistently and furiously that in the end there is only the outline, the shadow of him left, mouth open in complaint, ghostly teeth bared in protest at his captivity.

9

My father intends to paint the cat in later, but Barnstaple is a prodigious wanderer, and continues his campaign of resistance. Whenever my father has a spare moment, Barnstaple has gone mousing, and will answer to no calls or bowls of herring laid out tantalizingly on the kitchen step. And if my father spies him curled up in the kitchen and creeps in with a pencil to take a rough sketch, the unperturbed Barnstaple will partially open his eyes, leap down from his perch, stretch magnificently, and pad softly out the door.

When Lady Astor has vanished into the afternoon in her cloud of heavy silks, and my father has emerged from the studio, mopping his brow, and my mother has asked him forty questions about timings and payment, we rest for a little while in the sitting room, just the four of us.

We are lying on the floor building a palace from our old blocks, and my mother is at the table polishing a silver teapot with a pot of something so black that it does not look like it will turn anything silver, even if she scrubbed at it forever. My father sits, one leg crossed over the other, absorbed in his reading, fanning himself with a pamphlet.

Molly yawns, wrinkling her nose. I can see all her teeth in a neat little line, and her shiny pink and wet gums, and what looks like a piece of lunchtime ham too.

"What a sight, Molly Gainsborough." My mother looks up from the teapot in horror. "Close your mouth immediately."

Molly shuts it with a snap.

"Like a codfish," my mother says, shaking her head. "My goodness."

She comes and puts her hand on Molly's forehead, and I wish she would do the same to me, for it is so cool and comforting. "It is all your nighttime wandering that sets you off yawning in the day."

She looks at my father and shakes her head again, as if it is his fault, but he continues to read, unmoved.

"Thomas. I said it is the wandering at night that sets her off yawning in the day."

"Hmm," my father says, which is what he often says when he does not want to talk about something.

It is true that Molly walks in the night, slipping from the covers and disappearing so that I wake to find a warm, empty space where she is supposed to be, and even though it happens all the time, I am always frightened by it. Now I have started sleeping so lightly that I wake before she begins to move, and can catch her to avoid the fuss that will happen if she gets out and wakes my mother. The arguments, and the worries, and the violet shadows under my mother's eyes the next day.

Molly is only playing games, that is what I think, but no matter how much I beg her, she pretends not to remember anything about it in the morning. My mother says we should lock the door, but I beg her not to, for it gives me nightmares. I imagine us burning alive in our bedroom, screaming down into the road, or rattling at the doorknob while the flames eat us up.

"It is not right." My mother shakes her head.

"She will grow out of it," my father says easily. "It is common enough for a child."

"Not everything is easy, Tom," my mother says, rubbing hard at the teapot as if my father's good mood can be removed with the tarnish. "You walk through life as if everything fixes itself."

That seems to me to be a very nice way to walk through life, but something about it scrapes at my mother for reasons I cannot understand. They are like a pair of scales, I think. When he goes up, she goes down, and it is very hard to balance them.

"The girls are healthy. You overworry, Margaret."

She chews the inside of her lip. "Perhaps."

"We should be in a city." She puts down the cloth and looks

at him, a weary hand on her hip. "Where the girls may learn to behave in accordance with their class and lineage. And where you can get on."

"The time is not yet."

"You cannot stay painting in the backwaters forever."

My father only drums his fingers on the table, and stays silent. Why must my mother make everything difficult? I wonder. Why can't she let life be easy?

And yet sometimes only my mother will do, for all my father's good humor. The way she knows how to bandage up a cut without it being too tight, or make the right sort of hot milk and whisky to cure an earache just enough so that you forget about it. She is very good at that. Sometimes she tells us stories at bedtime, secret ones that she whispers into the dark. And best of all, when she is feeling merry, or if she has a moment to herself, she lets us open her locked drawer of treasures and take them all out. We put them one by one on her bed and hold them up while she sits and watches us.

There is a necklace of green marbled beads, and a hairpiece with silk ribbon shot through it, and a pair of earrings that look like drops of water. There is a looking glass, and a little gold box with the letter *F* on its lid and a swirling pattern all around it. The box is so tiny that it fits in my palm and disappears when I close my fist. I love to play with it, to look at the tiny hinges and the pattern of red birds and green flowers. It is so beautiful and precious that it makes me feel strange inside. It is also a mystery, for Molly and I do not know anyone beginning with *F*.

"It belonged to my mother" is all our mother will say. And then, when we press her, "It was a gift."

I try to grasp at the threads she leaves dangling, to find out more, for my mother's mother is never spoken of, and those particular threads are always pulled again before I can catch them.

"What was her name?"

Fiona, I think. Fiorentina. Francesca. Florence.

"Margaret, like yours and mine."

I must look disappointed, for my mother says, "My goodness, Peggy, it is a perfectly pleasant and elegant name."

Then she says, abruptly, "Put that down before you fiddle the hinges off." And she tells us, as she always does, that it is time to tidy up and put everything back neatly in its place, or the next time we ask we will not be allowed to play with it. Fun, with my mother, is kept tightly buttoned up in case it escapes and causes mischief. We put the treasures safely back into their drawer and turn the key.

The summer stays hot, so hot that in the kitchen the butter melts into greasy pools, and flies fuss stupidly around the meat. Molly and I creep in, shoeless, to try to cool our bare soles on the tiles, but our mother dispatches us with a single word without looking up from the puff of dough on the table.

"Out."

"But it's so hot I'm going to die," Molly says.

My mother gives a deft flick of her cloth, knocking a blue-bottle to the ground so that it lies stunned, its little black legs wiggling. Then she lifts the cloth as if she will flick us too.

"Out," she says again, and we dart away through the kitchen door.

I can still easily squeeze through the hole in the fence that runs along the back of the garden, but Molly is getting too big, and the edges scrape her arms, leaving chalky marks across her skin.

We are too hot to talk, and for a while we wander aimlessly in the fields behind our house. And then Molly finds something and calls out, crouching down in the long grass. At first, I think it is a poppy, a splotch of black and red in the sea of green, but when I go up close, I can see that it is a butterfly twitching on the ground. One wing is torn across, so it flutters in helpless circles on the summer grass. I cup my fingers and carry it back across two fields, its broken wing brushing so gently against my skin that I want to laugh and let go. But I keep it safe all the way to the kitchen door, where my father has come for a bite to eat, as he likes to call it, sitting at the rough table with flour falling onto his waistcoat as he chews on a bun.

He peers down at the butterfly and its ragged wing.

"A red admiral. An owl got at it, perhaps, or some other bird."

I imagine it with a tiny red admiral's hat, wounded in a naval battle with another military butterfly and left for dead.

My father fetches an old tin from his studio and empties it out, puts a hole in the top, and gives it to us. We carry it upstairs to the secrecy of our bedroom, hiding it behind our backs from our mother, who will say that insects belong outside. Once safe, we close the bedroom door, remove the lid, and stand in silence watching the butterfly's panicked flapping.

It is not white like the butterfly from the painting. Beneath two dots of red, its wings are a smooth, velvety black. Lamp black. My father sometimes tells us the stories of where paint comes from. Ivory black, from burnt bones. Vine black, from the charred stems of grapes. Indigo and madder from plants and flowers. Sienna and umber from the earth. And lamp black from the soot of the lamps that burn themselves out across cities. Molly does not listen, because she is not interested in that sort of thing, but I learn them all, and say them to myself in the dark.

"We must mend it," Molly says decidedly.

"How?"

"We must sew it up, like physicians."

"How?" I say again, because I am not very good yet at sewing cloth, never mind butterflies, but I like the sound of this game.

She sends me to fetch her embroidery, and I trot faithfully

downstairs like a dog to get it. When I return, I bark and stick my tongue out to pant.

"Good dog," she says, taking the needle and thread and snapping it from her work so that it hangs loose. "Now you must stop playing games, Peg, for this is a real surgery."

I crane my neck to watch as she threads the eye with a lick, then pushes the needle into the delicate wing. The butterfly struggles, its good wing beating frantically against the metal box, and Molly starts to draw the needle across it with a trembling hand.

"Lie still and stop wriggling," she says in our mother's voice, bending low over it, her brow furrowed. "Don't make a fuss, for it will not help you at all."

I stand with my arms folded in the sticky heat. When you are the smallest you often watch, instead of doing, and I like it that way. My fingers are clumsier than Molly's, and I always prick my finger just as the thimble falls off, and anyway I like to watch her cleverness. But my heart aches for the butterfly, trying so hard to escape while the needle pierces its papery wing.

"We are hurting it."

"We are saving it," Molly says, "and when you are saving something you have to make it feel worse before it feels better. The patient does not know what is good for it."

She looks at me, and then pauses the surgery, her needle poised.

"Remember when Papa had the toothache?"

I do remember it, very well, his furious row with the physician about the plan to yank it out with a metal instrument, and my mother intervening, flapping at him and telling him not to be a coward and how the pain will be worth the suffering. And then the silence after, and how relieved I felt when he lay in his armchair clutching the bloodied cloth to his cheek, breathing in and out as though he had run a race.

I nod, and Molly nods back, and carries on her work. But as the needle pushes the thread back and forth, the struggling grows weaker. I chew on my nails, hoping and hoping, but the painted wing begins to beat less rapidly. Then it stills. Molly puts down the needle with a click on the table.

"Poor butterfly," she says. "It was no good."

Hot tears bubble up from somewhere inside, and even though I know Molly will say that crying does not help, I cannot stop them. I am sad that the butterfly has died, but I am even sadder because I thought that we could save it.

"It is the shock, it is the shock, Peggy," Molly says, as if we have lost a relative. "Don't cry about it. We tried to make it better, that's all." She puts her arms around me, warm and damp with the heat of the day, and I let myself be comforted, my tears soaking her neck. All the time the butterfly lies limp in its tin, and I think about how strange it is that something dead can be so much stiller than something that was never alive in the first place.

When I have wiped my nose, and Molly has fussed over me, and kissed the top of my head although she cannot quite reach it, I am sent back downstairs again to steal a spoon from the kitchen so we can dig a hole to bury it in the garden. We carry the tin out to the elm tree, and in its shade, we scoop out the dry soil to make a hole. Then we tip the butterfly in and cover it over so that an animal can't dig it up and eat it, which, Molly says, is a very real concern.

We crouch barefoot over the tiny grave and recite a poem about a butterfly that my father showed us in a book, but Molly gets lost halfway through, so I do the rest on my own. Molly is better at knowing what to do, and at making me feel less worried about things, and at sewing, but words have a habit of skidding out of her mind.

Craquelure

When the summer heat fades, it is time to pick blackberries, which grow every year in a lane so narrow and scratchy it can hardly be called a lane at all. The September wind blusters across the fields, flapping at our dresses as though an invisible dog has got hold of the hem. We are wading through the slimy puddles, laughing and shivering as our feet sink into the muck. Bracing, Papa calls it.

"It's too cold," Molly says, pretending to chatter her teeth, which are still stained with purple.

"It is bracing."

Mud pushes its way up between my toes, squelchy and lovely, as we skirt along the edges of the lane, gripping the stone wall and trying not to slip.

"Where are they again?"

"By the white gate."

We have left our slippers and balled-up stockings under a bush. When the mud got too deep, Molly said we should turn back, but the blackberries are turning and will be gone soon, shriveled up or pecked away by birds. And I want them. So I nagged and pulled at her dress and called her boring and begged until she came too. It is always me who pulls us into trouble, one way or another.

17

I turn and see her behind me, ankle-deep in mud, her tin jug dangling at her side. The wind pushes her hair back so that she looks like a man without his wig on. I tell her, and she pulls a face. I do not know why I always want to say mean things to Molly, and sometimes I promise myself I will not do it anymore. But it always comes back like an itch, and when she is being quiet like this I can't help it.

"You look like Samuel Kilderbee of Ipswich," I say, and a bubble of mirth rises up inside me, delicious. Samuel Kilderbee of Ipswich is one of the portraits in our hall of people I always think my father secretly did not like, but had to paint as if he did. There are two paintings on top of each other, the one that Samuel Kilderbee sees, in which he looks very dignified, and the one containing my father's real feelings, in which he does not. In both, however, he has very funny hair.

I wait for Molly to pull another face, or tell me to shut up, or that my own hair is silly too, or that it is me who looks like Samuel Kilderbee of Ipswich. Instead, she only says, "I am too cold." Her voice is faint, and not her own.

"Come on, stupid, let's race to the gate," I say.

But she doesn't move.

"Moll. Molly."

She just stands, looking up at the white sky, the wind buffeting her blank face.

"Molly, stop it," I say again, and my voice comes out small.

Her eyes flick onto mine, but she is not there. She is not in her face. It is like when the shutters have been left open at night, exposing the squares of black window behind.

"Molly." My breath is shallow in my chest. "Why won't you answer me?"

Panic claws at me like a cat. I wonder suddenly if it is like the time I pretended to be dead. I lay on the bedroom floor and kept on pretending to be dead, until Molly stopped saying that she knew I was joking, and started to be afraid.

She is doing that, I tell myself. She is doing a trick, to make me frightened, although it is not like her, but perhaps I deserve it and she is teaching me a lesson.

"Molly, stop pretending." My voice is wobbly. I reach out and take her by the arms, which are icy, and I shake her, gently at first, then harder. "Stop it."

But she only looks at me with the same nothingness in her eyes, her slack mouth still stained with purple.

"Molly."

I have never felt so small, as if I am far away at the end of a tunnel. Tears are forming in my eyes, and they sting against the bite of the wind.

And then, somewhere in the distance, carrying over the fields, I hear another voice. "Where are your shoes?" the voice is saying. "Where are your *shoes*?" I look up, and there is our mother, beating her way across the wind-rattled lane, and the lean figure of my father somewhere behind, and relief at the sight of them floods through me so fast that I think I will fall over.

"You naughty, *naughty* little wretches!" she is calling. "Where are your shoes and stockings? *Where are they?*"

"In the hedge," I say.

And my mother's face, red and blotchy with fury and exertion, blanches as she comes close enough to hear.

"They are *where*?"

"In the hedge," I say again, and I start to laugh in spite of myself. Molly looks at me, and I see that she is coming back into her face again, confused, unsure. Relief hits me again in a great wave.

"What is *wrong* with them?" My mother looks back to my father. "What is *wrong*?"

But he only says, "It is cold, Margaret, and we must get them home. Molly is blue with it." He takes his coat and wraps it around Moll. "An adventure gone wrong, am I correct, Peg?"

I nod and rub my goose-bumped arms, and lean into his side, happy to be rescued. It is an adventure gone wrong, that is all. It is only naughtiness, and everything is easy, as my father wishes it. Things will fix themselves. But my mother rattles on and on, the wind tugging at her shawl, and although I try to shut it out, I cannot help it. For the first time her worries sink into me, right into the bottom of my stomach, and sit there like a stone.

"How are you to work," my mother is saying, "how are you to make a living if you must go roaming the countryside to sort out your wild children? This is what I feared when I—it will not do, Thomas."

My father walks on, an arm around me, and one hand in his pocket, as if he cannot hear her.

"They cannot be left to roam like this across the fields," she continues, breathless. "Shoeless! Shoeless and—and shivering like *urchins*. It is not *normal*, Thomas. This is not what young girls should be doing who wish to grow up well, who wish to have success and avoid—difficulty. This is why we must move to a city, to nip this in the bud, this—this *wild behavior*."

"Now, where exactly did you leave these shoes?" my father says to me, and my mother tightens her shawl around her in exasperation.

But when we get to the white gate, our slippers and stockings are nowhere to be seen. We search everywhere, until our hands are crisscrossed with thin red scratches from poking inside the hedge that runs the whole length of the lane, but they have gone. Perhaps they have been pinched, or hidden for a joke, but it is no use. They cannot be found, and we trudge home barefoot to sit on the wall while Sarah comes out from the kitchen with pails of freezing water to slosh the mud off.

The argument rages downstairs long after we are sent to bed.

Molly sits next to me, silent, knees hunched up against her chest. My mother says things she does not know we can hear. About how this is what she feared when she married my father. About the mistake she made, although I do not know what the mistake is, and about her father, God rest his soul, and our blood, all the words that tangle up and come out when the adults think no one is listening.

There is talk again of leaving Ipswich, leaving our fields and our house. But all I can think about is where Molly went. And what I will do if it happens again. Perhaps it was because I teased her. Perhaps it was because I told her we should take our shoes and stockings off and leave them by the hedge. I cannot help it. I am always having ideas, and itches of things I cannot resist. But then perhaps Molly was pretending all along. Playing a game to scare me. I wish my mother would come up and tell us one of her stories, drawing me onto her lap and tucking her arm around my waist so that I feel as if she is tying herself to me. But she is too cross.

I climb silently from my bed into Molly's and tuck myself up around her and breathe in her warm hair smell, and try not to think about the spidery fear that has found its way inside me. Of my mother's words. "It is not *normal*, Thomas." Of the shutter coming down over Molly's eyes. Of how small and alone I felt in the lane. Of the way she vanished from her own face, and how nobody saw it but me.

The next day we are brought downstairs and told that we are not to go roaming on our own again. I do not tell anyone that I do not want to. That I suddenly feel frightened of it and would rather stay in the house. But the sun has come out and turned the fields golden, and by the evening we look longingly out the window to where the swallows are playing their wild, funny games in the last of the light.

"We could go," Molly says hesitantly. "Just for a little bit, while no one is here."

"No," I say. "I don't like it when they are angry with each other."

Molly leans her forehead against the window. "Well, that's all the time."

"No, it isn't."

Molly rolls her eyes. "I suppose you're going to do another one of your *romantic drawings*."

I like to draw my mother and father together, happy, dancing, or getting married, although it doesn't look exactly like them, and it is not fair of Molly to tease me about it.

"Why didn't you answer me in the lane?" I ask suddenly.

"What?"

"I called and called you, but you kept playing your stupid game."

"Whatever are you talking about?" she says. I look into her eyes, right into them, to see if I can look hard enough to find out whether she is pretending not to know, but they are wide and shiny, and if they have any secrets, I cannot see them there. We look at each other for a second, and then she runs out of the room, kicking her heels up behind her and slamming the door with a bang.

I think about going after her and telling her that I know she is lying. But then I think perhaps, after all, it is best if we do not to talk about it. Perhaps, if we don't say it out loud, we can pretend that it never happened at all.

For three whole weeks, we are perfectly behaved. I begin to almost believe that it has worked, like one of my father's magic spells. That we have painted ourselves good. And then I find Molly in the hallway, in the dead of night, leaning down over the banister, and a few nights later I find her again, in the kitchen this time, walking round and round the table and rubbing her hands on her nightgown, up and down, up and down.

"Molly, come back to bed," I whisper into the dark. "Wake up."

She keeps moving about the room, as if I haven't spoken, up and down, past the clothed cheese and the skinned rabbits strung up in a line along the wall.

"Molly, you will wake Mama."

When I finally get her back into bed, tugging her, our hands sticky with sweat, up the stairs and drawing the cover clumsily over her, I climb in next to her and stare at the ceiling. Then worries creep into my mind like the shadows that creep across the wall.

I turn over to where Molly lies curled on her side, her mouth open and her eyes flickering as if she can see things even while she is sleeping. I pick a strand of her tangled brown hair as thick as my finger and wrap it tightly round the thin bar of the bed-post, again and again. Then I take another strand and hold it in my hand while I fall asleep.

In the normal, uncomplicated light of the morning, I look up at the painting of us, each doing the other's hair, on the landing. How pretty we look, I think to myself, and how good.

We are getting under everybody's feet in the house since the blackberries, and even Sarah has had enough. Then I get my hair caught in Molly's buttonhole, and the kitchen scissors have to be sent for, brown curls falling like feathers on the table.

"Now then," my father says, and I see laughter tickling at his mouth as he fetches himself a cup of water. "Can they not be occupied at home a little more, to avoid such unfortunate goings-on?"

"You can mind them, then, Thomas," my mother replies,

snipping furiously, "if it is so very easy to occupy them as all that." And my heart bounces at the thought of it, so hard that it almost makes up for my hair.

The easel is set up on the sloping bank of the Orwell in the last of the sun, so that he can paint the forest that fringes the field, and he stands over it, his eyes narrowed, moving back and forward as if weighing up the view.

Molly is making a town from things she finds washed up on the muddy shoreline, and I am up in the field by my father, gathering a few tall prickly weeds to make flags.

When my hands are full, I make for the riverbank, where Molly is waiting, her skirts hitched up around her knees. I hear my father's voice behind me.

"Wait, Peg."

I turn, surprised.

"Sit with me a moment."

I flop uncertainly to the ground, still clutching my straggly weeds.

"How is my Peggy?"

"Very well," I say cautiously. "A bit hungry."

I see Molly glance up, wondering why I am being so slow.

"You have eaten me quite out of bread and cheese, so you will have to wait until we are home for dinner."

"That's all right." I cross my legs and look at him expectantly. My father does not usually stop painting once he starts, not unless something important happens.

He watches Moll down on the bank, hunting for something where the water pools in flat puddles.

"And Molly? Has Molly been—quite herself recently?"

He says it carefully, as if he is asking something dangerous. My heart begins suddenly to jump about. He is supposed to be an adult who knows everything, I think, and I am supposed to be a child who does not.

"Yes," I say.

It is a lie. The first lie I have ever told him, that I can remember. But I cannot help the feeling that as soon as I say out loud that Molly is not herself sometimes, that something is wrong with her, it will be true.

"Yes," I say again. "She has."

He shifts position and picks a piece of grass and fiddles with it.

"And her—her walking in the night?"

I push down the memory. Molly in the kitchen, her eyes wide and blank. The pink, glistening skin of the rabbits on the wall.

"No," I say. "It is all quite well."

"It has not happened again?"

I look at Molly, her head bowed, mouthing something to herself, a stone in each hand.

"She is only a bit dreamy, that's all, isn't she?"

He laughs, throwing his head back so that I can see the straggly hairs under his chin where he has forgotten to shave.

"Yes. Always a dreamer, Moll. And nothing wrong with that, Captain. Long live the dreamers." I feel his relief like a breeze over me.

"I'm not a dreamer," I say, although I have only just decided it this moment.

"What are you, then?"

"I don't know yet." And then, trying the words out to see how they will sound, I add, "Perhaps a painter."

"A painter, eh?" He looks at me, his head tilted.

"Yes." I feel suddenly raw, like an onion with a layer peeled away. But somehow the way my father says, "A painter, eh?" makes me feel less silly. The way he is amused but also listening, fixing his eyes on me so that I know I am important. Perhaps

25

I will ask him to teach me now, here, and I am opening my mouth to form the words, but down on the bank Molly lets out a shrill cry.

I spring up and bound down over the sludge and pebbles, but when I reach the edge of the river, I see that she is only crying with disappointment, because her town has collapsed under its own weight. She stands with her arms folded, biting back tears, and won't look at me, as if it is my fault. I put my hand on her hot shoulder and tell her we will build another one, but she only slumps and says it will not be the same. My father puts down his brush and rolls up his britches and comes down to join us, his ankles shocking white against the mud.

"All empires must fall, Moll," he says when he sees the mess of sticks and broken bits of pot, and sweeps her, half laughing, half crying, to the bank nearby. We lie all three of us in the grass, and I breathe in the dank smell of the river, and of the faint tang of whisky on my father's breath. He points up at the clouds moving fast across the sky, his fingers mottled green and brown with paint, and he tells us about the winds, and where they come from, and how the sailors use them to navigate the water.

"The Romans called them the Venti, the four winds, from which we get the phrase 'to vent.' Do you know what that means? To vent? It is when one's feelings come pouring out. Whether one is very angry, or sad, perhaps, Molly, at the destruction of one's labors, out it comes with great force."

"To vent," I say, and blow softly into the warm air.

He tells us the old names of the sailing winds, the easterlies and westerlies and trade winds and the doldrums, and about how he once saw a man talk in London who had sailed so far he had almost never come home again, and then after a little while, he picks himself up and brushes the wet grass off his trousers.

"I must get on," he says. I want to leap after him and grab his shirt and pull him back and make him stay with us, make him not want to pick up his brush again, not for the whole day, but he is gone, back to his easel.

Molly sits up.

"Let's look for river creatures, I suppose," she says.

I watch my father, brow furrowed, dipping his brush into the pot he has brought and wiping it on the rag. The small canvas in front of him with its oily slicks of brown and yellow.

"Peg," Molly says again. "What shall we play now, then?"

But I scramble up, leaving her sitting in the grass, and follow my father to his easel, and then hang back, watching his thin hands. The cleverness of them. If I don't ask him now, I think, my mother will always be there, banishing, shooing, lamenting our naughtiness.

"Can I learn?"

He looks down at me as if startled to find me by his side.

"Later, Peg," he says, and turns back to his canvas. "I am behind now, and there are not many days left of this sort of light. Go and play, and I will find a moment to teach you another day."

I wonder why my father's love must come in doses, and why we can only be welcome until it runs out.

"Go along now and play," he says again, although this time his voice is not as soft.

I do not understand how grown-ups think that play can be turned on and off like a tap, instead of being something that curls up from inside you unbidden. I move away obediently. My father pats me on the head as I go, and says, "I am glad all is well with the two of you, my dear old favorites," but his eyes don't see me anymore.

For the rest of the afternoon, we play one of our favorite games, catching flies in our cupped fingers and trapping them in the webs that stretch across the gorse. We watch them twisting and buzzing in their shrill panic, and the spiders waiting, silently, with bulging jet-black eyes, to come forward and bind their prey. And then, when the last of the light dies, we walk home, crossing the broad, flat fields together, hand in hand.

Sold

When I open my eyes, the first thing I see is the strand of chestnut hair still attached to the bed frame. It is early, bluish autumn light bleeding weakly through the shutters. I am groggy from sleep, and for a moment I cannot understand what has happened. I sit up, my breath clouding. The thick strand of hair is still tied at one end to the bedpost, but the other end lies limp across the pillow. Molly is gone.

My heart thumps like a drum. Quickly, I swing my legs out of bed and move like a ghost through the sleeping house. The door to the garden stands open, letting a strip of cold light into the kitchen.

Molly is lying flat on her back in the chicken coop, her nightgown scrunched up around the tops of her legs. She is filthy with droppings and straw, whitish stains with smears of black spattered in her hair like paint. On the side of her head, where I had taken a clump of hair and tied it carefully to the bed frame, as I always do, there is a bald patch of scalp where she has ripped herself away from it while I slept, and tiny red bubbles oozing up from it. There are chickens everywhere, released from their box, more chickens than I ever thought we had, as if they have multiplied overnight, their scratchy feet wandering over Molly's hair and past her bare feet. I have never seen so many chickens.

The cock struts past, oblivious, stopping to peck at a stray grain.

Dread swells up inside me again like a creature under the bed. It is the same terror as in the lane, but stronger, as if somebody has fed it. There is something wrong with her, I know it. I try to swallow, but my tongue is as dry as parchment.

I press my hand to my mouth, hard, as if I can make my feelings go back down. I want to run away, as fast as I can, but I can't move at all. She is only pretending. She is only playing a game. Suddenly she sits bolt upright, pulling her legs around in front of her, and looks straight at me.

I could call for help. I could call my father. I hover over the choice like a fly, my mind buzzing, waiting to settle on the safest thing to do.

And then there is a tiny noise, like the sound of a creature being hurt. I turn, and there is my mother, dumbstruck, in the gray morning light. At the sight of her, the lie finds its way onto my tongue and slips out, trembling, into the air.

"It is a game," I say.

"A game?" my mother says.

"I dared her." My voice shakes, but I hold her gaze.

"You did *what*?"

My mother marches without saying another word into the muck of the chicken coop and pulls Molly out, bleary and soiled and pale as paper.

I hear a noise behind me, and there is my father standing outside the kitchen door, his arms folded tightly across his chest.

"This is the end of it, Thomas," my mother says, her breath a furious little puff of steam. She catches me by the arm with her other hand so hard that she leaves a row of little bruises, which I will discover later, locked in our room while Molly sleeps, with only a long observation of my own body to amuse me.

"A game," she says. "A *game*. They will send me to Bedlam,

these girls, they will! They will drive me past endurance." She stands before him, one hand clutching Molly and one hand clutching me, as if she is giving him a demonstration of our wickedness.

My body is shaking. I do not think she will whip us like the cook at the inn whips his son. But I am so frightened of upsetting her, of how she looks when she is angry. Of how my father is looking at us now.

He purses his lips, and then, without saying a word, he turns sharply on his heel and goes back into the house. I know, then, that that will be that. He will not tell my mother that it is only an adventure-gone-wrong anymore. He will not call it childhood mischief, and say that it is harmless, and that we do not have to grow up just yet.

This time there is not even an argument, only the murmur of hushed voices.

My mother has won. Everything will change, and Molly has made it so with her stupid, stupid games.

Late that night, long after we have been bundled up with hot bricks from the oven and sent to bed, there are voices in the drawing room, raucous but muffled. My father's friend Mr. Thicknesse is here, and some musicians, and there has been what my mother calls a racket. Now my father is playing the violin, his quick fingers sliding up and down the strings, while the others beat time with what sounds like the best cutlery on what sounds like the best table.

Our mother has retired, wrapped in so many layers that it is as if she is trying to disappear entirely, which perhaps she is, so as to avoid the sound of her furniture being ruined.

I slide my legs, one at a time, out of the warmth of the bed. Molly is curled into a small white ball, only the top of her tousled head visible. I do not want to wake or disturb her, in case she grows funny again. But I want to know what is going to happen to us, so I creep across the bedroom floor, and then down through the freezing house until I can perch alone on the bottom stair.

Through the door, I can hear the reedy voice of Thicknesse, drunk and in midflow. Something about taking rooms near an abbey, and then about living near a river.

"Come on, now, Tom, you know Margaret will be happy, and that is rare enough."

"Damned right it is."

That is my father's voice, which sounds the way it does when he has taken too much beer. The words make me jump, and I do not like them.

"Your girls will be the finest ladies of Bath," Thicknesse says, and begins to sing a snatch of a song about a lady, but I cannot make out the words, and my father cuts across him.

"I do not want the girls growing up in such a city."

"Better than them growing up in an Ipswich chicken coop."

The scrape of a chair. He has gone too far. Angry voices, a scuffle, somebody losing balance. Then calm again.

"I won't have it, Tom. You're too good for Ipswich and you know it. And . . ." There is a thud, as if Thicknesse has slapped my father on his back. "It will be good for you, to have daughters who can advance you. Accomplished, handsome, fashionable daughters are useful to a man."

"They can be accomplished without being fashionable. The devil take fashion."

"Fashion, and fashionable society, is your bread and butter, Tom. How else are you to keep all afloat? For God's sake, why do you delay and delay and always delay?"

"I owe too many people money, Philip," my father is saying.

"Then sell up and pay them off and get out of this hellhole."

"Shut up, Thicknesse, and let us play again," shouts a voice I don't know, one of the musicians perhaps, but he is ignored.

"And how to survive in Bath without a penny to my name?"

"You have Margaret's money."

"We have bitten into that too often."

"My God, but you are under the thumb, Tom. What is the point in having a wife with two hundred pounds a year from dubious means if you are too terrified to make use of it?"

What are dubious means? I wonder. I have never heard of them before. Or perhaps he is a person? I try to remember if my father has mentioned somebody of that name.

Thicknesse begins to sing again, a song about a man who is sat upon by his wife. The others take it up with a great muffled thumping. I crane my neck, leaning forward, straining to make sense of it.

Bath. What a stupid name for a place, I think.

I pad softly back up the stairs and push the door to our bedroom open, and there is Molly, perched on the windowsill, white and quiet in the moonlight.

"It is all your fault," I say. Tears burn at my eyes, which I try to blink away. "All of it. And now we have to go away from our house, and live in a city with the stupidest name I ever heard." I hate her, I think, so much that I could blow the clouds, fast and furious across the sky, all the way out to sea and farther, and farther, so that they never come back.

"I couldn't help it. I can't help it—when I—I can't . . ."

Her eyes are frightened. And all the anger goes out of me with a puff. I have no breath left in me then, no clouds to blow, and no sea, so I just sit on the floor instead and pick away at a bit of white paint on the skirting board, and don't talk, while she climbs back into bed and pretends to fall asleep.

And then, before another week has passed, the house is full of people wandering about, even in the very private rooms.

Dismantling us. Their hands rub over our furniture, over my father's chair, over the wardrobe in our bedroom with our things still in it. They examine it, hesitating over flaws in the woodwork, taking down my father's paintings, eyeing them with approbation, discussing this thicket or that plowman, until I want to wrestle each small frame out of their hands and smash it on the ground.

"Oh my goodness, look at you."

A lady bends down to pat me on the head. Thick powder cracks around her eyes.

"Aren't you the dearest little things?"

She is too close. The scent of lavender water and stale sweat. She straightens up and tilts her head to look at us and our butterfly on the wall.

"He has caught the very likeness of you."

She turns to her husband.

"Can't we take them, William? They are terribly sweet."

"We haven't the space, Dora."

"Perhaps the drawing room?"

"It is too large. And they are too melancholy for my taste."

William moves on, dismissing her with ease. I dig my nails into my hand so hard I think I will make myself bleed.

In the end it is a clergyman, a friend of my father's, who comes as the day draws to a close to cart us away, still chasing our butterfly, an old blanket thrown over us to protect us from the dust of the road. I think about us hanging on his wall, and all the pairs of eyes that will see us, while we are far away and don't know anything about it.

My mother has placed all the trappings of our childhood into two square boxes, which she is selling for a single price. My wooden horse that rolls along on four wheels is there, and our hoop, and six rather battered painted dolls of various sizes, and the few best dresses that we haven't destroyed. Our book of three hundred animals. The blocks our father carved the time he cut his thumb, a cut so deep it left the jagged ghost of a white line below his knuckle. A lady comes and rummages in the boxes and takes away half of what is there for half what my mother was asking. And the rest my mother sends for rubbish.

Our very last things are packed into traveling trunks, but they are only our copies of the Bible, two or three dresses, and a few little objects we have kept as treasures. We will have new in Bath, is my mother's constant refrain, when we lament the loss of this or that. New in Bath, new in Bath. All will be new in Bath.

They're only things, Molly tells me, on the last night in what used to be our bed. Only things, and everybody knows it is immoral to care about things too much. But they have our life in them, I think to myself. Our life too will be new in Bath.

The next day, the trunks are stacked high on top of the carriage, which waits to take us to meet the public coach. I am in the garden, keeping out of the way. I want to look at the trees with their familiar, tousled shapes, to run my finger along the stone walls of the house, to try and remember the shape of our bedroom window so that I can think about it later. But instead, I balance on the garden wall, placing one foot in front of the other, heel to toe, heel to toe, trying to forget about the sick feeling in my stomach.

Barnstaple, our fat ginger cat, watches me from the end of the wall. We look at each other. Even though it is terrible to move, it would be even more terrible to be left behind. I scoop him up and carry him, protesting, to the cupboard under the stairs, and climb inside, wrapping my arms around his thick fur. I stay there, tucked away, ignoring his increasingly frantic mews. When the clock strikes twelve, my mother and father and Molly all have to try to pull me away, for we cannot miss the public coach.

"Who is going to feed him?" I ask. "Who is going to keep him alive?"

"The next people, Peg," Molly says. I want to tell her that I do not care what she thinks. I want to say again that it is all her fault.

She reaches out and ruffles Barnstaple's fur, and he lets out a gravelly, undignified purr. My mother, who has been up since dawn cleaning the house and paying off the servants, is saying, "It is quite ridiculous, Peggy. There are plenty of cats to be had in Bath."

And then, because she nearly bangs her head on the shutter, which has not been closed properly, she adds, "I've had just about enough of it. You should be ashamed of yourselves. Weeping over a house cat. You don't know you're born, the pair of you."

"Perhaps you would like a dog, Peg," says my father, as he takes my hand. He rose at ten, and took his coffee to the garden, and has not banged his head on anything.

But I don't want a dog. I want everything put back in its place, everything we knew to be as it was, not this shabby, depleted shell. And only Molly knows this, because she knows my thoughts as well as she knows her own. So, in spite of myself, I let her wrap her arms around my neck.

"He'll live off mice, Peg," she says into my ear. And even though mice are not very substantial for a cat as fat as Barnstaple, and Molly knows this, I loosen my grip on his ginger fur enough to allow him to wriggle free.

We go out by the front door, the door we have almost never used in all our Ipswich life, and are folded into the carriage, two complaining concertinas clutching a picnic lunch. Up climb my father and finally my mother, who rearranges herself fitfully until we are all quite squashed. She does not like traveling, but she is smiling. We are saying goodbye to everything, and she is smiling. I want to cry, badly, but instead I let Molly take my hand and warm it under the traveling blanket.

The driver calls out to the horses, and we move off with a jolt, leaving Barnstaple sitting in the road outside our house, shrinking and indignant as he disappears from view.

The Watering Place

November is a bad time to travel. The roads are churned up with
months of rain. It is passable, says the coachman, but only just.
It will take us four days or perhaps more to make the journey,
depending on how many changes the coach must make, how
tired the horses become.

We lurch toward the tollhouse. A woman is waiting to take
the coins, a scrawny baby on her hip, and we pass through onto
the wide road ahead. We are a teetering contraption of boxes
and people, trundling past gaggles of houses, down jagged slopes
and up winding hilltops. Hidden in my hand is a stone from
the Orwell, a brown one, smooth and round; I keep my fingers
squeezed around it tight as we jolt along.

My father is next to the carriage window, and I see that he is
looking, always looking, at the countryside. His face is wrinkled
in concentration, and as the landscape rolls and changes and we
lurch across it in fits and starts I know that he is coloring it and
shading it and framing it, so clearly that it is as if he had his
brush in his hand.

As we leave London we pass the gibbets where they hang the
highwaymen, and my heart beats at the adventure. My mother
reaches over to pull the curtain so we cannot look out, but we
do, both of us, and see the blackened corpses twisting in the

breeze. There are five or six of them. One has on a pair of garish red-and-yellow britches, and I wonder why he did not choose to wear something less cheerful on the day he was going to be killed. Perhaps he was trying to be brave.

"It is ghastly, Thomas, to leave them there," says my mother, who has crumbs of cheese around her mouth from the picnic she has brought in a napkin. "It is quite medieval."

Early that morning she had stuffed her best necklace and several banknotes so far into the depths of her bodice that I feared they would be lost forever. Her hand goes instinctively to them.

"Better on the gibbets than on the road ahead," my father replies philosophically.

"On the road ahead?" Molly says, and I say, "Well, I expect they'll be hiding in the bushes, not on the actual road," but I am only pretending to be brave, like the highwayman in his red-and-yellow trousers.

My mother says, "Shush now, Thomas, for heaven's sake." She pulls the curtain across more firmly and says, "Now who would like to recite a poem?" We roll across the heath, past the bodies dangling like puppets, reciting Milton, Molly forgetting her place, the words sliding out of her mind as they sometimes do, and I pipe up to remind her, and the lady and gentleman who are squeezed in alongside us begin to look wan.

No highwaymen leap out at us, and we roll on, chewing on ginger biscuits, past Twyford and Slough and Maidenhead, as the black hills loom larger and the road narrows and widens and narrows again, like a snake that has eaten a goat. We grind to a halt again and again, clouds gathering in the darkening sky, and mud-caked boots stomp past us. All the men go down behind to join with shouts of push until we are thrown forward again, unstuck. On and on we are jolted, until our bones are sore with it. It feels as if we will be jolted forever. It reminds me of the Greek punishments my father told us about, the man forced forever to push a boulder up a hill, the water jar that never fills up, the liver pecked and pecked by hungry beaks, and us juddering on and on into the endless countryside.

On the third night, we pull in to rest at Reading, the horses muddy and weary, and all of us battered half to death. A blotchy and rather cross-looking king creaks in the wind overhead. Another King's Head. "How many heads can one king have?" I wonder to Molly, who rolls her eyes as if I have said something silly. A little dog yaps about our feet as we are helped down from the coach, and the gentleman traveler who did not enjoy our poems kicks it away.

"Come inside, girls, and bring your small trunks only," my mother calls as our father lifts us down from the carriage step. We jump over the puddles, murky in the evening light, and clamber inside the doorway to the chairs by the chimney. Molly tries to sit on my lap, which we both find hilarious, until I topple off and nearly catch fire, and our mother loses her last scrap of patience. Separated, we pull faces behind her back as she bustles about ordering dinner, which we eat away from the other travelers, tucked in the corner, where my mother tuts at their table manners and the traces of dirt she finds on the bread plate.

"Come, girls," my father says at last. Often he stays down, drinking with others, playing cards, while we are taken off to an early bed. But tonight he climbs the stairs with us to the poky rooms above, his knees as creaky as the floorboards, and when the candles are out we fall together into our usual traveling slumber, bodies still jolting with the restless memory of the road.

In the night I am woken by the snorts of horses passing below the window, the low voices of men giving orders. It is pitch black. My mother in the next bed is snoring, juddering in and out like a great machine under a blanket. I extricate myself from Molly, whose arms and legs are wrapped around me for warmth, and grope my way through the darkness to the small square of window on the other side of the room. Then I pull back the rough curtain just a little, enough to see the curl of the moon.

This is the farthest we have ever been. It is Molly's fault, a little voice inside me says, and I try to silence it, and remember how she looked after me in the coach, and how in Bath it will all be like that again, and how that is why we are going there. But I press my forehead against the coolness of the glass, and my body aches for Suffolk and our white house with its familiar smell, for the funny sound the wind made rattling through the windows, and for our old bed, where somebody else is now lying, fast asleep.

MEG

Harwich, July 1728

A spider winds its way across its web in the rough stone corner of the kitchen window. Meg Grey reaches out and closes it in her fist, knocking away the thin strands, then sends the spider spiraling down the sink with a jug of water. It hunches its legs as if that will somehow protect it from death, then is flipped on its side and disappears down the drain.

She has been working all morning, washing and chopping herbs, fetching gallons of water, jar upon jar of honey. Now, past midday, the mead is beginning to bubble. Drops of amber liquid crawl down the side of the pot and hit the embers where she has not stirred it carefully enough. They fizz and spark with a sickly, burnt smell, sending thin plumes of smoke twisting upward.

It can simmer now, this honey-sweet mixture, for the next

hour. She gives it one last stir as it begins to thicken, and leaves the spoon dripping on the side. Time to rest. She scoops out a handful of sticky salve from the pot she keeps nearby, and with the other hand she pushes open the door.

The sunlight seems to burn even through her eyelids. She moves across the courtyard to the opposite wall, where the afternoon shade is beginning to creep. Perching on the step, she rubs the blob of salve into the skin of her hands, tightened and blistered after a day in the heat. Mint, calendula, beeswax. They are big, her hands. She can open any jar, grapple with the largest barrel. It is not womanly, say the women, who seem to enjoy the narrowness of the box in which they place themselves. You'd better stop growing, Meg, they say, or the men will not like it. But to be tall, to be broad and strong, to be capable; she cannot see how this can ever be a failing. And she is admired enough by the men, although she sees a wariness in their eyes. They look at her shrewdly, as if trying to calculate the potential damage to their pride from her strength.

Around her, the garden throbs with life. Bees, flies, a tiny blue butterfly. The heat and rain, alternating for weeks now, has brought them out, set them mating, and now they scatter, giddy, across the garden, like drunk men who have lost their way home. Two greenflies, locked together, tumble onto her arm, and she knocks them away.

Behind her, on the other side of the wall, she hears the clunk and thwack of the stable boy, Hal, clearing the muck out with his shovel. Not so much a boy now. Nearly twenty, and suddenly looking at her like a man.

"That you, Meggy?" he calls.

She hears him stop for a moment to drink, and water from the pump spatters onto the dirt.

"Yes."

"Scorching hot. Don't burn yourself."

"Don't be daft. I'm in the shade."

"Good. Your face is too pretty for burning."

"Oh, stop it, Hal."

He laughs and picks up his shovel again with a scrape.

"True enough, though," he calls, before starting work again.

Everyone wants her to marry Hal. That's why they can't talk normally anymore, Hal and her, but instead have these half conversations with compliments stuck in them like pins. Hal wants it. Her father too. She's known him since they were born, the two of them tottering in napkins in the back rooms. Playing tag in the lane. She half wants it herself. It's hard to tell, sometimes, the difference between what you want and what you're supposed to want. Who else will she marry, anyway? What else is she going to do? He's gentle, Hal. Weak, but gentle. And with the two of them together, there would be more power, wouldn't there, against her father? Wouldn't there?

She closes her eyes and touches the cut, almost healed, where it aches along the edge of her eyebrow. In a minute, the next coach will arrive, another straggling line of horses blinded with dust, another crumpled, thirsty batch of travelers. And then later the boats will come in, bringing with them foreigners looking for shelter, returning merchants and travelers craving a pint of English ale. For now, it is only the afternoon drinkers. Resting sailors, mostly, who will drink at any time of day, their scruples, and their manners, left somewhere in the sea. Somewhere inside, she can hear her father coughing, hacking up his tobacco phlegm, serving up their sloshing tankards.

In the dark of the kitchen, forty lemons are waiting to be peeled. She likes that job, the smell of them, their color. It is one of the better jobs that fill her day, from the lighting of the fires before dawn to the cleaning up of vomit in the small hours. Before bed she goes out with a bucket and sloshes away the fresh piss splashed up the front wall of the inn. People are afraid of the sea, in her experience, and those who cross it drink heavily, from fear or relief. Either way, it is good trade for the landlords of Harwich, those who are not afraid of hard work, or those who have daughters they can beat into doing their hard work for them.

They live at the crossing point, the harbor, at the place where safety is left and found again. She feels the pull of it herself, of course. The crashing, desperate sea. Sometimes on a Sunday she walks up to the quay and stands looking out, eyeing the gray horizon, and wondering how it might feel to set foot upon one of the creaking boats, to set off blindly into nothingness. But she feels the pull of many things, in many different directions. Of anything that is not just more of the same.

Her older sisters are gone off and married, one with her husband working down by the canals, one at another inn on the road to Colchester, and one, the small, timid Kate, dead in childbirth. Word had come six months ago. Their father had taken himself off for days, and left her alone at the inn. He'd gone because Kate had been his favorite, and because their mother had died like that, in some agony that Meg can only begin to understand from the noises of the pigs giving birth in the backyard. Guttural, bloodied screams that she has always associated, secretly, with imagining her own entrance into the world. And she does imagine it, whenever that day of the year rolls round. Her tiny body yanked out like a sodden piglet. As a child she had willed herself to remember the touch that there must have been. A hand on her, gentle and soft. There must have been one.

The day, which falls in April, is not really her own. It is a day of loss, of grief and the way it hardens into bitterness, of her father sodden with drink, slumped on the floor of the inn, then hauled to his bed by the stable hands. And now Kate is gone too, the same way, leaving some small child to grow up the way she did. With a hole in the heart. Little Kate, although older than her, who always tied her hair with a loop at the back, who fell over everything and anything, bumping into doors and dropping trays.

So Meg, more than anyone, is aware of nature's indifference. Put yourself in its hands, borne on its sea, swollen with its off-spring, and take your chances. God may protect you, but nature will not. She likes its offerings, of course, and takes daily plea-sure in them—the pungent yellow of the lemons, the flowers in the garden, the fat buds of roses, the heady lavender—but she is not fooled. It is not harmless. She is quite aware, at twenty, that things are more complicated than that.

She hears a commotion on the other side of the wall. Horses, not just one carriage but two, or even three at once, then unfa-miliar voices. German, she thinks. It is early for the boats to have come in. She hears Hal trying his best with the smattering he's picked up. *"Hier entlang."* This way.

"Meg!"

Her father's voice.

"Get here, woman. Where are you?"

She pulls herself to her feet and makes her way back into the smoke-filled kitchen, ready to find out who has come, who needs to be tended to, ministered, fed and watered. And why her father's voice rasps with urgency, with excite-ment.

As the door creaks open to the gloom inside, she jumps, stu-pidly. There, framed in the doorway to the public area, a man is standing. He is immaculate. He is perhaps the cleanest person ever to have been seen in the Three Cups. Brass buttons like little suns up and down his frock coat, light bouncing off them through the open door. His face is soft. It reminds her of an apple, plump and round and rosy.

"Excuse me," he says, with a heavy accent. "Excuse me, but we are in need of a doctor."

The Painter's Daughters

In the front room of the inn, leaning back against the slanting wooden panels of the wall, a man is sitting, waxy, sweating. The skin under his eyes is so dark that it is almost black. Little beads of moisture bubble on his forehead. His hand is wrapped in a blackened bandage with a stain that spreads, yellowish, up his arm. More immaculately dressed men are standing by him, pouring cups of water, talking fast in German.

There is a terrible smell, like the wet, rotting stench of the rat that died under the floorboards last winter. She has sent the oldest stable boy flying down the road on his long legs to fetch the doctor, but there is no guarantee that the doctor will be found. There are only two in Harwich, and it is a town of comings and goings, of movement and all its perils.

Her father is going around evicting the afternoon drinkers, a firm hand on the shoulder, a hushed grip and twist of the wrist. "What the hell is this?" shouts one, snaking from her father's grasp. "Am I not good enough for you now, then, Thomas Grey? Is my money not good enough for you?"

Her father is expert in these men. It is in his blood. He knows how to incite them, how to pacify them, how to make them thirsty. She sees him fish out coins and press them quietly into the man's palm until he rises and staggers, muttering, to the door. He has kept his pint, but why wouldn't he? He has paid for it. He heads off into the road, slurping as he goes, his drink slopping all over the gutter.

The wounded man whimpers in the chair, a sickening moan that scrapes right through to her bones.

"Shall I bring something fresh to wrap it?" she asks the apple-faced man, who stands closest to her. But he doesn't seem to understand her, and looks instead to one of his companions, who translates.

"Yes. A sheet torn into strips."

"What happened?" she asks.

"An accident on the road into the port. In Holland," says the apple-faced man, then he falters. The translator continues, "The carriage overturned and his hand was caught beneath. It was seen to before we sailed, but it is not healing and has become worse on the voyage."

"I'm sorry," she replies inadequately.

Suddenly she is grabbed by the arm and pulled through the doorway into the hall, out of earshot. "Meg," her father hisses, his breath rancid in her face. "Do you not know who this is? It is Frederick. Frederick of Hanover. On his way to London."

Her face is blank.

"The Prince of Wales, Meg. The King's son. You wait on him hand and foot, do you understand me? Nothing is too good."

The King's son. She almost laughs. It is like the apparition of something one is supposed to believe in, but that never becomes a reality. Like God, she thinks, then realizes this is probably blasphemy.

"Jesus Christ, Meg, move. It is the Prince of Wales! Go and prepare the rooms! They need five between them."

"But the guests."

"Turn them out!"

"Into the street?!"

"Yes, into the street. They can go elsewhere. Move."

With a spray of warm spit, he shoves her on her way, and out of the corner of her eye she sees the apple-faced man has seen this. Frederick. She sees that he does not like it. And she sees how, unlike Hal, he will not bend to it. He doesn't have to.

"How long will you stay?" her father is asking Frederick, bending low in a contorted sort of bow. Bowing and talking, she thinks as she leaves, are probably best not attempted at the same time.

48

"We must see to Ainbach," Frederick says. "We must see to Ainbach before we can leave."

She turns and almost runs into Hal at the foot of the stairs. He takes her by the arm to steady her.

"This is a turn-up, eh?" he says, his face a little too close to hers.

"Let me go, Hal, I'm in a rush."

There is something about his face, the film of grease that shines on his nose, the strands of hair that fall lankly on his forehead, that she does not want to see.

"All right, then." He lets her arm go with a frown, as if she confuses him.

"It is a turn-up," she says as a sort of apology, and turns to climb the stairs with pretend haste.

The rooms upstairs seem dark and shabby as she moves about them, breathless. The furniture looks warped, the corners dusty. She cuts some flowers from the garden, sweet William and lavender, and puts them in each room on the sloping tables. She gets a rag and tries to clean away some of the muck that has settled on the windowsill, a child's greasy handprint on the glass. The former occupants, furious at their eviction, eventually take their bundles and trunks and are shunted down the road to the King's Arms. More coins from her father, more arm twisting. Down on the road, she stands and watches their coach move off and sees that word of the visitors has already gotten out. Women hang about in groups, children hopping and chasing at their feet. Someone calls to her, a woman she knows, "Meg, what's it all about? Is it true the Prince of Wales is dead in there?"

"No," she replies, and turns on her heel back into the gloom.

They move Ainbach, the wounded man, up the narrow stairs to the first room, and lay him down where he moans and sweats. She takes a bedsheet, one of their cleanest, and shreds it as best she can, then takes it up to them, hovering in the doorway clutching the thin, white strips.

Frederick looks up. "Come," he says. She moves toward the bed, although the smell is already making her feel sick. They are peeling back the stained bandages, which stick and cling where they have buried themselves into the wound. Her heart gives a great leap of fright at the mangled flesh, and she steadies herself on the little table.

Together they wash the wound, trickling water from a jug, and then the men stand back slightly to make room for her. She realizes that of course she is the only woman in the room. She must be the comfort giver, the carer, the placer of bandages. With all the gentleness she can muster, she presses the edge of the sheet down on the better part of his wrist. Air hisses in through the man's teeth in a noise more animal than human. The men have fallen silent, and there is only the faint sound of chatter from below the window, and the clenched breathing of the patient.

She holds her breath as she works, placing strip upon strip and securing them as best she can across the lacerated skin. The men begin to talk again quietly, in the German she has learned snatches of from travelers, but she cannot piece any of it together. How extraordinary to be able to sort this confusion of sounds into perfect order, and make sense of them, she thinks. She picks a word and silently forms her lips around it, trying it out. *Schmerzen.* An oozy word, like a wound. What could it mean? Sweat? Death?

And then she becomes aware that Frederick is looking at her, and that she knows the look. She knows it from half-cut sailors sagging against the bar, or from old men trying to catch her eye while she bends down to put their food on the table. But this man's gaze is clear. It is clean.

She recognizes the flicker of vanity in herself and looks away, finishing her work. And then she straightens up, just slightly, and looks back at him. Why not? she thinks. Must I cower away, when we are all standing here in this room, quite as real as each other? He is just a man, after all, a boy, really, who fancies an eyeful of me, not the first or the last. I will look directly at him, and we shall see what he makes of that.

She lets her eyes flicker up and over his face. He is young, perhaps a year older than her. Gray-blue eyes. Tallish. A long nose. A softness to his skin, as if he has been brought up in a cloud. It is like looking into the sun, too bright, and she turns away from the seriousness of his gaze. Retreating, with a half nod, half bob, she leaves the room and closes the door behind her, takes a deep breath, and grins. How funny, she thinks, standing in the hallway. What a joke, to look this man right in the eye, nearly the most important man in all of England. She will remember that moment. *Yes*, she will say to her children, *I looked him right in the eye, and I wasn't scared for one moment*. Which will only be half true, but that is the storyteller's prerogative.

A creak behind her on the stairs. Her father. Her body tenses imperceptibly.

"What did they say? What's happening in there?"

"They are just cleaning the wound."

"Does he need anything?"

"Other than a new hand, I shouldn't think so."

"You give them whatever they want, Meg, do you hear me? You find out what they want before they even know it themselves."

She remembers the keen look. The unguarded hunger of it.

"Of course," she says.

Down below, the doctor's carriage is pulling up through the arch. She hears the shout of the stable boy, then feet tramping over the floorboards. Her father watches her with bloodshot eyes for half a second too long, then turns and runs down the stairs, suddenly nimble. He pulls down his waistcoat as he goes. These days it has an unfortunate habit of riding up over his belly.

Meg stands for a moment, then, tucking her hair back up into its bun, heads back down to the kitchen, where the mead has been forgotten on the stove and is now a thick, blackened tar, ten minutes or less from setting the whole place alight.

PEGGY

The Headquarters of
Pleasure and Gaiety

The road to Bath is a mess of construction. Everywhere there are buildings, buildings, buildings—it is as if they will build on every square inch they can find, until the eye can see no farther. Brickwork, rubble, panes of glass, and frames for men to stand on. The whole city is a nest of ants, like the one Molly and I once found in the garden, wriggling and churning and alive.

It is the sixth day of the journey. There are two new travelers, a sullen boy and his mother, who slaps him about the face and arms when he complains, which he does with astonishing regularity. After a particularly hard wallop to the head, he falls silent and sits staring at us, pinched between my mother and his. We stare back. Molly, who has sung almost the entire way from London, says, "Let's sing some nursery rhymes," and even my mother, the most ardent supporter of traveling entertainment, visibly pales.

We are a disgruntled, irritable bunch as we roll down the final stretch into the heart of Bath. As we cross the bridge, I look out and see a man walking a stupid little dog in the evening air, a lady in an impossibly large hat giggling at nothing in particular, and a pair of gentlemen, both clad in purple trousers that make them look like footmen from a drawing. The men are frolicking like children on a patch of grass, and appear to be chasing each other about. I cannot fathom why these fully grown adults are behaving so idiotically. I look at Molly, and she grimaces, as if she is wondering exactly the same thing. What kind of city is this?

The coach draws up in a broad square of tall houses, taller than any I have ever seen. They look pretend, like toys. They are yellowish, like everything else in this city, the color of cream gone bad. Through the window I hear a voice calling out.

"Well, here they are! Here they are at last! I have been waiting for you near on two days now, Tom."

"Impatient as ever, Philip," calls my father, stepping down. "The road was dreadful."

"Molly, Captain, have you caused trouble all the way? Let me help you down, there. You have enough biscuit crumbs on you to feed a pack of pigeons."

Thicknesse lifts us gently down, and we stand on the pavement, our legs wobbly after so much sitting and bumping.

"Mrs. Gainsborough," he calls, "you are as ravishing as ever, even after six days on the road."

My mother, who is crumpled and rather sweaty-looking, says, "Thank you, Philip," in a voice so tight I fear it might snap the air between them in two. She disembarks, and the squashed boy is released from his compression and shifts up toward the window with relief.

"Now come in, the lot of you, and make yourselves comfortable."

He leads us through a doorway and up the stairs to his rather poky rooms, where we are to stay for the time being while we wait for my father to find us a house. Inside, it smells of soap and old cooking, and my mother draws a deep breath upon entering and says, "Girls, straight to bed, both of you." Our room is no bigger than a cupboard, but we play a game with two peculiar statues we find on the mantelpiece and then fall asleep on the bed in all our traveling clothes, Molly's arm draped over my shoulder.

The morning dawns, an unfamiliar gray light filtering through the blinds to wake me. Molly sleeps on, all rumpled and creased and still. I suddenly don't feel angry at all, just happy and re-lieved, that she is still in her bed and that I have her next to me, just old comfortable Molly. I tell myself again that she will be better here, as my mother says she will, and all the old confusion will be forgotten. I can stay close to her, as close as possible, then this strange new place, and its strange new smells, and its strange new people, will be all right. I wind her hair around my finger, first gently then tightly so that it goes pink and then white. I am attached to her. Suddenly she sits up in one swift movement, as if she's been woken up by a noise or a scare, and the hair cord between us tightens with a jerk.

She takes in the room slowly, her face as white as paper.

"Where are we?"

"At Mr. Thicknesse's new house in Bath." I squeeze her hand and smile my best smile, because I do not feel quite safe. Her face has lines on it from the pillow.

"It smells like kitchens," she says, wrinkling her nose. "I don't feel very well."

"Probably hungry," I say. I untangle my finger from her hair and unwrap my handkerchief to reveal a mess of crumbled gin-ger biscuits. We pick at them together in the muted morning light, and she makes me laugh about the squashed boy from the carriage, and about some of the silly hats we saw the ladies wearing, and we tell each other everything we have noticed without being able to say it. And then we hear our mother's harried voice, and her footsteps on the stairs, and she is upon us, flapping about crumbs in the bed, wiping at our faces with her handkerchief, and telling us off for sleeping in our clothes.

After breakfast, our father sets out on foot with Thicknesse to look at houses. Molly and I beg to be allowed to go. It seems only fair, when we are supposed to live there too. Instead, my father looks to Thicknesse for everything, as he always does, and Molly, my mother, and I are left behind to look out the window and sew things interminably until they return on the third day, toasting their find.

The new house is enormous. It looks like a great iced cake that somebody appears to have left wedged in a gap between a hundred other buildings. They lean in, crisscrossed all around by churned-up roads of whitish sludge. To the left, a vast cathedral looms, as though it is about to consume the house and everything around it in one gulp.

"It is a tremendous location, Thomas," Thicknesse says. "The very heart of the city."

"Look up there, girls," says our mother, and we follow her gaze, up and up, the white façade stretching all the way to the gray sky, where a grubby sculpted crest adorns the top in a confectioner's flourish. "The house was built, of course, for the Duke of Kingston." She lowers her voice to mouth the words *Duke of Kingston*.

I do not know who the Duke of Kingston is, but I nod.

"It is fitting, is it not?" she whispers to us. "Very fitting."

"A noble house for a noble lady," interjects Thicknesse, who is not supposed to have heard, and my mother stiffens and looks the other way.

I feel my father's hand on my shoulder.

"What do you think, Captain?"

"It looks like a cake," I say.

"No surprises, eh, Tom, for the city is built on sugar!" Thicknesse guffaws at his own joke and slaps my father on the back a little too firmly.

I look at the pavement. Built on sugar?

"Which is to be our bedroom?" I ask carefully.

"Whichever you like, Captain Peg," Thicknesse interjects, tousling my hair with his cold, dry fingers.

I move away, and my mother turns again to Thicknesse to say that such inquiries must come through her first, thank you very much, and that we will take the bedchamber we are given, and that her children are not for spoiling. Thicknesse gives me a wink of his frog-like eyes behind her back and goes to help with the bags.

Outside the house, attached to the black railings that run the length of the street, is a large sign: THOMAS GAINSBOROUGH, PORTRAIT ARTIST.

Its letters are a dazzling fresh red.

"I cannot for the life of me understand why we must be labeled like grocery salesmen, Thomas," my mother says, making her way to the vast front door.

"It is the way of the city, Margaret," my father says, somewhat wearily. And he is right. On every corner there are painted signs, for cheesemongers and pastrymakers and brushmakers and linen merchants and lacemakers and chandlers and watchmakers, and we are now among them, and are to wake and live and eat and sleep in a marketplace.

What I discover when I step onto the checkered tiles of the gargantuan hallway is that we can only afford a third of the iced-cake house. The rest will be rented out to other people by my father, or really by my mother, who will collect the payments and keep the accounts and reckon the totals. The paymaster general, Thicknesse calls her behind her back, which is an insult.

My father's sister is to take the whole right-hand side for her millinery business, for his family are as continually present in our lives as my mother's are absent and unspoken of. Except, sometimes, when we hear her heavy tread on the boards after we are tucked in bed, and she moves softly into the darkness and sits down to whisper us stories that she does not let our father hear. Secret stories, about people in her family long ago, although I do not know who they are. And even though my mother says they are stories that make Molly and me special, I think my father does not like it. There is something shameful about them.

"What is this place?"

At the sound of Molly's voice, distant and uncertain, I turn. She is standing apart, looking up at the white expanse, her face crinkled in puzzlement. Fear spiders through my veins.

"It is our house, Moll," I say. "You know it is our new house." And then after a moment I add, in a small voice, "Don't be silly. Don't play that game now."

Her eyes flicker onto mine. We stand for a second, the gray afternoon shrinking around us. My mother pokes her head out and calls from the doorway. "Come in, girls. For heaven's sake, stop dawdling about in the street!"

"You're being silly again. Stop it," I say. "Moll."

She only looks at me, the shutters open to the blankness behind.

"Molly." I take her hand and tug her. I must get her into the house, I think, and then she will start to be normal again.

"Come on, stupid," I say, and tug again, gently at first, then hard, almost hard enough to hurt her. And I say, "Ip dip sky blue, who's it? Not you," and tap myself when I say "not you." And then I pull on her hand with all my might, until her feet move beneath her in spite of herself, and I pull and pull and suddenly she is racing me through the doorway into the cold hall while I scream, "The biggest bedroom for the smallest! The biggest bedroom for the smallest!" and we fight each other to the second floor, tripping and stumbling over our hems, and it is forgotten; the clock has been wound up again, and the day runs on as before, as it is meant to.

When I wake the next morning in the stiff new sheets, it is still dark. There are noises on all sides. Half of Bath seems to threaten to break through into our bedchamber. I can smell the smoke of a hundred fires being lit in a hundred houses, thick and torrid and curling across the sky. The air in this city is bad, I think to myself. It is bad air. I don't know how it will make Molly better. But it must. I will look after her, I think, suddenly. I will do it. I make a promise, crossing myself and kissing my finger as I once saw the Ipswich dairyman do. I will look after her just the way Molly looks after me, and be the biggest, when I have to, and keep our secret close.

I pull back the scratchy blind, and below I see the most curious sight. All along the streets, ladies and gentlemen are borne aloft in chairs, hoisted above the rounded shoulders of their servants, garish in the gray light, all orange and pink and blue, entwined with birds and flowers in embroidered silk. Each chair wobbles its way past our house, past my father's new red-painted sign, and disappears through tall gates to one side. Where are they going? How strange adults are, I think. Much stranger than us. Why do they try to look so serious when they are doing something so peculiar? I watch them tottering down below until the sun starts to rise and the morning smoke becomes so thick I could not have seen my hand in front of my face. I hope to see one topple into the mud, but am disappointed, although I watch for half an hour or more. Then I crawl back into bed next to Molly, who shifts and rolls over so that her pale face is squashed up against mine.

She reaches out and brushes her finger to my lips.

"You'll be cut hard in the mouth," she says lightly. "You'll bleed and bleed."

I knock her finger away with a jerk, then remember myself and catch it in my hand and squeeze it gently.

"Shh, Molly. Go to sleep," I say in our mother's voice.

Her eyes are two blank stones in her face. I put my small hand over them and wait until they close and her breathing grows heavy with sleep, and I feel my stomach relax. Then I wrap my arms around the soft heat of her and lie, breathing in and out into the chill of the air, until a nervous girl with a maid's cap perched above her sallow face creeps in and crouches down to light the fire.

Show Pictures

In my father's new study, a dark, shiny sort of room into which he never goes, there is a set of prints upon the wall. They are a present from Thicknesse. There are eight of them, each in its own smooth brown frame, and they sit upon the wall in two neat rows of four. Each picture has a poem beneath it, which I struggle to read, for the writing is very small, and the words are complicated, but altogether they tell the story of a man. Molly tries for a while with the first one, then gets bored and goes to touch the row of crystals on a shelf, running her finger over the smooth, rosy spikes.

"I like these," she says. "They're fantastical."

"That's not even a word."

"Yes, it is. You're too small to know it."

I don't reply, because I know more words than Molly anyway, and because my eyes are fixed on the eighth picture. I cannot look away from it, or from the words written below in a looping script. "Madness, thou chaos of the brain." Chaos of the brain. I look at the picture, at blank eyes and leering faces and foolish antics, and the chains and bars and straw bedding, and the man who thinks he is a king but has no shirt. When Molly is not looking, I trace my finger over his gaping mouth. I try to understand the poem, but cannot. Shapes of horror. Shapes of pleasure. I do not like the figures in the picture at all, the miserable bald-headed clown or the little hunched figure with his fiddle, or the naked man who seems to pray and howl in his cell. But the one that truly frightens me is behind the door, where no one can see him. Hidden. And the fine ladies who simper behind their fans do not know that he is ready to jump out upon them.

The study is cluttered with papers covered in black scratchy notes, dotted minims and crotchets and semi-breves that dance across the page, and with the musical instruments my father loves to collect, but there are new, untouched things too. There is a this-o-scope and a that-o-scope, and a leather globe with countries pasted upon it, and all manner of things in which my father shows no interest, and I wonder why he has bought them. But Bath, I begin to realize in those slow first weeks, is itself a city of things. Objects are packed in together like the people, hundreds upon hundreds, all crowding in on one another for the holiday season. In Bath there cannot simply be a pot of tea. There must be a coffee cup, a chocolate cup, a milk jug, a pouring-cream jug, a sugar dish; there must be tea plates, there must be tiny silver strainers and tiny silver tongs, there must be a butter dish and a butter knife and a cake knife and a clotted-cream dish and a spoon for clotted cream. There must never be only one thing when fifty things will do. The shop windows stretch for mile upon mile with their shimmering glass, and inside each of them are more things to buy, all waiting, delicately labeled, jostling for position, for your eye to fall on them. Sometimes I feel relieved that we did not bring all our old things with us from Ipswich, for it feels as if one more added to the pile might sink the whole place.

Molly and I explore every inch of the house, and then run out of places to poke, and new things to touch. When we sit in the window during another interminable afternoon, I look down and imagine the whole city doing just that, sinking into the white mud of the roads. All of it, the abbey that looms like a monster over us, the ladies in their ridiculous hats, the foppish gentlemen with their thin little legs, the sedan chairs and the snide servants who look at you as if they know something funny about you, and the footman who picks his nose outside the gates while he waits for his lady to finish her bath. I watch them in my mind's eye, their arms flailing as they sink down beneath the airless limestone muck.

A maze of buildings boxes us in. I strain at the windows for a glimpse of the hill beyond, behind the farthest houses that fringe the white winter sky. Molly is not herself, and it worries me, gnawing at my insides when we are supposed to be being quiet, or good, or asleep. We are not allowed out into the streets, and the garden is not a garden, but a hard paved handkerchief with two stone acorns bearing balls of hedge, and a white stone bench in between, on which we are allowed to sit and think. My aunt is making arrangements for her business, and my mother is absorbed in the setting up of the house, and my father is seques-tered in his studio or gone for hours. Here, his door is heavy and does not stand ajar, but bangs firmly shut, and my father rides out to the countryside without us, on a large, rather frightening horse, his easel and paints carried by a mute manservant. Out-side, the city dances around us, late into the night, but we are too small to see it, and too big not to mind. We pace like caged animals at a traveling fair.

Then one afternoon we are playing kings in battle, our wildest game. It is a secret game, for my father does not like us to play kings. Once, in the Ipswich house, we stole some parchment to make a crown, and Molly was standing on a chair for me to bow at, and my father came in and saw her, and his face lost its fun as if someone had wiped it out with a cloth. He snatched the crown from her head and crumpled it and threw it under the table.

"I will not have you trying to be better than you are."

It is only a game, I wanted to tell him. We did not really think it, we were only playing at it, and that is different. Isn't it? But he had gone away to work again, so I couldn't ask him. The game of kings was banned, and the more we were not allowed to play it, the more we wanted to, so it became like biscuits, or running around when you are supposed to be still.

"Get back!" Molly says, brandishing her hairbrush at me. "I command you to get back into your stupid boat! I am your king, and you must do as I say."

Molly is always the King, and I am always a bad servant. Except sometimes, when I am a horse.

"Never," I shout, and run at her, and she leaps down from the nursery chair that is her boat, and we are both laughing, and we are both kings and not kings, and ourselves and not ourselves, and scared and not scared, all at the same time. I am lost in it, chasing her along the hallway, but she careers away from me, and we grind to a halt, stumbling across the landing.

"Never!" I say again, breathless, still laughing. "Surrender!" I take a step toward her, thinking to take her prisoner, but as I come close, she lashes out like a cat, and I stagger backward. A thin red line rises livid on my arm.

"Ow," I say. "You hurt me. Ow." I put it to my mouth and suck on it, and taste blood. "Molly, you hurt me," I say again.

She is not playing or laughing anymore. She is eyeing me, breathing hard in and out, and her hairbrush hangs limp in her hand. She is just Molly, I think, urgently. She is just Molly. I take a step toward her, when suddenly she draws back her hairbrush and throws it hard at a mirror. There is a crack like a bullet, and shards explode across the hallway.

"Molly, why did you do that?" I say in the seconds before the adults come, hot tears rising. "Why did you do that?" My voice sounds small and shaky. "You are so stupid." As the feet thunder up the stairs toward us to pull us from the shattered mess, I want to shout out, It was not me, it was Molly, it was Molly, it was all Molly. But I know that if I do that we will only be separated for the day, and there is nothing worse in the world. It is like a bit of me has been cut off.

When all the pieces have been picked up from the floor, and the mirror frame removed by three cheerful men who wink at us as they carry it down the stairs, my mother takes us to the drawing room and makes us sit next to each other on the chaise longue, which is pale blue and impossibly slippery. She is too roused to settle anywhere herself, and so paces in front of the windows, her apple cheeks flushed.

"This will not do, girls."

There is a tremor in her voice that I recognize from the history of our greatest misdemeanors. I stare at the painted wooden feet of the chaise longue, which are shaped like lion's paws, and wish the lion would rise up and carry us off down the stairs and out of the house.

"This absolutely will not do," my mother continues. "You are too old for this. Too old. You are so naughty. So disruptive and so—so wicked. I am quite despairing. This is a city of great promise, of great—gentility. Of great opportunity for your father, which we must all, all of us, set about procuring. Yourselves included. You are girls of lineage, of—of heritage you cannot possibly understand."

Heritage. Lineage. I think about my mother's whispered stories, of our blood, of our specialness, and wish I could make all the pieces fit together.

"Don't worry, I will fix her hair," Molly says.

"What?" My mother's brow creases. I feel that same feeling, the tightrope walker at the fair. It races across my stomach.

I am going to tell her, I think. Right this moment. She knows so many things about what to do. She will know.

65

"Mama," I say, and my tongue is dry in my mouth. "Mama."

"Yes?"

I can't find any words at all for it.

"Molly is . . ." I flounder. "Molly is . . ."

I feel Molly tense on the seat next to me, her breath quickening, but I push on, forcing everything out in a jumble.

"Molly is not herself. She is not playing games," I say. "She is—she has hurt me . . ." I raise my arm to show my mother the pink cat scratch on my skin. "I think she is—she is not quite—not quite—she is not behaving as she should—"

"My goodness, Peggy Gainsborough," my mother cuts over me, suddenly. Her voice is closed, like a clam. I look up, confused.

"How unladylike."

"I—"

"To blame your sister for your own naughtiness!"

"But I—"

"You were present when the mirror was smashed, were you not?"

"Yes."

"You were involved in yet another one of your games, of your wild, silly chases about the house?"

"Yes, but, Mama, I—"

"Not another word!"

I sit, miserable, clutching Molly's hand.

"I will have no more of this—this divisive talk! If this nonsense continues and you cannot get on with each other nicely, perhaps we would be better off separating you completely until you are properly grown up."

My mother's eyes are hard, like buttons in her face, and her voice is tight and shrill. I wish that I had never spoken. She looks at us sitting there, downcast, in front of her, and softens, just the smallest slackening of her mouth.

"I do understand that you have perhaps been a little forgotten in the clamor of the new arrangements. It is time we prepared you better. It is not good for girls to be left alone too long. It is not healthy."

She walks over to us and lightly touches the top of Molly's head, and then I realize, suddenly, that my mother is frightened too, about how Molly is, and that she thinks being good is the answer. She must be right, I think. She must be. I look up and smile sweetly, and I realize that I am still gripping Molly's hand so hard all the blood has gone out of it, and I can feel sweat sliding between our palms.

The next day, we are taken through the door to our aunt's slice of the iced cake. Her fabric shop is not quite ready for business yet, but already it is heady with scents of orange blossom and lavender water and peony. Rolls of ribbon are stacked in the corners, of every length and shade imaginable, and swathes of fabric, rich and delicate and extraordinary, pile up on tables. There are painted china bowls of buckles, staylaces, buttons, pins, and hooks. There are feathers and furs trapped under glass-topped cabinets like pinned butterflies, and bowls of dried fruits on the counter, cherries and apples and pears. The walls are covered in paper of the palest pink, like the inside of a shell. It is the most wonderful place I have ever seen.

My heart flutters inside me. This is why, I think. This is why we have come, and this is what will make everything better.

"Well, then," says my aunt, who is thin and beautiful and often holds pins in her mouth, "I hear you are come to be dressed as fine young ladies."

"Yes," Molly says, "and I should particularly like a blue dress."

"I see. And Miss Peggy?"

"I should particularly like a blue dress too." I don't have any preference, but only wish to look the same as Molly.

"Is blue in fashion this season?" my mother asks anxiously. "I had heard not."

"Oh, most certainly, Margaret. The paler blues are very modish, and suitable for young girls."

She moves to a stiff roll that is wrapped around and around with the color of the sky on a spring morning, not the hot, stark blue of summer, but something airy that makes me feel hopeful inside. Ipswich air in May when the rain might come later, and the sky hasn't decided yet.

"Perhaps this."

"Yes," I say, the words slipping out in spite of myself. "Oh, yes, please."

"Very good," my mother says, looking pleased. "I shall leave it up to you, Mary, as you know the fashions. Your aunt," our mother says, scraping back Molly's hair into a bunch so that the white skin tightens on her scalp, "is the finest dressmaker in Bath."

"Oh, I know fabric. Fabric is in my blood, and your father's, and yours too." She nods at us and pops a hot piece of crystallized ginger into each of our mouths. Then she hands a tape measure to our mother and disappears into the rolls of fabric. My mother helps us yank our girlish dresses over our heads until we are standing only in our underclothes behind a curtain. Molly folds her skinny arms and wiggles her loose tooth with her tongue.

"Stop that, Molly," our mother says.

"But it is so wobbly."

"Shall I tug it?"

"No! No! I will stop!"

Through the gap in the curtain, I watch my aunt's back moving between the shining colors.

"I wonder if perhaps I would like to be a lady in a fabric shop when I am older," I say, almost without thinking.

My mother nearly spits out her dried cherry.

"My goodness, no! Whatever are you *thinking*?"

My aunt glances up from her task, and I know that she has heard.

"But why not?"

"Because I am not raising you to *sell* things!" says our mother.

"Papa sells things."

"That is entirely different!"

"How is it different?"

"I am astonished that you even have to ask."

Her approval has vanished like kettle steam, and she winds the tape measure a little too vigorously around Molly's waist.

"It is different, because we are raising you for something quite else."

"For what?"

My mother looks as if she cannot believe the impossibility of the question. "To be in *society*," she says simply and finally, then turns me round and I feel the cold tip of the tape on my neck.

Molly looks at me in the mirror and puts her tongue on her wobbly tooth and wiggles it, pulling a stupid face, and I pull one back, crossing my eyes until I feel sick. Our aunt pushes back the curtain, armed with gauze and ribbon and flowers, like a drawing of a goddess from a book about the Romans, and begins to place them here and there. She winds tight strips of blue around Molly's waist.

Bleu de cendres, I think. The blue of ashes.

"Is that expensive, that blue stuff?" my mother asks.

"A little. It is the flowers that will cost," replies my aunt.

"Well. It is an investment."

"Oh, most certainly, Margaret." She places two huge flowers on Molly's head. "Girls are, are they not?"

69

We must wait a week for our dresses to be ready. While they are being made up, we are visited three times by a gentleman with long, papery fingers. He has enormous buckles on his shoes, and his cravat is a puff of pink lace. He tells us that we must never look too earnestly at a person who is eating, and that we must never sit down unless invited by a grown-up, and that we must never find fault with anything that is given to us. He shows us how to place our knives with the tip distant from the plate, and how to sit without getting our dresses in a tangle under us. He rounds out the last traces of our Ipswich vowels, the flat a and the short e and the rounded r, stretching the Suffolk out of them like dough on a kitchen surface.

"It is so generous of you, but I will not, thank you," we say, in unison.

"Generous," says the pink-cravated Mr. Tilbury.

"Generous," we repeat.

And Molly smiles, and curtsys, and is as perfect as if she had been painted new with varnish. We are being good, just as my mother told us to. Molly has whispered promises to me that she will be, crossed her heart and sworn. We have agreed it. Under my pillow I keep a thin strip of silk, soft and pink like roses, and every night I tie it carefully to my wrist and then to Molly's, so that when she wakes in the night I feel the tug and pull her back before she can escape the bed. And so far, it is working.

We do not see our father all week. He has gone to London, and I wonder if he was here whether he would banish the slender-fingered gentleman, or whether there is now no last trace of resistance to my mother's campaign. When he is gone, it feels as if a fence has been taken down.

At lunchtime on Friday, we are in the drawing room, practicing the politest way to refuse an offer of sweetmeats. Our stomachs are rumbling, and I am wondering if I can pretend to feel sick so I can escape upstairs, when my mother enters with shining eyes. She brings the chill of the fresh spring air with her from the outdoors.

"Well, girls. You will never guess."

We wait expectantly. The tutor bows.

"Lady Mary Campbell, the daughter-in-law of the fourth Duke of Argyll, is in town to take the waters, and came to visit your father's rooms. She has a little daughter of your age, Peggy, and has invited us to take tea with them on Wednesday afternoon." She has lowered her voice in the whispered tone she usually reserves for the names of the aristocracy, but finishes on a high-pitched note of triumph.

"It is time to go out and about, girls, and to make some suitable friends. It will be good for you both. A breath of fresh air. Are they ready, Mr. Tilbury?"

"Most certainly, madam." He bows again, and I wish he would fall over.

I do not want to have to go out with Molly all dressed up, and to see people, and to have them see us, and to make conversation and remember how to refuse sweetmeats in the correct way. I do not want to meet Lady Mary Campbell, or to take tea with her daughter. It gives me the old, uneasy fear of the games Molly plays, the way her oddness breaks the surface so fleetingly, then disappears, with only me to guard it from view. I wish my father were here, to say, *Leave them be, Margaret, leave them alone, they are too young. Let them be free.* But he is not. And my mother says that this, all of it, will make Molly better. So we must do it.

In the night, Molly whispers to me, her breath hot on my cheek.

"I don't want to go, do you?"

"No, but we must."

"What if I can't think?"

"I will speak if you can't. You know I always do."

"What if I—what if the other thing happens? What if I—if I . . ." She stops, unsure.

"I will pinch your hand," I whisper. "I will pinch it hard, and it will make you remember to be quiet."

I feel Molly hesitate. It is backward, this way of doing things. It is like we have made a silent swap, older for younger. I do not know if I like it, and I do not know if Molly does either. But I do not know what else to do.

"Yes," she says. "Yes, let's do that."

"Shall we practice? But you must not cry out."

"All right." She holds out her small white hand in the dark.

I steel myself and pinch it as hard as I can, so hard that I fear I will draw blood, and I see her face strain, the whites of her eyes glistening in the dying light of the embers. She bites her lip, but she doesn't cry out.

"There."

She snatches her hand away and puts it to her mouth. "It hurt."

"I know. But it is better than the other."

"All right."

"Do you agree, then?"

"Yes."

"I still don't want to go, though."

"We can wear our new dresses. And Mama says she has a dog to stroke. And perhaps it is better than being stuck here all day."

"Yes. Maybe." She rolls toward me and wraps her arms around my neck, and we don't talk anymore, apart from one moment a few minutes later when she says sleepily, "I do like dogs."

When our dresses are ready, we are summoned to put them on and stand in front of the great gilt mirrors in the fabric shop. Two flouncing figures, bedecked in flowers and bits of floating blue stuff, clutching small embroidered bags with nothing much inside them. I feel frozen stiff, like a flower caught in ice.

"It is so generous of you, but I will not, thank you," I say out loud to myself.

"Whatever are you talking about?" my mother snaps. Then, without letting me answer, she shakes her head. "Oh, I hope you will not be so rude this afternoon, drifting off with your nonsense, as if it is only the two of you that matter in the entire world."

In the mirror I watch myself raise my hand and fix Moll's hair back into place, and I see that our glassy images are caught, one reflecting back the other, in a perpetual line of Peggies fixing the hair of Mollies.

At two o'clock on Wednesday, we descend the steps of the carriage, flowers wobbling on our heads. My mother leads the way, in a gargantuan bonnet and an unusual dress that looks as though it has been wallpaper-pasted with lace. I look at her hands, and I see that they tremble a little as she climbs into the carriage, and when I see it, my heart starts to beat faster. She has commissioned an extra footman to ride at the back so we have someone to open the carriage door for us without an ungainly climb down from the roof.

We are ushered through an ornate entrance into a hallway hung with tapestries, then down a series of endless corridors with great, slippery, checkered squares on the floor, past the heads of bearded men teetering on pillars and a series of alabaster Greek gods. One clutches a discus as if ready to hurl it through the window into the neat gardens beyond. The walls are papered with tiny birds and flowers, which seem to gleam, impossibly tiny and perfect, and the windows are hung with pale loops of silk. Everything is porcelain and pastel and so fine that I can hardly breathe. I cannot squeeze Molly's hand, as she is ahead of me, so instead I watch the back of her head, brown curls bobbing along behind our mother and her bonnet, and I think about how I must make myself sit close to her, within arm's reach. So I can take her hand without being seen. Just in case.

When my slippers are beginning to pinch, and I think we cannot possibly go any farther without walking all the way into someone else's house, we reach an ornate set of double doors that open to reveal a tiny lady standing on an elaborately beautiful pale silk rug. She is middle-aged and as stiff as a brush, with a little spaniel jumping about at her heels. The spaniel, I think, has mean eyes.

"Stop it, Bartholomew! Stop it this minute or I shall put you outside."

The dog growls, a low warning note that I feel is directed particularly at me.

"Mrs. Gainsborough, I am enchanted," Lady Campbell says. She is so stiff and elegant that even her lips barely move when she talks. "What an honor."

My mother curtsies, a little too deeply, her face briefly entirely obscured by her bonnet, and says, "Oh, Lady Campbell, the honor is all mine. May I introduce my daughters, the eldest, Mary, and the younger, Margaret?"

We stage stiff, terrified curtsies of our own.

"Oh, such lovely girls. The painter's daughters. What a wonderful thing. I am very artistic myself." She points at a series of anemic, watery landscapes on the wall behind her.

"How *marvelous*," my mother says in a voice that is not quite her own. "What *talent*."

"This is my little girl, Anne, who is also an artist of most promising talent. We are thrilled to meet the Misses Gainsborough, are we not, Anne?"

"Yes," says Anne, who has a face like a dish and is entirely encased from head to toe in ruffles. She sits on a low stool, poking the spaniel away when he makes advances on her hem. The three of us survey one another.

"Come, sit," says Lady Campbell, and we all lower ourselves simultaneously and obediently onto various pieces of high-backed furniture. Everything is slippery and expensive-looking. In the center, just out of arm's reach and resting on the pale blue silk of the rug, lies a table bearing plates of sweetmeats. My eyes flick to my mother.

Lady Campbell begins to gush and praise and inquire about our father, and my mother talks away in her not-quite-own voice, and I am so relieved for the silence we are allowed to keep, for the way in which Molly can simply sit and look pretty like a doll, and that that is all we are required to do. Stay still, and do nothing, and be pretty. We can do that. I realize that I am tensing all my muscles right down to my toes, and think about how exhausting it would be to do this every day.

The pastries glisten on their blue patterned platters, glazed pecans and apricot jam and honeyed flakes moist with syrup, dusted with crumbs of crystallized sugar. Sticky dates, and candied apple, and pale pink Turkish sweetmeats rolled in icing sugar. I think of Mr. Tilbury with a sort of desperation.

Suddenly Lady Campbell breaks off. "Girls! You must help yourselves to pastries." She has seen my gluttonous eyes. I feel my stomach grumble.

"It is so generous of you, Lady Campbell," I intone, carefully, "but I will not, thank you very much."

"It is kind of you, but I will not indulge myself today," Molly adds, with only the faintest hint of rehearsal.

Lady Campbell's face falls.

"Oh, do have one, Miss Gainsborough. And you too, Miss Margaret. I shall be offended otherwise."

"I am most terribly full," I say.

"But I ordered them specially from Gill's. All girls like

sweetmeats, do they not? I should not like them to go to waste."

Mr. Tilbury's words desert me. "Will you have one, Anne?" I ask.

Anne opens her mouth to speak. "Anne has bad teeth," says Lady Campbell, and Anne closes her mouth again. "I ordered them for you. But if you do not want them, of course, it is no matter."

I become aware that my mother is glaring at us sideways. I am unsure whether her threat intimates what will happen if we do eat the sweetmeats, or if we do not. I begin to grow very confused. I look at Molly to see if she knows what to do, but she has grown rather pink in the face.

Uncertainly, I reach out and take a piece of candied apple, and my mother visibly relaxes. I pop it carefully into my mouth, and it is delicious, sweet and soft and melting on the tongue. I take another. Molly reaches, rather greedily, for a plum pastry. Anne watches us solemnly, and hungrily, from her stool. We chew and smile and make noises of appreciation, and Lady Campbell smiles indulgently and begins to talk again to our mother, who is saying, "Well, of course, with great artists one must be careful, but you will, of course, understand talent yourself, Lady Campbell, and of course . . ."

Just as I am wondering why she is saying "of course" so many times in a row, Molly spits a mouthful of blood down her pale blue dress. She makes a muffled noise, which stops my mother in her tracks, and then her bloodied tooth, which has been loosening all week, tumbles down across the handwoven rug.

Molly stands quickly, trying to reclaim the tooth in a panic, and as she does so her mouth drips rich red splats like thudding rain on the loops of silk. I have never seen so much blood come from a loosened tooth.

"The rug! Oh, the rug," says Lady Campbell, half rising to

her feet. The spaniel begins to bark, a series of high-pitched scrappy yelps, over and over again.

"Mary!" my mother manages to say. "Mary, sit down! The rug!"

Molly goes to sit, and Lady Campbell half shrieks. "No, no! The chaise! It was my grandfather's! It is from China!" and Molly bounces back up again like a firework.

I feel shrill, panicky laughter floating up like a belch from my stomach, and another glimpse at Molly, poised so uncertainly between sitting and standing, with her great gappy mouth dribbling blood and pastry crumbs down her chin, at Anne sitting agog in her ruffles, and I cannot contain it. I choke on my own sweetmeat, an uncontrollable explosion of candied apple. I snort, and a piece of apple shoots from my nose, and I convulse again with more laughter as it bounces along the rug. And then Molly starts laughing too, letting out undignified cackles, spraying flecks of blood and pastry and plum. We laugh and laugh and laugh. It is the funniest thing that has ever happened to us. Funnier than Molly's pig impression. Funnier than the time our father's chair gave way at dinner so that he landed in his own sponge pudding. It is the funniest thing that has ever happened in Bath. In our lives. In the whole history of the world.

My mother is on her feet, crossing swiftly to us, and the spaniel sees its chance and lunges, snapping its teeth around her gown. Somehow it is detached from her with a terrible ripping sound by Anne, and then carted from the room by the scruff of its neck, its yaps reaching an indignant and frantic crescendo. The rug is attended to by scores of kneeling footmen who swarm in and dab at it with faces of extreme crisis, which almost sets me off laughing again. One, his powdered wig bent low, is picking pieces of pastry out of an embroidered bird. Molly has her face stuffed with napkins so she looks like a gerbil, and she looks at me, and I convulse again, and so does she. We are taken from the room in a flurry of apology, but Lady Campbell is frowning, her attention fixed on the damage, and does not turn, or tell us that it is quite all right, and that no harm has been done, or suggest that we stay longer. "Roberts, can it be mended?" she is saying as we leave. "Roberts, what do you think?"

I do not think it is our fault. Molly can hardly help having her tooth fall out, because it is a perfectly natural thing, and my mother has a little pearl pot she keeps them in and about which she becomes very sentimental. It is not Molly's fault at all. And it was so funny that anyone would have laughed. Wouldn't they?

But somehow, watching my mother's pinched face beneath her ridiculous bonnet as she climbs into the carriage, and the tears that seem to prickle with a kind of violence in her eyes, I know that I have done something terrible. She is angry, but there is something beyond the anger, beneath it, something awful, and we have caused it, the same as we caused the incident in the chicken coop and the night-walking. I wonder for a second if she will simply open the carriage door and push us out into the road and go off home without us, we are so useless and shameful. Or worse, I think, she will take us away from each other as she said she would do if we could not be good enough when we are together.

Please, I think desperately, please let me try again. I will control Molly. I will make her good and well so nobody notices, and never play wild games with her again. I try to find something to say to that effect, but our mother's tearful anger is gaining force, and anything we say or do will be like fat falling on a fire.

"I cannot bear it. I cannot bear it. I am humiliated. You have humiliated us. Myself. Your father. You stupid, stupid girls. Dresses torn, blood everywhere, other people's homes ruined."

"It wasn't Molly's fault," I begin, but she runs over me.

"You understand nothing! For the daughters of a tradesman

to be invited into the home of a duke. To *finally* have the chances I have wished for you. Then to behave *thus*. You shame us. I shall go mad. I shall. I shall be taken away in a carriage to Bedlam with bars at the windows, and you shall never see me again, and I will be grateful to rest my banging head, and you shall be sorry then, with no mother, shan't you? Oh yes, you shall be sorry then, all right!"

I imagine my mother raving in a carriage, her face pressed against the bars, carted away down the road. Out of her mind. Out of control. A piece of candied apple comes free from between my teeth, releasing its cloying sweetness on my tongue.

"Mama—"

"I have given you everything different from what I had," my mother says. "Everything."

Different from what I had. The words jar with her lace, with her silk flowers, in a way that I don't want to hear, that makes me want to cover my ears.

"Mama—"

"Not another word!" She puts her hand to her forehead, as if I am making her ill. "Why will you never be *quiet*? You are a bad influence on your sister! There! I have said it. Molly is a *quiet* girl, a *soft* girl, and you are making her—making her wild."

Everything suddenly goes very small and faraway. I bite my lip and stare down at the carriage floor, at our six silk-clad feet peeping out from our dresses like silent creatures. It is me. She thinks it is me who is making Molly bad.

The carriage lurches to a halt, but before we can descend, an optimistic face appears at the window.

"Ladies, a ballad? Love songs, tragedies, perhaps a little London satire?"

The man waves his papers at us with a wink, then sees my mother's face.

"Get away! Get away!" she says, as if he is another nipping

dog, or a bluebottle, and hastily he retracts his hands and climbs down from the step.

She flings the carriage door open before she can be elegantly released and sweeps into the house in a tidal wave of fury, the footman backing himself as far as possible behind the door as he opens it to avoid being caught in the flood.

We are pushed up the stairs like cattle, our mother's dog-chewed dress trailing along the floor, then into separate rooms, and I hear the door to my prison being locked. I sit on the bed and think about what my mother has said.

Downstairs, she finds my father, who is newly returned from London, and probably wishing he had never come back, and begins to rage at him in turn, her voice rising through the floor-boards. When my parents argue, it is like someone is jumping on my insides. Arguments make my father leave, and I have caused this one. I push my nails into my palm as hard as I can. It was my idea to go into the lane for blackberries, with the wind so cold and wild. It was me who started laughing when the tooth fell on the rug.

"Because you would not let me treat them as *young ladies* but would have them *wild* and *uncivilized* and without *manners*, we have brought them here *too late*, and now we are a *laughingstock*, as I knew we would be, and you know their lineage, what it might get them, but because of your delaying and delaying, they are half-grown, halfway to marriage, and Molly is—and now they cannot even *hold themselves together in public for your sake*."

I will not let it be too late, I think. I will stop being a bad influence. I will stop talking and being wild. We will get better at it, together, at being perfect, like a painting, in *bleu de cendres*, in ruffles and flowers, and we will dance the quadrille without laughing, until we are just like the porcelain halls and puffs of pastel, the way we ought to be. I lie down and watch the shadow of the closet make its way across the ceiling as the light fades.

At dusk, the turn of the key. The door creaks open, and my mother stands, looking at me, her head tilted to one side. She puts down a plate of bread and meat on the little table, then sits heavily in the chair next to the bed.

We regard each other.

"Where is Molly?" I ask.

"Asleep."

"May I see her?"

"No. In the morning."

The morning is not so bad, I think. One night is not so bad. I swallow down the worry that churns in my stomach.

"It was not Molly's fault, about the tooth," I say.

"I know," my mother says. "I am afraid I lost my temper. I am not proud of it."

"Is Papa back?"

"Yes, but he has gone out."

"Oh." The last little bit of light I can find in the day vanishes.

"You will see him tomorrow, I am sure."

She reaches out and takes my hand.

"What is Bedlam?" I ask.

"That is not a thing for little girls to worry about. I should not have mentioned it."

"But what is it?"

"I have told you, it is nothing. It is not something for children to know about."

I open my mouth to ask again, but she cuts across me, her voice rising slightly. "I spoke out of turn, and I do not wish to speak of it again."

I heed the warning.

"I know it was all my fault for laughing. I do try to be good, and to get Molly to be good too, only I don't always know how."

"I know you do, Peggy." She sighs. "It is only that I wish you to be accepted. You will need to be accepted, later. All my life,

Peggy, I have . . ." But she breaks off, and changes her mind, and says instead, "The Duke of Argyll is so very influential. I can hardly bear to think of what people will say."

She pushes a rogue strand of hair back into her cap.

"We cannot afford—your father's position is precarious. It depends upon our reputation, you see, with the gentry. If he wishes to advance. You must be fine ladies, and we cannot make—mistakes—although your father will not concede it. And with my—family, it is a—a delicate balance which way it will be taken."

She catches my eye for a second, and then adds briskly, "Although you are too small to understand it."

I digest this news, and all the things that lie between the words. I think about my father, working away behind his door, and about what might happen if I make another mistake.

"There was never such a worry as being a mother," she says, rubbing her temples as if trying to erase something. "You will find that out yourself in time."

I do not know if I want to find it out. I want to tell her that I am frightened about Molly, that she is not quite right, and that perhaps it isn't to do with me after all. That Bath is not making her better as it is supposed to. But I do not want her to be more worried. I lean over and kiss her powdery cheek. "I'm sorry." She smells, as she always does, of roses and sweat.

"Will they really take you away?" I ask.

I know the answer already, or at least I think I do, but I ask so I can hear it.

"Take me away? Of course they will not! Of course not. My goodness. They only take away the insane, and I am quite, quite sane, thank you very much. My grip on reality is only too solid." Then she says, as if telling herself an amusing private joke, "Which, in this house, is both a blessing and a curse."

She stands up, weary, and tousles my hair.

"Get some sleep now, Peggy, and say your prayers. And for heaven's sake, pray to be good." She blows out the candle, and she has forgotten about the bread and meat, but I am too busy thinking to worry about it. The muffled medley of Bath sounds drifts through the window. Insane. I roll the word around my mouth. Insane. I think of Molly in the Ipswich chicken pen, on the pavement in front of the new Bath house. In the dark, I clench my fist, hard.

I kneel by the bed, and I pray until my kneecaps are sore on the floorboards, which is how you're supposed to do it, how it is in books. Make me good. Make me change. Make Molly good. Make Molly change.

The next day, in the afternoon lull, I sneak down to the kitchen. The cook is chopping fish, her knife splicing through the pinky-white flesh with a series of violent smacks. She has a soft spot for me, because she once had her own little girl my age, she says, although she never tells me her name, just pinches her mouth together when I ask, in a thin line that sits in her face like a sewn-up cut.

"If you're coming to distract me with your chatter, you can do the peas," she says, nodding at the bowl and its green pod mountain.

I pull it toward me and start shelling, my small fingers nimble on the rubbery cases. Then I take a deep breath.

"What is Bedlam?" I ask.

She stops and rests her knife on the block.

"Bedlam? Wherever did you hear about that?"

"My mother," I say.

"Your *mother*?"

"Yes."

"Whatever next?" She brings the knife down again and shakes her head. "It is not something for little girls, that."

"I know that."

"I wouldn't have thought a fine lady like your mother would talk of such things."

"But what is it?"

"Something that is not for your ears."

"Please."

She looks at me, resting one gelatinous hand on the hip of her apron.

"No one else will tell me."

"All right. But don't you go saying to your mother I've been encouraging you with such things. I know your tricky ways."

"I promise."

"Very well. It is a place for mad people," she says. "It is where they put you when you lose touch with what's real and what isn't. Lunatics." She taps her head with a blood-tinged finger.

"Lunatics," I say, sounding the word out.

"Yes, the ones what have lost it. They take them away, and they lock them up so as they can't hurt anyone or do themselves a mischief. I had a cousin who knew someone who had been taken in, because her family couldn't look after her in that state. Terrible, it was. She had gone quite mad. Couldn't recognize her own brother."

"Was it her brother's fault?"

"I shouldn't think so. Whatever gave you that idea? Such things are no one's fault at all."

"But why, then?" I ask.

"Not a soul knows, Miss Margaret. Perhaps it is a demon got inside them. Perhaps it is something got in their blood. It is the devil's work, that is certain."

Carefully I put the peas in the bowl, and the spent pod in the pile, and take another.

"What stops it?" I ask.

"Stops it?" She shakes her head as if the question is a strange one.

"What stops the demon in their blood?"

"Oh, not a thing can stop it once it's inside. That is what I hear." She looks at me, and changes her voice as if she has thought of something. "So you must be careful to be good, and not to let the demons in in the first place. That's the trick of it."

But it is too late, I think.

"It is a terrible thing, and it is best not to speak of it, especially not with young girls like you." She wags her knife at me, then brings it down again, splaying the backbone in two. "It is better if we all go on as if such horrors don't exist, for they have nothing to do with us."

I squeeze the new pea pod between my thumb and finger and watch it split open to reveal its shiny line of inhabitants.

"Thank you," I say.

"You can stay and help now, until you are called away." She shakes her head. "Whatever next, really. Curiosity killed the cat, you know, Miss Margaret."

"Did it?"

"Yes," she says with finality, and sweeps the fish guts away into a bowl in one expert movement, before turning away to the sink to wash her slippery hands under the pump.

MEG

It is rare, Meg thinks, that you do anything without thinking about the past or the future at the same time. You are always wondering what will happen, or making plans, and half your mind is on the future before you've even realized what you're doing. You mop the floor, but you are thinking about what you might eat later. You fall asleep, but you are thinking about the morning. Sometimes life feels like nothing but a series of thoughts about what might happen in the next five minutes, or the next hour, or the next week, as if people must keep one step ahead of themselves at all times in order to stay alive. There are very few things that do not feel like that. But this is one.

In the moments when she is with him, when he is pushing himself inside her with such force and such want, she doesn't think about the future or the past. The rhythm of it seems designed to stop such thoughts. And afterward, and in between, she doesn't think about it either. In case there is a consequence. In case it ends. In case she bursts out laughing at the thought of it. Somehow what they are doing, what she is allowing him to do, exists only in the very second that it is happening. It is, as the ballads said it would be, a momentary pleasure.

Such momentary pleasures, at least according to the ballads, don't fare very well when it comes to the future. The highwayman shoots his lover by accident. The farmer's daughter is betrayed. The maid hangs herself at dawn for her ruined virtue. Meg's virtue is ruined now too. But she's not going to think about that yet.

This thing between her and this man, whatever it is—a romance? An agreement?—began after a week. A week of washing and cleaning and tending to blood-soaked bandages gone crisp in the heat. A week of Ainbach groaning. The inn packed, the men bored and restless and drinking and waiting. And eating. The endless, endless eating and scraping of plates and mess on the floor swept up again. Standing in the garden after the worst of the day was over, her head pressed back against the rough wall, eyes closed.

Then the creak of the kitchen door.

Her eyes crinkle open reluctantly, ready to see her father on the prowl, or a customer stumbling the wrong way to relieve himself. But instead, it is him. Frederick, tall and sloping in the doorway. He has become disconnected from his title, from his corner of history, cut loose as he is from the pomp that keeps him aloft. He is a swimmer borne along on a tide then dumped awkwardly, abruptly, in the kitchen garden of a public house with everyone else. Only in a better jacket.

He stands looking at her, his broad face, like a fruit split open in the sunlight, asking permission. She gives it, or doesn't refuse it, and so he edges out into the evening sunshine, letting the door swing shut behind him. It's now, then, she thinks. They stand there for a moment. Then, without saying anything, he takes her hand and pulls her toward him, gives a fleeting glance upward, then presses his lips against hers.

She is startled by the pressure of them at first, having never been kissed in that way. She has only observed it, building up a little memory book of kisses she has seen, the rough and drunken and tender and lecherous. It doesn't feel the way it looks. She keeps her lips against his, carefully, though, as she decided to do in advance. His looks, his quiet nods to her, the keenness in his eyes. She isn't stupid. She's thought about it.

He reaches a white hand out and strokes the wisp of hair that has escaped from her cap. It is a small gesture, but so tender that it sends a shock of something through her body and makes her catch her breath.

Why is he alone? she wonders. What has happened to the bowing host of wigged men who circle him throughout the day? Perhaps he has asked them to leave him alone for a moment. Perhaps he has said, *I'm going to go and try my luck with the landlord's daughter,* and they have all laughed their thick, guttural laughs and are laughing now, as she stands stiffly in the evening sun with his lips locked on hers. Perhaps they are watching somewhere, through an upstairs window, one or two of them, jeering and cheering him on, as she has seen men do before. She breaks away and looks upward, but the window is empty.

He pulls her awkwardly toward him, and she follows the pull, trying to make him comfortable, to aid him, to demonstrate that she likes it, or welcomes it, at least. He puts his hands on her hips, his thumbs resting against her stomach, and smiles at her.

He won't force her, this man, she can tell that, and that is the highest thing you can say of a man, in her opinion. That he is not violent. Or that he hasn't had to be. Yes, she thinks, this is good.

"Do you like this?" he asks suddenly, and she is so surprised she laughs.

"Yes."

"Good. I like this. You. I like you."

"I like you too."

"But we have to be . . ." He stops and raises a white finger to his lips. "Yes?"

"Yes." She raises her finger to her own mouth, mirroring him, then places it on his lips.

"Good. That is good," he says.

He leans in to kiss her again, and this time she tries to think about how it feels. To see if there is any pleasure in it that is not just the pleasure of being wanted. She can't tell yet.

"Tonight, you come to my room. Late. Yes?"

For half a second, she hesitates. The future hangs over her, with its possibilities, its regrets, its disasters. She brushes it away like a spider's web.

"Yes."

PEGGY

Poison

Down in the street below, the oyster man is shouting about his fresh oysters to the boiled crowds emerging from the baths, and I am quietly mouthing his rhyme to myself along with him as I sew. "Oysteeeerrs, finest oysteeerrrrrs," I repeat soundlessly. "Most beneficial to the blooooood." I push my needle into the fabric, watching the blue thread trail after it as it forms the words.

> *Each Hour in useful Business spend*
> *For Time soon hastens to an End.*
> *Improve in each ingenious Art,*
> *Knowledge, like Beauty, wins the Heart.*

I am not sure whose heart it wins. It is strange that the moral lesson is that you should use your time well, because

90

you are shortly to die, as sewing is very boring. Perhaps it is a joke.

I have sewn three whole samplers since the trouble with Molly's tooth, one about the Lord being my shepherd, one about the importance of friendship, and one about suffering little children to come unto thee. I have plenty of time to spare, for Molly and I do not go out now, but stay in the house, and when our mother puts on her hefty best bonnet and goes visiting, the door closes behind her with a click. We do not play games at home like we used to, for I will not let us, but Molly and I have made a small world out of paper bits under her bed, and spend hours twisting parchment into little people to inhabit it. Our kings now are so small no one will ever know they are there, and so are our bad servants and our horses. So it is better than before, when we took up so much space and were so noisy.

When we are not playing with our tiny kingdom, we sing, or we sew, or do our lessons with the tutors who come and go through the big front door. I am satisfied, I think, that we are getting better at being good. We are making some excellent progress at it, although I cannot stop chewing at my nails. Apart from that, though, I am being careful to be a very good influence all the time.

I am finishing the *e* of "learning," and I have made a mistake and need to unpick it, when the door to my room swings open and there is Molly. She is holding out a chamber pot, her hands trembling.

"Look," she says, and her voice chokes on the word. "Look."

I stand up and go to her, uncertain, and peer over the bowl. Against the pale porcelain sides, I see splashes of grainy reddish purple.

"What is it?" She watches my face.

"I don't know," I say, because I do not. However much we stare at it, it does not change.

"Perhaps it is something you ate at dinner."

"I ate chicken, the same as you. I ate all the same things as you."

"Perhaps it is just something that happens."

"Perhaps."

There is a pause.

Suddenly I say, "Let's tip it away and nobody will know."

"But what is it?" Molly's voice is tremulous. "What is wrong with me?"

"It is nothing," I say. "We must tip it away."

She nods shakily, and a flood of relief washes over me. We will make it vanish. We will wash it away, and no one will ever know about it. I cross the room and peep through the crack in the door to the empty hallway.

"Let's go now," I say.

I ease the door open, and Molly comes, her hands clutching the bowl. We creep like thieves along the upstairs hall, our slippers shuffling on the carpet, and terror thrills through me at the idea that she might trip and drop it, and send the red stuff flying over the floor. First we must go down the main stairway, which is the most frightening part. Then we can slip out through the back corridors to the drains along the outside of the kitchen, and if we keep our heads down below the level of the window, and are lucky, we will not be seen.

We edge past the drawing room where my mother's voice holds forth, low and muffled through the door, giving instructions on dinner to the cook, and then down the second set of stairs that leads to the hall. We sneak with our bowl of blood below the unsmiling lords and ladies mounted on top of each other like acrobats in a tower, then flatten ourselves against the wall at the sound of voices.

My father is crossing the hall, and behind him is Thicknesse, on whose arm there is a tall lady with a thin mouth and a clever face. She is dressed head to toe in green satin. She turns and sees us frozen against the banister, Molly with her chamber pot pressed against her stomach. My heart stops.

"Miss Ford, it has been a pleasure," my father is saying. "Philip, I am not at all sure that you deserve her."

He kisses her hand, and as he does so, I see her eyes flick to us. We wait, rigid with fear. Thicknesse has his back to the stairwell, adjusting his cuffs. I grip the handrail behind my back as my father turns to show her a portrait somewhere above our heads.

"What is this?" the lady asks. "The paintwork is so light." With one deft remark, she draws my father back to her, and then turns with him toward the door, casting us only the most fleeting of amused glances as she moves out into the chill sunlight of the afternoon and the world beyond. In that moment I am more grateful to her than I have ever been in my life.

I hurry down the rest of the stairs, driven frantic at Molly's caution with the bowl behind me, and we are within sight of the back stairs, almost running across the hall in one swift movement, when we hear the front door open and our father's voice roots us to the spot.

"What are you doing?"

I cannot think of any useful words to say.

"Girls." His voice is a wire about to snap. "What are you doing here? What is that in your hands?"

He takes a step toward us and the flood breaks. Suddenly we run to him, and his face is hardening with fear as he looks into the bowl, and he is shouting for my mother, and Molly's knees suddenly give way under her, and the three of us are in a sort of scramble, with my mother hastening down the stairs toward us, her face blanched. And someone is sent for the doctor, and Molly is somehow got upstairs to bed, and my mother sits running her hand across Molly's damp forehead, and making shushing sounds. And I think, it is too late. This is the tangled, thorny path that I did not want to go down. This is the old nightmare, which I still wake with, sweating. Molly taken from me, Molly in the carriage, blank-eyed, forced away from me because we have been discovered. Because I have not kept the secret from the grown-ups.

When the doctor arrives, a thin spidery man in black stockings, I stay unnoticed in the corner while he examines Molly in silence. If he were a color, I think to myself, he would be ivory black, all made from the ground and charred bones of animals. He moves Molly's limbs and checks inside her mouth and nose and looks all over her for something. The hairs on the back of my neck stand up as if it is my body he is touching.

"She is only ten years old. It cannot be womanhood," my mother is saying in hushed tones. It cannot be womanhood, I repeat in my head to myself. What is womanhood? Something that comes in a chamber pot?

"No, no, do not alarm yourself. It is not that. I have examined her, and she is too young."

"Then what?"

"It is hard to say. Perhaps a passing childhood sickness. A taint in the blood. I would not worry yourself too much, madam, and it will not do to worry the child either. Plenty of rest. I have a very effective tincture, four drops a day to be given under the tongue, and a draft that has treated a wide variety of ailments with success—"

"I lost a child, once, you see," my mother interjects. I look up, startled. I have never heard her speak of it, only my father, to warn us not to ask any questions about it. "My other girl, my other Mary. My first. I was driven quite—quite mad with worry at first over her, but then I began to relax—to accept—that perhaps all would be well. So if anything should happen . . ."

She rubs her hands together, over and over, as if trying to

work something out of them. Molly's eyes are closed as if she is pretending to sleep, but I know that she is listening hard.

The other Mary, I think. The Mary we used to frighten each other with in the dark. The Mary we tell ghost stories about. "Go out in the dark at midnight," Molly would whisper to me under the covers of our Ipswich bed, "and say 'bloody Mary' three times and turn around with your eyes closed, and when you open them, you'll see her face right there next to yours. You'll conjure her up." Now we don't need to spin around. Now she has been conjured into this room by the sickness and fear in it.

Go away, I think. Go away, dead Mary.

"That is quite understandable, madam," says the doctor soothingly. His voice, like his fingers, is dry and crackly. "But you must not worry. These childhood peculiarities come and go. And you are in the very city of recuperation, of course."

"We brought the family here to—to improve a certain—a certain rustic quality in the girls, in—in Molly. A certain—distraction. We thought they had been too wild, left to their devices, and that perhaps . . ."

But the doctor does not want to hear about Ipswich, or motherly concerns, or to find what lies beneath her words. He is a busy man, and in Bath, illness is a business, like portraits, trinkets, or millinery.

"She walked—in the night, a little," my mother says hesitatingly, but he cuts across her.

"It is a common thing in childhood." He begins to pack his bag. "She would do well to take the waters twice a day, no more than a pint at each time, to be swallowed with some pills which I shall leave you, and to fully submerge at the King's Baths once every morning."

"And she will be well?"

"My remedies are known to be very effective against maladies of all types. This particular draft has cured everything from the ague to distemper. Of course, if it happens again, you must call me out immediately, and we will examine her further. For now, rest is the tonic. And keep the windows closed, for the air in the city is bad, as you know."

With a nod to my mother, and a glance at Molly, who is still resolutely pretending to be asleep, he vanishes downstairs on his spindly legs to be paid.

I sit by the bed, soaked in relief. He did not see bad things when he touched her body; he did not send her away. Our secret is safe, despite his prying hands. Despite our mistake with the bowl. I hold Molly's hand while the murky afternoon darkness settles across the room. I am left on the condition that I will be very quiet, and very good, but that is what I am trying to be all the time now.

"I will be all right, won't I?" Molly asks.

"Oh yes, it is nothing," I say. I don't feel smaller than her anymore, and I wonder if I ever will again.

"It frightened me," she says.

"I was frightened too."

She hesitates. "Is it to do with—with the other thing?"

That is what we call it, on the rare occasion that it breaks the surface into something we can talk about.

"Of course it isn't. That is nothing. That is just silliness." I push it back down, like a bag of kittens I once saw a man trying to drown. "Lie still, anyway, or you'll get me into trouble."

She closes her eyes, and I sit and wait until the worry leaves her face.

When the tea has been brought and left uneaten and cleared away again, our father appears in the doorway, filling it with his familiar shape.

"You worried us, my Moll," he says, leaning against the door-frame. The room feels lighter and somehow less frightening with him in it. He takes the other chair, his footsteps soft and quick as they always are, then reaches out and puts his hand on top of Molly's arm.

"You will soon feel better. Do you think you can rest without getting into mischief? Just for a few days?"

"And then I will be well again?"

"Oh, most certainly. It is something and nothing, Molly. Didn't the doctor say so? There are not too many advantages to having a dauber for a father, I know, but at least I can keep you in this city of wellness. The baths will sort you out. They are famous for it. Do you know what they call it here?"

Moll shakes her head.

"The Kettle."

We laugh, a bit, all three of us, at the idea of people bobbing about in a kettle, although having watched the kettle boiling on the stove more than once I am secretly a little alarmed.

"Will there be a . . ." Molly begins, but falters, her eyes losing focus, and before the silence can settle, I cut across it and ask instead, "Who was that lady?"

"Which lady?"

"The lady in the green silk, with Mr. Thicknesse."

"Oh, that was Miss Ford. Ann Ford. She is newly arrived, and Philip is very taken with her. She is rather scandalous, Peg, I'm afraid, so keep your distance, or your mother will have a fit."

"Will you paint her?"

"I hope to. She is most interesting, and I think people will talk about her, which as you know is very useful to me. And as work is nothing but face after face these days, it is nice to have a face that interests me. Like this one." He runs his hand across Molly's forehead. "And yours too, Captain, I must say is one of my very favorites. My soft, thoughtful Moll, and my determined Peg."

He looks at us and tilts his head to one side.

"Don't keep secrets from me again. Either of you. Secrets are a poison. They eat you up."

He kisses her, then squeezes my arm, and then he is gone.

I think about this later. All around me there are secrets. My father keeps them. I have heard him talking with Thicknesse when I am not supposed to, about women and the way their bodies look. Those secrets do not seem to eat him up. And my mother has a secret, her box with an *F*, her family who are all missing from our lives like the gaps in our teeth. Perhaps my father means do not be a *child* who keeps secrets because they don't belong to children. Or perhaps he simply means *do not keep a secret from me*.

I think to myself that I might just keep mine, after all, and that even my love for my father and his wry smile and his light touch are not enough to make me give them away. And I wish we had not been found out, because if we had tipped it away it would be gone, and Molly would not be in bed, quiet against the white sheets, being tended to like an invalid. Instead, it would all be forgotten, washed away down the drain with the kitchen slops.

MEG

For the rest of the day after their kiss in the heat of the garden, Meg is breathless. Not dizzy, like a lovestruck youth, but struggling to catch her breath fully, so that she feels she is not quite present as she moves about the inn. When darkness falls, the evening drags on, every minute an hour. Pint after pint is swigged and cleared. She serves and retreats, serves and retreats, watching Frederick laugh at bad jokes and slap his friends on the back and eat a pie, wiping crumbling pastry from his chin. Wordlessly, she clears his plate. He crosses his legs, leaning back in the armchair by the fireplace, which lies dead in the summer heat. They are carefully, deliberately disconnected from each other, the two of them. Only once does a glance cut through the hot air between them, running a direct pathway from her thoughts to his, rendering them both utterly transparent for a fraction of a second before it vanishes into nothing. She leans over and wipes down the wood of the bar with her cloth again, and watches, waiting for the alcohol to settle and turn heavy, waiting for the first stumbling retreat upstairs.

"'Scuse me, Meggy."

It is Hal, squeezing behind her to reach an emptied vat of whisky that stands upside down dripping on the side.

"They don't stop, do they?" he adds, rolling his eyes, and touching her softly on the shoulder. They are used to this sort of intimacy, the two of them, angling themselves sideways through the cramped space, making room for each other to pass. He comes closer to her body than any other man, right up against her, so close she knows the smell of his breath, and she feels nothing. And yet somehow the space between her and Frederick, half the inn away, is tight as string.

"You'll need a rest when this lot move on." He whips the cloth from under her hands, uses it to mop up the rogue drops of whisky, and passes it back to her. She takes it, impatient.

"Don't work too hard, Meggy. Don't wear yourself out." He touches her shoulder again.

"I won't," she says, her eyes elsewhere. He gives one look back at her then moves away, his slim hips vanishing through the back door into the dark.

At last they go, one by one, leaving a wreckage of tankards in their wake. Frederick stands and stretches and makes his way toward the narrow stairwell with his arm around the tallest and lankiest of the Germans. He doesn't look up, but talks intimately with his companion, as if whatever is being said is of the most profound and serious importance, leaving Meg alone to clear and wash and finally climb up to her room on leaden legs.

By midnight, the inn has settled into a loaded silence. Ale-fueled snores, the occasional fart. Meg undresses, then dresses again, then changes her mind and undresses, and sits in only her nightgown at the window, listening. A cat growls outside somewhere, a low, warning moan. She rises and moves softly to the door and waits, her heart thumping so hard she fears it will explode in her chest. She presses her ear against the gap in the door. A footstep? No. Is it? No. She hovers in the stench of the tallow from the candle. Nothing. With extreme care, she peels back the door and takes a step into the pitch-black corridor. She edges her way toward the room at the far end, every hair on her body alert.

Her father's door swings open. He is shirtless, his belly wobbling over his britches.

"Getting water. Parched."

"I've been for water too. To bed now." She steadies her voice.

"Good." He stares at her, his eyes unfocused. "Sleep well, then."

"Sleep well." She takes a step back toward her room, and he half topples toward the stairs, grabbing the rail to steady himself. "Tired," he says to himself. "Bloody hard work, this."

"Good night," she says, and watches him clump down the remaining stairs, grunting at each. As soon as his hulking white back is out of sight, she dashes in one swift movement to the door of the best room, and twists at the stiff handle. With relief, she feels it turn. There, in the darkness, is Frederick, somewhere between sitting and standing. She closes the door softly behind her, then places one finger on her lips in the light of the solitary candle. He lifts his finger in response, then crosses wordlessly to her, takes the candle plate from her hand, and places it on the low table.

They wait in the silence, listening to the crash of her father's returning footsteps and the slam of his door. Then nothing. Just the uneasy quiet of the night. She breathes deeply for the first time, her eyes taking in the shape of the room, the way his presence changes it. His clothes on the chair, his boots by the wall standing up as if he is still in them. The faint, still unfamiliar scent of him. He stoops to kiss her, his mouth finding hers in the dark, and she lets herself soften, feels her pulse slacken. His hands move to her body, and lift her nightgown up and over her head. She had not expected to be so vulnerable so quickly. But then why did she come, except to make herself vulnerable? She stands there naked, a fruit that has been peeled, her feet shifting on the uneven floorboards, and there it is, that strange sensation of time held, time suspended, a second stretching out beyond itself. She feels it as they move to the narrow bed, as he pushes her thighs apart and touches her. And then, more suddenly than she expected, he is fucking her. It hurts, a bit, but then she was expecting that, and it is hardly the worst thing. He is fucking her. It almost makes her smile. She says the word to herself again in her head—"fuck"—running it over her tongue to see how it feels—he fucks her, he fucks her, and it makes her feel like someone else. There is pleasure in this act, she thinks, but nothing as wild as was promised in the ballads, or in the winking of the women on her sisters' wedding days. It is probably better for the man, she thinks, but still, it is not a bad feeling. She puts her arms up around his neck and kisses him.

She wonders suddenly what he thinks of her, why he thinks she is willing to risk everything for this quick, hushed, animal encounter in the dark. Perhaps he thinks it is because of his power. Would she risk it for a normal man? A farrier or a servant or a sailor? No. So it is for vanity, then, or for pleasure? God knows you take pleasure where you can find it, but it isn't that. It is something else. Something is happening in this moment. She has chosen something, a series of events that will tumble one after another into being. He is fucking me, she thinks again, and is again exhilarated by the words, and then suddenly she knows with absolute clarity what it is that she wants. She wants to feel like someone else. She wants to be someone else. That is what she is choosing, right now, at this moment. For the first time, it makes sense. And then she stops needing to think about it anymore.

"What is this?"

Two weeks later. The candle almost a stub. His fingers trace over her rib. There is a knot in the bone, from the time her father knocked her over the table. She couldn't move for weeks, lying in bed watching the ugly purplish yellow swell and fade. That put him off for a while, the filth mounting with every passing day. She had watched him from the window trying to bring the washing in while the rain spattered on his head, and laughed, and winced. He had kept his temper then, for a few months, but the bump had hardened, jutting out of her rib cage.

"It was an accident."

"An accident?"

"Yes."

"Your father?"

"Yes."

"He is not a good man, I think."

"No, not really."

"My father is also not a good man."

She rolls over onto her side and looks at him, incredulous.

"Your father is the King."

Then she adds, "Of England." And laughs slightly, because it is ludicrous.

"I don't think that makes a difference," he says calmly, then closes his eyes.

"He doesn't hit you," she says, keeping her fingers wedged in the crack that has opened between them.

He opens his eyes again.

"He does not. But you cannot hit someone you do not see."

"How long is it since you have seen him?"

"Fourteen years," he says, and rolls over to face the window. She runs her hand over the rounded tops of his shoulders then buries her face in his back. They are letting the past in, she thinks. But the future, by mutual agreement, remains barred.

They don't talk much, normally. They hover mainly in the present, existing from day to night and back to day again, between two worlds. They kiss and fuck and lie together in the dark, until Meg shifts herself from their tangled heap and kisses him once, gently, on the mouth and leaves. And it works. By night, she feels like someone else. By day, they keep their eyes averted. They play their roles. Now, at this first sliver of light, she wants to ask him things, to find out about him, about his country, the other one, but she doesn't know where to start. She doesn't want him to think she's hoping for something.

She is intrigued by his body. The softness of it. He smells different, feels different, like someone from another world. Which, of course, he is. Her father has paid four of the biggest men in Harwich to stand outside on shifts to keep the townspeople away. They are a constant presence, trying to grab a glimpse of him, to press flowers into his hand, to grab at his sleeve and talk about how they once saw his mother in London on a fine chestnut horse, and how she was blessed to have such a tall, handsome son, and how the country was secure. It sends people mad, she thinks. Women cry. The same men who sat in the Three Cups making sneering jokes about Kraut princes and the sausage king now grin like fools. One old man, the grandfather of a girl she knows to nod at, brings his own kitchen chair into the road and sits outside day and night with a blanket on his knees. Frederick is escorted to see him, flanked by blue jackets, on the condition that the old man leaves once he has gripped Frederick by the hand and sung him an old military song.

Frederick, she notes with approval, is usually gracious. You have to be gracious all the time if you want to be important, Meg has observed, and when she sees him sit, weary, the door closing at last behind them, it makes her feel relieved that she will never have to bother.

"It was not like this in Germany," he says. His shoulders are slumped. "I was not *Fred*erick. *Fred*erick all the time. I was just Griff. Sometimes I wish I was at home. This place. The food. The language."

She takes a step closer to him and places a hand on his arm, conscious of the daylight, the uncharted waters. The voices next door.

"Sometimes I think—I think how can you be king of somewhere you have never been?"

"Because you have to be," she says, which is the common-sense answer.

He looks at her and nods.

"Griff?" she says, testing it out, still surprised.

"Yes. Don't you hear my friends call me Griff?"

"I don't understand anything you're saying at all," she says, making a helpless gesture with her hands.

"Why don't you call me Griff?"

"Me?"

"Yes."

She laughs. "All right. But don't have me beheaded."

"I don't understand you."

"It doesn't matter."

Everything between them feels suspended, waiting. Waiting for the end of the story, whatever it will be. The cautionary ballad of the landlord's daughter. The tragedy of the prince and his maid. The bawdy tale of the servant seduced.

Ainbach keeps his arm, just, and begins to mend, and the bandages come away cleaner day by day. There is talk of moving on before the weather turns. Frederick urges caution. Her father wheedles and bows and grins, trying to entice them to stay another week, then slaps Meg hard across the face behind the kitchen door when she knocks over a bottle of wine, her limbs heavy with lack of sleep. She feels as if she is stumbling through a dream.

The days roll by. The nights too. Hal lugs barrels of beer and tries to coax her into friendliness. She brushes him away. The scale hangs in the balance, waiting for the feather to land and tip it one way or another. And tip it will. It is only a question of which way.

PEGGY

In the Kettle

We do not have to take a sedan or a Bath chair for Molly to take the waters. We simply step out of our house and follow the narrow passage straight there by foot. We think our bathing costumes, fitted out for us in the scented cocoon of our aunt's fabric rooms, are absolutely hysterical, which greatly annoys our mother, so we do not tell her we think she looks funniest of all, her cap perched on top of her head like a flattened squirrel.

When I place my toe in the baths for the first time, the water seems like an alien thing, shrouded in steam, and I don't trust it. But then I venture a little deeper, placing one foot at a time on the hot stone steps. Molly too, holding my hand tightly, although as the oldest she should look after me.

The water creeps up my body like an animal. I have never known anything like it. The warmth of it and the way it pulls you down and down until you never want to leave it again, but to stay moving your hands and arms back and forth in the depths so that the current streams between your fingers. The baths are crowded with chatter, a hundred of us bobbing about in the steam. There are bodies everywhere, a parade of red- and pink- and white- and blue-tinged flesh, wrinkly and saggy and plump like pigs at Christmas. I see a woman whose eyes are sunken into her skull so far that they are almost not there at all, just great dark holes in the yellowish expanse of her face. I see a girl who has not a single hair, not even eyelashes or eyebrows, and her head is a smooth egg with eyes peeping out. I see a lady so thin she is only bones sewn together. And in between I see a great babbling host of people, their heads and shoulders all floating like ducks on the surface. Somebody passes round chocolate, and I lean back with the creamy sweetness on my tongue and listen.

All around us is talk of ailments, his weak stomach and his complaint of the lungs and her disorder of the skin.

"I shall take the waters at Bristol if there is no improvement, for my appetite is now so decayed I cannot even look at a bun, not even glance at one, without the most terrible sickness coming upon me, but I have heard that at Hotwells one can—"

"And it aches, oh, it simply will not let off, and in my bed I am tossing and turning—I have not known anything like it, and the tincture comes to nothing every time, so perhaps I am being taken for a fool again . . ."

The words drift over me, bubbling like the water. I look at Molly, who has her eyes closed.

"Do you feel better now, Moll?" I ask.

"I think so," Molly says. "But it might be the chocolate."

And then rising from the talk of rheumatism and deafness and stiffness and rash, like the steam rising into the morning air, comes another strain of conversation, which I lean to catch.

A plump lady, her face puckered in the heat, is saying a name I know, as if the words sound entirely foreign and not altogether pleasant in her mouth.

"Ann Ford?"

"Yes," replies her companion, not a little irritably.

"Miss or Mrs.?"

"Miss."

"An actress?"

"A musician."

"Never heard of such a person."

"Well, you are the only one in Bath who has not."

"Next month, did you say?"

"No, it is to be in March."

"Humph, a hundred years away. What instruments does she play?"

"Oh, several. The English guitar, the musical glasses, and"— the companion lowers her voice into a theatrical whisper worthy of my mother—"*the viola da gamba.*"

"The viola da gamba?! But that is an instrument for men! Why, the manner of holding it is not—seemly at all. One must—well, one must wrap one's legs quite around it. It is not an instrument for a woman."

The plump lady pulls herself to sitting as if thrilled at this prospect, sending sudden waves across the surface of the water.

"Yes, it is *quite* the scandal, and *everyone* is talking about it," the companion says delightedly. She turns herself over in the water and begins to talk with animation, which is hard as her teeth protrude at such a steep angle from her mouth that it looks as if she is trying to eat her own lips. "She will give several public concerts at the Haymarket. She *fled* her father's house, for he kept her much abused at home and forbade her to play in public, and had her *arrested* twice, and she was to be sent to the *West Indies.*"

"A punishment indeed." The interrupter rolls her eyes heavenward in horror.

"It is said," continues the companion, "that she had to *escape* from her home under cover of darkness, and that she has come to Bath to seek freedom."

"Freedom?" sniffs the plump lady. "How novel. Everybody else is here for a husband. Perhaps that's what she means. Is she a beauty?"

The companion considers. "I would not say so. Mr. Gainsborough is to paint her, and people will flock to see it, I should think, for she is ever so elegant, and her story is very romantic, and one hears her wit is very sharp, which is almost as good as beauty if you can dress well."

"It most certainly is not," replies her friend, taking a large handkerchief from the side and blowing her nose in it vigorously. "Still, I shall attend, if I return to London, for if everyone is talking about someone it is no good to be the one who does not know of them. I must retreat from the waters, Tabitha, for my physician says not a second longer than a half an hour, or I may do myself considerable damage."

And with that, she rises like a sea monster and wades toward the steps, leaving her companion to turn over again with a sigh and let her legs in their voluminous covering float upward toward the surface to kick gently at the water behind her.

I lie there, soaking, digesting my new pieces of information. I am a bird eating an insect, pecking over each morsel as a delicacy. Freedom, I think. In this smelly, cramped city? Freedom is a riverbank threaded with worms curling up like ribbons and mud between your toes. It is a lane of blackberries, a hedgehog drinking milk from your fingers, adults looking the other way while you push the back door and run. Freedom is not a place full of flies and silly hats where everyone talks about you as if they have bottled you to drink or dispose of at will. Where you are frightened all the time. Is freedom a husband? My mother seems to think so. I think about my parents, their raised voices and their cantankerous rows, and I am not sure. But even though I do not know Ann Ford at all, I know what it feels like to want freedom, and how you feel as though you cannot breathe until you get it.

On the other side of me, Molly is humming to herself. I lean my head against her shoulder and watch my mother adjusting her bathing robe, which seems to be trying to swallow her whole, and I wonder, idly, what a viola da gamba looks like, and what my father would say if I asked to play one.

A Worm i' the Bud

It is Twelfth Night. The house smells of cloves and rosemary and the fresh green boughs of ivy that loop across the doorways and above the fire. The long table groans under sweetmeats and sponge cakes and pies with carved pastry plums on top. My father's business goes well, and the house is full of guests, intimate friends, not anyone to worry about impressing tonight, but a ramshackle selection of musicians and tradesmen and men my father has taken to for no obvious reason, in the way he does. It is a family party.

Thicknesse has found the bean hidden in the plum pudding, a silly old tradition that I have never heard of anyone continuing but my father, for he loves japes of that sort. So Thicknesse is now elected the King of Christmas, and must wear a paper crown. He has no queen, for none of the ladies have yet found the pea. He rules alone. My mother is rather thin-lipped about this, for of course, she has muttered to us in a quiet moment, it would be Mr. Thicknesse who found it, a man who has no problems acquiring exactly what he wants whenever he wants it. And most certainly, she adds tightly, where your father is concerned.

Beside Thicknesse is Miss Ford, all in crimson silk, extending her hand so it can be kissed by a variety of obsequious mouths. I watch her through the banisters, noting the way she stands up

111

tall and doesn't stoop or let her shoulders go round like other ladies when they stop concentrating for a second on being attractive. It is like she is made of something inside that won't crumple.

Molly has not been herself tonight. Her eyes have been quiet. But no one notices quiet, because it is what girls are supposed to be. We retreat upstairs, and she ties a red ribbon in my hair to match the ribbons in the wreaths on the doors, only she is taking too long, and I am wriggling and wishing I were downstairs eating an orange.

"Don't pull so hard, Moll."

My head is yanked backward, and I cry out.

"Molly! Don't pull so hard."

"You must stop the black horse," Molly says matter-of-factly, tugging my plait back toward her.

"What?" The familiar chill.

"It cannot go any farther. It cannot. You must stop the black horse."

"Stop it, Molly." I pull away with difficulty from her grasp. "Stop that now."

"Are you listening to me? You must send for the stable hand. I command it."

"Stop it. I've told you not to play that game anymore. I don't like it." I grab her arm, cold and thin beneath its silken sleeve, and shake her.

She looks at me, half in, half out of focus. "You're not listening to me," she says. "You never do."

"Molly. I don't like it," I hiss, and this time I push her slightly.

"Stop the black horse," she says calmly, and blinks.

I reach out and pinch her hand hard, and she hits me square across the face, a clean blow that knocks against my bones. I reel, stunned, and then I come to, and push her so that she thumps backward into the wood paneling. Her head slams into the wall, and her face folds like a piece of paper. She starts to cry. I go to her, quickly, deftly, and she sobs and sobs, and I hold her and pat her on the back and shush her—"Shhh, shhh, shhh, crying doesn't help"—like our mother does. "I'm frightened," she is saying, over and over again, "I'm frightened," and all I can think is no one must know, no one must know, no one must know.

I rub her shoulders with my hands, while downstairs there is a chorus of an old folk song about a maid, the voices loud and raucous, my father's among them. No one must know. A taint in the blood, a demon got inside, my mother crying in the carriage. The pinching didn't work.

When she has stopped, I peel Molly from me and ask her how she is feeling, and she says, "Oh yes, I am quite well now. I am all right now." I say, "No one must know, Moll. You know no one must know when you are feeling funny, only me. You must only tell me," and then I go and splash both of our faces with cold water and take her downstairs, her clammy hand encased in mine.

When we enter, my father half rises from the chair.

"Captain! What has happened to your face?!"

"I tripped over our bed," I say promptly, and my mother clasps her forehead in mock despair while my father and his guests laugh. The air in the room is hot and orange-scented and laced with punch.

"My daughters," he says, and his words slur as if his mouth runs behind his mind, "are mischief. If there is an accident to be had, they will have it."

"They are quite in their own world," my mother interjects, her face more flushed than usual.

"I am sure you were not half so much mischief to your father, Miss Ford," my father says, "as my girls are to me."

Ann Ford's sharp eyes flash at us in the firelight, taking in the livid red mark I had hoped would not be noticed, then move back to my father.

"And you, Mr. Gainsborough? Were you much mischief as a child?"

"Oh, I was, and am afraid I still am. My Margaret will attest to that."

My mother stands behind him and snakes her arm around his shoulders, and touches the hair at the nape of his neck with a private sort of fondness. "She loves me still, though, you see, though I am not worth the half of her," he says, and he reaches up to take her hand and rub her fingers between his.

This is why I like Christmas. The muffled shouting and the raised voices and the disagreements we hear through the floor while we are supposed to be asleep vanish in the whisky haze. Tonight, because of Christmas, she is his Margaret.

"Come and sing us a song, girls," says my father, his cheeks flushed from the wine. "Sing us something pretty."

"The song you have prepared, the Twelfth Night song," my mother urges, and Miss Ford takes her lute and begins to play the first tangle of notes. We stand in front of the guests, exposed.

I open my mouth and sing, falteringly, alone, "When that I was and a little tiny boy, with a heigh-ho, the wind and the rain." I feel sick at the silence beside me, but then, with a rush of relief, I hear Molly join me, her voice piping over the harmony, clear and ringing like glass. It is only a sweet case of nerves for the adults to smile at. We are not musical, but we are charming, our mother tells us when we practice, quite charming, and that will do perfectly well. Molly is next to me, and her voice carries, and we are quite charming, and it is all going to be all right.

"And we'll strive to please you every day. Yes, we'll strive to please you every day," we finish, to a smattering of polite applause, and I sit with a puff on a footstool, relieved, feeling the attention pass over us again for the rest of the night. Molly's hand stays in mine, and it feels like a belonging I must tend to and not be separated from. For fear of what, I do not know.

"Play for us, now, Miss Ford," Thicknesse says, and I think that his eyes are hungry for something when he looks at her.

"Very well."

She smiles lightly and picks up her guitar, its honey sheen catching in the candlelight. She draws her fingers over it, and as the first notes come, something quivers inside me, like her hand on the string. And although nobody notices, tears I can't explain well up from where they have been lurking, unseen, all this time, without my knowing about it. They have been there ever since we left Ipswich, or before that, formed on the freezing path by the blackberries, in the kitchen by the skinned rabbits. They push themselves out as if they have been freed, rolling down my face and landing with a splat on my best Christmas dress. And when the song finishes, I am soaked in them. Molly leans in to my ear and whispers, "Why are you crying? It's only a song."

"Very nice," says Thicknesse, as Ann Ford puts her guitar away and stands, smiling, and I wipe my arm across my nose and face as hastily as I can so I will not have to explain myself. "Very nice indeed. But too mournful for a Twelfth Night. Come, Tom, let us have a ruckus."

And then my father gives the sign, and the rest of the musicians strike up a wild reel, and we eat again, and dance, and then my mother lets out a startled yell, for she has found the pea in the pudding, and shrieking and protesting she is hoisted into the air by my father and Thicknesse, and declared the Christmas Queen.

We are swept along with them around the drawing room, dancing and singing and sweating with exertion as my father fiddles, and my aunt laughs her gaping laugh, and everything is a single, perfect, dizzying moment. Molly's hand tugs on mine, and she pulls a silly face, as we spin across the room, round and round and round, chasing the tail of oblivion with everyone else.

Midnight. The yule log is burning its last embers. The guests, even my mother, slump, wine-heavy, as if they are drugged. The table of food lies in ruins, cheese hacked to crumbs with a knife, pies ruptured. Moll is asleep in a chair by the window. I am suddenly desperately thirsty. I feel like a dog I once saw trying to drink from a dry drain in the heat of the summer. I stand up, uncurling my stiff legs from beneath me.

Thicknesse sits in the corner playing with two of my father's musician friends, their three violins sliding over the notes. In the hallway the air is cooler, and I cross through it with relief, picking up my pace, thinking about the ice-cold rush of the kitchen tap. My best slippers pad swiftly across the carpet, and I swing round the corner and am stopped dead by the sight of silk and bodies clenched together, half-hidden by the clock that stands near the back stairs. I know instantly that it is Ann Ford, for I can see the crimson folds of her dress running like a river around her. And then the cold shock of realization hits me square in the stomach, and I know, without having to look anymore, who the other person is.

My father is embracing Ann Ford. It is not the embrace he gives my mother, a fond touch, the peck of a kiss. It is something else. They are moving together, too close, wrapped around each other. I press myself back against the wall and watch, my heart hammering in the swing of the clock's pendulum. I feel as if I am being pulled apart from the inside into two pieces, the fibers ripping with the force of it. Where is my mother? Where is she? I want to bring her running, to shout, to break something. But I don't. I stay, frozen, watching them twist together against the shadowy wall.

I can hardly tell where he begins and she ends, but I see him move one red, lined hand across her waist from front to back and draw her closer, and they have their mouths on each other, kissing. I think that is still the word for it, although it is in a way I have never seen. The bristles of his chin rub against her pale, delicate face, framed by strands of hair come loose. Then, in a single, shocking movement, he pulls down the silk at the front of her dress, and her breasts hang there, a fleshy, obscene white, and I don't know whether to stay or to run, as he takes her pink nipple in his mouth and bites it. I let out a muffled cry, which tears from my mouth in spite of myself. At the sound of my voice they leap apart like coiled springs, but I am gone, scuttling away back toward the drawing room.

Breathless, I slip back into the party, folding myself into the high-backed armchair by the glowing embers, and wait.

In a few minutes, my father enters, alert and owl-like, his movements cautious. Thicknesse and his friends play on, absorbed, oblivious. My mother snores slightly, the Christmas crown lopsided on her head.

He looks at me, my father, an assessing glance. I don't look up. Then he places himself with studious, careful movements in a chair nearby and crosses one leg over the other. A little later, Miss Ford appears, composed and serene. She picks up her lute and begins to play gently, and the notes fall light and soft and innocent, like petals caught in the breeze.

My father watches me out of the corner of his eye, but I stay curled up in my chair, a winter cat with a secret, my eyes narrowed, thinking about what I have seen.

Exhibition

Spring is coming, and with it the rain that turns the white sludge of the road into an unpassable swamp. The sedan chairs lurch and sway in the morning drizzle, servants wading knee-deep in the milky puddles. I watch ever more closely through my dawn window, waiting like a spider for one to topple.

I cling close to my mother. I wrap my arms around her until she shoos me away. I carry things for her up the stairs. I bake her little sweetmeats from mint and sugar in the kitchen. When I hover behind her as she does the books, she tells me I am under her feet, and ushers me out, and turns the key in the lock with a click.

"Go and sew."

I sew with a vengeance, as if I can sew my parents back together, as if I can sew up the gaps in Molly's mind.

I do not see my father alone. Once he tries to catch me, calling softly across the hall, but I twist away up the stairs, pretending to laugh.

Thicknesse comes, and says we look pale, and buys us a skipping rope to play with in our paved square of garden. But my mother and the thin-legged doctor say that Molly is not allowed to skip because she must not exert herself, so she sits on the white stone bench watching me as the rope lands with a smack on the paving tiles.

"Pease porridge hot," I chant. "Pease porridge cold."

Molly stares down at the bench, picking off bits of paint.

I stop and look at her.

"Don't do that, Molly, or we will get in trouble."

"I'm bored."

"Well, it's not my fault you're too ill to skip," I say, letting the rope fall slack to the ground.

"It's not my fault either."

There is a pause. A bird lands for a moment on the rosemary bush that Mrs. Hindrell keeps for cooking then takes off again, over the wall to freedom.

"I hate it."

"I know. But it is to make you feel better."

"I don't." She throws a piece of flaking white paint into the flower bed. "You said that Bath would make me better. And that the Kettle would. And the pump water. And the rest. And none of it works. None of it."

"Why don't you chant for me while I skip?" I say consolingly.

Molly looks up. "Because it is boring to chant when you can't skip." For a second I think she is going to cry. "It is boring."

"Mama says you must be careful."

"I'd rather do anything than be careful. I'd rather run away than be careful."

She wipes her nose fiercely with her sleeve.

"Don't be stupid, Moll," I say firmly. "Let's do the Samuel one that Mrs. Hindrell taught us." I pick up the rope and start to skip again. "Samuel was sent to France . . ."

But Molly doesn't join in, and only stares down at her knees, tucked tightly under their blanket. I carry on alone—thwack, step, thwack, step, thwack, step—until I can't skip anymore, until I run out of rhymes about Samuel, and how he learned to sing and dance.

In the house, our father is painting Ann Ford. I knew he

would, for Thicknesse has brought it about, with his knack for always working things out to his advantage while convincing everyone else that it will be to theirs. He hopes to marry Ann—I heard my mother say so. He always manages to profit from my father's talent, one way or another. My father looks to Thicknesse as if he does not have a mind of his own, and Thicknesse seems to guard him like a watchdog. That is why my mother does not like him. Although now, in my mind, they are linked as if in a story, Thicknesse with his bulbous eyes and my mother with her stubborn mouth and rounded head and the hairs that sprout on her chin. And then my father and Ann Ford, twisted crimson silk and white flesh. When I close my eyes, I see it.

Every morning at ten, the broad front door is opened, and my father greets Miss Ford with a kiss to her gloved hand. I watch carefully through the banister, my face still flushed from the morning in the Kettle. Molly has had another episode, and so is made to rest on our return, sealed stiffly and crossly inside an envelope of sheets with the shutters drawn, and I am left to myself. Each time Miss Ford appears, I creep a little closer, adjusting my perch a step at a time. One stormy March morning she spies me on the stair.

"Hello up there," she calls, raising a hand in greeting. "Perhaps you would like to come down and watch me sit?"

I am struck dumb. My father glances at me warily, then back at her.

"Would that be acceptable to you, Mr. Gainsborough?"

"Of course, Miss Ford, if you wish it." My father bows his slight bow, cautious. "Captain, give us ten minutes to set ourselves up, and you may come in to watch, as Miss Ford has given you a personal invitation."

He turns to show the way for her, and laughingly she moves on, the trail of heavy silk gliding fishlike behind her. The door shuts with a bump, muffling my father's small talk. For ten minutes I pace about, wondering if I want to go into this secret place of communion between this woman and my father, their private world of paint. I think I will not go, that it makes me feel sick, that it is disloyal, as if I am breaking everything apart, and that I will run away and sew moral lessons in the window seat on my mother's instruction until my fingers bleed. Then I walk up to the forbidden door and push it, and I feel it give way under the flat of my hand.

The studio is alive with candlelight. It catches the tumbling amber fabric that spills across the scene, morphing umber and Verona earth and ochre, making it flicker and glow as if it has a life of its own. At the center, one dainty yellow slipper crossed over the other, Miss Ford rests her gleaming hand on her cheek. White silk cascades over her body to the floor, layer upon layer of lace and translucent chiffon and brocade. On her lap, one hand rests on her guitar, and half-hidden behind the silk curtain stands the great hulking shape of the viola da gamba. I have never seen a woman sit for a portrait like this, spreading herself out across the canvas as if she has nothing to apologize for.

My father stands in front of a vast canvas, bigger than most I have seen, which stretches out across the width of the studio at an angle. It is already luscious with paint, layered whites and creams and yellows. To the right of it stands a large pencil-and-chalk sketch outline of the same scene from which he works, one paintbrush in his mouth and another in his hand.

Her voice cuts through the heaviness of the atmosphere.

"Are you Mary?" She is being careful. The events of Twelfth Night sit between us.

"No, I am Peggy," I say, my voice still timid. I cough. "Margaret, really."

"But your father calls you Captain?"

"Yes."

"Why is that?"

"I am not sure. Perhaps because I am the smallest, so it is funny."

She smiles. "Where is your sister?"

"She is resting. She has been unwell."

"I am sorry to hear that. She is a curious little thing. So pale."

"She is quite well, quite recovered," my father says, in the tone adults use with other adults when they want to make it clear that a child does not know what they are talking about.

"I am glad. She is Mary, but you call her Molly, do you not?"

"Yes. Because the other Mary died, and it makes my mother sad to speak of it."

My father frowns. "Sit, Peggy, now, and let Miss Ford concentrate, please."

I have said the wrong thing, but it is the truth, and that is why I think my father only wants us not to keep secrets when it suits him.

Miss Ford looks away, amused, and resumes her steady gaze. How much does she know? One word from me and she would be damaged in ways I am only beginning to understand. But I keep quiet.

I settle myself into a corner and watch my father's slender figure moving about in the half darkness. I wish more than anything that he would paint me again. I wish more than anything that he would watch me as he watches Ann Ford now, his eyes falling carefully across her face, as if he sees her in a different way from other people, and cares. Since we arrived in Bath it has felt even more as if he always has his back to us, as if he is always disappearing through a door. I think about us racing about on the banks of the Orwell, my father in his painting jacket, our picnic laid on the rug, and how he turned away again to the easel, and patted me on the head without seeing me. His fingers mottled green and brown and blue with paint. The Ipswich colors. Now I watch his keen eye rove over Miss Ford's satin

and lace, his fascination with the shine of it, and I think, it is silk
he wants now, and softly blushed cheeks. I burn to be grown up,
instead of sitting cross-legged in the shadows. I will wear satin
and lace, and I will wear all the jewels and bangles, and I will be
scandalous and clever with thin scarlet lips and sharp eyes. I will
get his attention back then—I will get everyone's attention, and
I will hold it in the way this woman holds it: lightly, easily, and
without effort. I will not be my mother, huffing and sweating
and storming in her hats, her waist too thick and her dresses too
wide, clumsily covering her badger-gray hair with black from
her pot. And then maybe he will help us. Maybe he will see us.

I study Ann Ford's hair swept back with pins, her subtly
reddened lips, the black necklace tight against her throat, the
bracelets dangling against the whiteness of her wrist. I stay for
an hour or more, crouching in my shadowy corner, watching,
until Miss Ford rises, stretches her arms above her head, and
gives her head a little shake.

"Will that do for today, Mr. Gainsborough? My neck is growing sore."

"It will, Miss Ford. We cannot have you uncomfortable."

"How much longer, would you say?"

He scratches his head. "A week, perhaps two. If I can, I will
show it at the exhibition."

"Tomorrow, again?"

"Tomorrow."

My father walks her to the door, and she stops and nods at me
and smiles a half smile with her pale brown eyes.

"It was nice to meet you properly, Margaret."

Margaret.

"Thank you, Miss Ford."

"You may call me Ann, if you would like. I hope that we shall
be friends in the future."

"Thank you." I try for "Ann," but it will not come.

123

And then she is gone in a rustle of silk.

Standing in the empty room, I say the word "Margaret" to myself, out loud, and for the first time it seems as though it might belong to me.

When my father returns, he stands before the canvas. He seems unsettled, his gray eyes flicking to my face and away again. I move toward him and put my hand on his arm, and then he rubs it softly, cupping it as he used to in his own lined, red one.

"I've missed you, clothes-Peg," he says.

My heart is still in two parts, both of them protesting at the embrace.

"I've missed you too," I say.

We are not going to talk about it. We are going to make it disappear.

"It is just one damned face after another."

"I wish we were in Ipswich." The words slip out in a rush.

He looks at me.

"Now, how can that be the case? In this city of fine dresses and fancy people."

"And bad smells," I say, and tears suddenly spring up and burn my eyes. I clench them away.

"Yes, it is a little smelly, that I will grant you." He reaches for a cloth and begins to wipe his brush. "How is Moll? Is she herself again?"

Why is he asking me? I wonder. Why is he always asking me, while Molly sleeps upstairs, and he has only to put down his brush and see her for himself? He turns the brush in his hand, fanning its bristles out gently with his fingers. I feel a sudden, stupid rush of hatred for it, for the brush itself, the way he treats it with such care, such attention. The way he never puts it down, but keeps it always near him, as if it matters more than anything else in the world.

"Yes," I say, biting down on my secrets like steel. "Yes, she is herself again."

"Good," he says. "If anything were to happen to my girls, I doubt I could survive it. You are my sunshine, the two of you, and when you are with me, you remove the shadow."

I am silent. We both study the ghostlike form of Ann Ford billowing out over the canvas in front of us.

Then he says, "No, it is no good."

"What is no good?"

"It will not do, that last bit, there, on the hem."

I look, confused.

"There is a taint in the oil, Peg. The color does not look quite as it should. Do you see, it is smeared, there, and there. I shall have to begin the hem again."

I move closer and squint, and see that there is the faintest trace of muddy brown running through the whiteness of the brushstrokes, almost imperceptible in the flickering candlelight.

He rubs his eye as if it is bothering him.

I stare at the painting.

A taint in the oil. A taint in the blood.

I think about Molly's blank eyes.

My father takes a brush and dips it in the white and paints over the hem until it vanishes.

We are in the street buying pastries from Gill's, and we are carrying them home in boxes tied with yellow ribbon. A busy Bath morning, ladies trinket-shopping in their March finery, dandies, for I begin to know that word, talking too loudly in the coffee shops. A pamphleteer stands on the corner, adjusting his wig against the blustery wind with one hand and handing out his papers with the other.

We are coming round the corner toward the great shadow

of the abbey when a figure tears out of a building onto the road in front of us, almost derailing a carriage. The driver gives a raucous yell, swerving round her, but she stands stock-still. A woman of perhaps thirty, her hair cropped like a boy's. Her eyes look wrong. She is screaming something, a high-pitched wail. A lady crossing the road nearby backs away, her face ashen, and a mother of a small girl turns round and pulls her smartly into a nearby shop. The pamphleteer freezes, uncertain, his papers flapping stupidly in the breeze.

"Keep walking, girls," my mother says, taking me by the arm and pulling me along like a coach horse. "Don't stare, keep moving along, that's right."

I look back, pretending to look for Molly, and see a stout, middle-aged lady running out from the same building and begin to grab hold of the escapee round the arms. The woman screams again, a torrent of abuse that gushes from her mouth like a pump on the street.

"Come!" my mother hisses, pulling the trailing Molly to her other side and linking her arms firmly through ours. We are marched briskly up the road, and she drops her voice so as not to be overheard. "It is dreadful, is it not? They are come from the madhouse at Box, I should imagine. It is a genteel establishment, by all accounts. I do not know why they could not keep her within. It is a most unfortunate incident."

I flick my head back, one more time, and see the two figures bundling through the door of the building from which they emerged.

"Such cases are terrible." She clicks her tongue in sadness, or disgust. "They have lost all touch with reality. Seeing things that are not there. It breaks one's heart. But in Bath, as a medical town, we must see the extremes of health, and I suppose there is nothing to be done about it."

"Why . . ." asks Molly falteringly, "why do such things happen?"

"Oh, who can say, Molly?" My mother shakes her head as if it is a distant, baffling problem. "Who can possibly say? Something wrong in the head. A punishment from God, perhaps. The sins of the fathers and so forth. It is best not to think too much about it."

We go up the steps into our iced-cake house, carrying our neatly tied yellow boxes, which swing, perfect and square and shiny, in our hands.

Late afternoon, the next day. The cold light of early spring leaks through the shutters. The house is quiet, for Molly is asleep, and my mother is counting the money upstairs, and my father has ridden out to paint near Bristol.

I push the door to the studio. All the candles are blown out. The brownish-red heavy silk has slipped down over the table and the unoccupied chair, an abandoned theater set half taken apart, the actors gone. The music papers are there in the same ordered disorder, and the books piled on top. The scent of Ann Ford still hangs in the air.

To one side is a canvas that stands unfinished. Three figures are sketched roughly in chalk—a woman and her two daughters, my mother, Molly, and I, from a sitting we had begun some months ago, but that my father had grown too busy to complete. Our faces are empty circles of dust with nothing in the center, our bodies a series of ghostly lines marked out and left blank, waiting.

Some of my father's paints lie abandoned on the palettes. I pick up a tube labeled VERMILLION and examine the red oozing from its opening, and rub my finger along it. Then I place my finger to my lips and smear the paint across them. I glance at the vast mirror that stands to one side by the wall, and see the alien red of my mouth leaping out from the white of my face.

In the corner, still half-concealed behind the drape, stands the viola da gamba, its bow standing at a coy slant. The floorboard creaks under my foot as I move softly across the room. Then, standing in the absolute quiet, I reach out and touch the warm wood of the instrument. I feel the way it curves steeply away from my fingers. I run them over the intricate carving where the shape gives way to the blackness inside, and then gently toward the strings. The sound thuds out in the still air, and I stop it with the flat of my hand.

Carefully I pick up the bow, which is longer than my whole arm, and with the other hand I drag the great hulk of the viola behind me to the chair. Then I sit and lean back against the give of the velvet, and I pull the body of the instrument to me and wrap my thighs around its smooth weight, my skin bare and warm against its limpid sheen. It is the most dangerous thing I have ever done. It makes me forget everything else, just for a moment. Molly, my shadow, is banished. It is just me. I do not have to be sunshine; I do not have to be good. I wonder, in the illicit silence, if this might be what adulthood, what freedom, feels like.

MEG

Meg places one hand on the trunk of the tree to steady herself, then vomits into the grass below. Her bowl of blackberries balances uncertainly on the slope where she has left it, threatening to tip its glossy contents into the dust of the lane. She steadies her breath, wipes her hands on her dress, and stands for a moment in the hush. Two fields away, the workers bend low over the crops, making their rhythmic way through the grain, their scythes flashing briefly in the evening sunlight as they rise and fall. Soundless, graceful. If you stood this far away from a war, she thinks, it would probably look the same.

She bends down on aching hips and collects the bowl before it tips. The blackberries are glistening, hot from the sun, and starting to lose their shape. Turning, like the season.

Walking back down the deserted lane, she wonders idly what it would be like to slash a scythe through a person. To see it slice through the skin, to see the look in their eyes. What it would be like to have someone slash a scythe through you. All the things you never find out, about being alive. Things you can never know.

She's not in danger from scythes currently. From perishing under a pile of sheets waiting to have the muck boiled out of them, yes. Sudden death from a tower of plates smeared with pie gravy, perhaps. God knows she has plenty to do at home that is not looking for blackberries, but she needed to get out. To think. To be sick in peace without the knowing glances of the drinkers as she hurries from view, yellowish, clutching a crop of tankards like a bouquet then letting them clatter down into the sink as she retches into the kitchen bucket. Again.

She has to make a decision, and fast. Frederick and the Germans have gone, on to London, on to their unknowable, unimaginable lives. She can stay here and raise the child at the inn, and manage the looks and the scoffing and the teasing. Not to mention the fury of her father. He will hate the child. Why wouldn't he? Her half-German bastard. Or she can trick Hal into marrying her. Or she can get out.

Nobody knows whose child it is. She is absolutely certain of that. They kept their secret, the two of them, tight and private and unseen by all the pairs of ogling eyes that surrounded them. Her father could try to beat it out of her, but he'd have no luck getting the truth, and she reasons that he can only beat her so badly before he creates more work for himself. There, at least, is a form of power.

She steps over a pile of horse muck and feels the nausea rising through her body again, threatening to bring her down in the fishman's slops that dribble across the dust of the main street. The world swims in front of her. She wonders when it will ease, all this. She is in no state to make decisions, to place her bets in this high-stakes game she is playing with their lives. Hers, and that of the tiny life-form sprouting inside her, barely visible under the soft slope of her stomach, but already capable of bringing her to her knees, of leaving her mouth dry and her head thumping, and her thoughts scrambled like eggs in a bowl. It doesn't seem fair, but maybe that's the way God made it. To stop this sort of thing from happening. A consequence for dis- obedience, a warning to other errant girls who let men lie on top of them in the dark.

She pushes the back gate with one hand, balancing the black-berries with the other, and suddenly, from nowhere, there is Hal. He always seems to be under her feet these days, in every corner, popping his wide face into the kitchen when she thinks she's alone, trying to squeeze too close past her in an empty hall-way. He comes toward her, his eyes hopeful, his hair flopping lankly over his forehead.

"Shall I help you with that, Meggy?"

"Oh, don't worry. It's only light."

"All right, then." He backs away, and his deference, which should feel so different from the brutality of her father, some-how makes her spirits sag.

She pushes past him into the kitchen and sets the blackber-ries down on the side. Carefully she moves around the room, gathering what she needs for pastry, but her head is filled with calculations of a different sort. Coach prices. Costs. She knows where her father keeps the cash. How he wraps it greedily in cloth with his fat fingers, and stashes it in parcels behind the loose brick, in the slit of the mattress, under a floorboard in his chamber. She knows how much there is. How long she could survive on it.

She has a plan, a wild, mad, laughable sort of plan, to find Frederick in London. It is the sort of plan that makes you sit bolt upright in the night gasping for breath at your own stupidity. To set off into the sprawl of the city, pregnant, alone, poor, in search of a man who has left you behind. These stories don't end well, everybody knows that. But, she tells herself, her eyes burning with lack of sleep, it's not the usual story, this, is it? She hasn't made the usual choices. Or at least, she hasn't made the usual mistakes.

She remembers being told once, about the old king, Henry, and his bastard, who became a duke. His favorite child, she heard. His only son. Women have borne kings' children out of wedlock, and none of them have died. At least, not the ones you hear about. She is not, she tells herself, just chasing some scoundrel who has run off in the night to God knows where. Frederick is, for a start, the most identifiable of men. She will find him through word of mouth, through whisper, through gossip, through the blue-coated fuss that follows him like a cloud. He cannot always be shrouded in palaces. And moreover, he is not a scoundrel. She knows that from his face. From his manner. From the way he spoke about his father. He minds. He is a man who minds. And, most important, unlike all the other young girls, clutching their round bellies in pursuit of their lamentable lovers, she is not seeking marriage. It wasn't a wedding she was after when she tiptoed, sweaty-palmed, across the landing. It's money she wants.

Money changes everything. It keeps you safe. It brings doctors running when you fall ill. It softens your sleep and cushions your fall. It makes people think that you, your body and mind and feelings and opinions, carry more worth. Women don't get it often, not their own money, but sometimes, just sometimes, they do. This baby is a consequence, a punishment, a warning to other errant girls. And, if the gamble pays off, it's a saving grace. When she said yes to Frederick, when she let him undress and fuck her while the rest of them snored, their breath beer-sour, she wasn't choosing anything, directly, that involved him at all. She only chose choice. Twist or stick, as she and her sisters used to shout, squabbling over the painted cards laid out on their bed. Twist, and peel away the tattered, colorful face of a king, and you win.

Somewhere out in the main room she hears her father's voice growl. "Meg! Meg! Jesus Christ, Meg, where are you this time?"

Inside her, the baby is starting to move, little bubbling kicks, like a fish alive in a jar. What if it's a girl? she thinks. What if it's a girl who spends her life readying herself against the next blow, steeling herself for the numb half second before the pain floods in? He'll die, though, won't he? He's an old man who spends half his life sozzled on cheap beer. His eyes are bloodshot, the skin beneath them purplish and thin. Of course he'll die. But when?

She leans both hands on the solid oak slab of the table, and breathes quietly, in and out, in the still afternoon air of the kitchen, and thinks.

PEGGY

The Blue Boy

When I am twelve and Molly is thirteen, a boy appears in our house. One day he is not there, and the next day he is. He has delicate features that look as if they have been painted on. Brownish hair framing a pointy face. He is very young, only a child, perhaps nine or ten years old, and his waistcoat is too short for him.

"This is your cousin Gainsborough," says my mother, her hand resting gently on top of his head.

Molly and I look at each other.

"Gainsborough?" Molly says. "Gainsborough Gainsborough?"

My mother's face wrinkles in parental warning. "No," she says, with studied patience. "Gainsborough Dupont. He is the son of your auntie Sarah, who married a Dupont. You remember her from Ipswich, surely. You will remember

134

Gainsborough too, I should think, although he will have been somewhat younger."

We do not remember him one bit. But then he would have been a great big fat baby, and therefore very boring. And there were aunts and uncles everywhere in Ipswich, Mary and John and Humphrey and Susannah and Sarah and Elizabeth and Robert and their husbands and their wives, beaky and broad and thin and pockmarked, the women all clutching toddlers and the men all patting us on the head while we tried to slip out and away through the back door.

"He is come to live with us," my mother continues, "to be of service to your father. To help him with his tools and so forth."

Gainsborough Gainsborough stares at his feet.

"Hello," I say, in a not entirely friendly fashion. "You're very welcome."

"Thank you," he says, and his cheeks flare with a violent red I recognize from my own moments of embarrassment.

I don't want this boy to help my father with his tools. I want him to slink back off to Suffolk and leave us alone with our father and our mother. I do not want him prying into our business with his staring eyes.

"How long is he staying?" I ask my mother.

"He will stay until we can see if he will be a suitable apprentice for your father, as I have given him no son to take the role. He shows some artistic talent already."

How does she know she won't have a son now? I wonder to myself. How did Molly and I come into being, but nobody else? Was it God? But the thought of it ever being anything other than Molly and me is impossible, and best not thought about at all. I link my arm through Molly's and do a sort of curtsy that says, *Welcome to our home*, and a face that says, *I wish you'd never come*.

I am very good, now, at doing one thing with my body and another with my mind. I am good at splitting myself off into different parts, the part that is seen and the part that is not. I spin lightly across the room in our dancing lesson quadrille, my stomach knotted at leaving Molly standing by the window out of arm's reach. My mouth smiles politely, and my fingers dig into her flesh. I have drilled her like a soldier. Trained her like a dog. Even when her mind slips, when she feels the pinch of finger and thumb on the back of her hand, she knows to be silent. I still tie her, every night, to myself, with my strip of silk. Molly's sleepwalking is lost in our Ipswich childhood, a forgotten thing, and my mother is pleased.

We are longer too, now, taller and all stretched out. Our knees under our dresses are like bumps halfway up the sticks of our legs. Our mother dresses these limbs in the finest silks, for we are walking advertisements, and begin to go out to concerts and to parties, and do not disgrace ourselves at all, but are quite charming. We do not speak much, but then girls who are quite charming often don't.

A woman comes to pierce our ears with a needle, giving us each a crumpled yellow square of cloth to staunch the blood and leaving golden hoops that I fidget with constantly until my mother threatens to remove them herself. I begin to follow the fashions, and to compare myself to the women in my father's portraits. To wish my feet were more slender, my wrists more dainty. We wear golden buckles on our shoes and flowers in our hair. One day my father uses us as models for peasants in the field, tucked onto the back of a wagon, and makes us swap our lace for smocks to sit for him, but we won't take off our gold buckle shoes.

"Do not be fooled by the fashions of the city," he says, frowning at the canvas. "Stay forever like this, my girls, simple and innocent in the country lanes."

But it was you who took us out of them, I think. There's no need to write a poem about it.

Now that I am twelve, nearly thirteen, I like to test myself. Sometimes I see how long I can go without eating anything, letting the hunger burn in my body until it is the only thing I can feel. It claws away at me, relentless. I think about it as if it is a person I must defeat, a monster I must control. At other times I let the monster out. I slide down to the larder, cold feet padding on the kitchen floor, and attack the cheeses that stand clothed one on top of the other, shredding them with my bare hands so that the cook shrieks about mice the next day. Then I make myself puke in the gutter outside. I wash the spongy, chewed-up mess away with water, and I creep back upstairs with a sour taste on my tongue. I don't tell anyone about it, even Molly, for it is a private thing. I want to climb in and out of her mind like I used to, but there are parts I cannot access, and so I begin to want to keep parts of my own mind private too. I cannot help it, although I wish with all my heart I could pull us back together again.

Gainsborough Gainsborough stays in the back bedroom near the kitchen and sleeps on a pull-out cot, and follows my father about like a tiny knock-kneed shadow. He is always behind him, around him, to one side of him. You cannot get anywhere near my father without him there, loitering, waiting to be told what to do like a diminutive, dim-witted footman. I give him angry stares when no one is looking, which seem to surprise him, but do not surprise me, for I always feel angry now. There is a sort of fury burning away in my guts with its own force that seems to come from nowhere. It just comes into being, like Molly and me, because God wants it to. And I am so angry with Gainsborough Gainsborough and with my father for wanting him near, for wanting a pretend son to follow him about carrying his paints instead of Molly and me. But I cannot do anything about it, for if I am bad, there will be an argument about us, and when there is an argument I feel sick with worry, so I swallow it down and am good.

In the afternoons, when the studio lies quiet, they saddle up two horses and take them out to the countryside, thundering off through the dust to the fresh air and the wild fields, and it makes me ache to think of it. I wonder what it would be like to ride a horse, legs flung over each warm flank, and the rhythm of its body, and the speed. One day I catch them when my mother is elsewhere, and suddenly I am clattering down the stairs to see the tail of my father's waistcoat disappearing through the door.

"Wait! Wait!"

"Captain! Whatever are you doing?"

I pull the door open, my head poking out into the street.

"May I come? May we come, Molly and me?"

"Not now, Peg, for heaven's sake," my father says. Gainsborough Gainsborough hangs at his side holding a folded-up easel. "And come away from the road!"

I step back slightly into the hall, away from the bright sunlight.

"It is too late today. Another time, perhaps."

"Now. Please, Papa. Now. We are always at dancing lessons in the afternoons or at our music. But today Mr. Fleming is unwell, and we could come. Please."

"There is not time today, Peggy. And what would you do? You cannot very well frolic in the lane." He eyes my glossy blue dress, my pale slippers peeping out from beneath its frills, and looks doubtful.

"I could paint."

"Paint?"

"Yes. I want to paint. Like you."

He sighs, and half smiles, as if baffled.

"You have never wanted to paint before."

How has he forgotten? My red cheeks on the bank of the Orwell. *Later, when I have some more time, Peg.*

"I want to now. I do."

He turns, distracted by something far beyond the door that

I cannot see, then he looks back at me and sighs again, as if he wants to escape and I am delaying him.

"Not today."

"Please."

"Go inside, Peggy. Don't let your mother catch you on the doorstep."

"Please."

"Enough."

His voice contains a warning. He blows me a kiss, then shakes his head and leaves, and the door clicks shut behind him.

I stand in the hall, looking at my feet and listening to the tick of the clock and the horses pulling away on the street outside. Then I go into my father's darkened studio, to the rail of fabrics that hang, puffy and flimsy and delicate and stately, and I try them on and watch myself in the vast gilt mirror to see which will make me the most beautiful to look at.

Spotted

One Sunday afternoon, we are sitting on the stone bench in the garden plaiting ribbons, when Molly starts to talk. She is listing, from memory, for no reason I can fathom, the three hundred animals from our three-hundred-animal book. There is no one around, so I let her. I cannot always be hurting her, or the effect will wear off. I have to choose my moments, so I keep plaiting, on and on, without looking up.

"The panther is in shape somewhat like a lioness, but not quite so large. His hair is short and moffy, his skin is of a bright yellow, beautifully marked with round black spots, and is said to send forth a fragrant smell, and bears a great price."

The door swings open, and I see Gainsborough Gainsborough is watching us. Our father has gone to London, so he has nothing to do. I do not care much, for he is only a child, so I keep quiet, my fingers still twisting over the smooth red strips.

"Hello," he says.

I ignore him. Molly rumbles on.

"He is a very fierce and cruel beast, greedy of blood, very swift—"

"What is she doing?"

"She is reciting about animals from our book. I would think that is obvious, should you listen." I say this as pompously as I can, as if to fight him off with the great seniority of my three years.

"Why?"

"Because she wants to."

"Why won't she stop?"

"Because she doesn't want to."

He looks at Molly, considering this. Then he tilts his head to one side. "Do you want to play?"

"No."

All the time Molly is talking, talking, talking on. "To hide himself among the thick boughs of trees and to surprise his prey by leaping upon it suddenly. His tongue, in licking . . ."

He pushes his hands deep into his pockets, and scuffs his foot back and forward on the ground as if he doesn't care that I don't want anything to do with him. Then he does something unexpected. He walks right up to Molly and stands close to her face. "Stop talking, Mary Gainsborough," he says. "Stop talking."

"Leave her alone." I stop plaiting.

Molly prattles on as if he is not there. ". . . grates like a file. The panther is—"

"Why won't she stop? Make her stop."

"I won't make her do anything just to please stupid little boys like you."

"You can't make her stop."

"Yes, I can."

"Prove it."

"No."

I can't pinch her hand now, or he will see our trick, so instead I say, as casually as I can, "Molly, do stop; this little worm wants to talk to you." But she carries on, on and on, about the panther and its tail, talking over us as if we are not here.

"She is mad, isn't she? Going on like that."

I rise to my feet, the ribbons slipping to the ground.

"Shut up."

"She's a loony."

"She's not."

"Loony Mary."

Before the words have left his lips, I run at him like a bull and throw myself at him, slamming my balled fist at him again and again, and push him down with a bang on the paved stones. There is, astonishingly, blood dropping with a splat on the ground from his nose.

Molly rambles on. "The tiger is in shape somewhat like a lioness, but has a shorter neck. His skin is beautifully spotted."

"Shut up!" I shout, and I do not know for a second if I am speaking to Gainsborough or Molly. "Shut up, shut up, shut up!" He lies on his side and my foot digs into the softness of his belly and he lets out a squeal. I kick him again and again and again. "It is very wild and fierce, exceeding ravenous—" "Shut. Up. Shut. Up. Shut. Up," I scream, and each syllable lands with a thump as my body connects with his.

Suddenly I am grabbed from behind by the arms and half dragged into the house, still wriggling, raw fury prickling fast and vicious in my veins, and the cook's voice is shouting at me, the words tumbling out in a high-pitched croak. "Just you—just you stop that this minute, you little monkey. You naughty little monkey!" She pushes me down hard onto a kitchen chair.

"He said that Molly—"

"It don't matter what he said." She is out of breath, pink with wrath. "Young ladies don't behave in such a way, not ever. What were you thinking? Brawling on the ground like that!"

"He said that Molly was—"

"Yes?"

I stop myself. "I'm sorry."

"He is a little boy! And you are a young lady! Nearly thirteen years old! It is a disgrace!" She wipes her brow frantically, as if my naughtiness has made her break into sweat. "I shall have to tell your mother."

"Please—"

"I shall have to. There's no doubt about it."

I begin to sweat myself.

"Please. Please. I promised I would be good. Please."

"I shouldn't have thought it of you, really I should not."

"Please." I sense a crack.

She hesitates, her head tilted to one side.

"I am always in trouble, but lately I have been so good and not in trouble at all, and it would worry my mother so. I will be good, I promise. I promise. I will be so good."

The gap widens, just enough.

"Very well."

"Thank you, Mrs. Hindrell."

She sighs and shakes her head again quickly as if trying to remove the thought of my wickedness from it and set it back to where it once was.

"I am shocked, Miss Margaret. Shocked, I really am. And on a Sunday too! You will apologize to Master Gainsborough this minute." She nods at Gainsborough Gainsborough, who is slinking into the kitchen with his hands in his pockets.

"There he is. Now. What do you have to say?"

I weigh up my options.

"I am very sorry."

"You oughtn't to have done that. It was quite unladylike of you," he says, staring at me.

"That will do, thank you, Master Gainsborough. I'm not sure who made you the expert on ladylike behavior."

The edges of my mouth crease in a stifled smile.

"Is everything all right, Mrs. Hindrell?" My mother appears at the door, a little out of breath. "I thought I heard a—a disturbance."

"All is fine, madam," the cook replies. "All is quite well. Master Gainsborough took a tumble in the courtyard and bumped his nose, and Miss Peggy was quite worried about him and flew into a sort of a panic."

143

"My goodness, Peggy, do we not have enough on our plates already without a fuss over a bumped nose? Master Gainsborough, you should not consider yourself unoccupied although your uncle is away. We must set you to something useful to keep you out of trouble. Mrs. Hindrell, will you find him something to do?"

"I can always use an extra pair of hands, madam."

"Good. And salmon tonight, yes? Now, Peggy, for heaven's sake, go outside and stay out of trouble."

She disappears again, tutting, which is a noise she seems to make almost without thinking, like a wind-up tin toy that tuts as it walks. I stand up and go out to the garden, where Molly is sitting on the bench still talking and talking and talking to herself.

Later. An uneasy after-dinner peace. My mother sits with the account books, rubbing her small nose as she always does when thinking carefully. The quill stands ready in the ink pot, waiting to mark its scratchy pounds and guineas against the sloping names of the aristocracy. My father, newly returned from town, is absorbed in a pamphlet by the fire. Molly and I read at the other end of the room in our favorite window seat. Molly is herself again, comforting and comfortable, her eyebrows knitted in concentration, her stockinged feet bumping into mine. I snuggle into the shiny cushions and let my thoughts drift over the wounds of the afternoon.

Gainsborough Gainsborough, who has been drawing something in charcoal at the table, rises softly and creeps over to us. He is sly as a cat, I think. There is a trace of dried blood crisping slightly on the inside of his nostril, which I regard with satisfaction.

He casts a cursory glance in the direction of my parents then bends down over me and, so quietly no one can hear it but me, begins to sing an old children's rhyme in my ear.

"There was a mad man,
And he had a mad wife
And they lived in a mad lane
The father was mad
The mother was mad
The children all mad beside
And they all got upon
A mad horse
And madly they did ride."

And then he looks at Molly, and leans in close and says, "Ride your mad horse, mad Mary." She looks up at him, her expression unreadable. In a flash, I reach out and kick his stockinged shin, a vicious, swift kick, as hard as I can make it in my stupid flimsy silk slipper, and he backs away like an injured dog.

My father, at the other end of the room, looks up from his paper and frowns. "Gainsborough. Come and help me with my brushes while there is still light. There is plenty to do before the morning sessions."

"Do be careful, Thomas, please. You have seemed under the weather recently," my mother says plaintively.

"Do not worry yourself so much, Margaret. It is only a summer cold," he replies, and casts a look toward her that I like. It is a warm look that tells of old love stories and secrets I want to exist but do not want to be part of. I do not want to see them, but I want to feel them, like glue.

Gainsborough Gainsborough skips off through the door with a quick, triumphant glance back at us, following my father down the stairs and letting the studio door thump shut behind him. But I do not care, for my father loves my mother, and so we are knitted together, the four of us, and no stupid boy can break it.

"I do wish you would not tease your cousin so," says my

mother, out of nowhere. "Poor boy, away from home, with only a pair of girls for company. He misses his mother, I should think. He is only young, after all. I do wish you would look after him."

I get up and go to her, and plant a small kiss on the top of her head where her hair parts in its thin white line.

"My goodness," she says. "Whatever was that for?"

"Because you look after us."

Her face creases in quizzical amusement, and she turns and blots a small, fat drop of ink that has escaped onto the surface of the desk.

"It is what women do, Peg."

I think for a second that I will wrap my arms around her and tell her about how frightened I am. Of not being good enough, of losing her, of her losing my father, of my father drifting away. Of secrets. Of Molly losing her mind. Of being so wild I let her down, or of never being wild at all so I become her. How it bubbles in my chest, the fear of all of it, all the time, every minute of every day of every week. But nothing comes out, of course, so I rest my head on her hair until she sends me away for being silly and stopping her from getting things done.

Later, when she has gone downstairs, I sit at my mother's broad desk, trying not to dislodge the tottering piles of accounting books, and pick up her quill. It is a fine one, a gift from my father, with a gold *M* on it. I dip the nib into the ink and write across the top of the paper.

Things that help

Then I write beneath:

Rest in bed

146

The Painter's Daughters

Being held so tight she cannot move

I think for a second, and then add in my scratchy, looping script:

Being hurt

Then I put the quill back gently on the table, pick up the paper, fold it into a tiny square, and tuck it in the top of my dress.

The next day, I wait. Like a creature hiding in a lair, ready to pounce. I have a plan to dislodge Gainsborough Gainsborough, and I am going to put it into action. I am the Panther, very Fierce and Subtle. I am the Tiger, most Terrible. I bide my time, hearing the hallway clock strike its lunchtime call, twelve solemn chimes, and then I see my prey, ambling unwittingly from the dining room, still wiping the crumbs from the corner of his mouth.

"Papa."

He turns, surprised.

"Peg?"

"You said you would teach me to paint another day, and this is another day. I have waited and waited, and I want to learn to paint." The words tumble out in a rush.

"To paint?"

"Yes." Does he not remember anything? Must he always be somehow absent? There, but not there.

"Is that what you want?"

"Yes, very much."

He regards me.

"It is true that I have had half a mind to teach you landscapes.

Your mother thinks landscapes are a more genteel pursuit. We had discussed it, when you were smaller, before things became so—so very busy. And I have some techniques, some new ways with landscape painting I could teach you, if you would like to learn them."

"Yes. I would. I would."

"Good. That's good."

It is as if he looks at me, really looks at me, for the first time since we were little.

"Would Molly like to learn also?"

"Of course." I have not asked Molly, who is upstairs trying to make her hair curl with pins. But I know she will not say no. These days it is as if somebody is rubbing out her definiteness so that she must borrow mine.

"Have you been keeping up with your drawing, both of you?"

"Yes," I say, which is a lie.

"I am so glad. I should have kept an eye on it, on you. But I spend half my life locked in a dark room with faces queuing to get in, and it never seems to end, by God, it does not. There is always another so-and-so with his great big face. And any time I get, I long to spend with my fiddle, for I am sadly out of practice these last months."

"I know how much you like to play."

"I do, Peg. And," he continues, a little uncertainly, "and you have seemed—distant—the two of you, lately. I thought I was losing you, a little. That you were growing up, away, perhaps from me. You have seemed, more than ever, in your own world."

"Us?" Us growing away from him? It is he who has gone away from us. He has everything backward.

"Yes."

"Have we?"

He is looking at me, his head tilted. "Is all quite well?"

I open my mouth, searching for words.

"It is—it is—"

"What is it, Peg?"

And there it is, suddenly, the old kindness in his eyes. At the sight of it, tears rise up and ache at the backs of mine. If I let them come, I think, they will not stop. They will roll on and on until there is nothing left of me.

"It is nothing."

He reaches out and touches my arm. We stand, poised, in the center of the hallway, the place of comings and goings, the in-between place.

"It is nothing," I repeat, and bite the inside of my lip. "When will you teach us?"

We make our way over the broad expanse, stumbling over the tufted grass and laughing. I glance at Gainsborough Gainsborough who struggles behind with three sets of paints instead of one and I smile, just a little bit. The wind catches my father's hair and ruffles it out of shape. Molly's face is pink with pleasure. We are out of breath, wild and happy under the fast-moving clouds, and the countryside stretches out beyond us, the sloping hills and patchwork fields and yellow wildflowers rioting across the grass.

We set up our easels near a fallen tree, and sit perched upon it in the shade of another enormous oak. I dip my brush into the sheen of the green and watch it move in careful circles, wrinkling the paint. I feel as though I can do anything, anything at all. Bath is only a distant, smoky white smear on the landscape, barely visible over the brow of the hill, and everything smells of summer grass.

"Now then," says my father. "We will start with the oak. The king of the English trees. This, my girls, is true royalty. Unchanging, unbending, stately." He waves his arms about exuberantly, and his shirt escapes from his britches. "You cannot paint landscape," he says, returning to his easel looking a little hot, "if you cannot capture the great English oak."

I look at the tree, its solidity, its confidence, and then down at the promise of my blank canvas. I pick up my pencil and make my first scratchy mark, a faltering line of lead. A beginning.

"You must loosen your wrist, Captain, there; loosen it so it is quite free, like this." He takes my hand and shakes it vigorously. "There, that ought to do nicely. And you too, Moll, shake hands with me." He cavorts over to Molly, and shakes her by the hand, and she throws her head back in laughter I have not seen for a while. I glance quickly at Gainsborough Gainsborough behind me as if to say, *See? See how happy we are. See how my father loves us. See how ordinary we are.*

We sketch out the shape of the trees that fringe the fields roughly in pencil, the height and scale of them, and my father praises and corrects and guides, and almost paints them for us, coming in with his delicate brush to show us the way the light dapples and distorts. One touch of white and the trees are alive. The slightest hint of gray shadow from a tool no wider than a pin, and they seem to move. How does he know? How does he know where to place these smudges, these whispers of color that breathe movement into something still?

"You have it there, Moll. That's it. Just a dab above, that's right. Now the ochre."

Our father shows us how the clouds are darker nearest the earth, how to underline them with weight and shadow, and how to find the gleam of their upper side where the sun catches them. He shows us where depth lies, and how to create light, and a thousand other tricks that are in his fingers, and not in ours.

Behind us, Gainsborough Gainsborough shifts from one foot to the next and watches my father.

And if we do not quite capture the way the light falls, we will learn it. If we do not quite seem able to render the movement of the trees, or their proportions, although we measure and squint and measure again, it does not matter. If we try hard enough, it will come.

He takes us into his studio two or three times a week, and now when the door closes it is with us cocooned inside, warm from the candlelight. And nobody minds, or ushers us away, or tells us that we are little girls and should be sewing out of sight. There is business here, there is money here, but it has come disguised as genteel accomplishment, and so my mother watches with her arms folded and nods. We hold our brushes very still in this meeting place of our father and mother's desires for us, and for one perfect moment, we please both.

"I shall paint the girls," my father says to my mother over breakfast one morning, with a new light in his eyes. "As artists. As painters of landscape. Something to show promise. It can hang in the hallway."

"Yes, yes," says my mother, the light from his eyes catching in hers.

"What shall we take down to make space? What could go? Ann Ford, perhaps, as she is to marry and leave Bath."

"Miss Ford is to be married?" I ask.

"Yes, to Mr. Thicknesse," my mother says.

I think about this news. Thicknesse, with his bulgy eyes and bad jokes. Why might she possibly marry him? Why does he seem to carry such power?

"He will travel Europe with her while she tours. A very good prospect for his career. For them both."

There is something behind my mother's words I cannot quite pick up on, a kind of satisfaction. And then I realize. She has deflected Thicknesse onto Miss Ford, and Miss Ford onto Thicknesse. The two great challengers to my father's loyalty. Perhaps, I realize with a jolt, it is not only Thicknesse who always manages things exactly as he wants them. Carefully placed suggestions, well-timed conversations. My mother talking confidentially to Ann in the drawing room, squeezing her hand. Talking of Ann's great success at dinner, of how she might capture Europe with someone to help her, while Thicknesse watched on, sly. Thinking that it was all his own idea.

"Yes, I shall feel the loss of Philip," my father continues, and I know that he is keen to draw the conversation elsewhere. "Now, who is sitting this coming Thursday, remind me?"

A nervous man with a permanently red face arrives to give us drawing lessons. He teaches us the poetic meanings of gestures, "raising of hands toward heaven for devotion, wringing of hands for grief, folding hands, idleness; scratching head, thoughtfulness; forefinger on mouth, silence." And for weeks one of us thoughtfully scratches our head, or artlessly folds our hands at dinner, and sends the other one into fits of silent laughter.

For the first time, we stand together in the hazy candlelight in the center of the Abbey Street studio, not watching from the shadows, or cast as extras in a scene. Fabric loaned from my aunt billows out over my arm, an unwearable, decadent explosion of azure silk placed for effect. I am in blue for continued affections, blue for loyalty. Loyally pursuing the art of painting, loyally thinking thoughts about paint. Molly is pensive, nursing her sketchbook, paintbrush raised. New gold rings glitter in her ears. I start off by looking toward her, but then our father changes his mind, and wipes me out, and turns me round, so that I face a statue he has borrowed from a friend. Flora, the goddess of spring.

When I am not being painted as a painter, I try to paint. I begin with a bowl of fruit. I think I do passably well with the apple. It is round and rosy, with a sheen to its skin. But then I add the next fruit, and the next, and it begins to lose its likeness, its depth, until it is abandoned, and I begin again, with a scene from nature. And then a rural cottage, and then a London vista, and then I try Molly at the piano, but the piano defeats me entirely, an unplayable construction of uncertain angles. A dog with legs too short for its body. The red-faced tutor makes weaker noises of encouragement. I can't do it, I think. I can't do it. Then my father talks excitedly over dinner about an exhibition for the three of us when we are grown up, "perhaps the Royal Academy, Margaret, although heaven knows they try my patience." I pick up my pencil and try again.

And I think, yes, very well, paint us, paint our faces, stage us in silks and twin us in the shadows, in gardens, by statues. Turn our faces upward, pose us, mold us and shape us in a future full of promise. And I will be patient, I will wait, and hope, and pray for something else to come and fill in the middle. For something real to color the blanks.

I have been woken by something, but I don't know what. I sit up, my heart pounding faster than it should. I find that I am listening hard, without knowing what I am listening for. The house sleeps on.

I think I hear a noise. A sort of moan.

I pull back the covers and make my way toward the hall, quiet as a mouse. There it is again, somewhere down in the dark of the house, a lowing moan, like a cow in a field. A few seconds pass.

I hear the unmistakable thump of a door. I think of robbers, of men with guns and grabbing hands, come to steal my mother's jewels, or worse, my mother, and I press myself back against the corridor wall. The lowing continues. Perhaps someone is ill. Hurt.

I imagine my father trapped under something heavy, his leg caught, sweating with pain, worried to wake us. I imagine the cook taken ill with a fever, calling out but lying stranded on the kitchen floor. I quicken my pace then stop dead at the top of the stairs.

A woman is moving silently through our hall. She glances round, and I see her sly eyes and her rough skin, the wrinkles around her mouth. She is not dressed like a lady. She is just a woman. She sees me on the stairs and winks, then she slips out into the dawn light, closing the front door to our house with a click behind her.

My father emerges from his studio and sees me with a start. One hand flies to his shirt, which is unbuttoned, showing the tufts of hair on the skin beneath. His eyes flick, almost imperceptibly, toward the front door.

"Peg, what are you doing up?"

"I heard a noise."

"There is nothing to worry about. I was working late. I had an idea for a painting. I did not mean to disturb anyone."

"It's all right," I say.

"Shall I take you back to bed?"

"I know the way," I say, because suddenly I want to hurt him, to spike him, in the small ways that are within my power. I turn away from his troubled, bleary face.

"Peg," he calls softly. "You are looking too thin. Are you quite well?"

"I'm all right," I say, and climb up the hallway stairs, feeling his bloodshot eyes on the back of my nightgown as I go.

"Shall we go painting tomorrow, clothes-Peg? Would you like that?"

"Yes," I say, but I keep walking up the stairs, and I do not think about the lowing, or about the woman winking at me with her painted eye inside my house while my mother and Molly lie sleeping in their beds above.

Wreck

Some weeks later, my father is in the hallway seeing off a couple who have come to have their little daughter added to their painting. The daughter, Selina, is waddling off on her fat little legs through the doorway and raising one hand in farewell to my father, who has made her laugh by juggling fruit. I am watching through the banister and waving too, when my father collapses on the rug like a piece of paper crumpled by an invisible hand.

The baby staggers backward and trips over my father's limp leg, then sits down with a bump and begins to howl, while the mother, slender in her silks, clutches a hand to her mouth and tries to pull the baby away. The father hovers, and I see cowardice flash across his face, for he is torn between the desire to help and the fear of contagion. I rush, stumbling, shouting for my mother. But when she comes, inky-fingered and bewildered, I see that she does not fall to the floor or shake him or feel his forehead or begin to weep in fear and panic. She glances down at my father's waxy face and says in a tight little voice to the maid, "Susan, tell Mrs. Hindrell to fetch the doctor at once." And she looks instead at Mr. and Mrs. George Byam and says, "I am so terribly sorry that Mr. Gainsborough has been taken ill."

I kneel and place my hand on my father's forehead, and all the while my mother is saying in her best voice, "I am sure it is nothing at all, of course. We will send for the doctor, but perhaps it is simply overwork, for he is very in demand, you know."

It is only when she has shown them out, and the screeches of the squalling baby are receding into the afternoon street, and the door is firmly closed behind them, that she turns and runs to the kitchen, shouting with a rasp in her throat for news of the doctor. She joins me on the floor, our skirts spread out like puddles, while Molly and two footmen and my aunt from her shop come running, and I look up and see Gainsborough Gainsborough hanging back by the wall. I see that he is watching and looking all the time, all the time, not at my father on the ground, but straight at me.

We do not see my father for several weeks. We are not allowed near, and only my mother sits by his bedside in an endless vigil, day after day, night after night, her face worn and the skin under her eyes dark with the strain. We hear her low voice through the door as she reads to him, letters from London friends, or the political pamphlets, or sometimes the Bible, although I have never heard my father express an interest in hearing the contents of the Bible in detail. He sits impassive in our abbey pew, one leg folded carefully over the other. When I listen to the sermons, I think that they are all about fear, so perhaps the Bible is what you need when you are very scared indeed. I begin to wonder if I should read it myself.

For weeks, we are left to roam the house and do as we wish. The adults were busy and distracted before, but now we are like animals when the zookeeper has left. There is no more painting. I ache for the open fields, but I cannot go without my mother's permission, and I dare not trouble her.

One afternoon we are lazing in the drawing room, and we do laze, for a person cannot be terrified all the time, no matter how guilty they feel about it. I am trying to sketch a cottage of the kind my father likes, but the roof will not come right, no matter how much I try to scratch it out and start again.

"Your cottage isn't much good," Molly says languidly, lying back on the window seat with her feet tucked up underneath her.

"It's only a first sketch. Don't be so rude, anyway, Molly."

"Do you think you're getting better at it?"

"At painting? Yes. Much better."

"I don't think I am."

"Of course you are. It is practice, isn't it? It is only trying harder, that's all."

"Then why isn't everyone a painter?"

"Because they don't want to be, so they don't try. And anyway, it is in our blood."

"So is selling dresses," Molly says, breathing on the windowpane and drawing an *M* in the cloudy circle.

"Oh, be quiet, Molly," I say. But I am discouraged, in spite of myself. I let the drawing flop down on my knees, and my pencil rolls across the floor and disappears beneath a chair. I am summoning the energy to go and pick it up again when our mother comes in. Molly springs up in surprise.

"Mama!"

Her face is haggard.

"You may come. He is comfortable and wishes to see you both."

We follow her wordlessly up the stairs, and she stops on the threshold outside the door of the bedroom where my father has lain all this time.

"This way, girls. Now, you must not be alarmed, for he is ill and does not look himself." She glances at Molly warily. "I expect you to be sensible about it, and not create a fuss." Then she stops and seems to wobble. "For it may be the last time you—it may be time to say goodbye, and it is best you do that before things become worse." And on the word "worse," her face constricts with sorrow and her voice swallows itself up, and she squeezes her hand against her face so that it pinches the tired, sagging skin of her eyes. We reach out and hold her, both of us, and she hiccups deep, horrible sobs that soak my neck.

I am trying to imagine a world without my father. But when I try, it is as if everything goes white and blank in my mind and I can't do it.

My mother turns away from us, wiping her bare forearm across her eyes. "But you are not to tell him," she says. "Or to talk to him of the end. For it may sap the last of his strength to think of it." We nod, and she places a hand on the doorknob and turns it.

The room is sweltering. It is July, but a fire rages in the grate, and the drapes lie thick over the shuttered and bolted windows. There is no air at all, none, and the heat of it rasps at my throat as I breathe in. It is like when you open the stove too close and a scorching rush from it escapes over your face. I pull at the neck of my dress.

My father lies on a stripped bed, a thin figure in a nightgown slumped against pillows and broiling in the heat. Around him are jugs and pills and bowls and books he is too weak to lift. I take a step closer, and I see that his face is yellowish, and so are the whites of his eyes, and that he has lost a tooth somewhere at the front.

"What a sight, eh, Peg? Can you bear to come close?" He speaks with difficulty, and I see that his mouth is spotted with livid red sores inside and out. "What a wreck of an old dad you have."

The sound of his voice after so many weeks makes my heart dance a funny little dance. I want to kiss him, feeling the old familiar tug, and I do not want to touch him at all.

He reaches out his hands, one for each of us, which is what he used to say when we were small and he was tugging us along a lane or through a field, our legs tired and our voices raised in complaint. *One hand for each of you and the old dad cart horse shall pull you home.* His hands now are marked with flaking yellowish bumps and patches. He looks like the cart horse we once saw put down. Shot in the head for his own good, the farmer said, chewing a piece of straw with his last three teeth. I see Molly hesitate.

"It is not catching, Moll. Do not be alarmed."

"What has made you ill, then, if it is not catching?" asks Molly.

"Stupidity, Moll."

Molly wrinkles her nose. Riddles and secrets, I think, and secrets and riddles. Always. So I say, out loud, "What do you mean?"

"Come, sit."

Tentatively, we reach out and take a hand each and sit on either side of the bed. To the side, on a low table, lies a broad shallow bowl, and inside it is a pool of liquid, molten metal, but it is not an oozing, glowing red like at the blacksmith's. It is the gleaming silver white of the moon. I am transfixed by it, the way it glimmers. He follows my gaze.

"That is only my ointment, Peg. They rub it into my skin to make me sweat. A rather pretty thing, is it not?"

I want to plunge my fingers into its swirling shine, to paint my skin with it.

"So beautiful," I say. "Like a liquid necklace."

My father laughs a weak laugh. "Oh, to put it into a painting, Captain." He reaches out and dips his fingers into the bowl, letting the silver run through and between them.

"What is that?"

"It is called mercury."

"Like the planet," Molly says.

"Or the messenger," my father says.

"Does it work? It looks like fairy stuff."

"I hope so. I need fairy stuff, as you can tell by the look of me, Moll."

"You look horrible," Molly says. "Extremely horrible."

"Thank you."

"Will you die?"

I glance at her, thinking she ought not to have asked.

He laughs a coughing laugh and wipes his fingers on a nearby rag. "Not if I can help it."

"Good," Molly says decisively.

"But . . ." He clears his throat. "But I have thought about my girls, these last weeks. About what would happen if I were not with you. And I began to worry, and to be clear that you must have some way to—support yourselves without me." His mouth distorts the words, trying to wrap itself around them without pain, and I lean forward to try to better catch what he is saying. "I have had time to think most seriously."

"But we are rich, aren't we?" asks Molly.

"Oh, Moll." His face sags, and for half a second I think that he will cry. "There is some money, but not as—not as much as all that. I am a stupid man. That is the—the long and short of it. A fool. Gambling and—and frolicking. I am so sorry to you both—to all of you."

He is looking past me, to my mother, who hangs back near the door, observing the three of us with her gray-blue eyes.

"To Mama?" I ask.

"Yes, to your mama. She is an angel. I do not deserve her."

I turn to see what she makes of these words. She has folded her arms across her chest as if trying to press her feelings back inside it. My father grips my hand more tightly, so that it almost hurts.

"I cannot help a good—a good time, you see. Peggy, you know this—of old—I think. I cannot help a good time, and now you see me, do you not?"

He laughs his rasping laugh again, revealing a wet flap of abcessed, toothless gum.

160

If ever there was a warning against a good time, my father seems now to be it. I stifle a shudder. So we are not rich, then. In spite of our fine dresses and silk stockings and iced-cake house with its chintz and its painted birds and its rotating door for decorated countesses. Behind the varnish, there is nothing much of substance. And without our father, brush in hand, the house crumbles. I turn to see if my mother is still there, but she has vanished, slipping from the room without anybody noticing.

"I have built a world I cannot support, my girls, for the work requires a level of grandeur that the money does not easily provide."

I think about the beggar who followed us once on the street, his teeth all gone but still gnawing on a crust. The stench of him. The filth. Women at the markets with pockmarked skin selling fish from a barrel.

"We have begun well with your craft," my father says, "but I want you to work hard at it, for you may need it. I have engaged a new drawing tutor, and I want you to practice daily. Do you promise me you will?"

"But we might marry rich men," Molly says, and I glance at her again. She is saying unspoken things. Things that are only thought about and imagined. It is true that we might. But how will we ever let anyone see through the cracks? How will Molly ever manage on her own with no one to squeeze her hand, and hang by her side, and fill in the gaps in her mind? It is an impossibility. Can she not see that? And yet not marrying, to be a grown-up woman who does not marry anyone. That feels like an impossibility too. And if we do not marry, and our father dies, we will have no money. We will have nothing at all.

"Perhaps you will, Molly, or perhaps you will fall in love with a shepherd and live in a hut and eat only lamb chops."

Molly pulls a face.

"Promise me you will practice."

"I promise," I say, and Molly nods, her thoughts clearly still on eternal lamb chop dinners.

"Good. Now go, so I can sleep. I love you both."

We kiss his clammy forehead and leave him, his eyes already closed against the great effort of being with us. In the hall, Molly doesn't look at me, and I don't look at her. What my father has said is only words. Nothing real, just words. But they creep like a rot under everything, and leave the foundations creaking and groaning beneath us.

I go straight to my sketchpad, holding the floppy, awkward weight of it in my hands, and without saying a word I pick up my pencil and begin again.

Molly sinks into a chair at the bureau, her head slumped over her hands. We stay like that for a few minutes, with only the sound of the hushed tick of the clock and the scratch of lead on paper.

"Can't we find something else to do?"

She raises her head and looks at me, but I ignore her.

"Peggy. Can't we find something else to do?"

I keep my head down and shade in the little bricks of the cottage one by one, concentrating hard. From the corner of my eye, I see her stand and move about, turning her hands over and over again and rubbing them down the front of her skirts. She is getting agitated, I think. I will have to go and calm her down. I will have to leave what I am doing, again, and go and soothe her, and stroke her hair, but for now, I am so tired of everything and so angry, so angry at her for all her needing of me that I do not want to. I want her, as I hear my father shout when he is drinking, to go to hell.

"I can't stand this house," she says suddenly. "I can't stand it. All this stillness and illness and—misery and waiting, waiting, waiting for something to happen! And all you will do now is draw forever, because all you ever want to do is please Papa like his little pet. I can't stand another minute of it."

162

"Someone must please Papa," I say carefully, and the lid I have placed upon the bubbling fury deep inside me begins to clank and jump around. "Someone must please him, Molly, for what do you think will become of us if we do not do as he says? What choice do we have beyond pleasing Papa, who keeps us all alive with his work, and who is thinking of how we will survive without him?"

"We will marry, of course!" she says, and her voice is shrill. "We will marry!"

I stand. The pot boils over. "Do you really think you will marry, Molly? Do you really think you will marry a great, rich gentleman with a great, rich house?" My sketchbook slithers to the ground. "Do you think you will run a great household and host balls and have a hundred little children to manage?" I go over and take her by the shoulders and shake her until her teeth chatter. "You . . . cannot manage . . . half a day alone—not . . . half a day."

She is limp under my hands, drooping like a rag doll when I let her go. We stand, my hands on her shoulders, shock on her face. Then she turns and runs. I hear her feet patter over the floorboards and up the stairs, and then the slam of the bedroom door.

For a couple of moments, I feel terrible. Guilt and nausea are washing over me, sloshing at my stomach. I will scream, I think. I will scream. But instead I pick up my pencil and my sketch-book with a wobbly hand, and begin again carefully to shade in the bricks of the little cottage on the page in front of me.

Correction

The *Bath Gazette* announces my father's death. Then, in the next edition, a correction. The correction is at the very bottom of the page, and somewhat hidden, so no one sees it.

Within hours of the death announcement, mourning gifts begin to arrive at the house. Callers leave black-edged cards and send pairs of black gloves. A bunch of black silk roses. A signet ring with a pair of black hearts entwined upon it. My mother is at first flummoxed, then tearful, then furious, raging at the boxes and letters of condolence as if it is somehow their own fault that they have been delivered. Gainsborough Gainsborough carries them all solemnly upstairs and piles them up on the table where my mother does her accounts.

Every time the doorbell chimes I want to burst out laughing, except that it is not funny at all, but awful, for all the while that the mourning tokens arrive, my father still lies on the very edge of death. If he did not, I think to myself, he would laugh harder than anyone.

Molly and I do not speak for the rest of the day after our fight. In the morning she does not come to breakfast, but remains sealed in her room with a headache. My mother is asleep upstairs, the faint rumble of her snores audible from the corridor. I nibble the edges of my kipper, making a collection of fine bones

164

in the corner of my plate. It is only Gainsborough Gainsborough and me at the table, eyeing each other across the breakfast china.

"Where's Molly?" he asks.

"She has a headache," I say.

"Oh, a headache," he replies gleefully, and takes a mouthful of egg, the soft yellow of the yolk dripping down over his napkin as he grins.

I look out the window. Everything is beginning to slide and slip like a tilting carriage, and I cannot keep it all in place. Down below, on the street, I see two girls with their parents making their way past the hawkers to the crowds milling at the doors of the abbey. It is Sunday. I have forgotten it, and there is no one to remind us. The family looks so very ordinary, I think. The younger girl is laughing with her mother, and the older hangs close to her father's arm, looking up at him as if he has the answers to things. I look down at my plate again and rearrange the kipper bones with my fork.

"Want to play a game, if Molly isn't coming down, then?"

I glance up at Gainsborough Gainsborough, startled. There are two burning red patches on his cheeks, but he looks at me with a sort of fierce defiance.

A game? I think. For a moment an ache springs up, for the old things. To build a den, to play at kings, to chase and be chased until my chest hurts. The Ipswich things.

I put down my fork and place my hands on the smooth pink sheen of my dress.

"I'm too old for games," I say, ice cold. "And so should you be."

I see him flinch although he tries to hide it, but I don't care.

After breakfast I hover outside Molly's door listening to see if she is making noise she should not be. There is only the faintest sound of tapping, as if on wood.

"Moll?" I call. "Moll?"

165

Nothing.

I wait for half an hour or more, but she will not answer me. The key is always to keep her close, and I have made a dreadful mistake. I go downstairs to the drawing room and start to sketch and sketch until it hurts, until a great bump rises up on my finger where I grip the pencil. I sketch all day, my mind on Molly, as if it will save me from something. Then I go into my father's studio. Everything stands untouched. Paint hardening on the palette in shiny little swirls. His waistcoat slung over the back of the chair. His brushes gone solid.

"Cousin Gainsborough," I call imperiously into the hallway. "Cousin Gainsborough!"

Gainsborough slinks from the back room where he spends his free time, hours and hours of it, playing a stupid game with cards and pebbles. He looks at me, his nose wrinkled.

"What?"

"My father's brushes need cleaning. Everything has been left, and it is quite ruined. Go and scrub them in turpentine until they are soft again. I shall need them this afternoon for my work."

I say "work" with as much importance as I can muster, but the word falls flat and doubtful into the air. Gainsborough Gainsborough considers his response. Then he shoots a quick glance toward the kitchen, turns round, pulls down his britches, and waggles his small, white bare bottom at me. I open my mouth to shout out for an adult, for anyone, but the shock of it makes my mouth run slowly, as if it is moving through mud.

I cannot get the shout out before he pulls his britches up and runs off back into his room, laughing. I look around wildly, desperately for witnesses, but we are, as always, quite alone. I take a deep breath, wipe my clammy hands on my dress, and steady myself against the wall.

I spend the next two hours scrubbing brushes. My fingers

shrivel, turning a translucent white, and begin to sting. I clear and tidy the whole studio, scouring the palette, rearranging bottles and instruments, throwing away empty tubes, and then put paper on the easels and draw until I want to scream. I tear the paper into a hundred pieces, and then I tear it again, and place some more on the easel, and sketch again. Then when the trees look more like a gray scribbled mass of clouds than trees, I select a newly cleaned brush at random, dip it in the oil, and begin to paint. I become absorbed, blindly focused, adding layer upon layer, trying to catch the way the gray must sit upon the green to make the movement come just so. And every time it does not. And I tear away the paper, and start again with another, until the room is littered with aborted glens and rivers and trees and thick messes of brown, and I forget about Molly, and my ruined father in his hot, deathly room, and all I can think about is why it will not come right. I am trying to paint something I cannot see, frantic with my own blindness.

The clock is striking for lunch when I hear a noise, a sort of scuffling sound, and footsteps out in the hallway. Someone is coming down the stairs, and it is not my mother's heavy tread. I drop my brush and race to the door in time to see Molly, dressed only in her nightgown and one of my father's gray wigs, disappearing through the front door of our house into the road.

I run. Slipping on the polished floor, I try to catch the back of her, but I am too late—she is gone. I hear a snorting come from somewhere up on the landing. Gainsborough Gainsborough is standing at the top of the stairs, winking at me and laughing as if he has never seen anything funnier in his life. I look wildly around, see my mother's long black cloak on the peg and tug it down in a heap, then open the great front door and tear out into the street, squinting against the sudden rush of daylight.

I look left and right, and there she is, a white afternoon ghost making her way down the middle of the road toward the abbey. A sedan chair swerves to avoid her, its bearer letting out a shout. Molly walks on, perfectly straight, through the piles of horse and dog muck, through the butcher's offal. I see his back retreating with his empty buckets down the lane. The tipped-out mess swills outward, turning everything to paste, and now Molly moves through it, her bare feet poking out from the frill of the nightgown's browning, bloodied hem, the little gray wig bobbing up and down on her head.

"Molly!" I call. "Molly!"

My thin slippers slip on the sludge as I reach her and throw the cloak over her shoulders. "Stop now," I say, my breath coming so fast it makes my chest hurt. "You must come home."

She looks at me, docile, compliant. She lets me turn her round and yank the wig from her head and pull the cloak tight across her chest, tugging the hood up so that her matted hair is out of sight. There are pairs of eyes on us all around. A furniture mender has set up on the corner, and sits waiting for custom on an old dining chair, his bony legs stretched out, one crossed over the other. He chews on a piece of tobacco, watching us as if amused. An orange-seller no older than me sits with her feet tucked up under her in a doorway, taking a break, her tray of oranges balanced on her lap. I stuff the wig inside the cloak.

"You all right, love?" she calls. "She not well?"

"She is quite all right, thank you," I say, and then turn and pull Molly back toward the house, pinching her hand viciously the whole way. My breath is tight in my chest. I bundle her up the steps and through the front door. I have saved her again, I think. The familiar sick feeling in my stomach is suddenly somehow comforting. I am relieved it is back, like an old friend. I pin her to my side and grip her so she cannot twist away again.

In the safety of her room, my heart still thumping, I take the cloak off her, throw it on the bed, and sit her down firmly on the dressing-table chair. I cannot have her out of my sight again now, I realize. We will have to stay together every moment. I tug off her nightgown, and dress her, and brush her hair, pulling back the strands and smoothing them down so she begins to look almost normal again. Her old self rises up in her eyes. There is Molly, I think. There she is. I only need to hold her close and she will come back to me. But every day, now, she seems to vanish more quickly, sinking away from me as if beneath the water.

I wake in the night with an idea. I remember my father's medicine, the silver swirl of liquid. How powerful it looked. Mercury. Even its name is powerful. Perhaps. Could it? Might it?

I take a small cup and spoon from the kitchen, bury them in the folds of my nightgown, and slink across the house and up the stairs to where he lies. They are snoring almost in unison, my mother sitting upright, and my father slumped back, mouth hanging slack, the bed-curtains only partly drawn. I tiptoe through the sweltering heat to the bowl that stands on the side. I dip my spoon into the mixture, metal on glimmering metal in the light of the failing candle. Then I carry my cup of stolen magic carefully up to Molly's room and shake her awake.

"What? What do you want?" she says blearily. "What have I done?"

"Nothing. Nothing."

"Have I wandered again?"

"No. Shh. I have an idea for making you better. Look." I hold out the cup. "Lie back and I will try some of Papa's medicine."

She sits up, unsure. "I don't know."

"It might help."

"It is not meant for me," she says, peering into the cup.

"No, but it is worth a try."

"Do you think so? I think it looks frightening."

"That's because it's powerful. Lie back now."

I push her back down onto the pillow and wonder where to put it. She lies, stiff, her eyes open. On her head, I decide. After all, it is her head that is wrong. It is telling her body to do strange things. I take the spoon and push her hair back and smear silver across her forehead, then on her temples and down her cheeks.

"Now," I whisper, "we must leave it on for a while, then wipe it off with a cloth."

We sit and wait. I think about her brain and what it looks like inside. About the pig brains I saw in a bucket in Ipswich. A human brain must be different from that, for pigs only think about food, whereas humans are full of words and ideas. I imagine a human brain is silver too, a mass of beautiful, shining connections that make thoughts come. I imagine the silver making its way into her head and mending all the parts that have gone wrong, coating everything inside her in its metallic glow. But in the gloomy light it doesn't really look magical anymore, just a gray slime across her face. I take an old muslin from my drawer and wipe it off and place it, along with the half-full cup, at the very back of my locked drawer, where no one will ever find it.

The next morning Molly is very sick, which I think is a good thing, for everyone knows sickness is the bad stuff inside you being forced out. Her bedclothes are soaked, and my mother is furious, and we are sent to the dining room and told not to leave under any circumstances. Molly sits, pallid, in a chair, while I practice the harpsichord, hitting notes that jar, and starting over and over.

The door opens.

"I am to sit with you until lunchtime, Mrs. Hindrell says." It is Gainsborough, scratching his nose.

"We don't want you," I say.

"Don't care."

He slumps down into one of the chairs, lets his head flop back, and stares up at the ceiling.

For a while, we sit there, the three of us, listening to the footsteps above us as Molly's bed is changed. Rain hammers outside, slicing down to the street below. I can see through the window into the drawing room of the house opposite, where a small boy is blowing into a French horn, his face contorted in a burst of mute effort. Full of sound and fury, signifying nothing, I think, which is something I have heard my father say. Then I notice Molly is crying. Fat tears are soaking her face while she sits, motionless in her dining chair. I glance at Gainsborough, who has not moved, then go to her and bend down toward her chair and put my arm around her, but she leans forward so that my hand drops and she is doubled over, her face hidden in her hands. She cries and cries. Gainsborough stares at the ceiling still.

Then Molly stands and starts to walk in an endless circle around the table. Round and round and round.

"Molly," I say, "sit down."

She ignores me.

I look at Gainsborough, who is tracing a pattern on the table with his finger, his eyes on Molly.

"Molly," I say again, trying to take her by the arm, "sit down, now." She pushes me off and keeps walking in her circle.

"Do you like to dance, mad Molly?" Gainsborough Gainsborough says suddenly, grabbing her by the hand as she passes and pulling her round toward him. He stands up and swings her arms back and forth roughly.

"Stop it," I say. "Molly, come here." But she laughs. As I step toward her, he pushes her away so that she spins, and then he starts to beat a drum rhythm on the table with his bare hands.

"Dance, mad Molly, come on, dance!"

Molly laughs again and starts to clap her hands, and then

suddenly she is dancing a quadrille, moving in wider and wider circles as if guided by a partner who is not there, her head turned toward his imaginary face, smiling and laughing and making conversation and switching direction back and forth to music that is not playing.

"Oh, the weather is fine, the weather is fine, the weather is fine, do you like cards? I like cards."

"It isn't funny! Stop it!" I reach out to grab Molly, but she tears past me, knocking a little statuette of a shepherdess to the ground. Its pink-and-blue arm breaks off and skids beneath a chair. "Someone will come! Someone will come!"

"Shall we dance a gavotte? Do you like cards?"

Gainsborough Gainsborough makes the noise of the band, narrowing his mouth into a trumpet, and it is a game, a stupid game among three children, and at the same time it is not, and Molly spins and reels, her dress bumping into the table and sending papers flying.

"Stop it," I say again, desperately, trying to catch her as though we are playing chase, trying to get her away from him, but I do not dare to pull her out into the hall in case we see an adult. She climbs onto a chair, wobbling on the padded seat. She is singing to herself, something about a gay deceiver, a song Ann Ford once sang.

"Molly, get down from there."

"Mad Mary Gainsborough, mad mad Moll," sings Gainsborough Gainsborough. "Sing songs, you loony lunatic."

"Molly," I say, my voice trembling. "Molly, get down from there this minute. Mama will come. Molly. Mama will come."

She ignores me, pulling at her hair so it comes half loose on her shoulders, singing to herself on the chair. Gainsborough is laughing a high-pitched laugh, pointing at her and bending over double as if he is hysterical. I go over to her and hit her legs, slapping at her skirt. "Stop it," I say. "Stop it!" Then in a violent tug she yanks down her dress, the pins falling from the stomacher like rain on the floorboards below, and exposes her small white breasts.

"Oysters," she is saying. "Oysters, two for a shilling."

Molly, I try to say, but no words come out. Gainsborough Gainsborough stands silenced, his mouth agape, his eyes two staring beads.

"Oysters, two for a shilling."

There is a numb sort of silence as Molly sways on the chair, and we stand watching her, and both of us are suddenly nothing but a pair of aimless puppets hanging limply in this empty moment. Somewhere, at the end of a long tunnel, my brain is saying to me that I have to grab her, that I must control her, somehow, right now, right this minute. I think about the piece of paper folded into my bodice.

> *Being held so tight she cannot move*
> *Being hurt*

My mother's voice outside somewhere snaps me back into my body and in a single leaping movement I rush to Molly and grab her by the arms from behind then slap her face and pinch her hand hard, twisting her body and holding her as I saw the woman do from the asylum at Box. "Quiet," I hiss into her hair. "Quiet, quiet, quiet, be quiet, hush, you must hush," and at the same moment Gainsborough Gainsborough runs to the door, but before he can place his hand on the handle, it opens.

Standing there, a dustpan and bucket hanging low in her hand, is a maidservant, the sallow-faced girl who lights the fires. Bessie, or Betsy, or something like that. She looks at us, slack-jawed. At the tableau. At Gainsborough Gainsborough's startled face as he pins himself back against the wall, and at me, frozen, halfway through pulling Molly's clothes back up around her, and at Molly balancing unsteadily on the chair, her shoulders bare.

There is a horrified stillness.

Then the girl averts her eyes, and with that one tiny movement, Gainsborough Gainsborough bolts through the door like a dog. She moves to the fireplace and kneels. I bundle Molly into her clothes, trying not to catch her skin with the pins I collect from the floor, talking all the time in her ear, and then push her firmly down into a dining chair.

"It is quite all right," I say. "It was only an accident. It only came loose; you must not be embarrassed."

I glance at the servant to see if she can hear me, but she has her head bowed low over the grate. She begins to clean. Metal hits the stone hearth. *Clunk, swish. Clunk, swish.*

"Next time we must make sure it is secured more firmly if we are to dance. We all need tea."

Molly looks at me, her eyes out of focus.

"Stay there, and I'll bring you some."

Clunk, swish. Clunk, swish.

"Molly, I will bring you tea. Do you understand?" I pinch her hand hard, and there is a flicker behind the shutters.

"Do you understand, Moll?"

"Yes," she says faintly.

I put my hand on her cold arm.

"But you must stay here, and stay quiet."

She looks at me, pale, unsteady.

I turn and leave her to go to ask the cook for tea, but the kitchen is deserted. I remember that it is Wednesday. She has gone to the market. I cannot lift the great black kettle on my own. She may come back at any moment, so I wait, glad for the excuse to be there, where it is silent, where I do not have to be constantly thinking what to do, what to do, what to do.

The kitchen is my favorite place in the house. The rough

sloping walls, the pots hanging scrubbed and orderly on their rails, the fire always burning in the hearth. Things always seem simpler when you step onto the chill of the flagstone, as if it is a reminder that the earth is still there under your feet. Today, the pastry bowls are laid out on the broad table waiting for their afternoon use, a recipe scrawled on a piece of brown paper in a hand I do not know. The sugarloaf stands wrapped with a cloth. I lift the cloth and scratch some away, and then lick my finger, press it into the crumbling sugar, and bring it to my mouth. Comfort. Then suddenly, before I know what I am doing, panicky as a thief, I am unwrapping the cold chicken that stands covered with a napkin on the side. I push huge chunks of it into my mouth, barely chewing it, forcing it down my throat, licking the grease around my lips and wiping it with the back of my hand. It tastes wonderful, meaty and rich and sticky and satisfying. For one minute, everything is pleasure. Then I stick my fingers down my throat until I vomit in the sink and wash it all away.

When I climb the stairs again with a glass of water, I find my mother leaning over Molly. She turns as I come in.

"Something is wrong with Molly."

"No, no," I say quickly, "she is all right."

"Peggy, she is clearly not well. She will not speak to me. Molly. Molly. I cannot manage it, I cannot, Peggy, after everything that is happening with your father, after—I cannot manage it." Tears spring into her eyes, and I take a step forward.

"Mama, she is quite well."

"Feel—she is clammy. She will barely talk to me. Molly. Papa warned me; he said he felt—Molly."

"I must be very quiet," Molly says. "Very quiet, or—"

"It is only that she felt faint. I went to fetch her some water," I say, talking smoothly over her, as I do. "It is nothing, Mama, really, it isn't anything at all. We were dancing too much, that's all. Practicing, and then suddenly she lost blood to her head, and had to sit down, and her dress came loose—it is only that."

Over by the fireplace, head bowed, the sallow girl keeps on working.

"Peggy, do stop speaking for her. One would think Molly hadn't a voice of her own. Molly. Are you feeling better?"

Speak, Molly. Speak, I will her, silently.

"Yes," Molly says. "Much."

"To bed," my mother says. "Immediately."

I take one of her arms, and my mother takes the other, and gently we bring her to standing.

"You are too much alone. I know it. Your papa said so too, but it has all been so dreadful, and I have been quite at my wits' end with—Jones, stop that horrible clattering and fetch some tea."

The sallow girl looks up, and I see her lips part as if she is going to say something. She looks from my mother to me, and back again, then gives a jerk of the head and leaves the room.

Molly is wrapped in a nightgown and sheets and topped with an eiderdown, and tea is finally brought, then the tinctures the doctor left are administered again, and there is more talk of the Kettle, and finally my mother draws the bed-curtains and shoos me away. Later that day, when she is busy with my father again, returning to his bedside like rubber snapping back into place, I creep back in and part the curtains and crawl into the bed next to Molly.

We lie in the boxed-in gloom, looking at each other's ghostly outlines.

"Why does it happen?" Her voice is quiet, soft.

"I don't know."

"My mind goes blank and I—I cannot remember."

"I know."

"There is something wrong with me."

She looks at me with a sort of pleading, as if, somehow, she is

176

hoping that I will say, *No, there is nothing wrong with you. There is nothing wrong with you at all.*

"It is only sometimes," I say.

"Perhaps . . ." She hesitates, her voice barely above a whisper. "Perhaps we should tell Mama."

I lean forward, gripping her hand urgently in the dark. "No, Molly, we should *not* tell Mama. We absolutely must not tell Mama, do you understand? If we tell anyone, anyone at all, they will take you away. They take people away who cannot think straight and cannot remember, and they put them somewhere terrible."

Molly's breathing quickens, the thick fabric of her nightgown rising and falling swiftly. "I'm scared," she says. "I'm scared."

I squeeze her hand. "I will look after you. We must be very, very good for Mama."

"Don't ever tell anyone, Peg. Don't ever."

"I will never tell anyone, and I will never let anyone find out. I promise. It is about being very careful, and very quiet. You must just do as I say. You must do everything I say. We must not argue anymore."

"I promise. I promise I will do everything you say."

"Good. I may have to hurt you, sometimes, but you know that," I say carefully, "it is for your own good. It is not because I want to. It is because I love you and I am trying to keep us safe. Do you understand?"

"Yes."

"Good. Now go to sleep."

She shuts her eyes obediently, and her sobs judder more slowly, her face pressed into my chest, my arms locked around her neck. She cries for perhaps ten minutes, until the pillow is sodden with tears, and then she stills. I shut my eyes too, and lie awake trying not to think about the net that feels as if it is closing in around us.

MEG

It is, of course, raining. The thin, shivery sort of rain that prickles on your face and makes you close your eyes involuntarily against it. It's already leaving a fine wet web on the wool of her cloak. Another ten minutes and she'll be damp and uncomfortable all the way to London. She hurries, sliding on the mud and skirting round the black shine of the puddles that are forming in the dips of the day's carriage tracks.

The public coach leaves at five, but the inn will be waking by then, so she left an hour earlier and stood in the chill shelter of a nearby house waiting for the church bell to strike the quarter hour. She has lain awake all night, too frightened to go to sleep in case she didn't wake again, and now her limbs are stiff and sore and her head pounds at the temples. She turns the corner and sees the coach waiting outside the Black Horse inn, and the men standing with candles in the mottled dawn light. She squints, trying to identify them. It's the blacksmith's son, Tom, she thinks, relieved, and his brother. These two will see her right. She has brought money to give anyone who keeps quiet until she is safely away, but in reality, no one in Harwich has much loyalty to her father. She picks up speed, but a hand catches her on the upper arm and pulls her back so she flies round, knocked out of kilter.

"What in hell's name are you doing?"

Hal, the whites of his eyes gleaming in the half light.

"Let me go."

"Where are you going?" He grips her, insistent.

"Hal, stop it." She yanks her arm away from his and he lets it fall.

"Tell me right this minute where you're going, or I swear, Meg Grey, I'll . . ." His eyes are pleading, his threats more desperate than ominous.

"It's not your business."

"It's—you're my business. You're—"

"I'm not your wife yet, Hal. I'm not anyone's wife, however stupid you may think me."

"What do you mean, stupid?"

"Nothing, it doesn't matter." They stand there in the rain, miserable.

"You're running away."

"I'm not, I'm . . ." But she doesn't know what she's doing. Perhaps she is doing exactly that.

"I'll have you, Meg. I want you. We can—we can say it was mine. I don't care that it isn't. I don't want you to leave."

He knows, then. She wonders who else does. She looks at Hal, his head bowed in the drizzle, offering to raise the bastard child of a German. He's chased her out into the night like a man in a poem. He loves her. He'll have her at any cost. She knows enough to be grateful for that.

"Hal."

"Whose was it, anyway? Which one of theirs?" He brings his eyes up to hers, as if ashamed to ask.

"I can't—it's—it's not your business."

"Please, Meggy. Please."

Day after day looking at this face. Feeding this mouth. Washing these britches. Walking the same safe square route from inn to church to market to inn, like a mouse in a cage.

"I'm going to miss the coach." Immediately she wishes she hadn't spoken.

"The coach? For God's sake, Meg. The London coach?"

"Yes."

"Then I do think you stupid. Bloody stupid."

"It's not your business, whether I'm stupid or not." It stings, though. Her boots, already past their best, are starting to sag in the mud, letting the creep of water into her toes. Doubt too is beginning to edge its way in. She readjusts her pack on her shoulder. Hal shifts from foot to foot, beads of rain settling in his hair.

"Please, Meg. Please don't go. It's dangerous. It's so dangerous. Please."

Suddenly she wants to drop to her knees in the mud and sob. She wants him to pick her up, and take her home, and put a blanket on her, and for nothing else to follow after that, for time to stop with her sitting there, warm and rescued under her imaginary blanket.

He takes her arm again, more gently now.

"You don't have to run away. You don't. I'll have you."

She can't think of anything to say that won't insult him. That she doesn't want him to touch her in that sort of way. That she doesn't want to touch him either. That the thought of spending her days seeing him every minute, in her bed, in the kitchen, in the bar, morning, noon, and night, makes her feel so sad and weary that she will not want to rise and face the inexorable burdens that a normal day will bring.

"I know," she says. "I'm grateful. But I don't want you."

She has calculated the sting of the words to leave him reeling and give her time to stumble away across the mud toward the waiting coach, but she feels them like a physical pain as she moves, as if she has cut herself on her own cruelty.

As she pulls herself up the ladder to the roof, where the cheapest fares are, her feet slipping on the rungs, she looks back at him standing dejected in the whitish-blue light, then turns and sits, facing the road ahead.

The journey is brutal, but then she had expected no less. On the roof she can lean over the edge to be sick, but it is too wet and too precarious, each jolt threatening to turn her out into the mud. At the first stop she accepts defeat and pays to join the others in the interior of the coach, which she finds, too late, stinks of garlic and fetid morning breath. When she can't hold her vomit down anymore, she unfolds the small bag she has brought to be sick into, and hides her mouth with one hand as she retches again and again.

"Bloody hell," the man next to her mutters. "Jesus."

A fat man nearest the door stares down disconsolately at his chicken legs, grease still shining on his lips.

After four hours of repeated retching, she leans her head back against the rattling carriage wall and lets her eyes droop shut. Tonight, she has a bed at their stopping place. For now, she is warm enough. One moment at a time, and no more. She lets herself think about Frederick, and blue coats, and dark nights, in the same way that, when she was small and woke with a night terror, she used to let herself think about fairies, and comfort herself with the thought of their delicate, iridescent wings.

"All out, all out."

Meg staggers, dazed, into the darkening afternoon of the next day. Smog hangs like a drape over the buildings, over the brawling men slamming one another against the brickwork, over the beggars and the hawkers of vegetables and the man asleep under a cloak on a basket. Her fellow passengers filter out and away and disappear into the crowd as if they have been dissolved into the watery day. There are taverns on all sides, crowds around their doors, spilling out into the road, where coaches stand waiting in the dinge, a long snake of them stretching round the corner and away. London seems to pulse with life, like the summer garden in Harwich, with its fucking and fighting and industry, the same force of nature made big and played out on its grubby stage. Another scrap is on the verge of erupting between two drivers who both seem to blame the other for blocking their way. Meg swerves as something is thrown. An onion. It bounces a couple of times and rolls under a carriage. She shifts her pack onto her back and looks both ways, to each end of the street. Cripplegate looms to her right, a vast guardian of the city entrance. To the left, the road bends: more sludge, more chaos.

"Know your way from here, do you, sweetheart?"

She turns round to see the driver is eyeing her. He dismounts and jumps down from his perch with a splat, sending more mud flying up his spattered britches.

"I'll go tomorrow. To my aunt, I mean."

"Your aunt, eh?" He looks at her doubtfully.

"Yes. She's unwell, so I had to come quick."

He eyes her pack. "What will you do for a bed tonight?"

"Is there—is there somewhere I can stay nearby? Not too expensive. But clean enough. Respectable."

"Within or without?"

"What?"

"Within or without the city gates?"

"What's—what's best?" She is aware of how stupid she sounds.

"Try the Swan with Two Necks. That'll do you for a night."
He turns and stomps through the slush toward the yard where
the boys are pulling the horses in to rest. "Keep yourself to yourself, mind." He shakes his head, looking back and calling over
his shoulder, "No place for a girl on her own, this, if you ask me.
Didn't you have a brother or something what could have come
with you?"

"No," she starts to reply, "I never had . . ." and then trails off,
as he has disappeared into the yard without turning back to hear
her answer.

All right, she thinks. All right. She looks left and right again,
at the motley collection of painted pub signs up and down the
roads before her, fear pumping through her body. What is she
doing? What was she thinking? She could stay one night, only
one, and take the morning coach back, and take the beatings
that would come for a few days, and beg Hal on her knees for
a wedding. She thinks about Hal's wounded-dog eyes. And she
thinks about her father's bulging, yellowish ones as he comes
at her with his fist, with his elbow. Somewhere deep inside
her, beneath the layers of wool and linen and whalebone and
skin and fat and muscle, the baby is still, quiet in its cocoon.
She takes a deep breath and begins to pick her way between the
crowds and coaches, heading to her left.

PEGGY

Burned

My father begins, slowly, to mend. He sits, pale and shaky, wrapped in a great Indian dressing gown and tucked under the thick blanket my mother brought with us from Ipswich. Molly fusses over him and smooths his hair. He looks like one of Mrs. Hindrell's pastries, enveloped in layer upon thin layer, ready to be popped in the oven. The sight of the Ipswich blanket always makes me feel better when I am not myself. It is brown and red and rather ugly, and reminds me of our white house on Foundation Street, and of how our mother was always there to place her big hand on my forehead, cool and certain. I thought it had magic powers. Perhaps it does, I think, for it has cured my father.

After a couple of days, he comes downstairs and discovers the pile of gifts to commemorate his death. He asks my mother what they are, and then laughs for almost an hour, reading out commiserations and condolences and letters that say he was the greatest artist of our time, and which set him off laughing again for another ten minutes. He asks to see the cutting from the *Bath Gazette* and sends off for it to be framed. Death seems to go from the house, leaving its ruins and ravages but taking its chill with it.

I dose Molly nightly with the medicine, then wipe it carefully away, and she seems to grow less sick, and sleepier each time. In the middle of the night, I creep down to the great bunch of keys that hangs in the kitchen on a hook, and carry them upstairs, muffling their treacherous jangling in the fabric of my nightgown. I try all the small keys until I find the one that locks Molly's door with a click of steel. Then I pull it from the ring and hide it in my bedroom along with the cup of mercury and the cloth. Any moment when Molly is not with me, I lock her in. I am pale from not sleeping, blackish-purple shadows under my eyes. My mother notices and tuts and frets and feeds us cheeses and extra eggs and makes us both drink pump water twice a day.

Our lessons have begun again, so we move from drawing to dancing to harpsichord to French to Bible studies to embroidery. I tuck an embroidery needle in the hem of my dress, and once, when Molly begins to act oddly before the French tutor arrives, I take her hand when no one is looking and push the needle into her finger, just enough to make a bubble of blood, and she becomes quiet again, quiet enough to sit by me. I can only do that once or twice, every now and again, for it is messy and risks drawing attention, but I keep a needle with me always, so I know we can be safe.

One afternoon, Molly and I are having our dancing lesson, our favorite bit of the week. Mr. Fleming is here, leaping about the drawing room with every part of him wobbling, even his hair. It was once a joke of ours that Mr. Fleming's chin lands several seconds after he does, but we do not tell the joke

185

anymore, for his wife has died and we feel so sorry for him. His solemn oldest daughter plays for us, peeping over the top of the harpsichord at him with her big, sad eyes. I do not like to look at her, although she is only our age. Instead, Molly and I make each other laugh with our terrible country dancing hops. I am thinking about how everything feels better when you hop about, and wondering why that might be, and am about to say so to Molly when I hear a fuss downstairs. My mother's voice remonstrating, my father swearing, the banging of doors.

"Dear God! Dear God!"

"Oh, for heaven's sake! It is far too soon for you to be thinking about such things, Thomas!"

I fling open the door and see, with a rush of panic, that, for the first time since his illness, he is at the studio door. I remember that I have not had time to tidy it for him after my practicing. But he will be proud of that, at least, although I have been messy. He will see how hard I have worked.

"Peggy Gainsborough!" he tries to shout, his voice still hoarse. "Margaret Gainsborough! Where the devil are you?"

He is in the hall, the door to his studio wide open, and his face is written all over with fury. He sees me appear at the top of the stairs.

"Come down here this minute."

I go down, running my sweaty hand along the banister, until I am standing with him at the studio door.

"Goddammit, Peggy, what is this mess? What in God's name has gone on in here?"

"I—I tidied up for you—"

"Tidied up?! The place is a wreck. My paint is dried out! My brushes are utterly ruined, cleaned with God knows what, then left to rot. And these bloody scribblings everywhere! The waste! The waste of it!"

I look beyond him into the darkened studio. My paintings,

hundreds of them, fill every corner. My attempt at a canvas stands in the center, a muddy mess of murky browns and greens. Everywhere there are matted brushes, used cloths, tubes of paint abandoned on surfaces. I think, desperately, about blaming someone else. Molly? No. The boy. I open my mouth, ready to form the lie. But then I remember I have signed them all, Margaret Gainsborough, Margaret Gainsborough, Margaret Gainsborough. The room is littered with my name. And I can see, suddenly, how terrible my paintings are, and what a mess I have made.

"My God, Peggy." He tugs at his hair, desperately. "I am already so far behind with my work I shall probably never leave the studio again, and you have made everything a hundred times more difficult. What were you thinking?"

"I—I thought to practice."

"Gainsborough, go and take these to the stove and have Mrs. Hindrell burn them."

The humiliation is white hot. I turn and brush past Gainsborough, who is making his way to gather up the first piles of my drawings in his arms as rubbish to be disposed of.

"My God, Peggy," my father says as I go, "you have set my apprentice a dire task with this childish mess. It is a mercy I have him to help me restore order. Women! Why must it be my fate to be surrounded by women who interfere so incessantly in a man's business!"

I am stung, and go out, past my pale, exhausted father, past my mother, who stands with her lips pinched, hurt again, troubled again, and up the stairs to my room.

I lie on the bed, face down, until Molly slips into the room, quiet as a ghost. She slides onto the mattress and wraps her arms around me and tells me that they will forget about it all soon, and that my pictures were very good, and that he did tell us to practice, so it is really all his fault, actually, if you think about it, and that everything will be all right.

Once he is on his feet again, my father is busy with the many missed commissions he has to complete after his illness.

One day I find him and try, tentatively, to show him a drawing of some elms I can see from my window, but he says that he has no intention of dying, after all, and that there is nothing wrong with a hobby. Perhaps some things are best kept that way, he says, for he sees that recently I am looking very pale and worried. He agrees with our mother, he says, that it is not good for girls to be burdened with such things.

He is less energetic. There is a weariness to his gait that wasn't there before. He doesn't speak of painting lessons again. He smiles at us more.

He gives us money for new dresses for the winter season.

He buys us a pair of singing birds, each in its own cage.

Breakfast. The smell of haddock and egg. The sallow-faced girl stands in the corner, head down, waiting to refill the hot water. Gainsborough scribbles away at something next to me, his hand shielding the work as though I might copy it.

My father crosses the dining room, wrapping the folds of his dressing gown around him as he takes his coffee to sit in the far corner and reply to his letters.

"My goodness, Gainsborough, that is not bad at all," he says, pausing at the table to examine a drawing. He holds a letter and a letter opener with the head of a tiger, his inky thumb rubbing over the tiger's ears as he stands looking down.

"There is a talent here. Most certainly. It is very good." He nods. His eyes are careful, examining. "Yes. There is promise here. Good."

My father taps him on the top of the head and nods again.

"He's caught you, Peg."

He winks at me, a casual, cheery wink, and goes to his chair and sits to read his letter, rubbing his chin. Gainsborough Gainsborough shifts in his seat and picks up his pencil, then looks up at me. Our eyes meet, and I hate him, but this time with a defeated sort of hate. A half smile plays on his lips as he glances down at the drawing and then back up at me, as if to indicate something.

I look down at the paper.

He has drawn me.

The house lies quiet. I turn the key to Molly's room and bury it in the front of my dress, then go downstairs and push open the studio door and stand in the familiar half-lit hush. My heart beats in my throat, quick and insistent. It is not like the kitchen, a place of safety and calm, this. It is a secret world that pulls me in. And now it is forbidden, more dangerous than ever. Once it was the world my father drew us into, and now it is the world he wants us out of, but still I am always there in spite of myself. The portrait of Molly and me, styled into artists, stands in the corner. Only a few strokes away from being perfect. My hand, hanging loosely to one side, is thin, almost translucent. He has seen that. The way I am trying to make myself vanish. I can hide it from him in life, but not in paint.

There is something else in the picture I have not seen before. The ghost of my old profile, before my father rearranged our positions and began again, is still visible through the paint, rising to the surface.

I shake my head, to knock all these ghostly selves away, the real and the pretend and the imagined, so I don't have to think about which is which. I move instead to the slick curls of leftover paint and dip my finger and paint my face in my now-familiar secret ritual, a layer of chalky white beneath, then the smear of vermillion on my cheeks and Titian red on my lips. A smudge of black beneath my eyes. Lamp black. The color of the butterfly's wings as it fluttered helplessly under the needle. I smudge it across my eyelid. Then I look at myself in the mirror and pull at my dress, sliding the fabric down so that my shoulder is bare.

There is a noise, the creak of a footstep. I freeze. A pale face appears at the edge of the back curtain. It is the boy.

I know that he has been watching me. Watching my private moments. Watching me smear the crimson paint across my lips. I look back at him, fixing my eyes on his. I more than anyone know what it means to be looked at. We stay there, suspended in hostility. It is as quiet as death in the room, his eyes boring into me, and mine staring into his, a pair of cats about to fight. I feel the solid weight of the look as if it is a physical touch. Without even knowing what I am doing, my hand disconnected from my body, I reach for the front of my dress and slowly, deliberately, I pull out the pins, one by one, and put them on the table. I do not stop looking at him. I want to make it so that he cannot look away. And then I pull down the stiff, resistant fabric of my stomacher and let it drop to the floor. The key to Molly's room falls too, with a clatter on the wood. I let it go and do not stoop to pick it up. The air is cool on my skin. My breasts are exposed, like Molly's in her wild dance, like Ann Ford's with my father, and his eyes are fixed on them, on me, and he cannot stop it. *Shapes of horror, shapes of pleasure.* Slowly, I pull the folds of my dress up over my slippers, then over my ankles, then past my knees and up to my thighs, so he can see them, so that his eyes fix on the little hole in my stocking and the pale, exposed oval of skin beneath it. I can feel my heart racing in my throat, and I can see his breath fast and panicked, and I know that I am winning something. I have made him panic, made his palms sweat, and the moment is pure power, stretching out and out into infinity, and I stand, my chest rising and falling, and in that long, single moment, I do not notice that his face has changed. I do not notice, immediately, the light, a tunnel of bright, unbearable daylight, that seems to have appeared from somewhere behind me.

Until I hear my father's voice. It cracks on the note like a broken instrument.

"Peggy?"

And then the bottom falls out of the world.

Dislodged

I lie, my cheek squashed against the floorboards, listening to the argument raging on through the afternoon. I can hear everything, the shrillness of my mother blaming everyone but herself, and the agonized voice of my father blaming nobody but himself. It is a runaway horse I cannot stop.

"Thicknesse knows nothing of my family! My girls! Nothing!" my mother shouts.

"He has warned me before, he has—"

"He meddles and he meddles and he meddles!"

They are performing a duet, I think. The soaring, furious soprano, and the lamenting tenor.

"He is concerned, Margaret! He is a concerned friend. He sees that things are not—not—"

"Not what?!"

"Not quite—right—with the girls, with Molly, and worries that they are too much alone."

"I cannot bear it! A stranger *speculating* on our children, on how I manage our children! *Secret* talks!"

"No, no, it was not that. He worries that Molly is not—not well."

"Molly? Of course she is well. Of course she is quite well! There is nothing wrong with her! Except idleness!"

"Margaret—"

"Nothing but wickedness comes from being idle, and not being given a purpose. And this is wickedness. What you have told me is nothing but *immorality*. They need to be thinking about husbands, about marriage, although you persistently forbid it."

"Goddammit, Margaret, I will not have them grow up good for nothing but tea-drinking and husband-hunting!"

"Then what?! Turn them into a pair of—of bluestockings?"

"Hardly that!"

My mother is pacing, her tiny little feet in her tiny little shoes click-clacking up and down under her weight, stopping and starting in their tracks with each fresh burst of feeling.

"We tried it your way: we set them painting, and nothing came of it."

"They did not have the talent I had hoped."

"So you will not have them painting, and you will not have them married! What will you have them be?!"

"Happy! I would have them be happy!"

The words are like a sip of a hot drink in a storm. I savor the warmth.

"You know who my father was! You know what is in their blood! What they might expect. What people will say if they are brought up wrong."

"Nobody knows, Margaret. The secret went to the grave with him."

"But still. Beaufort is alive."

I turn the word over in my mind again and again, but I have never heard it before. Who was my grandfather? What is Beaufort?

"This is not about Beaufort, Margaret," my father is saying. "Molly is not—not well. Something feels wrong."

"She has seen a doctor! They can find nothing wrong with her!"

193

"It was not normal! She was—it was not—"

Suddenly my mother's voice, so carefully put together, comes apart a little at the seams, and London vowels squeeze their way out in a low warning. "You just be very careful, Tom Gainsborough. You be very careful what you say about my daughters."

There is a long pause. I turn my head over on the floor so my other cheek presses down against the wood. I can see a hairpin lying forgotten under the dressing table, glinting forlornly.

"Molly is not our concern here, in case you have forgotten! It is Peggy and her wickedness!"

"I know. I know that." My father begins to sound defeated.

"I have warned you and warned you! They need a guiding hand. They absolutely must have a guiding hand. We have no man to lead us. Women will fall apart without men. A household without a man's strength is no good! You are too weak with them! You always have been!"

"Not every woman is like your mother, Margaret. Not every man is your father."

"My mother has nothing to do with it! Nor has my father neither! You are the head of this household, and I wish you would act accordingly!"

Nor has my father neither, I think, and pull a face to myself on the floor. She sounds like Mrs. Hindrell.

There is a long pause. Then, my father, very low. "How can I when you will not let me speak?"

I have to strain to make out my mother's words. "Speak, then."

A sigh. My father stands, and his lighter footsteps move a couple of paces below.

"I am concerned. I do not know what causes it. I agree something must be done. Thicknesse thinks that we should send them away."

"Away?"

"To school. Somewhere with other girls and laughter and noise. Where they can become less shy. Less—reclusive. Where they might learn how to behave, and become ready to enter society."

"That is what we said of Bath! That they might be made ready to enter society."

"But it did not work!"

"I have failed, then. Perhaps someone else will manage them better, for you see for yourself what a fine job I have made of it. I cannot manage them, Thomas! I do not know what to do with them!"

There is a pause. I feel like I have swallowed a stone. We are so bad that my mother has given up. She cannot cope with us. And she does not know the half of it.

"Very well."

Away, I think. Away to be surrounded by terrible, frightening strangers and their staring eyes. By a thousand Thicknesses and Gainsborough Gainsboroughs and Ann Fords trying to see if we are normal. I am panicked, trying to pull my thoughts together. Trying to work out my next move.

Suddenly, from nowhere, the sound of my mother's rasping sobs. "I am sorry, Tom. I am so sorry," she hiccups. "It is all me. It is me. I could not manage with you unwell."

"There, there, Margaret," my father is saying. "There, there. We have fixed it. It is only a childish nonsense upon which we shall look back and laugh. All will be well."

I stand in the thick October light, which pours through the window of his study and lights all the little specks of dust dancing in the air.

"Please don't send us away."

My lip trembles as it did when I was a child with a sore knee.

I want him to notice, and to pull me close. To give me a sweet from his tin. A kiss on the head.

"You are not going as a punishment, Peggy."

My father finds it difficult to look at me. His eyes will settle on anything that is not my face. The curtain rail. The ink pot, its quill poking out askew. The curled edge of the rug.

"You are not thriving, it is clear to see. What I saw—I cannot easily dismiss." He swallows, as if trying to swallow down the memory.

"Why is *he* still here, when we are sent away?" I throw the challenge at him, because my face is burning with shame. I will do anything for us to be allowed to stay with my parents, away from the terrible, frightening danger of strangers and their staring eyes. Anything.

"Your cousin?"

"Yes."

"I need an apprentice. It is as simple as that, Peggy. His mother paid me many kindnesses when we were children. And he has talent. He has the skill for it. I have no sons, and I have half trained him up already. He is only a boy."

He runs his fingers over the top of the old globe on its stand by the window, tracing the thick leather with its swirl of places we will never go.

"And you are different," he says. "Different things are expected of you."

"Who was our grandfather?"

He looks at me with a kind of helplessness.

"He was—a duke."

A duke. Jewels, and powdered faces, and satin trousers. My head spins. Things are shifting, gaps filling; things I have never been told but always known are floating to the surface. The letter *F*. Francisco. Felice. Francis.

"And our grandmother was a duchess?"

My father bites his lip. "No."

"Then—"

"Stop asking questions, Peggy." His voice is hard. "Stop asking questions, and do as you are told for once."

It is a riddle, a duke with no duchess, and there is something shameful in it, or he would not try to silence me. Of course, I think. We are sullied in some way. I have always known it.

My father places his hand on mine, then takes it away again quickly as if it will burn him.

"My two lovely little girls are changed," he says, "and I do not like it. I do not like the way things are, and there must be action taken. It is too quiet for you here. Too somber. And, as you now know, there are reasons for you to behave in a way that is fitting. More so than other girls."

"Please." I cannot think of any other way to be heard. "Please don't make us go."

Finally, he turns and looks at me, and I know it is no use.

"It will be good for you."

And his eyes snap away from mine again, as if he is unable to bear the contact for more than a few seconds. As though I am too shameful to look at anymore.

The trunks are piled up high, many more than when we came all those years ago from Ipswich, for now we are young ladies of thirteen and fourteen and have more things. Petticoats and bonnets and trinket boxes with a memory of the fine city of Bath painted upon them, and five pairs of slippers each, and a hairbrush our mother has had engraved with a sentimental message about fond hearts and absence. Embroidery rings and brand-new prayer books with stiff spines and our names written on the front as gifts from Thicknesse, who watches us depart, his shrewd eyes on the carriage as it rolls away.

Molly is crying, stupid, hopeless tears, her face pressed against the carriage curtain. I squeeze my legs together under my skirts, trying not to think about the blood that has suddenly started flowing between them, or about the wad of bedsheets I have torn up and stuffed in my undergarments to stem the flow, or about how terrified I am, or about whether any of it will find its way through to the pale yellow silk of my dress. My stomach aches with dull, spidery twinges. We are falling apart at the seams, both of us, our bodies betraying us, and now we must find a way to hold ourselves together on our own in the world without a home to hide in.

I look back, at the iced-cake house, at my mother on the steps with her arms folded, at Thicknesse waving his handkerchief. We have been dislodged. That boy has dislodged us, just by being a boy, and now he stands, my father's hands on his shoulders, waving us off as we trundle down the road and away.

PART TWO

PEGGY

Six Years Later
Pentimento

"Is it silly?"

Molly watches herself in the great gilt mirror, turning her head from left to right. The feathers suspended over her forehead quiver softly, wishing, I suppose, that they were safely back on the ostrich from which they came. A mother and her four girls behind us look up briefly at her question, and then avert their eyes.

"It is quite silly, yes," I say.

She looks at me, rueful. "It is the fashion." She reaches up and unpins the hat. "One must try it, I suppose."

"I think it looks perfectly à la mode." It is the youngest girl, who is running her fingers carefully through a ribbon drawer. She cannot be more than thirteen, and the French words are self-conscious on her lips. She looks at Molly, her height, her trailing silks, her exquisite coiffeur, with a look I recognize from my own childhood, part admiring, part covetous. We are the Ann Fords now, I think.

"I am afraid my sister does not like it," Molly says, placing the hat in the arms of the servant who waits, deferent, to take it. "And perhaps you do not know it, but one must always, always do as my sister says."

"What will happen if you do not?" the girl asks.

"Oh, terrible, unspeakable things." Molly pulls the hood back over her head and, turning toward the door, she whispers, "She is very violent."

"Molly!"

The girl stands uncertainly, a crimson strip in her hand. She does not know if my sister is joking. I smile at her, a reassuring, easy smile, and shake my head a little, and follow Molly out into the September morning.

"Why ever did you say that, Moll? You frightened her."

"It was a joke, of course."

There is not quite space for two to walk abreast, and the fashion for dresses is now so broad that I struggle alongside her, trying not to be bumped into the sludge. I feel like one of the cartoons the men draw to make fun of us.

"Who is it arriving, do you suppose?" Molly asks over the clamor of the bells, pulling her fur hood closer as we make our way home past the coffee houses of West Gate Street. We are a little breathless, stumbling past the sedans returning from the Pump Room and the crumpled travelers emerging from the Bear like newly hatched chicks, trying to gain their orientation in the hum of the city. We have been back in Bath three weeks— three weeks of buying things, fitting things, readying things, and it is all beginning. Our first real Bath season. I have the feeling of a carousel that's beginning to gain speed.

"Perhaps the Duke of Lancaster and his wife. I have heard they plan to stay for the whole winter."

"I cannot wait," Molly says. "I cannot wait for it all." I see that there are two high spots of color on her cheeks. I put my arm through hers, firmly, and we turn a sharp left into the Circus.

Our new house, at number seventeen, is finished so recently that I can smell the paint on the railings. It is rented, of course, for there is still not the money to back up the style in which we live. However much my father rises, he remains a trades-man, and my mother must balance his books. And yet ours is the most fashionable address in Bath, and we are powdered and curled and polished to match it.

I cannot understand how anyone can build houses so per-fectly into a circle, what measurements must be rendered into stone to make houses, which are square, into something entirely round, without anyone inside them noticing. The Circus is so well paved, so perfectly even and clean, that carriages may pass with ease. The rest of the city is left below to battle through the mud and puddles. The new house is full of tall, low windows, of glassy mirrors reflecting wide, airy rooms. It is not like the iced-cake house; the way the air hung heavy there, the way the abbey loomed like a monster over us. When I look out the window at the Circus, I see a broad expanse of wealth and space. A gen-tleman touring its perfect circle with his gold-topped walking stick. A satin-clad child, her face puckered in outrage, sitting on the wall beneath the railing letting out gasping howls, while a maid fusses at her with a napkin. A lady trotting along beside her dog.

It is immaculate. But I cannot quite shrug off the old sense I used to have as a child that in Bath the world has tipped. That someone has taken the line of the landscape, which should be flat, and bent it into all sorts of shapes, and put the city in the center, on its own slanting line, so that everything, even a per-fect circle, feels as if it is not quite straight. It is an illusion, I tell myself, but I am not sure what the illusion is—that the city is not quite steady, or that the circle is not quite perfect.

Our father is now the most fashionable painter in the city.

Visitors come daily in droves to view his paintings, traipsing in and out as though we are a china shop or a milliner's or a ruined castle they must visit in order to check off their list of Bath attractions. They wear the gay, painted faces of those at leisure, for everything done in the spirit of holiday must be smiled through, even if it is not particularly enjoyable, I have noticed. The ladies catch their reflections in the great hallway mirror and their laughs grow a little more tinkling, and they turn to their companions, seeing how they are seen. Even at the very heart of our house there are always people looking at themselves being looked at. "People, and their damned faces," my father says, as he stomps away from the music room and into the darkness of the studio, clutching the tonic my mother has made him up for his sore head. He keeps himself to himself in the daytime, a mysterious figure, the great artist, calculated so as to rouse the curiosity of the visitors and also to avoid overwhelming him and his bad head (for it is always bad in the mornings) with endless showroom chatter.

We sit, all four of us, sipping our morning tea in the sitting room above while the autumn sun comes flooding in. I am thirsty for such moments of pause. I feel breathless, always, since we came from school, and I do not know why, for life is only pleasure.

Tristram lies panting on the rug at my mother's feet in a great heap of white curls, for he will not be parted from her. When she leaves the house, he sits howling at the door, his tongue hanging out like a slab of meat, sometimes for hours, until my father comes out again from his studio, red in the face, and calls him a monstrous hound and says he will kick him to Bristol. Then Molly, who is always soft on animals, goes to the kitchen for scraps and feeds them to Tristram until he gives up and lies dejected on the hallway floor, his chin on his paws.

I look at him now, nestled against my mother's skirts, and

at the little mess of stray hairs he has left across the silk. My mother wears her finest clothes, even at breakfast. Even her day cap is a puff of silky pink London lace on her head. The servants snort when her great embellished bonnets arrive and they think no one is looking. "She thinks she's quite someone, doesn't she?" "Another package for Lady Muck." And worse things, sometimes. Even my father will say, "For God's sake, Margaret, there is no need for all this fussy dressing when there is nobody to see you." But in my mother's mind, her blood and her fashion match each other; the inside and the out must sit aligned. And because it is so in our mother's mind, so it is in our lives too. Our house is as much a house of fabric and feathers as it is of paint and brushes. Now that we are grown up, we have our own maidservant between us whose only job is to keep us immaculate. In order to paint beauty, my mother says, my father must have beauty to paint. I love to visit the scented shops to choose laces and damask silks of the palest and richest hues, yellows, blues, and greens. I have always loved colors. It is like each one changes the way you feel. But sometimes, when I am having my hair molded and styled and tugged and wound through with flowers, or when I am being pinned and adjusted and tucked into a new stomacher, I look in the mirror at all the beauty and feel a great wave of sadness I cannot explain.

I reach for the teapot, so delicate, hewn as fine as the sugar upon which the town is built, and pour myself a cup.

"One more for me, Captain," my father says, "and then I must get on."

Molly is chattering away, reading about a breakfast concert from the paper, and beneath her words, as if in duet, I can just make out the footman's voice through the floorboards, reciting his script, as he does every morning. I almost know it by heart.

"To the far right, the Duke of Northumberland, three-quarter length. Directly above, Sir Robert Fletcher in his Regimentals.

To his right, Mrs. Hudson of Bessingby. On the far wall, Lady Sussex and her little daughter. To her right, Lord Radnor . . ."

And then Molly, her voice piping above his. "A winter concert to begin the season at the finished Assembly Rooms on Bennett Street, with dances to include the cotillion and the quadrille, Mr. Wade to visit with tickets. Did he already call, Mama? I think he already called. Did we miss him?" I watch her face, the flush that has risen to the surface of her cheeks. Is there an unsteadiness in her eyes? I fight the thought down. No. It is only that we are at home again, so I am afraid that it will be as it was before. But nothing is. Nothing is.

"And then there is to be a dance," she says, "followed by a break-fast concert at the Bagatelle with dancing the following morning, and then a cotillion rehearsal for ladies at the Pump Room, and then the Waterloo Gardens for fireworks on Saturday evening. I shall wear my *polonaise* to the fireworks, if only Williams will get it ready, and I shall get her to *frizzle* my hair, and . . ."

I cannot keep up with it all. I imagine our sedan bearers running themselves into ever-increasing circles, faster and faster, sweating into their blue coats; Williams running up and down the stairs with armfuls of baffling objects with French names. And Molly chatters and chatters and chatters, and I long for the calm of school, for its silence.

When we arrived at the dark gray frontispiece of Miss Edgar's School for Young Ladies, we were half-frozen in fear. I was holding Molly's arm so tightly that I would not be prized away. We were a forlorn sight, a pair of thin, pale little things, Miss Edgar says later, for two girls of such a great age, huddled together in the back of the carriage as if we had been sent to our deaths. She gave us some bread and pease, which I do remember, and decided that she must feed us up, which of course I do not.

On the first night, I only remember the terror and the pain in my stomach, nagging at me like an ugly thought. When the candles were put out, I slipped into Molly's bed, burying my face in her hair, so that I could not tell which of the brown curls were mine and which were hers. The way I like it to be. When we woke in the unfamiliar morning, I helped her dress, and took her arm, and made sure to stick close to her side at every moment with my iron grasp, ready to speak over her, to close the gaps. But when we sat down to work after breakfast, Miss Edgar set Molly apart, and gave her a desk at the front of the room. I sat, my heart in my mouth, shredding my nails with my fingers. Waiting. But Molly, obedient, subdued, stayed silent at her desk.

That night, and every one after, I crept into her bed, and wrapped my arms around her tight. And then one night, I fell asleep before I could go to her. In the morning, I woke in a terror. But nothing changed. Molly was still good. The next night, I did not go either. She did not walk in the night, or scream out, or say things that frightened me. She simply slept, the white heap of her nightgown moving up and down in the darkness.

Then, slowly, so slowly that I cannot remember it happening, something began to unfurl inside me. Inside us. The knot loosened. Imperceptibly, my panic settled, buried beneath the steady pattern of the school day. We woke. We slept. We ate, studied, and sewed. The handbell rang at dawn, and it rang again at night. Miss Edgar made her trudging lap of the bedchambers, the clattering jangle rising and receding with perfect regularity. I waited, waited, all the time, for danger. But it did not come.

Molly became proficient at the harpsichord. She was complimented for her French. She memorized the Kings and Queens of England to recite at will. My muscles began to soften from their state of high alert.

We began, tentatively, to laugh with the others, although we were shy, and clung mostly to each other. To make friendships, of a sort. I began to talk, here and there, about fashions, and dresses, and silk, and husbands, things I do not have yet but want, or say I want. I began to curl my hair, and to send away for feathers to dress it with, and to wonder if perhaps I look a little like a duchess, or if Molly has a touch of aristocracy in her nose. And then Molly began to talk too, about the same things. Softly at first. Then with more confidence. Until she felt older than me again. Until what had happened before began almost to feel like a dream. Molly, in my father's wig on the street, white as a ghost. The bubble of blood on her hand from my pin. The boy's eyes on my exposed skin. My father's face. These woke me in the night with a sudden gasp, but then I remembered where I was. I saw the shadowy forms of our schoolbooks, our unremarkable bonnets draped over the chair, our friends tucked into their beds, normal schoolgirls, plump and thin and tall and tiny, all in a row. No, I thought. It was a childhood fancy. Only that.

And now we sit in the painted Circus room, quite grown up, and quite perfect. But I can feel something stir beneath the surface that I thought was buried with our childhood. Something in Molly's brittle chatter. Something in the color that rises to her face too fast. We have used our most delicate brushes, our most sumptuous colors, to reconfigure the canvas, to wipe out the mistakes, to create something more beautiful. It is very effective. But here is what I know about a painting that is formed on top of another: You may glaze it and varnish it and fix it in its ornate frame. You may display it in the best room of your house. But there is something which my father calls the pentimento. It is the rising up of the old picture under the paint. You think you have got rid of it and started again, but there it is, the ghost of what was there before, surfacing, making its way back into the frame. And no varnish, no satin sheen worked in with a cloth, no brittle layer of gum sandarac and Venice turpentine, can keep it from view.

Tristram sneezes one of his strange little sneezes, and my mother tuts and blesses him as if he were a person. Below us,

I can almost make out the shuffling of the visitors' feet across the floor, the low murmur of appraisal, and then the way their voices rise once they are back on the street, and think they can speak without being heard about what they did and did not like. I am quite relieved I am not hanging in the portrait room, and that people cannot say, *Oh, but he was rather overgenerous to his daughter, was he not? She is not quite such a beauty as all that.*

"Will you call chairs to go to the Pump Room, girls?" my mother asks, resting her book on her lap. "Perhaps I shall join you."

"One would think you had no legs of your own," my father remarks, "the amount you three are borne about by chairmen."

"Now, now, Thomas, don't be bad-tempered." My mother readjusts her cap complacently.

"Mrs. Haverley is borne to church on Sundays in her sedan," Molly says wickedly, "and does not step out even to receive communion, but is carried down the aisle like the Queen of Sheba to be blessed."

"And if the sermon is too boring she closes the curtains and nods off," I add. Mrs. Haverley, we always think, is a Sunday highlight.

My father looks up with sudden sharpness. "I am not raising you to be Mrs. Haverleys."

Molly widens her eyes at me, and we both look away. Aren't you? I think. You are not raising us to work in dress shops, nor to be artists, nor to be Miss Fords, nor to be Mrs. Haverleys. For what, then, are you raising us?

My father's dog, Fox, moves to lick himself, and Tristram lets out a low growl.

"Stop it, you naughty boy," my mother says lazily, placing her hand on his side.

"It is not very nice of you to talk to Papa that way," I say. "He was only a little bit grumpy." My father snorts. My mother

209

shakes her head. I like these mornings. The four of us, sitting together. I like adulthood, and being nineteen. We are not shushed and hushed and locked in our rooms, but part of the world, and perfectly trained to play by its rules.

"And on the twentieth of November," Molly continues, "it says that a tragedy and a farce are to be performed in the same evening."

"Aren't they always, Moll?" my father says, and my mother shakes her head again as he swings his legs over the side of his easy chair to avoid the dogs and leaves the room with a quick wink back at me.

We were careful with each other, to start with, when Molly and I descended from the carriage onto the broad pavement of the Circus, schoolgirls fresh into the world. Into our new life, our new beginning, with our trunks standing piled in the glossy hallway. A new brush carefully painting out the old mistakes. I saw the relief pass over our parents' faces, a glance between them quick as a ghost. We have drawn a veil over it, all of it, and live in the comfortable day-to-day reality of practical arrangements. I am full of joy and fun and laughter and chatter. Aren't I? I talk of balls and concerts and I have a sharp wit, and play pianoforte, and do everything a fashionable young lady ought to do.

And yet he finds excuses not to be alone with me, my father. Perhaps I imagine it. Perhaps it is only a holding back. A slight wariness. As if something has changed between us that will never quite be restored. I do not try to hang about him as I used to, to gain his attention with my silly ideas. I have left all that behind. But every time there is a space in the day where we might find ourselves together, perhaps when the others have left breakfast before us, or when we run into each other in the hallway, he winks, and then he always, always leaves.

I have seen Gainsborough Dupont only three times since our return. It was the thing I was most dreading, the thought that woke me with a cold horror in those last slow weeks at school. He is my father's apprentice, a perfectly average portrait painter with perfectly average success, although my father tries all he can to promote him. So that something of his artistic talent will survive him, I suppose, as it is not in my fingers, nor Molly's.

The first time I saw him, I glimpsed him coming back from a ride. His face was flushed with the outdoors. I panicked and ran, two stairs at a time, like a great child, to hide in my bedroom. The next time, I ran almost straight into his arms as he came in through the door. He pulled back sharply, narrowly avoiding a collision. I stepped away, heat flooding my face, and he bowed, a low, slow bow.

"Cousin Margaret," he said.

"Cousin Gainsborough."

His face is longer, thinner, now, and it sits atop the lanky frame of a seventeen-year-old. His eyes are still sharp, so sharp that I cannot quite look into them still. Fringed with dark lashes, just as I remember. The same sly look. For a moment, the old fear thrills through me.

But then I begin to realize that things are different now. I did not know it before, but I have layer upon layer of protective shell. Finery—that is one layer; our father's status—that is another. Molly is herself again; that is a third. And being quite grown up, in a grown-up woman's body, when he is only a painter's apprentice—that is one more. And then there is my beauty. The way I wear the secret of my lineage with ease at last. The rules have changed.

And he will have to play the game that we all play, the game of blanking out the things that are not convenient to remember.

The season gains momentum and carries us along with it, and we are thrown from concert to ball to exhibition like the dice at cards. Our days follow the Bath rhythm, and so we move with the dukes and physicians and heiresses and Quakers and members of Parliament and countesses as they come and go, from the dawn baths to the garden breakfasts to the Pump Room, from the Pump Room to the coffeehouse to the abbey for the midday service, to dinner and to the evening entertainments. And all the time, Molly pulls away from me, dancing and laughing and twisting away, as tightly coiled as an overwound clock, and I have to work harder and harder to keep her in sight.

"You are so lucky," our school friend said, lying on the damp summer grass. "I can't believe how lucky you are, that you will live all the time in the city of leisure. Your life will only be pleasure, pleasure, pleasure. Whereas I shall have to live in dirty Manchester, where there is only a ball once a month."

Before bed, I watch Molly taking the flowers and pins from her hair in the flicker of candlelight. She is pale, paler than she should be, with delicate purple shadows beneath her eyes. Cobalt violet. Our box of silk flowers is on the dresser, embossed with an *M—M* for Margaret, *M* for Mary. It plays a tinkling tune as it stands open, clicking its way through the notes mechanically. I have the feeling of too much sugar.

"Do you miss school?" I ask suddenly.

She looks up. "No."

"Don't you ever feel . . . dizzy with it all?"

I have chosen the wrong word.

"No." She says it with a definite firmness, and turns away, closing the box.

I climb into bed and shut my eyes and see dancers moving in their intricate circles of color, like cogs in a machine, spinning and spinning across the floor.

MEG

On the first London night, Meg lies on a straw mattress, tugging the blanket up around her ears to block out the sounds of the other sleepers, and counting her remaining money in her head. When she wakes in the uneasy quiet of the dawn, she makes her way straight out through the low-ceilinged inn into the air. Coaches are being readied to go back again the way they came, drivers yawning and pissing against the wall, horses stomping on the chilly cobbles. She sees the Harwich coach, and the driver leaning against its door, bleary-eyed, chewing on a breakfast bun.

"You coming back?" he says, laughing, as he sees her.

"No."

"Can't tempt you?"

"No," she says again, although her eyes flick briefly to the coach, its entrance open, waiting.

"Best wishes to your aunt," he says, holding her gaze.

"Thanks," she replies, and walks on past him to the broad expanse of Cripplegate as the sun climbs its way into the dirty London sky.

She walks all morning, only sitting to rest on the steps of a building near the livestock market when her legs sag beneath her, then getting up again and pushing on, stepping over streams of fresh piss and onward through the packed passages between the pens of sheep and cows bleating and lowing helplessly. She feels like one of them, jostled, clueless, lost in the heat of bodies.

She finds the river and sits breathing in its stench, watching the oysters coming in off the boats. Then she turns away from the fetid dampness, back past the women screeching their cries and cackling with one another, the trays strapped round their necks loaded with eels and herring and crab. Past a horse trapped beneath its toppled load, eyes bulging, hooves kicking out, men frantic about the lost produce, filthy boys grabbing their loot and tearing off into the shadowy maze of buildings with it. The driver stands poised with a rock to bring down with a blow on the twisting head of the animal. She is frightened, exhausted, nauseous, but her heart pounds with it all, an answering echo to the city's thumping energy. She asks, "What area is this?" everywhere she goes, and then puts the names on a shelf in her mind to keep them safe. Billingsgate, Bishopsgate, Smithfield, Leadenhall, Fleet. All she can think is that the only way she can survive here, thrive here, is to shrink the city by understanding it.

At the end of the day, wrapping her cloak around her against the sudden chill of the turning season, she returns to the Swan with Two Necks with something that is almost a plan. She eats a bowl of grayish vegetable stew, hunched over in the corner by the fireplace, trying not to be seen, before crawling to bed on blistered feet, her boots flapping at the seams. She wakes the next morning, stiff and nauseous with hunger, and after throwing up the meager contents of her stomach into the open sewer that runs the length of the street, she makes her way straight down the road away from the city toward the rows of taverns. Summoning all her strength, she goes inside and asks for work.

They don't need anyone, nor do the next, nor do the next. In the fourth, a dirty-looking man who peers at her from beneath eyebrows that project out in triangles over his eyes sends her to a cookshop that his sister owns on the edge of Smithfield market. The pavement-pounding of the previous day pays off. She knows Smithfield; she knows the way to it, just. She counts the buildings running on the opposite side of the long hospital, until she finds what she is looking for: a low, narrow doorway with a board leaning against the wall bearing scrawled chalked prices.

She pushes open the door into a suffocating haze of smoky, smoldering flesh. One wall is a huge, open fireplace with whole pigs stuck across it, metal bars down their open snouts and coming out of their behinds. Smoke pours from their charred bodies, up the chimney and thickly across into the room, and the fat spits and fizzes as it falls on the fire. A man so fat his body tries to escape from his clothes like a badly stuffed sausage straining at its skin is standing, turning the handle slowly to stop the pig skin blistering. Meg weaves her way over to him through the maze of small tables laid out with salt and pepper and napkins, where two or three diners sit with their forks stuck in plates of pork.

"I'm looking for Liz," she says. "About some work."

Up close, she sees the man is drenched in sweat, which seems to pour from him as if he is a tap, and she feels her own upper lip bubbling with moisture, her cheeks starting to redden from the sheer force of the fire. He has a rag in his hand, and wipes his face and neck and the top of his chest, and then reaches under his shirt and wipes his armpits.

"Out back," he grunts, and as she starts in the direction of the small door he gestures toward, she sees him reach out and wipe down the pigs with the same soggy, sweat-soaked cloth.

In the kitchen, she finds a lean, tough woman with her hands deep in a bowl of meat and flour.

"Yes?"

"I need—I'm looking for work. Your brother sent me here."

The woman stops tossing the meat and watches her, one hand on an aproned hip, pushing back her stringy hair with the other.

"I have experience." Meg keeps her voice as steady as she can.

"Don't need experience. Need a hard worker who'll wash the dishes. Married?"

"No."

The woman's small eyes narrow.

"Why not?"

"I ran away."

Unexpectedly, the woman laughs, a harsh, sudden sound. "Did you, now?!"

"From my father, I mean."

"I don't need details. Cook?"

"Yes. And clean. I've served at the bar of an inn, and served ale, and—"

"It's washing dishes I need."

"I can do that. I'm a hard worker." She keeps her head up and sets her jaw.

The woman, Liz, eyes her one more time then sucks air through her teeth. "All right. Three pence a day, and you work till the last customer leaves. Pig for your meals. Get an apron on and start now, if you want. There's plenty needs doing."

"Thank you. Thank you." Meg, doing frantic calculations in her head, looks around and sees a grease-stained apron on a peg. She takes off her cloak, puts her pack down in the corner, and ties the apron over her bodice, pulling its tatty gray strings behind her and in front again. That's dinner, that's a shared room for tuppence a night, that's possible. She can eke out her father's money, and that will give her time, all the time she needs for her search. She moves to the sink, which sits full of stagnant water, piled high with plates smeared with meaty remnants, and pulls them out one by one, while Liz turns away to her bowl of meat and starts to pound it with her small, balled fist.

Eight hours later, she trudges home, stinking of pig, three pence in her pocket. She is breaking with tiredness, her body, and her boots, almost falling to pieces. She tumbles onto the mattress and drifts into a welcome oblivion. She has a way to survive, however meager, for just a little longer, while she works out her plan.

PEGGY

Spun

Standing on the grand sweep of the stairs, which do not, of course, creak in the Circus, but lie as solid and new and immaculate as the house itself, I can hear music. It is pulling me toward it.

There is nothing unusual about that, for music is as much the sound of our house as the gong for dinner or the crackle of the fire. It lies beneath everything. The house is full of instruments new and old, for if my father hears a new instrument played well, he will try to buy it for himself, as if he thinks the talent lies somehow in the instrument itself and not the player.

"Dear God, Thomas, we could stage an orchestra of our own with all the servants on strings and the family on woodwind at this rate," my mother will say in exasperation, as another huge

218

wooden box packed tight with paper is carried through the door. "Where on earth do you expect us to put this one?"

"I have never heard such a sound as this viol can make!" he will say, attacking the box with his penknife. "I will play for you and I defy you not to say so!"

It is not only my father, though. I jangle daily upon the harpsichord, and Molly too, and even my mother has been known to sit at the pianoforte and sing an old folk song from her childhood, although not when anyone is listening. I once heard her sing a ballad quietly to herself, a sorry tale of a sailor wooing his maid in Harwich Town, but when she heard my step she stopped and shut the lid with a bang.

This music, though, is like nothing I have heard before.

It is not only strings, the familiar strains of Abel and my father's other friends who haunt our house at all hours, but another instrument, something low and sonorous. It is a wooden instrument, and it moves over the notes with a soft grace, climbing the scale then falling then climbing again higher and higher. It has a kind of certainty to it, this instrument, a kind of confidence, unlike the tremulous, hesitant violin or the lugubrious cello. It is clear and crisp, and will lead you where it wants to take you. I move closer to the door and look through the gap into the room beyond. The fire burns low, and the musicians sit on chairs gathered close in a circle, my father with his eyes closed.

The player is the tallest of the men. Gray hair. Gray eyes. He sits on his chair as if he is too big to be contained by it, his limbs too long. His suit is a soft, worn velvet, and his face is creased in concentration. Suddenly he glances up, catching me quite unawares, and seems to look directly at me. I back away from the door as swiftly as I can, meaning to go up to Molly. But I cannot help myself, and pause for a moment in the hall instead, listening, with Fox at my heels. When the piece ends, I realize that we have been stood there for ten minutes together, as still as the portraits that observe us from the walls.

"Did you like that, Fox?" I say, bending down to tousle his small ears. "Did you like that?" Fox rubs his head against my hand, straining for the affection.

"Does he?"

I snap back to standing so fast that my stays leave me dizzy for a moment. The gray-haired man is there in the doorway. He must have moved as stealthily as a mouse, and yet there he stands almost as tall as the frame itself, and stooping a little beneath it.

He smiles at me, and there is something clever about the smile.

"I had a dog as a child who did not think so much of my playing. Fritz. He would howl along with me so loudly that my father put him out of the house."

His accent is not English. German, I think, or perhaps Hungarian, like the dancing teacher at school. I look at him, this stranger, at the way his smile creases the skin around his eyes, as my father's does. He is Venetian red, I think. Rich and earthy.

"If that had happened to me as a child, I think I should have refused to play," I say.

"Perhaps you did not have a great love of music."

"Perhaps you did not have a great love of your dog."

He smiles again, a different sort of smile. More interested, more curious. It is the sort of smile that makes me feel as if I should turn and walk away. But I smile back, cautious. Just beneath the skin, my pulse quickens.

"Fish, whatever are you doing here loitering in the doorway?" My father appears, tousled, at his shoulder, a glass of claret in his hand. "And you, Peg, more to the point, whatever are you doing loitering in the corridor? Aren't you supposed to be at some ball or other?"

"I was fetching my cloak, Papa, but your music stopped me."

"Not my music. Fischer's." He pats the oboist on the shoulder. "Come back and play again, Fish."

"Very well." The man speaks quietly, amiably.

"He is quite the composer, is he not, Peg?" my father says, taking a swig from his glass. "And not bad company either."

"It was beautiful," I say.

"Thank you, Miss—"

"This is my Peggy," my father says, nodding in my direction. "Miss Margaret to you, Fish."

"Of course. Miss Margaret." He bows carefully, and I watch him as he does. The elegance of it.

"Captain, may I introduce the great oboist Johann Christian Fischer." I give a nod, and my father turns to him again. "Now get back in here and play again before the rest of us fall asleep, you old German slacker. And Peg, for heaven's sake, hurry up, or you will be so late back that it will be time to get up again. My girls, Fish, delight in burning the candle at both ends." My father pats him again distractedly and disappears toward the waiting musicians in search of more claret. For one suspended moment, we are left alone. He looks at me. I feel my breath rising and falling, and Fox waiting at my feet, still and alert. Fish makes a small bow, just the slightest incline of his head, keeping his eyes fixed on mine. Then I hear Molly's footsteps on the stairs behind me, and she is there, bowing to Mr. Fischer, telling me to hurry or the cloakroom will be too full and we will have to queue. He looks at her for a moment with his quizzical gray eyes, then back at me, then turns and moves back into the music room without a word.

"He is the handsomest man I have ever seen," Molly says as we are undressed the next evening.

"Who?" I ask, a little too quickly.

"Captain Wade, of course."

The scarlet Captain Wade. Of course. My father is painting him for the Assembly Rooms, which are soon to open, and a vast canvas sits in the studio waiting for its finishing touches. His shining eye, his fine lip, are the talk of the ladies boiling in the Kettle. Bath's most fashionable painter paints Bath's most fashionable man.

"Oh, Captain Wade. Yes, and he knows it rather too well."

Molly turns, her panniers swinging so vigorously that they almost knock Williams to the floor. "He is quite charming! Don't you think so, Williams?"

"He is very handsome, miss. Stand still a minute if you don't mind, please."

"See," says Molly, raising her arms compliantly, "even Williams thinks so."

"It is not my place to say, miss, of course." She turns, head bowed, to place the discarded panniers on the bed.

"We still like to hear it, though, don't we, Peg?"

"He is too handsome for me," I say. I don't much like the delicately painted face of Captain Wade. How he stands as if always on display. The way his hair twirls so perfectly into its little coils. I think of Fischer, with his worn velvet at the knees. The lines around his mouth. Captain Wade is a new, brash red, the kind that light bounces off. But Fischer's red is the mixing of colors on a palette, the depth and the light together, so that you cannot see all the parts at once, and must try instead to piece the story together.

"Too handsome?!" Molly flings herself onto the bed in disgust. "Did you ever hear such a thing, Williams?"

"No, miss," Williams says, her fingers working away at the knot in my pocket bags. She is so close to me that I can smell the smoke of the kitchen fire on her skin. Suddenly I want to grab her and speak right into her face. *Did you really never hear*

222

such a thing, Williams? I want to say. Do you really have any thoughts about Captain Wade at all? And us? Do you think we are nothing but a pair of Mrs. Haverleys? What is it that you really think? But the knot comes loose in Williams's hands, and she slips away with a nod, impassive, decorous, so that we are left alone to forget that she was ever here, or had any thoughts at all.

I search for Fischer among the crowds everywhere I go, but he is never among them. I think I glimpse the back of his head, or his faded velvet suit on the other side of a room, but they only vanish like a magician's trick, and I am left to make conversation with a dull boy with hungry eyes, or an inquisitive lady who wishes to have her portrait painted by my father but cannot afford it. I scour the newspapers for mentions of oboe recitals. I attend concerts when I would rather dance, just in case, and then sit, gloomily, while a portly oboist stands for a solo. Once on a Sunday evening I hear oboe music drifting up from the floor below, but Molly is mixing a new pomade and using my head as an experiment. I sit, chalky slime sliding down my neck, furious at everything, baffling Molly with my sudden bad mood.

I will see him again, I tell myself. I can feel it. It is only a matter of time. And then, of course, I do see him, some months later, and am struck dumb with fear, and half wish I hadn't.

Molly has a head cold, and has been packaged up by my mother with a poultice on her head and made to stay in, despite her violent protestations, for she has given up Captain Wade, and now speaks only of a Mr. Whitchurch, a violinist with a dazzling array of embroidered waistcoats, who is playing at the dance.

"It is unfair," Molly says through a blocked nose, as Williams finishes my hair. "I am perfectly well." She is almost in tears, and

I do not understand why. It is not about Mr. Whitchurch, that much I know. By the time she got there, I think, she would have found another one anyway, a fellow with particularly handsome calves, or a pair of blue eyes she cannot stop comparing to the sky, and Mr. Whitchurch and his embroidered waistcoats would be dropped before the second dance. It troubles me, this depthless flitting between, but the sedan men are here, and I leave her with a kiss to her furious, poulticed head.

My father is gone to London, so I am quite alone at Harrison's. As I make my way across the room, I feel the absence of Molly at my side, as if I am a shadow come loose from its body. And then I see him, breaking away from his gaggle of acquaintances and coming toward me. My heart starts to race, as if I am frightened. And I am. But there is something else too, lapping at the edges of my fear. An exhilaration. A kind of freedom I have not felt for years, as if perhaps I might, after all, be able to leave the life that has been written for me.

As we meet, he bows low, and then his gray eyes fix on mine.

"Good evening, Miss Gainsborough."

"Good evening." I steady my gaze.

"Do you remember me?"

"Yes, of course. You are a friend of my father's."

"I am."

He looks at me, a measuring look. Perhaps he is only that, I think. A friend of my father's. Taking an interest in his friend's daughter out of kindness. Is that what it is?

"It is Margaret, is it not? Or, as your father calls you, the Captain?"

"Margaret, thank you," I say stiffly.

"It is most strange to see you alone."

"It is quite strange to be alone."

"It is good to be alone sometimes. If you fill every gap with people, there's no space to live."

"Molly doesn't feel like people to me."

"You are close."

"Yes."

"You can see it. Those paintings. Breathtaking."

"Yes," I say again, because I cannot decide if the compliment is for me or for my father.

"You are celebrated."

"We didn't really do anything."

"That is not true, Margaret. Inspiration is not something to be undervalued, I think."

"Thank you. He loves us." I don't know why, but I make it sound almost like an apology.

"That is certainly obvious. You glow in his paintings. Both of you. There is something intangible, something beautiful. Twinned perfection."

I stare at my feet, in their pale blue silk slippers. Blue for continued affections, blue for loyalty. I don't know what to say to this man. His confidence pulls me toward him like a magnet.

"He is fond of musicians, my father," I hear myself say.

"He is a good musician himself. But composing is the magic. Perhaps we might call it painting with sound." He smiles.

"Yes, perhaps."

"But music is better than art. Art plays with the eye. Music plays with emotion."

"Are emotions something to be played with?"

He looks at me, amused.

"What do we have without playfulness, Margaret?"

"Playfulness is—for children."

"Is it?"

A beat passes between us, and I try to think how I can move the conversation away from this strange, disorienting territory. I open my mouth to ask him something about music, about the

225

rumors I have heard that he has played for the Queen, but he speaks first.

"Will you dance, Margaret?"

My first name feels suddenly naked, intimate. This is not avuncular; this is not paternal. I long for the arm's-length formality of Miss Gainsborough, for Molly as my shield.

Perhaps it is his age. Perhaps it is because he is my father's friend. Or perhaps there is something else. The unsettling stirring of a secret freedom, something pushing up involuntarily, like a bulb from under the dark earth.

We dance, and dance again, and he leaves me reeling, my forehead warm to the touch. As the carriage rumbles home, I lean my head against the window and think of nothing but the look in his eye, cool, penetrating, and the way his hand rested on mine as we said goodbye, so fleetingly, so casually, that it might almost not have happened.

When I enter the darkened house, I can hear my father's violin, low and mournful, and I pause for a moment to listen, drawing closer to his study. He stops playing and catches sight of me there in the doorway.

"Hello," he says.

"Hello."

"Spying on me and my scraping?"

"It's not scraping."

I hang back, cautious, ready for him to make his move away as he has done since that night in the old house, but instead he rests his violin gently on the pianoforte and looks at me.

"How are you, Peg?"

"I'm well."

"How was tonight's dance?"

"It was busy. Almost too busy to dance."

"Was the music good?"

"It was. I didn't mean to stop you playing."

"It's quite all right.

"It's a while since I enjoyed a dance," my father adds. "Too many commissions. Too many silks and satins and impossible dogs lined up. I'm surprised I don't step outside the house to find them queuing round the corner."

"You've been so busy."

"I have." He sits on a low stool, and picks up his bow, winding it down. I venture farther into the room.

"Do you enjoy it?"

"Some parts of it, yes. Other parts, less so. You know I'd only paint landscapes if I could. Landscapes and you, my dearest two. But it gives me something besides money, Peg. And sometimes precious little of that, as your mother will attest. It gives a satisfaction, a purpose."

He looks at me, tilting his head in the old way. "It is something I wish for you two more than anything else," he says. "I watch you with Moll, sometimes, Captain, and I wonder if you are restless. Bored. Are you happy, Peg?"

I am struck dumb by the question. "I—I don't know," I say stupidly. I think of Fischer, and my heart hums, again, inside me.

"I've seen too many young girls of your class drift blind into womanhood, into wifehood. They come in to me with their vacant faces. They can't string a sentence together without a simper. But your mother, you know I rely on her to hold us all together. Without her, the business would have been sunk long ago, for all my talent with a brush."

"I know." I do not know what he wants me to say. My mother says we must not learn numbers and figures, that it is beneath us, that she does it so we will not have to. And yet my father praises it.

"She has been a good mother to you both."

"She has; of course she has."

"Of course, they say motherhood itself is purpose, and perhaps it will be, Peg, for both of you, one day. But for now, I long for you to find something that absorbs you, that makes the time fly, that makes you wake up and want to hop out of bed and begin the day. Not to drift through it, letting it pass you by. Try to find a purpose, Peg."

"I will." I watch a coal slip and crumble to ash on the cooling fire.

"I'm lecturing you, Peggy, I know."

"No."

"Since you came back from school, Molly is—is quite herself again. She seems on fire with it all. Which is how it should be. A young girl, at her first Bath season. It is no wonder she chatters so. It is good to see, is it not?"

I am not sure if it is a question, or if I am only to confirm what he would like to believe.

"But with you, Peg," he continues, without waiting, "it feels—it is as if I am watching a butterfly trapped under a glass dome. I want to see you free."

There is a long pause.

"I know, I . . ." I say, but I don't finish my sentence. I am not sure how to.

"I don't mean to corner you when you only came to say hello." He stands, rubbing his back. "It is late."

"It is."

"Head up to bed and rest."

I don't want to go. I want to stay and talk to him some more. To tell him the things that lie in the gaps. I feel as I did when I was a little girl and trying to catch the back of his waistcoat to stop him moving away across the grass back to his easel. But I nod, and he blows me a kiss, and gives me a wink, and I make my way up the stairs to slide in beside Molly, and I lie awake, watching her breath rise and fall. I think about the way I would smear the silver fairy liquid on her face at night when we were young, dipping my hand into the cup and drawing it over her soft skin. The way she would hold my hand and ask me to make her better. How scared I was, all the time. How I did not expect to find freedom, of any sort, and yet now, without my doing anything about it, it seems to be calling me. Asking me to remember who I am. Or who I might be.

Fall

We are at the newly opened Assembly Rooms. The chandeliers bear so many candles between them that it seems as though the ceiling is on fire with trembling light. They are the most beautiful I have ever seen, each as big as a man, dripping with quivering crystals. The air is thick with heat and punch and sweat. My head swims with the sweetness of it all.

There are people everywhere, more than I have ever seen in one room, bodies careering up and down the floor, bodies pushing past one another and bowing low, bodies pressed against the windows to watch the dancing. The older ladies are packed together on benches, flapping their fans like weapons against the warmth. My mother holds court among them, her small round face atop an explosion of lace. Next to her, a cousin visiting from Suffolk sits agog at the sight of it all. I pass them, trying to see where Molly is, for she left me to find refreshments and I have not seen her since.

"I merit such dress, you know, because of my *lineage*," I hear my mother whisper to the cousin theatrically. "It is only fitting that I should dress according to the rank of my father, is it not?"

The cousin nods, overwhelmed. I keep moving, looking around me, and see eyes snap away when I meet them. A young man in a red jacket blushes as I pass him. We are being watched, weighed up, for marriage, I think, however much my father talks against it.

I catch sight of Molly in the thick of the dancers, forming a round with some girls from school who are visiting for a week or two. They are excitable, almost hysterical with it all, and Molly is at the center. I see her appear and disappear and reappear again, her mouth open in a laugh I do not recognize. I look at her again and I wonder if she is too pale, if her eyes don't look quite right. And then I see her stop dead, for a moment, near the card table, breathing rapidly. Panic begins to surge, the old, familiar panic. I make my way through the crush of bodies, trying to reach her, skirting round the side of the dancers. Her friends are still laughing, fixing one another's headdresses, and have not noticed. How could they notice? They have not seen her like this; they do not know her. It is only I who know her. I quicken my pace, but I do not know what I will do even if I get to her, for it is the worst Bath etiquette to interrupt a dance for any reason other than the direst emergency.

"Molly?" My pulse skids. "Molly?"

"Steady on there!" A gentleman to my right strays into my path as he tries to brush past me. The glasses he is carrying tip and slop a crimson splash of punch over his waistcoat. "Dammit!"

I apologize and push past him, and he exclaims again. Molly looks up. "Molly!" I call out. "It is all right, I am here!" But as I approach, she twists away, laughing. "I was only out of breath!" she says. "Go away, Peg, and stop fussing. I am showing Marianne and Sarah everything there is to see, and if you won't join in the fun then just go."

"Molly, wait," I call, but she is in the crowd, moving away, mouthing something at me, and I can just make out her voice. "I am going to dance!" she is saying. "I am going to dance!" She is always trying to get away from me, always, and she must not. It is dangerous. Why can she not see that it is dangerous? I fall back, nearly toppling into a clergyman carrying a small dog, and he moves the dog out of my way, lifting it high into the air, as if I am a danger to be near. I stumble, apologizing, back to the side of the room, and stand there, leaning against the painted wall, watching for Molly, while the women swing past me, dresses swaying and spinning, and the men clap and bow and call out in time to the music.

I see Fischer, over by the window, in conversation with my father. And then I think perhaps it isn't dangerous. Perhaps it is all right. To dance, and to spin, and to laugh. To be without Molly at my side.

I begin to make my way across the room without quite knowing what I am going to do when I get there, but suddenly Molly is at my shoulder again.

"Peg, I do not feel well."

Her face is feverish.

"Peggy."

"It is the heat of the rooms," I say. "You will feel quite all right when we are out in the air."

"When?"

I look around again for Fischer, and see that he is now dancing in the center of the throng. He takes the hand of a girl I know is newly arrived and draws her to him, in and out and round. I look back at Molly, at the two spots of high color dotted on her cheeks.

"Two more dances."

She nods, and I see her chest rising and falling as if she is trying to steady her breath.

"Only two, and we will leave," I say. "Shall I bring you tea?"

She nods again, and I step away from her toward the refreshments, feeling the music pulling me. I turn, my sight fixed on Fischer's lean form as it moves across the room. My father has joined the dance, leaving his violin on the side, and now jigs across the room, dancing, as he does everything, with his own type of exuberant vigor. The eyes of the onlookers turn toward him, his fame rippling through the crowd like a whisper. In the corner, I see Gainsborough Gainsborough, red-cheeked with the heat, stooping over a richly dressed old man. He is trying to drum up business, as he always does, for his talent cannot carry him far.

I quicken my pace. To find the tea and sweetmeats, I must make my way around the entire circumference of the hall without tripping over anybody or upsetting the dancers, and such a task is not easy on a night as busy as this. The windows are wet with steam.

If I can only get there and back before the dance ends, I will find him, or he will find me, before we have to leave. I am thinking wildly about what I will say, and how it is possible that we can be alone, when I hear a groaning, metallic noise. I look around, but I cannot place it. I look toward the musicians, but they play on, oblivious. Light seems to move and tip sideways. I see a candle fall, then another, and another, raining down like stars on the heads below. My father dances on, left, then right, left, then right. Then half of a vast chandelier rips away and falls, missing my father's skull by a hair. He staggers back, struck dumb by the force of it. The dancers trip and shriek away; candles break off and go rolling across the floor. The music grinds to a halt as if it has been broken up by the screams. The chandelier lies, a wreckage, bent and smashed in the center of the room. There is a single suspended moment of pure shock. Then those beneath the other chandeliers, still iridescent and glittering above us, begin to look up and back away in haste as if they will descend upon their heads at any moment. Young men escort their lovers to safety. People flock to my father, the owner bowing and pressing my father's hand again and again. And Molly stands, white and waxy, pressed back against the wall, her eyes blank.

I know with absolute certainty that I must get her out. I push my way toward her, laugh too brightly. "Did you see that? What a fright."

She looks at me, unfocused.

"Come, Molly." I shake her arm.

"I don't—"

"We must find Papa before the whole building collapses," I say, and I give a little laugh, for someone is passing close and looking at us awry.

She doesn't move.

"Come, Molly." I pull her across the floor through the chatter of the dispersed dancers. She follows, her hand limp and hot in mine.

"Miss Gainsborough." It is Fischer at my shoulder. "Are you quite all right?"

I look from him to Molly's face, as pale as parchment, and at the beads of sweat on her forehead.

"It is my sister. She is in need of air."

"Take her out. I shall tell your father," he says, and as he bows and moves away, I feel him touch his hand to my back, just above the place where my skirts splay out.

When Molly and I surface into the ice cold of the atrium, the color seems to come back into her face.

"Did you see it fall?"

She nods, catching her breath.

"Did you see how the ladies screamed?"

She nods again, and suddenly we are laughing, lightheaded and dizzy.

"Do you feel better, Moll?" I ask. "You look better. It was so hot inside."

"Yes, I—I don't . . ."

And then my father is outside with us in a gaggle of friends, and my mother, who is half furious with him still without even

234

knowing why, and people are calling him the luckiest man in England, slapping him on the back, and others are talking about the builders and the man who made the chandeliers, how they cannot be trusted again, and how it must be looked into. We are merry, the four of us, soaked with relief, laughing our way into the street. It is only the shock, I think. Nothing more. As I climb into my sedan, I realize that Molly and I have left our dress hoops in the changing room, but I am too wild and silly to care. I will send for them tomorrow. I lean my head back and close my eyes while the bearers hoist me up, and let the world pitch and roll as we move along the street, thinking about the way Fischer rested his hand so lightly on the small of my back.

And then we arrive home, the bearers pulling up in the Circus with a jerk. I see my father climb down, and then my mother, and then last of all comes Molly, but as I see them approach, I know instantly that something is not quite right. I look through the dark window and see that she is lolling forward, knocked limply from side to side by the motion of the chair on the cobbles. For a moment, I stand motionless, as though a shutter has come down over my mind. My father has seen the same thing, and he lets out a shout to the bearers. And when they set down the sedan, she is not conscious at all.

Gap

For the first few weeks, she raves. She cannot be brought back with a pinch, or a shake, or a slap. It is not only moments now. She has slipped, and cannot adjust herself again. She is held firm by Williams and my mother, screaming that she is of royal blood, that they wait for her at Windsor. That her blood is blue. I begin to understand, now, something of my mother's secrets, or the layers of them. Of who her father really was, and who we are. I cannot see how Molly knows it, or what she knows. They are like everything in our family: an illusion of something, its substance hard to grasp. They mean everything and nothing together. And now they are surfacing from the depths, distorted.

Molly rides a horse around her room by day, shouting like a child, until she is hushed back to bed by my mother, who plays along and talks of stables and grooms. She touches herself until we bind her hands, horrified. My mother cries almost every day, and my father takes so little care of himself that he too falls into a fever for a while, and the house is run half-ragged. But I only feel numb.

"I cannot understand it," my mother says, wiping the tears compulsively, for they never seem to stop flowing. "I cannot. Where is my Molly? Where has my Molly gone?"

This is your Molly, I want to say. This always was your Molly, but you would never see it.

Physicians come and go, bringing tinctures and poultices. They draw the fever, they bleed her, they apply hot cups, until I hear her screaming in pain and have to put the pillows over my head. They talk of humors and fevers and disorders of the blood. They talk of choler and palpitations and tension of the fibers. But not one of them will mention madness. For my mother will not tolerate it. The doctors know this; they can read her as they read their written bills, or their neatly printed pamphlets on modern medicine. They know that to say the word, even once, will have them sent from the house unpaid. And, worse, it will mean admitting that they do not know what to do.

When my father is away, my mother calls a priest, who comes stealthily into the house by the side entrance, a thief in reverse. He brings a bag of candles and incense and metal things on chains he swings about. And Molly lies, fat tears seeping from her eyes, while the priest closes his eyes and tells the devil to leave her. But the devil wants to stay.

Thicknesse, briefly returned from Europe, comes to visit. My father has told him of it all by letter, pulled him into the family secret in the old way that leaves my mother furious and my parents divided. I do not know why my father must always look to Thicknesse for answers he cannot find in himself.

"She must be sent away," Thicknesse says sagely, sitting cross-legged in the best chair. "She must be sent somewhere to be taken care of. There are places that will do the job. None of this barbarism you hear of. Only minimal restraint used."

I grip the curled arms of my chair.

This is what happens. Thicknesse's thoughts pass into my father's head and become his own.

"What places?" my father says.

My mother sits motionless in the corner, head bowed, miserable.

My father is going to do it again, I think. He is going to betray us all, to run roughshod across our lives, for another man's opinion, because he cannot trust himself. Because he cannot place his love for us ahead of his work, his worry, his need for money.

"Discreet places," Thicknesse says.

My father shakes his head. Thicknesse watches him, as if he cannot understand him at all.

"You know as well as I do, Thomas, that this cannot continue. She will bring you down if word gets out. You cannot afford it. We have built it all on your reputation."

"I would rather lose it." My father stands. "I would rather lose the whole damned lot."

"You cannot be serious. For God's sake, Tom, have her taken away and be done with it. I can arrange it, quickly, easily. A madwoman in your home will do you no favors!"

"Get out."

I look up, startled. I have never heard my easy, gentle father speak like this. My mother rises from her chair.

"Get out," my father says again. "Before I throw you out."

"You are a sentimental old fool." Thicknesse doesn't move, as if he cannot quite believe it. "Tom. She is mad. She has always been mad. For a man who looks for a living, you are blind."

"I will not ask again."

"You are a fool, Thomas." He rises at last, backing away toward the door, shaking his head. "Ignore my advice at your peril. If not for my advice, you'd be in Ipswich painting hedges."

But it makes no difference. Something has changed. Perhaps it is the distance my mother has placed between Thicknesse and my father. Perhaps it is that Molly and I are grown and cannot be dismissed for naughtiness or willfulness any longer. Perhaps, though, it is only that his pictures now hang in royal palaces, so he thinks that he matters more. Whatever it is, my parents stand at last united, protecting us.

My father will not show Thicknesse out into the hall, so he is left to make his own way back out into the bright morning air. My mother watches him go from the window, savoring the final victory. We do not see him again.

His words, though, linger behind him, like the swirling smoke of the priest, creeping under everything. Sometimes, for a moment, I imagine myself, with Molly gone, vanished, and the freedom seems to tumble out into the future, multiplying itself. Marriage, children, Johann's head resting on my chest. I had felt desire for this life rise up like a bird before the chandelier tumbled, quivering inside me with its possibilities. I close the thoughts down and seal them away where they belong.

Slowly, Molly's raving recedes, and is replaced by blankness. Whether it is the leeches or the cupping or the priest that has abated the screams, I do not know. When I sit with her, it is like half of myself has got lost somewhere, and left an opaque, unknowable space. The gaps in her mind feel like gaps in mine. I hold her hand on that first day, and hold it every day until she begins to sit, to eat, shakily, before collapsing back into a sleep.

When my father recovers, I hear Fischer downstairs with him, hear the strains of the oboe I have longed for, and stay resolutely where I am. I do not want Molly to wake up and find that I am not there. The days blur together.

I hold her hand in the shuttered room, the great ugly blanket slung over her legs.

"I don't—I am."

"What is it, Moll?" I lean in close to her.

"I don't feel—myself—at all."

"I'm here," I whisper to her. "You are yourself. And I have brought you some yellow cakes from Gill's, the kind with the cream. They are a bit old—they are from the day before yesterday, as you were not well enough—but they are still good. Would you like one? Shall I send for plates?"

"I . . ." she says, her face wrinkled in confusion. "I . . ."

I put my face close to hers.

"I will look after you. You are yourself."

"Yes," she whispers back, with frightened eyes.

Day by day, week by week, she is stronger. We begin to walk down the road to the river and back. We walk to take tea. My world, which has shrunk with hers, begins, slowly, to expand again. But all the time, all the time, I know that something has changed, and that the brightness of her, the sharpness, that came for a while at school, will never quite be there again. It is like a plant that begins to grow but yellows, and you can see how it might have been, but not why it has failed. You only see that it has, and that nothing you try, now, will restore it. And my life, at least the life I had planned but that never quite seemed real, is now yellowing and failing with it.

We are sitting by the canal, watching the barges come in and be loaded up, which we are not really allowed to do, for it is not a very proper place. The grunting of the bargemen, the stench of coal fires, the horses stopping to shit their steaming piles. The women eye us from the hatches, then whisper and laugh, and duck back inside. We liked it, before Molly was ill again, because it made us feel alive, so I guide her by the arm and we slip carefully away from the shops and the promenading beaus and ladies and rakes and sit together on the wall.

"I think I am mad," Molly says suddenly. "Or mad in part."

"Molly, you must not say such things. Of course you are not."

"No one else will say it. Not Mama nor Papa. And we never say it, we never talk about—it. The way it was when we were small. We just pretend it never happened. But, Peg, I am not quite right."

"You have been unwell again, that is all."

"No, it has come back."

I don't say anything, only look down at the intricate pattern of flowers on my slippers.

"Do you remember the pictures in Papa's study? The set of them. Madness, thou chaos of the brain. And that picture, of the man behind the door, waiting to leap out. I used to creep in and look at them to scare myself, because I knew. I knew it was me."

"If you were mad, you wouldn't know it."

"I only know it for a moment, like this one, when everything is completely clear, and then the colors run. If you see."

There is a silence. A duck bobs in a circle on the water, herding her bedraggled ducklings.

"It will go away again, when you are recovered," I say.

"I don't want it," she says, and starts to cry. "I can't. I don't want it."

"I will take care of you," I say, and put my arm around her, strong and reassuring. "As I used to."

She only nods, but as I bring her to standing, and weave my arm through hers as tightly as I can to take her home to rest, her eyes are wide with fear.

MEG

At first, on Sundays, Meg takes herself to the church, as she has always done, for fear of being fined, but then realizes in the crush that no one will notice whether she is there or not. She can do as she wishes. No one is watching her. In this city you can arrive and hide and mill unseen. You can falter and die or thrive, and not a soul will watch you do it until you cause them some inconvenience, or have something they want. She is learning that the best thing to do is to fall into neither category. It suits her very well to be invisible, for now. She flits away from the crowds under the looming tower of St. Giles and goes down to the river, leaning over the rail to listen to the maze of masts clinking in the crisp November breeze. The problem, she thinks, is that if she is undetectable in the vastness of the churning city, so is he.

She is exhausted, either chilled so her bones feel like iron, or sweltering in pork smoke. She is bruised and battered, by turns desperately hungry and then nauseous. She is fright-ened, viciously lonely, lost, on the edge of retreat. But there's something about the city that runs through her, that keeps her moving. Its variety. Its wildness. It seems to hum, waking something inside her. When she walks home from the cook-shop she sometimes goes out of her way, to where the squat gray Tower stands by the river, and stands and listens, and if she's lucky, she can hear the lions roaring inside. A man once tells her that if she brings a dead cat or dog to feed to them, she can get in for free. God knows she hasn't got time to go scouring the streets for the corpses of small animals, let alone to take an afternoon to pet lion cubs for pleasure. But she can stop, rest her aching back against the wall by the river, and hear them roar. It is as if life has been calling her, and she didn't know how to answer, but the answer is here somewhere, and even though she is exhausted, terrified, and alone, she is closer to it than she has ever been.

She has found a shared room in a boardinghouse, cheap and clean enough, on the recommendation of the girl who worked behind the bar at the Swan with Two Necks. Two women with missing teeth take the other beds, and mercifully they are hardly there. She hears them clack across the floorboards in the middle of the night, and smells their stale gin breath as they pass her mattress. Then she rises and leaves them with their mouths hanging open in the dawn gloom. Ships in the night, her father would say. But maybe that's London. Everybody is a ship on their way to somewhere past you.

For four days a week she scrubs the greasy plates, stopping only to sit and eat twice a day at the smoky table, and to help carry the dead pigs in from the street. Her hands slide on the coarse ginger hairs, their bellies still warm against hers. After two weeks, the sight of a pig turns her stomach, alive, dead, or roasted. She cannot turn down free food, so she forces each forkful down her gullet, watching the pork man sweat into his shirt. She survives the four days every week, so that she can have the three free, rambling ones. To begin with, they stretch out before her, filled with promise.

She pieces together her plan from gossip. From snatches of conversation that hang in the air. London loves to talk, she realizes. It's full of lonely people. So if she sidles up to one and smiles, and says she is newly arrived, and might she meet the King, she will soon be laughed at. And once she is laughed at, a friend will be brought over from the bar, and it's *My God, did you hear this one, Willem, freshly arrived in the city and wants to know when she can meet the King*. And then another friend will slap his leg in laughter and draw up a chair, and another, and another, and it is only a short step from there to what she needs. Where does Frederick go? What does he do? Where is he seen? How might she know his carriage?

As they wave her off laughing into the dark, this countrified idiot who wants to meet the King—*Look out for his blue-and-red carriage, won't you, my darling*—she savors the nuggets they have given her.

On the first day, she half expects to find him. She believes, somewhere in her mind, that she will walk for an hour, perhaps two, in St. James's Park, before his carriage draws up beside her. He will step down, and there she will be, and when she calls out to him, he will take her up into the quiet, warm carriage, and lament over her plight.

She stands outside St. Paul's and St. James's Piccadilly for Matins and Eucharist and Evensong, rubbing her pinched, icy fingers together over and over again to keep the blood in them. In total she does that fifteen times. She waits all day at a tavern where he is reputed to drink, standing on the opposite side of the street, then sitting on a doorstep until she is moved on by a sour man with dirty hands who gives her a kick in the back for loitering. She moves to a doorway, and is approached by two men as a whore, and has to push the second away with as hard a shove as she dares, but not before he pushes his thick, sour tongue into her mouth. By dusk, her hair, dampened by the earlier rain, starts to freeze with the dropping temperature. She goes inside, buys a tankard of flip, and drinks it as slowly as she can, hunched in the corner by the fire, letting the hot alcohol soak into her stomach. Then she trudges home with the ghost of another wasted day on her shoulder.

Twice he is supposed to be somewhere, but he is not. She waits at a Twelfth Night pageant, hope fading, watching a parade of stubby little Christmas angels picking their noses, eyes wandering to find their parents' faces in the pews. Once, on a dark street, she sees his carriage flash past, horses clattering on the paving stones. Before she knows what she's doing, her feet are running beneath her, slipping on horse shit, skidding through the late-night crowds, faster and faster, until she slams full force into the broad body of a man who is backing out of a coffeehouse. The carriage rattles off round the corner, and she bends double in the road, her chest stinging, her pulse drumming in her neck. Gone.

She goes back to the tavern that boasts his favor seven more times, until even the tavern's owner thinks she is a whore and threatens to chase her off unless she goes with him upstairs for six pence. Two whole days' work elbow-deep in slime at the cookshop. Sixteen hours with her feet burning and swelling, her hands softening like bloated white fish in the grimy water, then turning stiff and cracking until they bleed. For ten minutes of closing her eyes against his grunting weight. She says yes, if he will let her sit in the tavern once a week without charge. He laughs, and says he doesn't run a whorehouse, and she can take the fuck and the six pence or leave it.

She mounts the stairs to the room above, sick to her stomach, and prays he will not notice the swell of her belly, but he doesn't want her naked anyway. Not like Frederick did, vulnerable and present, as if her body is part of what is happening. This man wants her to bend over the bed and let him strike her with his hand, which she submits to, because it feels better, somehow, than the other thing. She keeps her face pressed into the bed-spread, breathing in and out the scent of stale cooking fat, thinking that it is only like a beating from her father, really, but not as bad, just the sting and slap of his thin hand against her buttocks.

Then he opens a cupboard and brings out a willowy stick. She sees him approach her through scrunched-up eyes and tries to stand without even knowing what she is doing, instinctively flinching at the sight of it, but he pushes her face back into the mattress. He brings the stick down on her six, seven, eight times, and pain floods her body until she is crying, begging him to stop, fearing for the baby. She hears him swear and take down his britches and try to fuck her, wrapping his hand across her face to stifle the protests. She starts to kick so hard she catches him in the kneecap and he reels back. She scrambles up, her face a mess of snot and tears, and stumbles toward the door with the wool of her stockings sagging around her knees. He catches her by her arm.

"What kind of a whore are you?"

She closes her eyes against the flecks of spit and writhes to get free. His hand springs forward and smacks her hard across the face. Everything goes white. Then she gathers herself together enough to run, clattering down the stairs and out into the bright day, head spinning, without her payment. She squeezes into a piss-dank alley and pulls up her undergarments, wiping stupid, fat, hopeless tears away with the back of her hand. Then she walks the three miles home.

Tied inside her skirts, she keeps a separate purse. Her return fare to Harwich. If it gets bad, too bad, there's a way out. But still, there is hope. She can feel it, stubborn, solid, inside her, the way she can feel the baby. And although while the baby grows, the hope shrinks, both just a little, every day, for now it is so slight that she doesn't have to notice.

PEGGY

Mirrors

In the showroom of the new London house, there is a vast full-length portrait of Molly and me, arm in arm, Tristram at our heels. It is the largest in the room. It is the first time my father has painted us together since we were young, and we are all porcelain skin and silk against the woodland murk. That is how my father paints beauty, always in contrast with something else. Something darker. Translucent sleeves tumble down, embroidered with gold thread. Seed pearls glint on satin. We are immaculate. But my father is too good a likeness man to be able to conceal the truth. His talent betrays him. And so the painting, designed to show the glory of his daughters, their beauty and elegance, shows only the strange, brittle sadness it was intended to hide.

If you glimpsed us, fleetingly, you would think that we are

two fashionable young ladies, a little haughty, perhaps, but to be distant, after all, is very elegant. But when you look closer, we are stiff. There is a blankness to us that beauty cannot hide. I can see it.

There is something funny about the eldest Gainsborough girl, they sometimes say. Is there something behind her eyes, a glaze, an oddness? But then the music starts, and they glance away, distracted by the musicians. They glance back, but I am laughing with my sister and they think, no, perhaps she is shy. Perhaps it was nothing. She is only a little absent. And absence suits girls; absence is encouraged—an absence of thought, of idea, of trouble. Much better an absence than a presence. A presence is a frightening thing, a thing that carries you off in the night. A Bedlam thing. But no. An absence is nothing that can't be covered with silks and ribbons and fine reputations, and a clever comment. It is only a lost thought. A lost moment. Until the fog lifts and she is back where she was.

What cannot be hidden is that we are getting old. Turning, like fruit in a bowl, unchosen. Questions are asked. Eyebrows are raised. And Molly walks in the night, a white ghost in the drawing room, sweating, telling us that she is royalty, that she is going into battle, breaking things against the wall and screaming when her armor is not brought. And we cover and we soothe and we shush, and we hide the evidence.

My mother is frightened that I have not married. Her fear is tangible, prowling the house like a cat. Who have I spoken to? Who was near me at the dance? I must marry a wealthy man, not an impoverished musician. I must make eyes behind my fan, to a future for Molly and myself, not to a man as old as my father. She would be horrified if she knew. I hear their voices in the drawing room, muffled, low.

"If Peggy marries well, the problem will be solved."

"I will not have such a thing forced upon her."

"Then what would you have, Thomas Gainsborough? You are not immortal!"

"I do not claim to be immortal, Margaret." His patience is straining.

"Then what if your eyes go dim? What if your hands start to shake? Don't turn away from me! If anything should happen to either of us, the girls will have nothing! The figures do not add up! We must have a younger man in the family. There is no choice."

"There is Gainsborough."

"He has no talent, and you know it. And regardless, he will have his own family to support. The only way the girls can thrive without you is through marriage, and it must be Peggy!"

"Molly may yet recover further."

"You are a dreamer! You always were a dreamer! Why can you not see it?" My mother's voice is rising, hysterical.

And then my father's footsteps, and the slam of the door.

I cannot tell my mother that no one is near me at the dance. That I draw a circle around the pair of us, invisible but there as surely as if I had drawn it in chalk. Men feel it and do not dare approach us. Girls turn away, withdrawing their gestures of friendship. I am an expert at the smile that deters, at the casual closing word, at brushing them away so that their advances fall like raindrops on oilskin. But Fischer does not have to find his way across our circle. He is in our house, visiting my father, playing his music, coming and going as he pleases. He is unavoidable.

And perhaps he knows the way things must be, for there is no clumsy scramble. There are no hurried declarations of want, no lovers' notes in sloping script. It is like him, elegant, sparing, in its taking root. It is nights of aching, days where nothing happens, months where he is away in Germany, or in London. It is weeks of waiting for one evening of watching him across my father's dinner table, six such evenings for one look, quizzical, intimate. It is a delicious tension, so thick you could snap it; it is the air before the storm, the match before the ignition.

We are standing in the half dark. I have waited, hidden, for everyone to go, for he caught me before dinner and asked me to, whispering in my ear with his hot breath, and while I have waited, the candle has melted away almost to nothing. In its flickering light, I see that his hands bear calluses from the oboe, as my father's do from his brushes and tools. I want to reach out and run my fingers over them. Instead, I grip the base of the candle tight and hover, on edge, as if I might suddenly bolt away back up the stairs to safety.

He takes a step toward me in the dark. I feel that I can hardly breathe. That the air has turned solid and I cannot catch enough of it. He lowers his face to mine and then holds it there, his mouth an inch from my cheek.

I am alert, readying myself for his kiss. Willing it.

His lips touch mine. I am upended, spun like sugar.

I think of Ann Ford in her crimson dress, of my father's mouth teasing her nipple, of Molly's blank face, and I try to get the thoughts out of my mind, but they keep coming, playing themselves out again and again, until I pull away suddenly from him and stumble backward in the dark.

We stand there for a moment together, and then he reaches out his hand to me, but there is a noise outside, a call. Someone is coming. He places his finger to his lips, and slips out wordlessly into the hallway. I wait in the silence. Five minutes pass, then ten. The candle snuffs itself out. A thin plume of smoke moves upward into the darkness, and I watch it curling into nothing. Then I slip out of the room myself and climb the stairs to bed.

Nothing can come of it. Nothing. He has no money. I have

heard it too many times from my father. That he wastes his earnings. That he misses his chance at court. I know that if I marry him, I will live in poverty, with a man who loves the gambling tables too much. And where will Molly go then? Who will hold her arms and force her nightly back to bed? Who will let me? For I will not let anyone else. I cannot, and if I marry Fischer, I will not be able to afford to anyway.

When he touches me, it is right and it is wrong. It is desperate want, and it is nausea, my father's yellowed eyes, his wet, flapping gums on his sickbed, warning me against a good time. Warning me against pleasure. It is the woman in the hall slipping away and my father's hand moving instinctively to his shirt, to the dark hairs beneath, and it is Ann Ford, beautiful, destructive, pulling my mother and father apart in oil and varnish.

But I cannot stay away.

At the heart of the Pleasure Gardens there is a swing. It hangs low, and has a seat of intricate white metal, and I am sitting on it like a little girl, knowing that I should get off, that I have been on it too long. A couple loiter nearby, the woman giggling. Two girls of about fifteen watch me, one whispering to the other. I can hear the band playing somewhere in the distance, and the splash of oars on the dark lake, but they are far off, for the swing lies at the center of the maze, boxed in by hedges. I must stop and go back to my mother, for we take turns to walk a little and enjoy some freedom while the other sits with Molly, who is feeling well enough to be out. But I love the way the breeze pushes through my hair, the way my stomach feels as though it has been left high in the air as I swoop down.

I stop the swing suddenly, my slippers scuffing the checkered tiles, and stand, adjusting my dress, breathless. The young couple edge forward to take my place, and I slip past them, for there is Fischer waiting for me out of sight at the edge of the maze, where the fire lanterns cast long, flickering shadows across the ground.

"Good evening, Miss Margaret."

"Good evening."

I cannot help myself, but look around quickly to see if anyone is watching us, and I see him do the same. He places his hand gently on my arm, just below the sleeve, then moves it away again as a couple come round the corner, absorbed in each other.

"You were enjoying yourself on the swing, I think," he says, when they have passed us.

"Yes." I don't know why, but I feel embarrassed. It is a Pleasure Garden, after all, I think. What else is one to do in it? And yet I feel caught out, as if I have been watched doing something I shouldn't. "I must go back to Molly. She is not feeling well this evening."

"Yes," he says. And then, as if I had not spoken, he adds, "It was nice to see it."

He takes my hand again, and we walk, losing ourselves in the twisting pathways. I could not tell you which lead toward the world and which lead deeper in, but I don't feel afraid. There is something about being with Fischer that makes me feel as if I don't have to think, but only follow. It intoxicates me. I have not felt like this since I was a child, following Molly from room to room, or my father through the lanes with his easel. As though wherever I go, it is another person who will choose the path, and I have only to rest my gloved hand in his and put one foot in front of the other.

"It is pleasant to be lost, is it not, Margaret?" he says, glancing sideways at me.

"Only because I trust you to lead us out into safety."

"Let us hope I can." He seems amused, but I do not quite understand why.

We walk in silence, our feet crunching on the gravel, until I can hear the band growing louder somewhere on the other side of the hedges. He stops and looks down at me.

"Do you hear the music?"

"Yes."

"What do you think of it?"

"It is pretty."

"But music should be more than pretty, don't you think?"

"Yes, I—yes." I do not really know what I think.

"You are agreeing with me for the sake of it, I think. I do not want that. I want to know what your thoughts are, Margaret. I want to hear them."

I look at him, his head bowed, his eyes on mine, and I realize that I cannot remember the last time a man asked me what I thought about something.

"I think music should make you feel," I say carefully. "Like a painting. That you feel as if you experience not only—not only what is there, but the person who has created it. As though you can see them, the ghost of them—but only reflected in a hall of mirrors."

"Yes," he says. "That is how I feel also. And sometimes I feel, myself, like the ghost in a hall of mirrors. Perhaps you know what I mean when I say this."

I nod, the smallest hint of a nod. Beyond the maze, the music loops and falls and chases its frantic melody in the night air. Checking that we are alone, he reaches out and runs his fingers gently down my cheek. And then he speaks in his low, soft way.

"Have you ever been to Germany?"

"No. I haven't been anywhere."

"It is beautiful. A beautiful country. I travel there often, and to other cities, to Vienna, to Paris. I want to take you there."

I imagine it. Stepping onto the boat, wrapped in furs. Setting off across the sea, Fischer's hand in mine.

"My home in Munich is near the opera. There is the most

253

beautiful palace in the city. The Nymphenburg. I want to show it to you. To watch your face as you see it for the first time."

I think of palaces, of opera. Of what Germany might be like. Of who I might become there, in that impossibly faraway and unknowable place, without my family. Fischer takes my chin between his finger and thumb and draws my face up toward him.

"You worry for your sister, I think."

"I do."

"You miss her."

"Yes."

"But your life matters also. Your happiness."

I want him to kiss me again, more than anything, so that I can let my mind soften into the kiss in the way it does, and so that I will not have to think about whether my life matters. But he only looks down at me.

"I think there are things you long for, Margaret."

"I am quite happy," I say, and it sounds so weak I am embarrassed.

"Perhaps I can give you some of them."

He kisses me once, softly, and straightens.

"I will see you tomorrow night."

I move out alone into the raucous night, my head spinning, my body already aching for his touch. I had thought there would be more time before he spoke of plans like these. Time to be sure of his poverty, not just to guess at it. To press at my father to see what the resistance will be. Time to think. It feels real, suddenly: a life of travel, a life away from home, dislodged from everything I know. And I want it, and I don't.

Without warning, the fireworks start, cracking open against the night sky, so that I can hardly hear myself think. I push through the crowds, narrowly avoiding a bowing gentleman who seems to want a conversation, back to my mother and Molly, who sits, vacant, on a bench.

My mother rises to her feet, clawing at my arm, and I can barely make out her words under the riot of sound and color above us.

"Margaret! Margaret!" she seems to be saying. "Whatever were you thinking? Whatever were you doing?"

I smile and look up as if I cannot hear her, as if I am entranced by the display above me, but she grabs at me, trying to draw her mouth close to my ear.

"What were you thinking, Margaret, ignoring the Viscount Cranborne? You brushed him away as if he were—as if he were a—an oyster salesman!"

I look back and see the bowing gentleman I brushed away, and the fine cut of his coat as he walks away.

"I did not know . . ." I say, but it is no use, and she cannot be stopped, but talks on and on, pecking at me about young men and beaus and marriage and the Viscount Cranborne. As the final firework leaps into the sky, as we jostle to locate our carriage, as we trundle down Pall Mall, where the cows low in the darkness waiting for their morning milking, my mother is still talking. The three of us, my father, Molly, and I, sit exhausted. My father's eyes are closing in the half light, and I am thinking about Fischer bending his face to mine. I think there are things you long for, Margaret. I want him, I think. I want him at any cost, at any price.

"Margaret!" my mother is saying. "Margaret!"

"What is it?"

"My God, you do not listen. It is so disrespectful! Why can you not respect your mother?"

"Perhaps she is not worthy of respect!" The words flash out of me, white hot, before I can help them.

"Peggy!" my father says, jolted from sleep. "Margaret! Enough of this!"

"Stop it, Peg," says Molly quietly. "Please stop it."

But I cannot stop.

"I have had enough of it! Marriage this and marriage that! You are brainless. It is all brainless. You know nothing of the world! Of what I want!"

"Peggy!" Molly says again. "Peggy!"

"Won't you ever leave me alone? You will pick and pick at me until there's nothing left but a pile of scraps to serve to the nearest eligible man!"

My mother is so red with fury that I think for a second she will lean over and grab me by the cloak and shake me.

"It all falls to you!" She almost hisses it. "You are a stupid, selfish girl, and always were! It all falls to you—why will you not see it? If you will not marry soon, no one will want you, and then what will become of Molly? What will become of you both, after everything we have tried to do for you?"

She starts to sob. Molly leans her head against the carriage window, her eyes closed as if she can make us disappear, and we ride on, the four of us, in misery, until we pull up with a clatter at the house.

In the hallway I discard my cloak and run, two stairs at a time, to the safety of my room. As I go, I hear my father's voice over my mother's muted sobs as the footman takes his overcoat.

"Come now, Margaret. It is like the fable of Aesop. The harder you blow, the more she wraps her coat around herself. Perhaps you should wait for the warmth of the sun."

"This is England, Thomas," replies my mother between sniffs. "The sun is almost never visible."

Upstairs, I throw my muffler down with such vigor that it bounces from the bed and rolls away. Williams undresses us in silent, unquestioning neutrality, prizing feathers from tangled curls and unknotting petticoat strings with her thin fingers, and all the time the anger boils inside me. The injustice of it. Molly climbs quietly into bed, her knees tucked up in front of her like two mountains, and she does not speak until Williams has closed the door softly and left us with a single candle on the bedside cabinet.

"You should not have spoken that way to Mama."

Her voice is gentle, but it is firm. A glimmer of the old Molly. The lost big sister. But she is hardly that now. *You*, I have the sudden urge to say, *you, of all people, cannot tell me how to behave. You, who must be watched constantly, for fear you will shame us all.*

"She infuriates me," I say instead, sliding between the cold sheets. It is not wise to upset Molly at bedtime.

"You infuriate each other." Molly looks at me. "Don't you wish to marry?"

Words burn on my tongue. *I am loved*, I want to say. *I have been asked. And I love in return. And it is so beautiful and so intoxicating that everything else disappears. Colors grow muted when he is not there. My worries, all the old pain and fear, melt into nothingness when he is. But to choose him means to leave you, and so I will not do it.* All the words are there, waiting to spill out, but I push them away so they cannot hurt her.

"I—I don't know—of course," I say. "I only wish to decide for myself. And I wish to take care of you."

"Isn't there anyone you like?" She asks the question tentatively, unsure.

"It doesn't matter who I like. Only who Mama likes."

"She will let you choose. She is only worried, that's all."

"I wish she wouldn't. It is constant. I feel I cannot breathe. You are so lucky to escape it."

"Am I?" The words shoot like a dart, sharper than Molly ever is now, and I glance up, confused. "Am I lucky to escape it?"

"Oh, Molly. I am so sorry."

She sits glassy-eyed. "What do you mean?"

"I have been thoughtless." I reach out and touch her arm. "To speak of such things, when you cannot expect—I am sorry."

At first, she does not respond, just lets me keep rubbing her arm gently, apologetically.

"Oh, that's all right."

"But it is not all right, and I should not speak of such things. I will not again. It was selfish of me."

"You don't have to be sorry."

"I do. I am. Moll, I will take care of you. You know that. I have promised it." I stroke her hair over and over, smoothing it down, and she does not resist, but only looks at me.

"You are right. I should not expect it, should I?" she says, and I cannot make out the expression on her face. "What right would I have to expect it?"

She turns away and extinguishes the single flame, then lies like a stone, unmoving, pulling her nightgown tight around her body.

I take down the great books in my father's study in secret. I touch the drawings of the great buildings, the opera and the gardens of Munich and Paris and Vienna. I imagine myself there, strolling with Fischer along the white gravel. A wife. A newly freed Ann Ford, floating across Europe in a gown of spring colors.

Later that day, I find a little packet in my cloak, wrapped in tissue paper of the palest pink. Inside is a little palace, the most beautiful I have ever seen, and a note. *The Nymphenburg, Munich.*

I go into the music room, where Fischer is waiting to see my father, hoping to catch him alone, but I find him stooping over Molly at the harpsichord. He is showing her, softly, how to play his melody, the symphony he has written, tapping out the rhythm on the side of the instrument. When she stumbles over the tune, he laughs gently and corrects her. I wait, the palace in my pocket, watching his kindness to her, and loving him more because of it.

————

Midnight. The candles are fiery pools of liquid. We thread our way through the heat of bodies. I catch my breath in the heady scent of the room; sweat, perfume, the spice of the punch steaming in great silver bowls. I nearly lose sight of him, the pale velvet of his frock coat twisting and turning through the crowd, through the nascent love affairs, the bored wives, the sardonic husbands, until we are somewhere dark, somewhere quiet, where the air is clear and cool, and the music and laughter as distant as if they are coming from a different world.

Somewhere through the thickness of the doors, the dance is in full swing. The laughter of the women. A man's sudden raucous shout. It feels as if we are underwater.

And then the heat of his hands. The shock of it, and the urgency. Touch like nothing I have ever felt. Ungodly, indecent touch in the dark.

He tells me he will take me away to Italy, to Switzerland, to Spain. I say the place names after him. Madrid. Naples. Lausanne. We talk of his apartment in Munich, of its yellow walls. I imagine it: waking beside him, falling asleep next to him. Traveling across the broad expanse of the world, and never looking behind at what is left.

"This is how life feels, Peggy," he whispers. "This is how it should feel." When I close my eyes, I am somewhere else. I am somebody else. Perhaps that is what I am choosing, in the end. To be, for a moment, somebody else.

When I return home, the house is quiet. Just the sound of my father's violin, sliding up and down the scales, fingers quivering, practicing, practicing.

He has painted me alone for the first time now, my father, against a backdrop of perfect clouds. There is a black ribbon tight against the whiteness of my throat. I am looking up, away,

259

a stubborn refusal to engage. Gone is the directly challenging stare of my childhood. Now I will not divulge my secrets. I cling firmly to my black silk shawl, pulling it tight across my chest. Black gauze and lace, treacle hair pinned up. A fine lady, a Bath lady, no longer the little Ipswich scrap chasing cats in the kitchen.

But my father is clever. He sees people, although he does not always know what he sees. There at the bottom, almost imperceptible at first, away from my determined gaze, bloodred folds of fabric spill, in spite of me, out of the perfect oval frame, toward the onlooker. Toward you. Not everything can be contained. Not everything can be hidden. I am a trompe l'oeil: I cheat the eye. My secrets won't stay where they are supposed to. Secrets never do.

I knock once, then twice, a tentative knock, although my heart is racing. I do not go into the studio often now. I hear my father call in surprised answer, and push my way into the gloom. The air is stuffy, the windows hung with thick black drapes.

My father is wiping his brushes.

"May I come in?"

"Of course, yes. I am just cleaning up. One more sitting should do it." He looks at me. "What is it, Peg?"

"It is Molly. She isn't anywhere to be found."

"She must be somewhere about."

"She isn't. I haven't seen her since dinner. I thought she was in her room reading, but she isn't."

"How long has it been? Two hours?"

"Three at least."

"I shall send someone out to look for her. Don't worry your mother yet."

"I am worried enough for both of us. She promised she would not leave without telling me. What if she were to become—confused?"

"It is a rare enough occurrence."

"It is not, recently."

"I will send out." He takes a step toward the door, but before he can open it, my mother appears, harried.

"Where is Molly?"

"I don't know," I say. "I think she has gone out."

"She has gone out alone in this weather?!"

"In the carriage, I am sure," my father says.

"The carriage is still here," I say, and I feel my palms start to sweat.

"She has gone out alone without the carriage?" My mother is panicked, shrill.

I begin to imagine Molly caught alone, where they would take her, if she cannot remember who she is and where she comes from, and the door swings open and there is Molly, bright-eyed and damp from the rain.

"Molly!"

"My God, Molly," my father says.

"Where on earth have you been?" My mother starts to brush the raindrops from her cloak, ushering her inside.

"I don't know why you are all in hysterics. You may call off the search."

"Where have you been?" I ask as she shrugs me away.

"Walking." She takes off her bonnet, leaving a spatter of drops across the floor.

"My God, I was so worried about you," I say.

"There," my father says, shaking his head. "All is well."

"It was always well," Molly says.

"You didn't say anything about going out." I can see that she does not want to talk to us, that she wants to slip away and to be left alone, but I cannot let her think that this is all right. She cannot go wandering like this.

"I know. I wanted some air, and didn't see why I should bother anyone."

"You worried me terribly."

"I knew it would be like this, which is exactly why I didn't say anything."

My mother reappears, a blanket in her hand. "Whatever were you doing?"

"I was walking."

"It is the middle of winter! You cannot get ill again!" She rubs Molly's hands, drawing them to her, while Molly stands, passive.

"I'm back now," she says, "and rather cold, so I wish everyone would stop making such a fuss."

"I will never stop worrying about the pair of you as long as I am alive," my mother says.

And what if you are not? I think. What if you are not, and it is only me, and I bring Molly with me to a husband? There will be three of us, always, in the marriage. There will be sleepless nights and ravings and screaming. And everything will sour.

There is a sharp rap at the door, and my heart leaps at the sound of Fischer's lilting voice. He comes toward us, his head bowed.

"Good afternoon, Mrs. Gainsborough, Miss Margaret."

"Good afternoon," I say, and our secret binds us in the way it always does, so thick and private between us that I can almost taste it.

"Miss Gainsborough, you look flushed." He stops at Mary's side, his head tilted. Are you in good health?"

"In perfect health. I have been walking, that's all."

"You must excuse me. I have an appointment to see your father." He looks back at me, and then says casually, "That is a beautiful dress, Miss Margaret. A Titian red."

"Thank you," I say as lightly as I can, and I see something pass across Molly's face that I do not quite understand.

Fischer turns to her. "Miss Mary."

"Mr. Fischer."

And then I know it, and it is unvoiced, unspoken, but I know it. She loves him. We, the fluid, shifting we, love him. And for Molly, it is hopeless, so hopeless that I cannot bear to think about it. How did I not see it before?

It is not the way it used to be, with Molly's rootless, frantic switching between eligible men, whipped up by the Bath froth. She is vulnerable now, soft, a tight mussel shell split open. I wonder if, like me, it is his surety she longs for. His certainty. The way he is not caught in any storm. If, like me, it is his strength she wants, when everything is so frightening. Or if it is only the tragedy of her isolation that has led her to him.

He is in the house constantly. He catches me for a moment, he walks with me in the garden, but he always takes time to be with her, to be kind, so that no one notices. With me, with her, with me, with her. With my father. And I see Molly look at him, and in the look is everything I feel, so much so that I feel the look has come from me.

I toss and turn in the dark, imagining unseemly things, night-time things, things no one should talk of, things I wouldn't tell a soul, and cannot now ever tell Molly. It is me he wants. But she loves him, and I love her most, so I am caught. And sometimes when we are there in bed, wound round each other for warmth, I feel that we are so much the same I can't begin to tell where she ends and I begin, where one arm clasps and merges with the other, where one brown curl becomes another, that there is no beginning and ending with the two of us, so that when he has one of us he has the other, when he touches my hand he touches hers, and when he looks at her I feel the weight of the look.

MEG

The baby is growing, poking out from beneath her stomacher. Reluctantly, Meg uses three pence to find herself a new one, scraping through the piles at the Rag Fair for something that doesn't stink of grease or dried piss or some dead woman's sweat. She ties it loosely, bulking out her skirts at the front, and stands hunched forward when under scrutiny as if she has an affliction of the spine. Christmas has come and gone fast, pulling time toward it like a magnet, and the deep, uneasy fear that sits in her belly rises up so that she begins to count the days and make her calculations. She has a month, perhaps two, until she cannot hide it any longer. She pushes the fear back down, and tugs her cloak around her, and plunges her hands into the greasy scum that rests on the surface of the sink water.

One evening she is crossing back through the city from one side to the other, from the cookshop to her new lodgings in the west, when she turns into Drury Lane and sees the blue-and-red crest of Frederick's carriage. It brings her to a halt, sudden, violent, like horses rearing up in fright. She looks left and right, panicked. A coachman sits atop the carriage, rubbing his hands miserably against the cold, but she doesn't like the look of him. Then she sees a woman coming out of the building, the tall, narrow façade outside which the carriage waits. Meg pounces.

"Excuse me."

The woman clacks past her, her mouth downturned like a trout.

"Excuse me, is the Prince of Wales in there?"

"Aye. He's never out of the place, is he?"

"What is—what is the place?"

The woman turns with a clatter on the road. Meg feels the weight of the look, its delight, so familiar now, at her stupidity. There's nothing like stupidity to make people stop in their tracks and talk to you.

"The theater. Do you live under a rock, my darling?"

Practically, Meg thinks, yes.

"Can't stand it myself. Load of warbling. I'd rather be in bed. What do you care about the Prince of Wales, anyhow?"

Meg flushes.

"Oh, I don't, I—I only wish to see him, as he is newly arrived. To admire him."

"One of those, are you?"

"I'm curious, that's all."

"Well, go in now and it's half the price. You've missed the first half."

"How much?"

"The cheap gallery's a shilling, so I daresay they'd let you in for six pence."

"And the Prince of Wales is inside? Watching? Frederick?"

"I don't know how many Princes of Wales you think we've got, but yes."

"And is it lit inside with candles? So you can see him? And he see you?"

The woman looks at her oddly. "I should think so."

Meg looks up at the theater, its broad façade.

"You don't mean him harm, do you?"

"What?"

"You aren't part of a plot or some such? You're acting odd."

"Oh no! No! Of course not! It is only that I admire him, that's all."

"You're not a Londoner." Her eyes are narrow, uncertain.

"No. I'm visiting. I wanted to catch a glimpse of royalty, that's all, and saw the carriage."

The woman, uneasy, looks to the driver, who appears to be nodding off, one hand still clutching the reins, then back to Meg.

"Well, get in, then, before you miss it. Down the side alley there, and they'll give you your token."

"Thank you." Meg turns and darts across the street, the woman's eyes on her back. He is inside. She is moments away from him. She buys her ticket for the price of two days in the kitchen, and grips the little metal circle like a magic lamp. Then she is tripping up the narrow stairs, giddy, breathless, and numb. She has spent days chasing Frederick, hunting him, straining to catch a trace of his movements across the vastness of the city, and now she has walked straight into his carriage, standing there in front of her as if it has been waiting for her to arrive, and up the stairs into his presence. With clumsy hands she passes the token over at the door to a pock-marked boy who nods her through, and then walks straight into a wall of heat and noise. The theater is thick with bodies, cheering, cackling, hooting. Down on the stage somewhere far below are players, singing and shouting, and a band scratches beneath them, but she cannot look down, for the height makes her palms sweat. She tries to force her way to an empty seat but loses her balance and half topples over the balcony. Arms grab her, and voices shout at her to be careful, to sit down and shut up, and she lands with a thump on the empty seat, her eyes frantically roaming the vast hall.

Then she almost cries out. In a painted box, suspended like a church angel. His round, white face. The familiar softness, the brightness, that seems to surround him like a cloud. He is gleaming, all blue brocade and alabaster skin. He will never see her. She is lost, faceless, above him.

He's still there, she thinks, as if she had begun to doubt that he had ever existed. There he is, his body, the long legs that slid up against hers in the heat of the night. She wants to scream out to him, but the crowd, the music, the performers are deafening. He is not going to hear her. He is not going to see her.

She turns her face to the stage, where a woman is singing, shrill and hysterical, about her love being madness and folly. The audience whoops and howls and catcalls. A few ruddy-faced figures in the gallery behind her stand up and start shouting at her. "We'll ride you, Polly, don't you feel lonely." "Do you take it all ways, Polly? Tell us how you take it!" until they are pulled down by the people around them and drowned out by groans. Her eyes flick to Frederick. He is laughing.

Meg feels something and she doesn't know what. Then she recognizes it. Humiliation. In church, she thinks, in the long, somber sermons from the wan Harwich reverend, fallen women, the kind of woman she is, now, were derided or pitied, but they were never mocked. Now she is reflected back, paraded onstage as stupid, useless, and conniving, a wanton hussy, a sorry slut, to gales of merry laughter. And there, Frederick in his gilt balcony, guffawing at the whores, rolling around, his mouth hanging open with thigh-slapping snorts. "Our Polly is a sad slut," they all sing, "our Polly is a sorry slut," and the audience roars.

Meg sinks lower in her seat, the only face not stretched with laughter, feeling the baby kick with sharp little thumps at her bladder as the women sing about how they love to ride, and ride, and ride. So this is the world he comes from, she thinks, and she, his cast-off whore, is going to come to him and press him for money. There is nothing serious about it. It's only funny. Our Polly is a sorry slut. She is so tired, so exhausted, and she has had to pay to come here to be insulted, and it is all hopeless.

She thinks about trying to leave, her face burning, wanting to get out, away from it all, into the air, and looks for her best route to the exit. The girl next to her, bored, has torn the peel of her orange into tiny pieces, and is engaged in flicking them one at a time over the edge of the balcony with considerable force. She notices Meg watching her and leans toward her, shouting, hot-breathed, in her ear, "One point for a gentleman's wig, two points for a lady's hat. Want to play?" Meg laughs and nods, and the girl tips a portion of peel into her hand. Meg sends her first piece ricocheting down into the pit, and sees it bounce on the bare shoulder of a plump lady, who swats at herself as if she has been stung by a wasp. The girl, eyes round with glee, turns to Meg and pulls a face, and she laughs in response, the first real, stupid laugh in weeks. The smell of the peel in her warm hand is like Christmas. One small piece of kindness, she thinks, one stupid little moment of togetherness, and her heart is on fire with happiness.

"Oh, you gentlemen," shouts a petulant character, preening and strutting in the footlights, "take pleasure in insulting the women you ruin," and the band strikes up, and Meg uses her forefinger to send another piece of peel onto a ribboned wig, where it remains, bobbing about each time its owner laughs.

Pull yourself together, she tells herself. It's only self-pity, after all. And didn't she know it already, what the world thought of foolish girls who got themselves in trouble? She was hardly born in a barn, as her father used to say. She has one task. She needs money. And for money, she needs to find Frederick. She leans over to the girl.

"That the Prince of Wales there?"

"Yeah, why?"

"Do you know how I can get a glimpse of him, after?"

"Why? He a pal of yours?"

Meg rolls her eyes. "Just want a look, that's all."

"His carriage waits out front. If you want to gawp at him, wait by the stairs, not in the yard. Not much worth looking at, if you ask me, but maybe you like that sort of thing. They say he's a no-good," she continues, her eyes amused. "Always at the gambling tables and the theater."

"*We're* at the theater," Meg points out.

"*We*," says the girl, "can do what we bloody well want. Perks of being a nobody. Two points for me. Right in the bonnet."

When the play ends, Meg pushes her way out, moving against the tide of bodies like a salmon. The corridors are packed, hazy with candlelight, full of chatter and laughter and snatches of song. She jostles and pushes, through the reek of stale breath and old booze and sweat and mingled perfumes and pomades, one hand around her stomach to protect it, trying to break nearer to the stairs. She sees their red curve, the carved handrail, but the crowds are too thick. Then through the ornate doors she catches a glimpse of his coach waiting on the street outside. There are footmen all around it now, the horses stomping and snorting clouds into the cold air, and Meg starts to push the other way, to get out. She is halfway there, tripping over cloaks and feet and someone's small dog, which yaps at her skirts as if it will fight them. Then suddenly there is a murmur from the crowd, and she sees him. His long legs are tripping down the stairs, his broad, open face pink with laughter, surrounded by guards who push the crowds back as he and his friends make their way out, heads down, eyes averted. He is almost going to pass right by her. She is two, three rows of people away from him, and she presses forward, knocking a cup of nuts from the hand of a man who turns, shouting in an angry shower of spit. "Frederick!" she calls over the shouts and the whoops, "Frederick!" *Shut up*, she wants to scream, *shut up, all of you!* Words rise up into her mind, vile, insulting words she wants to hurl at them all, at the man who is shouting at her about the cost of nuts. She raises herself up on her toes and tries to get her face clear of the man in front of her. "Frederick!" If he turns, he will see her face, see her eyes, hear her call, but just as she does so, and takes a breath to shout again, he passes by and is gone, out into the night. She is left, jostled and alone, to fend off the man who insists she pay him a penny for the nuts, which lie scattered across the floor, trampled into dust by the churning crowd.

PEGGY

Tempest

One winter's evening, late, Fischer catches me as I leave the drawing room. He always seems to know how to catch me, but then, I am always waiting to be caught.

"Margaret."

"Yes."

He reaches for my hand, his gray eyes darting across the landing, and pulls me into the darkened music room. It stands silent, deserted, with only the looming shapes of the instruments, which seem to watch us like a crowd.

"I was thinking about you today," he says. "About our little apartment in Munich." His mouth is urgent on mine, so urgent that it feels more like a battle than a kiss. "About our life together."

I close my eyes and let myself sink into the thought of it. The apartment, with its yellow walls. Its tiled fireplaces. I can see it.

"I will come home to you," he says, his hand working its way toward my breast, and under the ridge of my corset. "I will come home to you, and you will be waiting for me."

I begin to feel breathless and pull myself away for a moment, back into the house. I hear the heavy trudge of my parents next door, drawing the curtains, readying the house for bed. I think of Molly lying upstairs, waiting for me to kiss her good night.

"Let us talk it through," I say. He puts his arms around my waist, firm and insistent, and kisses me again, and I wriggle free. "No, Johann, let us talk through how it might be."

"We have so little time together."

"It will not work to travel," I say. "You know it will not work."

"What are you talking about?" He kisses me softly on the head.

"It is not possible, Johann. It is not as simple as . . . it is—it is the money—I do not know your circumstances."

He hesitates for a second, his mouth an inch from mine.

"I did not think of you as mercenary, Peggy."

"I'm hardly—I . . ."

"I am teasing you."

"It is more complicated than you think. Molly—Molly cares for you—"

"Does she?"

"You must see it."

"I am flattered."

"Please don't joke." I pull away, and he catches my hand and tugs me back.

"Come here, Margaret. Please. We have so few moments together."

"Someone will come." I don't like it, being here with people so close. I feel a sort of panic rising in my chest, but he kisses me again, a series of small kisses around my mouth and across my face, and I close my eyes to receive them. I have the old feeling that he will solve everything, give me an answer to everything, if I only bury myself in him. If I only say yes.

"I want you, Margaret," he says. "I want you to be able to live. You deserve to live your own life. To experience everything life has to offer."

"I know, I—"

"I have a place we can be without interruption."

Suddenly I find strength, and bring my hands up and push at his waistcoat. "You cannot ask that of me."

"Then decide what you want."

I hear his footsteps descending the stairs, soft and quick, and then the click of the front door.

I stand motionless in the dark. My head is still full of the taste of him, the roughness of his face. His thin musician's hands. The way they push back my hair, tuck a rogue strand behind my ear. The heat of his mouth on mine. I want it all, so badly, the life he promises. All of it. To be free.

And then there is a scream, somewhere above, and movement, the running of feet, a shout, and Molly bent double again, screaming blindly into the thick, shuttered bedroom air. Screaming wild things, mad things, things that would have her taken to Bedlam if anyone heard them, but nobody will, because we close around her like a clam. And the bang of my mother's bedroom door as she moves, bleary, across the house. And the doctors are called again, and the voices are lowered again, and a door opens and someone scurries past, and I glimpse the chamber pot they are carrying and what is in it is red, rich earthy red urine splattered up the sides of the bone-white china. And I know it cannot continue.

I move silently from the study, closing the door behind me, past the muffled screaming and commotion and Williams, impassive with her pile of sheets. I walk into the darkened drawing room, remove a piece of paper, light a candle, and begin to write.

Dear Mr. Fischer,

I hope you will forgive me for corresponding by letter with regard to such a delicate personal matter.

My sister is so very unwell. I think perhaps you do not know quite the extent of it. I have promised her that I will stay with her, and I cannot break my promise.

I would beg you if only for my sake to remain distant from our household until sufficient time has passed to render the decision less painful. I assure you that it has not been taken lightly.

I remain faithfully,
Miss Margaret Gainsborough

The next day I seal it and send for a messenger. I watch as he disappears up the street, the back of his head bobbing into the distance. And then I turn back into the house, back into its slow rhythms, its dim, shuttered afternoon light.

The crisis has passed, I think, and this is where things will remain, in care, in quiet, in steadiness. I do not want tempests. I look into the drawing room, where Molly sits, better again for now, and I wind my arms around her neck and breathe the soft indoors smell of her hair.

It has been a bad night. I am perched on the bed tending to Molly while she is sick into a bowl. Her shoulders heave as she retches, and the lank tail of hair I have gathered jerks suddenly out of my hand.

She turns her face to me, loose strands around her face spattered with vomit.

"Why can't you keep hold of it?"

"I am trying, Moll."

"Try harder."

She slumps backward onto the pillow.

"I am so tired of this." There are tears in her eyes.

"I know," I say. "Lie still." I dip a cloth into a bowl of water and dab at her hair and mouth as she lies, passive, like a baby.

"I want to go out."

"Of course you cannot go out."

"Downstairs, then."

"No."

"Fischer is coming to play with Papa, I am sure of it."

"Oh, Moll," I say, because of the secret hope that has crept across her face. "No."

"I cannot stand this." She twists her face away from me. "I am trapped here."

"You are not trapped."

"I am."

"Oh, Molly," I say, because I cannot help myself. "It will pass. I promise you it will pass."

"It always comes back."

"Not that."

"What, then?"

Her eyes are fixed on mine.

"The way you feel," I say carefully. "About him."

"What?" she says, as if she will cry again. "What?"

"About Fischer."

"What?"

"I see it. And I am so sorry, Moll. I have failed you, I think."

"How?"

"I have tried to protect you from this. To protect you from— from things you cannot hope for. But he is here so often, to see Papa, I mean. I did not see it. And he is kind, and I understand it, but it is only that. It will fade away, I promise you. And you will feel better. And I will be here."

She stares at me with such fierce sadness that it almost feels like hate.

"You know nothing. You know nothing about it at all."

And she turns her face and will not say another word, so I put the cloth down, dry my hands, and leave her to sleep.

The first moment that I know that something is wrong is when I hear the sound of my mother crying.

I am coming home from town, boxes tied with string in my hands, and my cloak pulled up against the winter chill. A footman opens the door to me, and I pass him into the hall, and then I hear it. A desperate sort of sobbing. It is Molly. It can only be Molly. I go quickly to the cloakroom and am pulling at the ribbon of my cloak with numb fingers when I hear the front door slam, and see my father cross the hall, sweat shining on his brow, and take the stairs, two at time, without seeing me.

I follow him softly. The sitting-room door is closed, and I hover near it, listening.

"I came at once," my father is saying. "I came at once. Now, now, Margaret, now, now."

"I cannot—I cannot bear it." My mother's sobs rack her body. I place my hand on the door handle, thinking that it would be better to go and comfort her myself, for whatever it is, it is surely better faced by all of us together. And then she says, "He is twenty years her senior!"

"He is a composer, and much—"

"A second-rate composer of oboe concertos!"

My hand freezes. How do they know? How can they know?

"His talent is undisputed," my father is saying, but my mother weeps again. I think of my note, running through it in my mind, and try to understand how it can possibly have been misconstrued. Is this some ploy to get me to consent? What has he told them?

My father raises his voice to be heard.

"Margaret, listen to me. I had not the least suspicion of the attachment being so long and deeply settled. It is too late for me to alter anything."

"You have known him all these years and should have—"

"I refuse to doubt his honesty or goodness of heart." My father is defiant. "I have never heard anyone speak anything amiss of him."

And then my mother speaks, and I begin to see.

"She is not well, Thomas."

A beat passes, and in it, my brain seems slow as mud.

"Does he know that she is not well? Does he?" my mother continues, plaintive and childlike. "How can he know it? She is unmarriageable. You know it as well as I. He cannot know the extent of it! He simply cannot know it. We have hidden it away, covered it from view, and now look!"

The pieces of the jigsaw shift into place, and with them the ground shifts too.

"I agree it is alarming," my father is saying, "Of course I agree."

"This is your fault! Your fault! You brought him into the house, when he is well-known as—as a philanderer."

"He is nearly twice her age! I had no idea that she would consider him in this way! I thought he would be like a—like a father to them. I am furious with myself. Furious with Fischer."

"Then stop it! Stop them!"

"It is too late, Margaret."

"And what does he say of it all?" my mother asks.

"He says that he loves her. That he understands his responsibilities and is able to provide for her comfortably. He says he

277

understands that she has been previously unwell, and that he will care for the delicacy of her situation."

"She will be miserable." My mother's voice is tremulous.

I stand, frozen, at the door. I want to run, but my feet won't move. How is it possible? How can it be possible?

"He is a dissipated wretch and you know it." She is crying again.

"You have been happy all these years with a dissipated wretch yourself."

"It is not what I wished," I hear my mother say helplessly.

Molly, I think. He is marrying Molly. Fischer is marrying Molly. No. It cannot be.

"And there is something else," I hear my father say. "A reason to suspect there may be no—choice in the matter."

"Molly?" My mother's voice is small, uncertain.

"So he says."

There is a pause.

"She is—no. It cannot be so. She is—unwell. Who would—?"

"I believe it to be the case."

"The foolish, foolish, foolish girl. I have done everything to avoid this." The tears come again, muffled through the door, and suddenly I understand everything, and I think I will be sick.

"What is wrong with us?" my mother is saying through her sobs. "My mother first, and then me, and now Molly. We are fools, all of us."

"But we have been happy, Margaret, in spite of the way we began. I would not have chosen another woman. It is not unusual to begin a marriage in such circumstances. It may do Fischer a power of good, as it has done me."

I hear my mother make a little noise of unhappiness, and my father's low voice soothing her.

"Come now, Margaret. It is too late. It is too late."

I reach out, stupidly, to put one hand on the wall to steady myself, but the wall itself seems to move. Why has he done this? How? It is me he loves. I know it. He told me so.

Oh God, I think. Of course. Of course. It is a stupid, comic tale of seduction. It is a sordid little story. Two sisters in love with the same man, like an old Irish ballad, or a comedy at the theater, gales of laughter from the crowd.

A movement on the stairs. Molly is behind me, with a look in her eyes of mingled fear and triumph, and I turn on her like a cat.

"What have you done?"

"Nothing at all."

"What have you done?" I say again. My voice shakes. It does not sound like mine.

"Only fallen in love. Didn't you think me capable?"

"I—you can't . . ." I try to steady myself again somehow, but the world is spinning and all is upside down, and I fear I will be sick.

"You didn't think me capable, you see," Molly says. "You didn't!"

"You aren't—you cannot—"

"I cannot what?"

"This is impossible. It is impossible. You have destroyed everything—the family, everything. Mother is beside herself . . ." Even as my mouth forms the words I know that I am lying, that it is not our mother for whom I am angry.

"Poor Molly, who can never be loved," she says. "Poor Molly, who can hope for *nothing*."

"I didn't—"

"Who would have thought that she might have secrets, and a life, and something to hope for. That she might be desired instead of just pitied! Not you, for you prefer me ill! It suits you better!"

"No," I say. "No!"

"I shall be traveling now, like Miss Ford, traveling across Europe. I shall have a new life, and you will not have to worry about me anymore."

My mind feels its way across everything that is happening, the layers of injustice falling one upon the other.

"It is all ruined," I say. "Everything. You have—"

"I have only fallen in love with someone. It is perfectly normal, and nothing to be hysterical about."

She pauses, her breath coming thick and fast, her cheeks flushed.

"You are not normal, Molly," I say, and my voice is soft and low.

"Yes, I am," she says, and I see tears spring into her eyes. "I am."

I take a step toward her, cautious. "You are not well enough to leave us all to go and make a life with him."

"What else am I to do? What else do women do?" she says, and I see that she is trembling. I take another step.

"You are not well enough for this, and you do not know the cost of what—"

But she steps away. "How can there be a cost?" she says. "A cost to who? To yourself, because you are frightened you will never be wanted, and because you only think of yourself—"

"I think of you! I only think of you! You are not well enough for this!" My voice rises, panicky. "But he is not—he is—I would never damage us, I would never separate us or divide us, I would never have done it!"

"Of course you would! If you had been in love, or had any desire for a life at all, or a chance at it. You with your *pity* and your *care*." She spits the words at me as if they are poison.

"That is not—"

"Are you so much more sensible than me that you would remain here unmarried, childless, being painted in pairs until we die, because no man is ever to your liking or you to his—"

"That is not—" I try again to intervene, but she will not listen.

"Johann loves me, has loved me in secret, with such passion, and he sees me as a woman, not as a—child, and you are jealous, I know it! Because you will not see me happy when you are not—"

"He has not!" I almost shout it, and she stops dead. "He does not! He is not honorable, Moll! He would have had me, all this time he has wanted me, but I would never have said yes, never. He has made fools of us."

There is a pause that stretches out in front of us, endless and horrible, and I see her reeling in it. Her mind tumbling over a thousand things. And then she looks at me, pale as ash.

"Will you take everything that is mine, because you cannot have it?"

I open my mouth to reply, but she cuts over me.

"We are not the same person! I am not you, and you are not me! I have a right to a life of my own, experiences of my own. You think because I have been ill that you can own me. You smother me! When we were children, you—you hurt me, you would hurt me, if I did not do as you wished. Do you remember it, the blood on my hands, the way you would pinch and stab me? *Do you?*"

"I—"

"You creep up on me and into me, always touching me and stroking me and trying to keep me like a pet! And now you are trying to do it again, because you are too frightened to go yourself and want to keep me as you want to be kept, to manage me as you have always—you cannot! I won't let you. I won't let you."

I am suddenly aware that Williams is standing at the bottom of the stairs. I see that she has heard everything, the humble

Williams, that she has listened to it, and that the power was never ours at all. My father has come from the sitting room and is watching us too. He opens his mouth to speak, and I think of his words, a tragedy and a farce in the same evening, and how he winked, and I laughed as if I knew everything about the world, and I turn and run to my room and lock the door and lie flat on the rug as I used to when we were little, and cry.

It is the humiliation. It is the shock of my own shabby little story revealed to me. The pomposity and foolishness of my little note. I burn with the shame. Two squabbling sisters in a jealous rage. I hate myself. I hate both of us. They will ruin us, I think, ruin our lives, these virtuosic men who surround us, and all we can do is turn on each other.

And yet I remember his seriousness. His delicacy. *I want to know what your thoughts are, Margaret. I want to hear them.* He did not seem to be one of those men. The rakes, the dueling fools I read about in the papers, seducers of sisters, abandoners of young maids. But perhaps those men do not seem it either. Perhaps that is exactly why they are desired in the first place.

I know then that that is the end of it for me, that I would rather die untouched than have everything I am and value and love stripped from me in a game played by these rules. And I know, with a hard, cold clarity, that if words don't match actions then there's nothing worth having in either.

Before the wedding, my father paints Johann Christian Fischer, as a mark of faith, or approval perhaps. As a sign that all is well. A bad marriage is bad for business. But my father loves his hidden messages, to make himself visible even when it is you, and you alone, who fills the canvas. And so, although perhaps only he and I will ever understand it, he chooses to reuse an old painting for his base. It is a figure of Shakespeare, who stands poised between Tragedy and Comedy. "They always are, Peg."

He will not look at me, Fischer, as he takes my fragile sister's arm and brings her out into the winter sun. Her hand rests lightly on her stomach, and he places his over it, as if proud. As if he will keep her safe. I feel contempt, rage, righteous fury. But later, as we sit for the wedding feast, his gray eyes search for mine, and meet them, and I think my heart will crack in two with sadness.

MEG

"I can't." Meg's voice is a croak. She tries again. "I can't."

The man is crouching near her, close enough that he can probably smell the stale sweat on her, his stockings thinning at the knee where he bends.

"It's a short walk, and I can show you the way. They'll take you in, if you'll work once the child is born. You must not remain on the street in your condition."

Meg squints up at him in the morning sunlight. His eyes have a kindness to them. They crinkle at the edges. It is too hard to explain, all of it. She cannot tell him that she must stay on the street, that she must keep looking, until the very last moment, until there's no hope at all. Because she doesn't know if she will survive the birth, and it is she, and she alone, who is the link between her child and its father. If she is not there, the chain breaks. But the words won't come, and anyway, he would dismiss her as a fantasist. Perhaps she is one. She has nothing left, only a single shilling, and can only surrender to that risk, or beg. So she will beg.

"I can't."

The man removes his hat, and scratches at his head, then puts it back on again. He lets out a heavy sort of sigh and brings himself to standing with an audible creak of his knees.

"Very well."

He reaches into his purse and leans down to put a single coin into her hand, pressing it in with his own warm fingers, then walks away down the street. A shilling, glinting, perfect in the early spring sunlight. She would cry with relief, and with gratitude, but she's too tired. She grips it, weeks of survival shrunk down into a tiny, hard circle, then pulls herself to her feet.

She finds a place that serves her a steaming bowl of porridge, and sits nursing it, hiding her bitten, cracked fingers, their blackened nails, in her skirts to avoid attention. Each spoonful slides warm and thick down her throat, and with the nourishment the hope comes back. Food and hope. She'd never have thought they were connected, back then. But now it seems obvious, like a lot of things she never knew.

The worse things have gotten, the harder it has been to avoid suspicion. It has made it more difficult to access the places Frederick might be found. Poverty brings fear with it into a room. As if it is contagious. When you are wealthy and stand for a moment in the street, you are lost. You are someone to be rescued, to be helped. When you are poor, you are someone to be feared. Even a woman is feared, which is not something she is used to. To be kicked at, to be spat at, or only shifted quietly away from. And it has become more and more impossible to think about returning, swollen and defeated and dirty, to Harwich.

It had begun to turn in February, when the ground was frozen and the baby had finally pushed her skirts out so far and hard that it was as if it had grown overnight. Liz had stood in the center of the kitchen, her weary face cracking with a sudden, violent hostility.

"You little slut."

Without a word, Meg had grabbed her things and left. Not much point fighting about it. That was what she was, after all, wasn't it? She'd known it was coming, of course, and had saved her wages for it. She would be free, at least, to find Frederick with every waking minute she had. But that was more than a month ago now, five long weeks, and her penury has crept up on her, her filth, like a disease claiming its victim.

She thinks she has perhaps one month left before the baby comes. She has heard he will be at a cricket match at a village outside the city, and that anyone may attend such an event for no fee. The next day, she walks for seven hours. She has done such things before, walking for a whole day to a village fair near Hampton Court, only to arrive, sore and broken, to find no sign of him. She doesn't cry anymore. She simply eats something, rests, and returns. It feels sometimes as if the object has become no longer to find him, but simply to keep on with the search.

As she nears the village of Kew, she joins throngs of people moving toward an expanse of grass that stretches out under the patchy April sky. There is a juggler standing under a tree, sending balls flying upward so high they seem to brush against the branches. A band. Courting couples who can't see beyond their own noses. All the usual paraphernalia of a gathering. She looks past it all, looking forward, looking onward. There, at the far end of the green, stand two tents, with little flags fluttering around them. Behind the tents, Frederick's carriage horses graze. At the sight of them, the tatters of hope somewhere inside her rise up. They are still there, then, after all, fluttering like the flags in the light spring breeze.

She makes her way to the front of a thin crowd that has gathered by ropes at the tent's exit. An old woman stands with three children who won't keep still, but who tangle themselves in her skirts as if trying to lose themselves. "Stop it, Bess," she is saying. "Stop it, or I'll take you home and your father will whip you. You are a wicked child. John! Stop it and stand still." Meg looks at the wicked Bess, who grins back at her from the tent she has made of her grandmother's cloak. The three children are like snakes all trying to bite one another. At least she will only have one, she thinks. And there will be no father to threaten a whipping from.

"Is the Prince of Wales inside?" she asks a greasy man to her right.

"Yes, love. Waiting for the match to start. Keen to see him, are you?"

Meg almost laughs out loud. "Yes."

Her palms are sweating, her breath is coming shallow and rapid. It's too easy. Will he just come out and walk past her, Frederick? Will he just emerge from the tent, as simple as that, and see her there in the sunshine? It's impossible. Could she find her way into the tent? It is not like a palace, after all, with gates and walls and guards and a maze of rooms to navigate. It is only one flapping piece of fabric. But the risk of it. She is too dirty, too poor, not to be arrested and dragged away at the first second of discovery.

Suddenly a shout goes up. Her heart hammers at her ribs like an iron bell. She rocks back and forward on her heels, as if readying herself to run, to race, and the opening of the tent is pulled back.

A blue-coated man emerges, then another, and she is taking a breath to shout, when she is shoved hard from behind. She almost falls over the rope, clutching at her stomach to protect the baby, then is pushed back behind a group of women who press forward, laughing and calling out. She can't see, she can't be seen anymore, and she fights to get forward again. People have come from nowhere, hundreds of them, pushing and shouting. She should be used to this now, the way the crowd surges forward at the thought of him, the way reasonable men, intelligent women, lose their senses and start to grin and cheer. They become stupid, like children, pushing for a glimpse, clinging to the chance of finding some meaning, some significance, in the flash of royalty as it passes. There are shouts of "God save the King," and the band is somewhere behind her with its brassy din, and everything is chaos. The guards press them back, but the more they are pressed back, the more they push, groveling, forward.

"Frederick! Frederick!" Voices cut over hers from all sides, drowning her out when she tries to speak. She will not be heard; she cannot be heard. It is hopeless. If she screams, people will think her mad and remove her by force. She pushes forward, scratching like a cat, knocking the child Bess to one side, seeing the fright in her upturned eyes and feeling nothing, then she is elbowed hard in the side. "Steady on, darling," says the greasy man in her ear. "Watch the children." She ignores him. She is too far back. "Frederick!" Panic rises in her chest. He is walking, head down, in that loping way he has, the bat hanging low in his hand. He will pass her just once, close enough to hear, and then he will go on walking, taking with him the last traces of hope that still cling on inside her. She is filthy. Exhausted. Almost broken. There is just this one single moment left. She summons all her courage. All her breath.

"Griff!"

His face snaps up instantly. He scans the crowd. As if he is scared of that name, and the people who call him by it.

"Griff!"

His eyes lock on hers. Something floods her body. An emotion that is not quite relief, not quite fear. Then he is backing away, and for a moment she thinks he is leaving. He turns and heads back, away from her, away from the pitch, toward the tent.

"Yer for it now, darlin'," says the greasy man, eyeing her with bafflement and rising panic. "What the hell d'you do that for? Griff?! Jesus."

She wipes her palms down her dress, trying to see over the head of the woman in front of her. He is talking to someone, one of the blue-coated men she remembers from Harwich, and she sees him point. Then she loses sight of them for a moment, jostled from behind, looking left to right, straining on tiptoes in her pattens, until a tap on her shoulder makes her turn.

"Come, please." She sees that it is the tallest of the Germans from Harwich—Kleist? Klast?—and she wants to embrace him like an old friend. She wants to fling herself on his blue jacket and cry. She sees his eyes flick down to her belly, and something like contempt, or perhaps just weariness, passes across his face.

"Hey, she didn't do nothing wrong," the greasy man says, although she can see he is nervous. "She didn't say nothing."

"It's all right," she says, touching him on the shoulder. "It's all right."

"You can't just take her away like that," he says, defiant. "Hey!" His voice wobbles slightly. "Hey!"

She follows the blue-uniformed man through the crowd, which parts before them, and re-forms again almost instantly. They walk, the two of them, away from the brawling, seething mass, across the damp grass, its wet shadow creeping up her skirts. The tall man stands back with a nod and pulls open the tent, and she steps inside. She has never been in a tent before. In its cool gloom, everything smells different. Earthy.

She stands, waiting, although there is a row of ornately carved cream chairs along one side of the canvas. She feels too dirty to sit on one. One blackened, cracked hand sits instinctively on her belly, in some sort of private, invisible communication with the baby inside, as if she is trying to say that she will protect it from whatever's coming. Or perhaps the message is for her. Perhaps she is reminding herself that she isn't alone. That there are two of them. Strength in numbers. She has played a gambling game with their lives. That has been her first act of motherhood. And now the cards are about to be revealed.

"Meg."

She looks up, and there he is at the entrance to the tent, his face creased in a frown. The moment, so long anticipated, feels unreal. Like a dream. In the dreams she's had, when he has found her, he has kicked her to the floor, or taken their baby in his arms and kissed her, or the baby has become a fish, or died, or run away on strange baby legs, and each time she has woken, disorientated, grasping after the vanishing images. Now Frederick stands before her, real, neither kicking her nor kissing her, but looking at her, serious and confused, in the shade of the tent.

"I'm sorry," she says, and then wants to kick herself. "I mean, I'm sorry for—coming here—but—"

"It's all right. No, no, it is all right." He takes a couple of steps toward her. "My God," he says, "a child."

"Yes." She looks down at the hard bulge of her belly under her skirts, and fights down the urge to apologize again.

"*Ach. Mein Gott.*" He rubs at his forehead, at the line where the gray strands of his wig meet his skin.

"I know."

"My father will not be happy."

"Neither will mine," she says, half smiling.

"Couldn't you find someone to marry?" he says. "The boy who always looked at you with the stupid eyes."

"Hal?" She laughs in spite of herself.

"Yes, him. Hal. Or anyone. To take care of you."

She looks at him. "I didn't want to," she says simply.

He rubs his forehead again. "This is not good for me, Meg. This is not a good thing for me."

"I know. I know. I need help. I've come for help. I don't want

290

anything apart from money." Red heat rises over her face at the words, but she clenches her jaw.

"Money?"

"Yes. I need money. To get the baby away from my father. So he's safe. And then I'll leave you alone, I promise."

"I will have to talk to people. To my advisors. To my father's advisors, as I am his—his *puppe*, his puppet. For now."

"Do you have—do you have money now?" Her face is burning, but she will not, she cannot, leave here empty-handed. With only a promise.

He sighs. "It is difficult, Meg. Everything is difficult. I lose money at the gambling tables. And they do not want to give me more."

"I have nowhere to sleep."

"You should not have left your home."

She stares at her hands. Anger is starting to rise up inside her like a sea, and she has to control it. She has to. Can she really blame him when she's gambled so wildly herself? She lifts her head and looks him directly in the eye.

"I need money."

"Wait here. Wait for a moment." He goes to the opening of the tent. "Kleist!" he calls, and almost instantly the tall man appears. Listening at the door, she thinks. He always was loitering near them, watching them. Frederick begins to talk in German, and Kleist listens, frowning, making the odd terse interjection. The way their mouths form the words, the way their tongues fit around the sounds, reminds her of those days in the inn a lifetime ago. The heat and his long white body in the dark.

Kleist disappears, and they stand looking at each other for a moment.

"It is my first child, this," he says, nodding at her stomach.

"Mine too," she says wryly.

"I do not—I did not want you to suffer."

"It's the way of the world," she says, and turns away, shutting down his attempt at tenderness before all the things she carefully stores away, the anger and the fear, come bubbling up again in response to it. "But I need—I need practical help."

"It is my duty," he says with a courtly nod, as if someone has prepared him on what he must say on the day when this, inevitably, came to pass. This is what she has gambled on. On courtliness. She has staked everything on it, and she feels, for the first time, a flicker of possibility. Of victory.

Kleist returns with something in his hands, and Frederick turns to him with evident relief. They confer again in German, and then Frederick presses into her hands a purse weighted with coins. She wants to tear it open, as if it's bread that she can shovel into her mouth; she wants to count it and touch it and feel it, and calculate, quickly, how long she can survive on it. But she holds it tight in a clenched fist, dignified, and keeps her eyes fixed on his, while he passes her something else. It is a scrap of paper, on which is scrawled an address.

5 Grosvenor Square.

And beneath, in a sprawling script, one word.

Beaufort.

"Go here tomorrow, at two o'clock, and I will come. Yes?"

"Yes."

"Good."

"Thank you," she says, and attempts what she hopes is a curtsy. The words are harder to say than they should be, so she says them again, summoning all her relief and turning it into gratitude. "Thank you."

He smiles, a tight, worried smile, and she turns to go, but he calls her back.

"Meg."

He reaches into his pocket and passes her a little gold box, so

tiny she can close it in her fist. She examines it, the intricacy of
the engraving; the florid letter *F* on its lid.

"Just in case," he says.

In case of what? she wonders. What is it? A warning, that he
may not be where he says he will be? A gift, to protect them
until he sees them again? She opens it. There is nothing inside
but some traces of black powder, and anyway, he is turning
away, dismissing her. She pushes her way out of the tent into
the sunlight, dizzy with triumph. She can feel Frederick and
Kleist watching her as she goes, thrusting her bag of money and
the little golden box down into the pocket that hangs from the
belt inside her skirts, and burying them deep in the folds of the
wool. The day is dazzling, and she shields her eyes for a second, disorientated and reeling with the possibilities of food, of
warmth, of safety, that spin before her now. The gamble is not
quite won, of course. Not quite. But almost. She looks around
at the spring day in full swing, at the people passing by on their
way here and there, at the children who play sticky tag on the
edge of the common, who scream and yell and scuffle, who
don't know that everything has changed forever.

To her surprise, the greasy man from the crowd is loitering,
hands in pockets, a wary distance from the tent's entrance.
When he spots her, he hurries across the grass, his face wide
with relief.

"By God, girl, you had me worried there."

"Oh—thank you for staying."

"I was sweating it, I don't mind saying."

"I'm all right, I really am."

"If you have any bother on the way home, you give my name.
John Burr. I can't do much now, but I'll do what I can."

"I won't, I'm sure."

He pulls out a ratty piece of fabric from his sleeve and mops at
his head, and she wonders what it would be like to have a father,

or a husband, like that, who waited and worried and sweated for you, so much that he had to mop his brow, not because you were useful, but only from care. From kindness. Hal would have done it, she thinks, and feels a brief pang of something.

"They didn't give you hell, did they?" he asks, tucking the handkerchief back into one grubby cuff with some difficulty.

"No, no. No. It was—it was only a telling-off, you know."

He shakes his head. "You want to watch it, love. They don't muck about with that sort of thing. Too many threats on the old Kraut's life. I wouldn't be a king, me. Being shot at. Loonies shouting at you. Not you, I mean," he adds hastily.

"I know," she says, smiling.

"Good. Now get home to your husband and stay out of trouble."

She laughs and waves, and he raises his own hand in response, then moves off, shaking his head. Meg turns away across the grass toward the street, her heart beating a riotous tattoo of freedom and relief, keeping her hand tight on the warm, solid weight of the gold in her pocket.

She spends the night at the Swan with Two Necks, and as she walks past the coaches snaking their way round the corner, past the drivers bickering and swearing and spitting in the gutter, it feels like coming home. On her way through the streets, she was seized with a mad desire to buy everything she saw, cakes and shawls and salve for her hands, to have her boots mended, to neck the foamy bitterness of a pint of ale, to buy oysters from a street seller and let their salty coolness slip down her throat. But she must be careful. She can survive now until the baby is born, but the rest is still uncertain.

She bought only one thing, from a man with no legs who sat in front of a collection of carved items spread out on a grubby

294

cloth. A small hairbrush with a smooth wooden handle. Then she slipped into the dank gap between two buildings and pulled it through her matted hair, over and over again.

In the loft bedroom of the Swan, the straw mattress feels like feathers, and the blanket like silk. She takes out the tiny gold box and runs her finger over the *F*, over the delicate red birds and green flowers along its edges. It is so beautiful it makes her feel strange inside. She wonders how much she can sell it for.

Before she falls asleep, one hand clenched around the money folded snugly into her body, she thinks to herself that it is almost worth the suffering. To understand the pleasure of something that, before you lost it, didn't seem very much at all.

She wakes early. The sky is still cracking open. She picks her way through the sleeping bodies and out into the morning air. Cripplegate stands like a guardian to the city, and as she passes through it, Meg touches the rough stone wall for luck.

She makes her way to Mayfair by a long-winded process of asking passersby, working through the maze of the city from road to road, taking directions from anyone who will give them. At least twice she finds herself going in a circle, sent on a wild-goose chase by a prankster or an overconfident shopkeeper, but slowly she edges closer and closer and the roads grow wider. She walks the length of Bond Street, her pattens clattering on the stones, past the waiting hackney carriages, the jewelers and tailors and hatters and music shops. There it is again, that something thrilling through her, that energy, like the pull of the Harwich sea but less melancholy.

She buys herself an apple from a seller on the corner, weighing it in her hand, examining it for bruises, ignoring the gnawing hunger building in her stomach, and sits and eats it on the steps of the church, savoring the sweetness. Still not safe. Still not sure. Her ankles are swollen now when she walks anywhere. She looks at them peeking out from under her skirts as she chomps on the flesh of the apple. Two bloated fish. It's getting close, her time. A few more weeks, maybe. Yesterday's money will have to see her through to that, so she can have a room for the birth, and perhaps a woman, and then—but if Frederick gives her nothing, she suddenly realizes, if he has nothing to give, there isn't any hope at all. There is only Harwich.

When the church bells strike half past one, she crosses Oxford Street and finds herself in a mass of opulent houses laid out in grids, some half-built, some finished and lying empty and vast under the heat of the London sky. There are gardens at every turn, but freshly planted, so everything feels underdeveloped and fragile. Wet piles of earth around the base of box hedges. The evenly spaced stubs of nascent rosebushes formal in their neat little rows.

"Excuse me," she calls to a gardener bending over a line of anemic lavender bushes. "I'm looking for Grosvenor Square."

He wipes soil from his hands on the leather of his waistcoat and straightens up. "Well, I'll tell you one thing, it ain't Grozz-vennor." He points. "Left then right. You can't miss it. Huge great square. Grove-nor. Don't want to look like an idiot, do you?"

"No," she says. "I don't. Grove-nor. Thank you."

"It's only half-finished, mind. Best be quick in these parts or they'll build on you where you're standing. Lie down for a rest in a field and wake up in somebody's drawing room."

She laughs and makes her way down the street until she reaches a broad square, wider than any she has ever seen. It is empty in the middle, a desert of paving stones, and one or two people crossing it. A man on foot, a letter in his hand. A servant walking a handful of small cream dogs.

Funny how rich people always buy space, she thinks. More air, more room between them. Is that what she would choose?

She finds it frightening, in a way, this man-made quiet. Not the broad, sweeping space of nature, but something artificial.

There are no instructions about which door to go to, about what to say, about who to ask for, beyond the one word: Beaufort. She looks again at the scrap of paper in her hand, at the *B* and the *F* and the *T* spreading forth across the page as if announcing the great significance of their formation, and tucks it back in her pocket. Beoo-fort? Be-ow-fort? As the gardener said, she does not want to look like an idiot. She makes her way up the white steps to the pillars which stand on either side of a gleaming black door and knocks. When the door is opened by an immaculate, impassive footman, she presents him silently with the piece of paper. With a nod she is ushered in, through the hall, which stinks of fresh paint and newly finished woodwork, and into a room walled with books. It is a man's room. All dark varnish and knowledge.

Frederick stands, restless, at the window, and near him, in a high-backed chair, there is another man who sits, one leg resting on the other, drumming his white, ringed fingers on the leather. He is the same age as Frederick, she thinks, perhaps twenty-one, dripping in ribbons and velvets and silks and jewels. He makes Frederick look like a footman.

"Meg," Frederick says quickly, and gestures to a chair opposite the stranger. "Sit, please. It will not do to keep you standing."

Courteous, always. Gingerly, she crosses the room and perches on the edge of the cushion, which squeaks beneath her shifting weight like a complaining animal. She feels mucky, sweaty, in the stiff new finish of the room. She grips the tiny gold box in her pocket, rubbing its fine etched lines as if they will bring her luck.

"This is Henry," Frederick says. It feels odd to Meg that someone so utterly refined, so lofty, should have such a simple name. Henry. Hal. "He is the Duke of Beaufort. He is—a good friend of mine."

Meg looks at the white-fingered man. His eyes are soft almonds. Bow-fort. Friend or foe? she thinks.

"I am—I am in a difficult position," Frederick continues, pacing. "My father will not let me sire a child."

"That's a pity," Meg says, in spite of herself, and the Duke of Beaufort gives an explosive, surprised sort of laugh.

"You are never—what is the word—humble, Meg," says Frederick, turning away to the window as if exasperated. "You must be more humble."

Meg bites her lip. To survive this, to get what she wants, she must be a thief, a cleaner, a navigator, a fighter, a cook, a whore; she must be a sufferer of blisters and loneliness and pain, she must be a hard worker, she must be tough and determined and unbreakable, she must not be an idiot, and now she must be humble.

"I'm sorry," she says.

Frederick runs his fingers over a collection of rocks that sit on a low table, pinks and purples and greens, a fantastical landscape in miniature. The Duke breaks the silence, his voice soft. "She doesn't have to be anything, Fred, except discreet."

"All right." Frederick turns. "I wish to do my duty by you, Meg, as you know, but I am not in a position to offer a—my father will not let me, for now, acknowledge or—or give money to—an illegitimate child."

Her heart begins to race.

"He considers me too newly arrived, too unknown by the English people to begin my time here with a scandal. And as I am unmarried, the acknowledgment might—what word does he use, Henry?"

"Impact."

"Ah yes, impact."

I'll impact you in a minute, she thinks, if you don't get to the point. She is sweating, fine beads on her lip.

"He fears it will impact the Crown. It is not considered— possible."

She is frightened now. The baby pushes inside her, squashed in his cocoon, landing small, hard blows on her guts. She waits, for both of them.

"I do not control my money. It is all my father. I have made some—debts—here in London, and he does not approve."

God, she thinks, I don't care.

"Henry is not married. People will not talk. These things happen. It is not of significance. He has offered to take— responsibility for you and for the child."

The two men watch her carefully. Her eyes flick to Henry and lock on his. This new father for her baby, who until ten minutes ago she had never met. Does it matter? Should it? She is unsure if she is somehow being duped.

"Why?"

"Because he is my friend," says Frederick.

"Because I wish to help," says Henry, calm. "It is something I care about, the protection of mothers. And naturally I care for Frederick too. I simply wish to help."

"Henry," Frederick says, "is a—*ein Philanthrop*." He shakes his head, frustrated by himself.

"A philanthropist," Henry says.

"A philanthropist."

She nods, still looking between them. This was not what she expected. She is disorientated. Why will no one speak about money? she wonders. Money is everything, it is crucial, it is life or death. It is why she is here. And then without even realizing what she is saying, the words slip out. "And the money?" she asks, because she cannot bear to wait another second in uncertainty, and because she is beyond pretending.

"Henry will provide two hundred pounds a year, which will be settled upon the child until its death."

Her hands start to shake. She wants to jump from her seat, to pace the room, to run out into the street. Two hundred pounds a year? She has been surviving on two. Two hundred pounds will bring private rooms. A servant. Clothes, food, her own fireplace. Medicines. Safety. She will not need anything. She will not have to scrub dishes until her fingers crack and bleed. They will not be hungry. They will not be beaten. She can feel her pulse in her neck, throbbing rapid and wild. Tears spring into her eyes, and she blinks them back down. Get control, Meg. Get control. It will seem like greed.

Frederick is still talking. "When I come into my own titles, I will repay him. But nothing must be spoken of. If it becomes known, if it is even whispered about, I will cease the arrangement immediately. Do you understand?"

Meg nods. "Yes," she says in a whisper, to reinforce that she does understand, she understands perfectly. "Thank you." She looks at this man, Henry, who has come, from nowhere, to save them, as surely as if he had pulled her from the edge of a bridge, or bled her with his own hands. And then she says, "But," and they both look up, surprised. "But how can I trust you?"

The Duke of Beaufort looks at her with his soft eyes. "How can you not?"

She buys herself a wedding ring from a pawnbroker, a sliver of thin gold, and slips it on her finger. She stops and has her boots mended by a boot man at his stall, his nimble fingers working the leather, bringing it back together, strengthening it again. She goes to a shop with a glass front and buys herself a new spring cloak with a ribbon around the hood, just one strip of triumphant color threaded through its dark folds. She eats a meal of pie and beer and soft bread with a pat of butter, and lets the heat and creamy richness slide down her throat. She buys a traveling bag, puts the rest of her things in it, and throws her old pack into the river.

She goes to a boardinghouse in Chelsea.

"I am a widow," she says, "on my way to my mother's house to find respite, and must stay in London for some days first."

The woman's eyes slide up and down her body. They take in the fine yellow ribbon that snakes along the cloak, the wedding band, the traveling bag with its newly waxed sheen.

"Very well, Mrs.—?"

"Burr," Meg replies. "Mrs. Burr." And the woman stands back to allow her to pass into the softly scented hallway.

She is shown up to a small room with a bed in it, and a low window looking out over the cobbles. Outside she can hear the street sellers, and she thinks about how she can step out and buy anything they offer, and sit in the April sunshine, and savor it. The woman closes the door behind her, and Meg is alone in the stillness. There is a small looking glass in the room, only the size of her hand, hanging by a chain on the wall. She can't remember the last time she saw her reflection. She positions herself in front of it, and her eyes jump back at her, sudden and startling. It's like seeing a stranger. Hello then, she thinks. You again.

She puts her bag down, lets her new cloak slide to the floor, and climbs up onto the bed. She lies there on the smooth sheets with her eyes closed, and feels that the world is still spinning and squalling and rioting around her, but that she, finally, is not part of the storm.

PEGGY

Empty

When I wake on the morning after the wedding, for the first time I can recall, I do not know where Molly is, or what she is doing. When someone gives an opinion, and asks for mine, I cannot first look across at her to see what hers is, to see what we think, whether we find it amusing or odd. Instead, I falter and realize that I don't know. I don't know what I think. The scaffold is removed, and the walls won't hold.

For weeks I don't see her. I attend balls, because my father, for once, wishes it, and I stand rigidly by the wall and make rigid conversation, while my eyes are fixed on every opening of the door, every couple emerging from the dark night outside.

My mother invites the daughter of a friend to spend the after-noon with me, a thin girl with a scattering of smallpox scars, and we talk politely, stiffly, about balls and hats and other people, and when she leaves it's getting dark and she says, "Oh, you must come to the dance next week," and I say, "Yes, I must," and off she goes. And I sit in the drawing room and watch the fire dying out and think about him, and her, and them. I think about where they live, and what they eat, and how they talk to each other when the candles burn out. I think about whether he knows to put his hand on her forehead when she wakes, sweating, to soothe her cloying screams. I think about whether he is kind.

My parents try to cajole me to visit Molly, to go with my mother, to make the best of things.

"It breaks my heart to see these divisions between you," my mother says as I sit stiffly at the pianoforte, bashing out a waltz, my fingers sticking on the keys. "You only have each other, Peggy. You will only have each other when your father and I have gone."

"Not at all," I reply, turning the sheet music without looking up. "Molly will have Mr. Fischer, and a dozen oboe-playing infants."

"You know quite well what I mean," my mother says, but nothing will draw me.

The missing is like a physical ache. Half of me torn out, like a tree split by a storm. I think about his hands on her. What was I doing at that moment? Sitting, a devoted lamb, watching listlessly for his carriage through the window, guarding his empty words like my own little girlish secrets.

When I think about it, I do not burn with rage. This anger will not exhaust itself in a flash and be gone. It is a hardening, a constriction, that grips the center of me. It is something cold, a punishing, unsatisfied, internalized fury, fueled by sadness.

I realize that I live with it now, lying beneath everything I do and think. I wake in the night with a shout, something grabbing at my chest. It will not pass. It is cankerous, and feeds on itself.

And I think about the absences, the engagements, the trips to Germany, and I wonder, was he there? Or was he pulling Molly to him, in some shabby room, or some other entranced girl, hungry for something to make her feel alive. It is not fury with his lust. It is not the humiliation, as I had thought at first. It is fury with what he has debased. Trust. Faith. Honesty. It is fury that he has wasted those things in me, and that I have let him.

A school friend of mine once told me, in the dark one night, that you should never let your head fully empty of thoughts, or the devil will enter your mind. I thought about the devil, then, waiting there in a constant vigil, poised to wriggle up into my mind and wreak havoc. About Mrs. Hindrell in the kitchen all those years ago. *A demon got inside.* And now, I think, my anger is like a devil, waiting, waiting, in the space below, for the first moment my thoughts still to push his misery into my head.

I wonder if I will be angry forever.

Weeks pass. Clients come, are painted, and leave. I walk, and visit girls I don't want to talk to for tea, and sew things badly, ruining embroidery with blood spots and botched stitches. I hear a rumor that no one wants me to hear: that Molly, at a ball, claimed loudly, shrilly, that she had been made a duchess, that the Prince of Wales was in love with her, growing wilder and wilder until pulled from the hall by her husband.

I do not tell my mother. She will be beside herself. She has buried the lost truth in layers of finery, embellished it with bows and lace, but in spite of it, her whispered stories push through ours like tangled weeds. I hear my father's voice. *Secrets are a poison.* A letter comes addressed to my mother, marked with a crest, and she takes it away to open it in private, her mouth tight.

Too much alcohol, the onlookers say. Poor Mrs. Fischer. Not uncommon.

I feel a pull, the elastic that binds me to Molly made taut, but I resist.

A week later, she is rescued from the water at the Pleasure Gardens. A boating accident, they say, when Mrs. Fischer seemed to stand in her boat, then fall. She must have tripped, for when one is with child, one can suffer from clumsiness. My mother comes and goes, her face pinched, and I hear her lament through closed doors about the poverty of it all, about Fischer's absences in Germany, about the lack of servants, the blank look in Molly's eyes. About the letter she received, and its warning. I turn my head away.

And then one day I am sitting in the drawing room, a book unread on my lap. The house is empty. Only my mother's little dog asleep on his silk cushion, snoring weakly. A knock at the door. A message, the handwriting sprawled, off kilter, but unmistakable.

Just two words.

Please come.

And then a line of address written beneath.

I stand, unsteady, and the book falls with a slap to the floor. The dog starts awake and resettles himself with a disheartened sigh. The carriage isn't there. Mother has taken it out somewhere, on some pointless errand, and there is nothing to do but run. I run. I run like I haven't run since I was a little girl in a muddy Suffolk lane, heels kicking up against my dress, stepping in puddles that soak my blue silk shoes, *blue for continued affections, blue for loyalty*, following the elastic pull that brings me back, always back and back, until I round the corner and see the narrow street where Fischer's apartment is. I am let in by a ruddy-faced boy, and nearly shake him until he tells me where Mrs. Fischer can be found, and I bolt up the stairs, and burst into the shabby room, and there is Molly, covered in blood, dripping, sodden like a butchered pig.

She is pacing, back and forth, and I go to her, trying to scoop her up in my arms before she collapses, shushing her and bringing her head close into my chest as if I can mend her if she will only get close enough. "It's the baby," she is crying, "it's the baby."

"I know. I know," I say, and I see that the blood is trickling onto the floor from under her dress. "You need a doctor, Moll," I say, and she bends double in a sudden scream of pain.

"You need a doctor."

"I can't afford one."

"My God, Molly, let me send out."

"We haven't got any money." Her voice is weak. "Johann hasn't . . ."

I look around, desperately, at the peeling wallpaper, the windows with their film of grime. I cannot believe what I am hearing. Surely there must be money enough for a doctor.

"For God's sake, Father will pay—let me just go and call down—"

"No, no, don't leave me." She grips my arm.

"Molly—"

"Please, please don't leave me." Her eyes are so frightened, and I fear she will have a collapse, that her mind will go, and I do not know what I will do then.

"Where is Fischer?"

She doesn't respond. I shake her, only slightly.

"Molly! Where is your husband?"

"He is gone out."

I drop my cloak to the floor and try to guide her, gently, to the bed, but she cries out again and bends low over the back of a chair.

"Let me at least go and send for Mother."

"No—please—no," she says. "Don't leave me."

"Here, sit for a moment."

"I can't. I can't. Oh God, Peg, I don't want to lose the baby, I want the baby, I want it."

I can feel her fear coursing through my own veins, as I could when we were small and she hurt herself and I had to cover my ears so I couldn't feel her hurting.

"There's so much blood," she says.

"Shh," I say, "shhh, now," and carefully I get her to place her arms around my shoulders, a little at a time, and we shuffle bit by bit to the bed.

"I want the baby, Peggy, I want to be a mother, I want to be its mother," she is saying.

"There, now," I say, "gently, now," and together we sit.

"It hurts," she says.

"I know."

"It hurts so much."

"You're the bravest of us, you know. It was always me howling and you quiet and good. Just be brave now, Moll."

"I don't know if I can."

I look down at the mess of skirts, at the bulge of her belly.

"I'm going to try to see what is happening. All right, Moll?"

"Yes."

I give her hand a quick squeeze, and then I lift her skirts, pushing fold after fold aside, thick with blood, until I can look. I don't know what I will do next, but I know that I will have to look. And suddenly there it is, sliding out so easily onto the sopping crimson sheet, a mess of clots and flesh. A little aborted half human, wrapped in its bluish sac. Unformed, translucent. Pity sinks in my stomach. For a moment we are there, the three of us, suspended in time, a little trio sequestered, private, impenetrable.

I find a sheet, and wrap it, and try to take it away so she will not have to see it, this futile attempt at life, but she clings to me and holds the bundle in her arms, and howls with grief while I sit, arms around her shoulders, cheek resting on top of her head, until it gets dark. I remember how when I was little, I thought

307

that babies were willed into being. That God decided on each one, on Molly and me, and made us grow. I wonder if He has decided this. To will something in and out of life so fleetingly, so that it has no chance at all.

Later, washed and clean, Molly falls asleep. I look around at the shabby apartment. At the flaking paint. If this had been mine, would I have been happy? Do I envy her? And despite what I know of his exposed cowardice, despite the callousness of his brutality, I know that it would be a lie if I did not say yes.

When she wakes, it is so late that the noise of the street has fallen silent. My body is stiff from sitting upright. Her eyes flicker open.

"Hello," I say.

"Hello."

"Mother is on her way."

"Thank you."

There is a silence, as we sit together in the blackness.

"Thank you for coming," she says.

"Don't say that. Of course I came. I will always come, Molly. Always."

"I know."

I find half a tallow candle in a drawer and light it so that it sends shadows flickering across the room, and makes everything around us giant. And then I sit and take her hand.

"How are you feeling?"

"Empty."

The word is so small, and the feeling of it so big, that I don't know what to say. I want to press her hand to my cheek, to kiss it, and rub it, and soothe her, but the easy physical intimacy of before is gone, so I only say, "I'm so sorry it happened."

"I wanted it." Her voice is small.

"I know."

A carriage passes in the street, the horses rattling over the cobbles, and I wonder if it is our mother come at last, but on it goes past into the night without stopping. As I look toward the window, I see the two oboes that stand on the desk, surrounded by their little piles of yellowish reeds, and around them the mess of shavings on the floor.

"Are you happy, Molly?" I say.

I don't know why I ask it. The words slip out in spite of me. She turns her head toward me.

"Am I happy?"

"Here, with—being married."

And beneath my arms I feel her stiffen, just the very slightest movement, a warning, as she says, "Yes, very." Just that. "Yes, very." And then she says she will be all right now until Mother comes, and I pick up my belongings, left scattered in the crisis, my gloves still on the floor by the bed, and I go to kiss her. But there it is, the barrier, placed gently, impermeably, again between us, and I put on my hat and let myself out into the street and begin to walk home, the ghostly imprint of her blood across my dress.

MEG

She is going out of her mind with pain. She is going out of her mind so that she is only body, only rocking, swearing, gripping body, all thoughts wiped out by its force. It is a violence. It will tear her limb from limb. She is face down on the rug, biting on a piece of twisted cloth, and when the midwife tries to bring her to the bed, she lashes out blindly. It is as though if anyone takes her from the floor, she will lose the last shred of control, of whatever it is that keeps her intact.

Time has dissolved. There is the pain, and then there are the moments between the pain. When those moments come, she is back in the room, the thick drapes drawn and the shutters closed and barred. The fire crackling in the May heat. She can wipe sweat from her face; she can think about her mother dying, like this. About little Kate, her body bloody, mangled, dying this vicious death, from this vicious pain, but before the image is even formed in her head, it has got her again, bending her double with a cry that comes from the pit of her stomach, and the world goes black.

It has been hours, nearly two days. The midwife, and the young, nervous girl she has brought with her to assist, pace and fold sheets and remove old water for fresh, and then sit, with pale, drawn faces, waiting for something to change.

At dawn, it does.

"I'm going to die," she says. "I'm going to die." Her breath comes in short pants, sweat seeping through her nightdress, her legs pulled up around her chest. She is so tired now. The midwife stands, suddenly alert, and comes to the foot of the bed.

It has been inevitable from the start—Meg's death. She knows that. She has felt it, almost her whole life, without knowing why. She is saying it now as a warning, because she can feel it coming soon, so that the midwife knows what to do, so that the plans she has made will be put into action. She has found a family who take in orphan babies as long as you can pay their way. In the city, in one of the better areas, a sensible woman and a placid man. It was the man she had watched. It is to be raised as a gentleman or woman, the baby, and its money kept apart. She has agreed that with Henry's lawyers, who wrote everything up so that it cannot be challenged. The child will be protected financially if she cannot protect it in any other way. It is the best she can do.

It is nearly noon, the summer sun arching across the sky, when something gives in a slithering, agonizing rush. Meg throws her head back and screams. This is it, she thinks, this is death, and she waits for it to take her, almost wishing it would hurry up, because she has been waiting for it for so long, for months, even years, imagining this moment coming, anticipating it. But in the sudden stillness she opens her eyes, and when she looks up and behind her, there is a baby, round, purplish gray, silent, dangling in the air. The midwife grabs it firmly by the legs as if it is a skinned chicken to be put in a pie, and Meg opens her mouth to cry out, no, no, you'll hurt him, but she cannot get the

311

sounds out, she is too confused, and instead of her voice a wail fills the room. It is a furious, indignant wail, a railing against life and this sudden immersion in its cold, uncomfortable troubles, and when the baby is put on her chest, bloodied and crusted with something like milk or perhaps wax, it opens its black eyes and looks straight at her.

"A girl," says the midwife, as if it is a casual matter. "A pretty little girl."

Meg looks at the furious, squashed face, the wet slick of black hair. She is disorientated, baffled. The baby doesn't feel like a different person. More like a part of her own body, her own soul, come away and wrapped in a blanket. When she cries her screeching cry, Meg feels a sickening tug in her own stomach. They are linked, she thinks, in the guts. For now, and perhaps forever. I'll call her Margaret, like me. Me, but not kicked in the dirt. Me, but a prince's daughter, not a thug's. I'll bring her up differently. I'll bring her up so she knows what she is.

She pulls the blanket up and over their bodies, a new one she has bought for the two of them, brown and red and rather ugly, but somehow comforting, and puts the baby to her breast. They are both alive. Meg savors the miracle. She doesn't look down at the blood-soaked rags, her bulging, flabby belly, the mess of her body. Things that keep death near, just over her shoulder. She looks at the baby, and only at the baby. Freshly grown, like a turnip just dug up, or a chick cracking its soggy, wobbly way into the air outside its egg.

There you are at last, she thinks, tracing a finger over the creased forehead. There you are. I gambled everything, and I won it for us. And you were supposed to ruin everything, but you saved me. And they don't sing about that in the ballads, do they, Margaret Burr? They don't sing about us.

PEGGY

Promises

One night, weeks later. We are woken first by a knocking, once, then twice, then nothing. I am fuzzy-headed, befuddled. It is pitch black. Another knock, insistent and sharp. I fumble in the darkness to light a candle. My room is at the front of the house. No one else has heard, I think. Why has the boy not woken? I wait until I am sure no one is coming and prize myself out into the icy air and down through the silent house. I pull back the bolts and open the front door. The sun is just beginning to rise, the very faintest tinge of pink at the sky's edge.

And there is Molly, half-dressed, standing in the light drizzle, confused, barefoot. Her gown is slipping at the shoulder, unfastened. She looks at me and I can see that she is not with us, that she is not here. I look down the road, empty in the half light,

313

and just catch a glimpse of the wheels of his carriage flinging mud up as it rounds the corner and vanishes.

"Molly."

She turns her vacant face to me. "I didn't. I don't."

I pull her toward me, and breathe in the scent of her damp hair, with its beads of rain settling lightly. I wrap my arms around her, gently, so gently, and then my mother is at my shoulder, and "Oh my God," she is saying, "Oh my God, Molly." And my father, tousled in his nightcap and socks, behind us in the hall, and he says, "What is it? What?" and sees her, so bedraggled, his Moll dumped on the road, and says, "Molly. Oh no, Molly."

"I . . ." Molly says, "I . . ."

"She is near frozen," says my mother.

"Bring her in," my father says. "Bring her in, and I shall have Fischer before the courts, my God. My God."

"Molly, Molly, my darling," my mother is saying. "Come here."

"Bring her off the road."

My mother's face is lined and worn in the dawn light. "My God, Thomas, look at her."

"Bring her in here, that's it."

We half carry her into the sitting room between us, and one by one the servants begin to join us. We bring blankets and shawls, and send for the doctor, and make hot tea with rum in it, and Fischer's name is cursed, and Molly says things that do not make sense. I am full of sisterly concern, of regret and kindness, of dismay at her treatment. I am altruism itself, holding her while she sobs, reassuring her when she is confused. I am unimpeachably kind, caring to a fault. And I try not to think about the thin streak of triumph that is rising through me, of ownership. Of vindication. She thought she did not need me, but she does. I do not like it about myself, not at all, and I push it away, and think only of Molly, but it is true. She has come home

314

to me, in the end, where she belongs. Back into my frame. She won't go out of it again.

I sit with her for an hour, and then I squeeze her cold hand and tuck it under the blanket, and leave her bundled, safe, shrouded in the shuttered room. I give instructions that she is not to be allowed to leave under any circumstances, and then I walk straight down the steps and call the carriage.

By the time I arrive, the sun has risen above the London fog. The ruddy-faced boy is terrified. "Mr. Fischer is packing," he says. "Mr. Fischer is not—" But I push past him, and up the stairs, to where Mr. Fischer stands openmouthed near his traveling bags, a dress shirt in his hand.

"Margaret! For God's sake!"

"Running away?"

He drops the shirt onto a nearby chair, the chair over which Molly had leaned, blood-soaked, as she stood, alone, losing their child.

"Not at all. I am not—I am not running away from anything. I have urgent business in Germany."

"Is that so?"

He puts up a hand as if to defend himself from me.

"I had no choice in this. I had no choice."

"You had every choice."

"She is insane."

"She is your *wife*." I almost hiss it. "You left her on the doorstep like a bag of unwanted goods."

He moves then, gathering more clothes from the wardrobe and beginning to fold them with unnecessary precision into the open bag. The same impenetrable calm that once so intoxicated me is now anathema. I want to scream at him, shake him, hit him out of it.

"The marriage is not legal," he says curtly.

"On what grounds?"

He pauses. "She is insane. You concealed her madness; you hid it between you."

I cannot believe he is saying these words. That I have so misjudged such a person as to consider marrying them. What can be trusted, if not my own self?

"She is a madwoman! I have no obligation; there is no child. It was a false engagement; it was on false pretenses."

"The false pretense of your seduction?"

He pushes past me to take something from a shelf behind, and I smell the fragrance I remember from his clothes. Fleetingly, I am transported to the cool darkness of my father's study, to his lips on mine.

"No one can prove such a thing!"

"Do you expect sympathy?"

"I expect nothing from you," he says tightly, "but to be left alone."

"Why couldn't you leave *us* alone?"

"I have been well and truly punished for failing to do so." He pulls the traveling bag shut smartly, and turns to face me with such bitterness that I cannot believe how our two versions of events can be so utterly different.

"*You* have been punished? *You* have been?"

He tries to move past me again, but I am not finished yet and block his way with my words. "It is not good enough!"

"I have done nothing wrong! I married her! I had never intended to marry at all! I took her home to raise the child, and I was happy to do so. I was tricked, and so the marriage ends, and any man would do the same. In the eyes of the law—"

"You had never intended to marry at all?"

"No, not seriously."

"But you—you asked me."

I hear doubt creep into my voice even as I say the words.

"I did not ask you, Margaret."

"You did, you—asked me to—to travel with you, to live with you."

He looks incredulous.

"That was not a proposal. Did you think that I was proposing marriage to you?"

"You did—you—you talked about where we would live. You gave me the palace."

He looks as if he cannot remember.

"It was a gift—a pretty little thing. I meant nothing by it of that kind. You are a grown woman; you must know the ways of the world. Do you think I would have been catching you in darkened cupboards if I had been looking for a wife?"

"But . . ."

His eyes are quizzical, the way they were when we first met each other, when he seemed so sure, so curious and clever, as if he could see things about me that I could not hope to.

"I had not even spoken to your father," he says gently. "You could not have thought . . ."

I see, then, that it has all been in my head. How easy it must have been. How much I wanted to be saved. He caught me, and I fell, like a shot bird.

"But my father," I say in a low voice. I feel like a child, the power weighted hopelessly away from me. "My father is your friend."

Fischer lets out a wry laugh.

"On that score, he is no different, and a damned sight worse than me." The colloquialism sounds strange in his accent, as if he has borrowed it. And then I realize, of course, that it is my father's. They have sat together, the two of them, and drunk toasts to their conquests. Fischer's hand pushing its way beneath my corset. My father's teeth on Ann Ford's breast. All of us hidden from view, in darkness, in secrecy. I have sought a man who reminds me of my father, and I have found exactly that.

317

"I cannot stand it," I say, the anger rising fast and hot. It is anger at both of them, at myself, at Molly, at everything and everyone. I throw my words out wildly, as if I can wound him to the death with words, because they are all I have. "I cannot stand it! You act as if it has no consequence, as if people have no—feelings! You break words away from their meanings, until nothing holds true at all."

"Not at all."

He takes a step toward me, as if he is going to explain myself to me in the way that only men do. "Love is not always marriage, Margaret. You are naive! It does not have to be eternal promises and fat babies in a basket."

It is not fair, I think, with a kind of despair. You may take what you want. My father takes what he wants, and he is successful. He keeps my mother, to dab at his forehead when he is unwell, and to exhaust herself at his bedside. To manage his children, his accounts, his household, his best shirts.

"The way you kissed me. The things you told me. The vows you made to Molly. All of it is come loose, and you do not seem to care at all about the damage you do. It is—immoral!"

And then I see that he is looking at me with something that is almost pity.

"People are not good, Margaret," he says quietly, as if he is teaching me something I have not already learned. "Promises are broken. People will take what they want. It is naivety to expect anything more."

"Why . . ." I say, and as I do, I feel tears somewhere behind the question, so long held. I hate him, and yet still I burn to hear the answer. "Why Molly? Why did you choose her?"

"Because she wanted me," he says simply. The room is so quiet I can hardly breathe. So quiet that I want to cry. "Both of you. You wanted so much to be loved."

I remember myself. A tinderbox of passion, waiting to be

ignited. I saw only what I wanted to see, like my father's subjects looking at their own portraits. Like my mother looking at Molly.

"But you didn't love us."

"I did. I do love you, Margaret, in my way. Still."

I look down at his fingers, the way they rest lightly on my glove. And then, slowly, carefully, as if I am extricating myself from something tangled, I say, "No. You have no idea of what love is. None at all. It is—it is giving your life to someone. Helping them. Putting your own desires to one side. Caring for them when no one else will. You have no idea of it."

"That is not love, Peggy." He looks at me, baffled. "That is self-sacrifice."

"The two are one and the same," I say, but my voice shakes.

I stare at him, and he at me, two animals from different species encountering each other for the first time.

"Do you think that is what Molly wants?" he asks. "Your life ruined on her behalf? As your great act of charity?"

"She does not know what she wants! She is not fit to decide what she wants."

"My God, Margaret, that is what you think? You speak of her as if she has no will of her own!"

"You have seen her! How can she have any?"

"It is no wonder that she said you stifle her!"

I try to unravel his blame from mine, but I cannot, caught in the echo of old betrayals. He takes a step toward me so we are close again.

"She only wanted a life, Peggy. Some pleasure. A chance at living. And God forgive me, but I will not ruin my own because it was not possible."

"God will not forgive you for it," I say.

"She will end up in the madhouse," he says. I can feel his breath hot on my cheek.

"I will keep her out."

319

"Then that will be all your life amounts to." He says it softly, as if the thought saddens him.

A beat passes. I steel myself. Against the way he sees me. Against his sadness. The way he tries to tell me my own story.

"I will tell you why I have come," I say. "To see your guilt. It drips off you. The terror in your eyes when I walked in, as plain as day. You are a coward. And the rest is just words."

And then I turn away from him, and walk down the steps past the flummoxed boy and climb back into the carriage and the horses jerk away, back toward Molly. I look out into the bright morning, and in spite of everything, my triumph rises like a bird through all my sorrow, the pounding of my heart its wings beating hard against the winter wind.

When I get home, I go up to Molly, and sit by her side. She is awake now, and knows where she is, which is half pinned to the bed by blankets in my mother's old vigorous style. The faded red-and-brown blanket lies on top of them all. She lies passively there, her face placid.

"Where did you go?"

"Out," I say. "I won't go out again now."

"To see him," she says.

"Yes."

"To take your terrible revenge?"

"Yes."

"Did you take a pair of scissors to his best coat? Did you skewer him with his oboe?"

"I should have liked to."

She looks at me. "The fault is not his, Peggy, not really."

"The fault is entirely his."

"No, I am going mad. It is more all the time, and I could not—I cannot trust myself. I cannot remember what I have done, what I have said, or even where I have gone. My mind is not what it should be. I don't know if it ever has been quite correct. Do you remember when we were little and I would forget? And you would pinch me."

"Of course," I say. "I have always protected you."

"I hated it," she says. "But now I think it is for the best."

"Get some rest, Molly," I say, placing my hand on her forehead.

"I wanted a life."

"You have a life. This is a life." I bring the sheet up tightly over her body and tuck it in where she has wriggled loose.

"Do you ever wonder why?" she asks. "Why it has happened to me?"

I don't answer.

"Papa says it was the fever after the ball. But you and I know it was not, don't we? It was something in me. Something in my blood. From the very beginning."

"There is nothing to be gained by asking it," I say. "You will tire yourself out. Now close your eyes, and be sensible."

She closes them, obedient, and I stroke the hair back from her forehead. "I will protect you now, as I did then," I say. "I promise it." I bend to kiss her, her face still and pale against the pillow. Then I leave her to sleep, locking the door on my way out.

We wait to see if there is to be another child, but thank God there isn't. Perhaps people talk of her mental fragility, of the marriage and its scandalous end, but if there are rumors, they don't reach us.

And so we begin our cloistered life. I become her shadow again, and she is mine, just as when we were little girls, together, always together, no intruders upon our intimacy, nothing between us, not a sliver; heads together on the pillow, tangled curls.

I hold it at bay, the advancing darkness, as I promised I would. I have kept my promise; I will keep my promise.

My father doesn't paint us again. Too painful? I wonder. Too difficult to face us, to frame us. Two daughters, one wasted, one mad. No promise now, no bloom. He loves us too much to cast his painter's eye on us, to dip his brush and see my hard face, my lined face, and Molly's absent one. Or, says a little voice I cannot unhear, it is because we will not sell.

He ages, and the sickness that has danced around him these last years, come and gone like a visiting ghost, settles again for the final time. I sit with him when I can, keeping the fire burning, keeping watch, while my mother and Molly sleep upstairs.

"Peg," he calls. "Captain, are you there?"

"Yes," I say, pulling myself from sleep. "I'm here. What is it?"

"Come closer. I can't find a way to lie. To be comfortable. Every which way is pain."

I move the poultice a little so that it covers the swollen mound of his neck, and he winces. "There," I say, standing, "keep it on your neck and I will go down and make you a fresh one."

"Don't go yet."

He takes my hand and holds it in his red, lined one, still callused, still a working hand.

"Is it beginning to swell again badly, do you think?"

"I don't think so," I say, but it is.

"It feels as if it is worsening."

"Keep the poultice on it. There." I place my hand on the soapy surface of the linen. He makes a guttural noise of pain.

"How I long to be on the coast at Norfolk. I long for the bluster of it. It is funny what illness does. I feel quite childish again, Captain, so childish that I could make a kite, or catch goldfinches, or build little ships and set them sailing."

"All the things we used to do in our Ipswich days,"
I say.

I want him to say, *Those were the best days, Peg, although perhaps
I did not realize it at the time.* Or, *I wish we had never left Ipswich,
but that we had stayed together, the four of us, living our unfashionable
country lives. I wish I had stayed with you more. I wish I had not let the
studio door always swing shut with you outside it.*

But instead he says, "I must see Reynolds."

"Reynolds?" For a moment I do not understand what he
means. And then I do. "The artist?"

"I cannot stop thinking of it. How much better I might have
been. How much more I might have done. There is so much I
want to talk to him about—to ask him about. Will you get him
a message, Peg?"

"I will write."

"Do you promise it?"

"I do."

He shifts on the bed, grunting with the effort.

"I could have done more. Worked harder." He looks at
me with yellowish eyes. "I have left you with nothing. Fit for
nothing."

"Don't be silly, Papa."

"I have not shaped you into any way of life that helps you."

"You must not worry," I say. "Mama has put away a little,
over the years, as you know, and if we sell some paintings, we
will manage well enough."

"Molly's mind. The waste of it."

"Papa."

"It is not what I wanted for you. None of it is what I wanted."

"I have Molly, and that is quite as I wanted it."

"Yes."

There is a long pause. We sit there together, the fire crackling
in the grate.

Then he says, "I wanted you to paint."

"I know," I say.

He is buried at Kew, in the shadow of the church. His grave is set near to his friend, as he asked. "Social to the last," my mother says, drawing her black veil down from her bonnet. As we each throw our handful of earth and hear it land with a dull thud, I think of his violin, his fingers skillful on the strings. I think of those fingers reaching lightly out and holding mine inside them.

We take a small house in Acton when our mother dies. It is set far away across the fields, away even from the church and its clutter of cottages, where there is nothing but birds, swooping low over the grain, and sometimes the small figures of the workers bent in toil. It is a stifling quiet. It muffles the sweats and confusion and the nighttime howls. Our chaos is absorbed, like sound.

We are quite respectable, two spinster ladies, past our best, the painter's daughters, yes, of Thomas Gainsborough, don't you know, very fashionable in Bath at one time. Dead now, of course, and one doesn't hear much about him. And the older one was married to a musician, one hears, but it all ended very badly.

One evening, in the final throes of the summer of 1816, I stand alone on the cobbles in front of the Ipswich house. I look up at the window where my mother banged her head on the shutter on the day we left. At the place where Barnstaple sat, fat and deserted, in the road, watching us judder away. I run my hand over my stomach.

"Are you all right there, ma'am?"

A man is at my shoulder, a rustic sort of man, his face red and coarse.

"I am, thank you," I say stiffly. I am not used to talking to strange men, not these days. He has the round Suffolk vowels of my childhood.

"Mr. Gainsborough, the painter, lived here once. Many years ago. The likeness man. Is that why you've come to see it?"

"Yes," I say. "That's why I've come to see it."

He squints up with me at the white glare of the house.

"A fine house, no question about it," he says. "There's a painting up at the vicarage, one of his. Two little girls with a butterfly. Very nice thing. You might knock and see it if you like."

Something rises in my throat.

"No, thank you. I must be getting back," I say.

"Very well, ma'am."

I nod to him, and turn and walk away from the white stone house, away from the little ghosts of Molly and me, still grasping for our cabbage white, still clasping each other's pearlescent hands somewhere in the gloom. Instead, I reach into my pocket and finger the key to the room where Molly is safely locked away, where no harm can come to her. I wrap my hand tightly around the key, feeling its coldness, its solidity, and then I climb up into the waiting carriage, and the horses lurch forward and carry me away toward Acton.

MEG

Her husband's ginger chin rises and falls, slack and flabby, like one of the dead pigs she used to haul into the cookhouse with their mouths flopping open. She has always marveled at the variety of snores Samuel is able to emit in one night, from thin reedy breaths to sudden snorts that seem to shudder through his whole body. Meg reaches out and jabs him with her foot, and he grunts and rolls over, pulling the cover with him. That's marriage. You know exactly what the other one is thinking, even in your sleep. Even without words. It's funny, she thinks, that you can love someone rather well, yet also compare them in your head to a dead pig. That's marriage too.

She married Samuel because Margaret was a girl. The money will pass with her to the man she eventually marries. Meg has always known that. It is Margaret's money, in her own name, until it isn't. She doesn't want her daughter to marry anyone at all, and there is no need for her to do so, but children are stupid. She was stupid herself.

So she had to protect herself somehow. She built a life for

Margaret, and then it was time to think about her own. Having known poverty in youth, she knew enough not to want to experience it in old age. And Sam was gentle, and hardworking, and could provide a life for them, and was willing to take her on with someone else's child in tow. And even a duke is still someone else, to a man, because men are like that. He is kind enough to her, Sam, in spite of it all. She would not have married him if she hadn't felt he would be kind.

"She's a lovely little thing," he had said, leaning over the cot. "Hello, Margaret. Hello, little one." He had placed a small blue rabbit next to her on the pillow then looked up at Meg. "I don't like to think of the two of you alone."

She had not said, *But we are never alone. We have each other.* Sometimes it was better to be quiet. They had married quickly, and nobody would know to look at them that they weren't a simple family of three—mother, father, and child. Nobody would know.

"Here," a man at a stall had said, a few months after their marriage, passing Margaret the little wooden toy they had bought. "Here, show your daddy." And Sam had put out his hand. "Show me, Margaret," he had said.

Yes, she had thought, her heart singing a quiet little song, yes, this was the right choice. And they have been happy enough, although the sadness of the children who have not come hangs about them, now, in the air. The house is full of ghosts, the ghosts of the babies who died before they could be born. Margaret too is a ghost, in a way, of the time before they met. Samuel cares for her, there is no question. But there has always been something not quite there. Or perhaps some resistance she cannot place, that has grown with each failed pregnancy of their own, each lost chance. He tolerates it when Margaret takes his arm and hugs it to her, gripping its warm weight to her chest. When she hangs near him, Papa, Papa. He stays for a moment, then is already turning away, with a job to do, or something to call him away, tugging his arm from her grip with a smile with only the faintest trace of stiffness in it. He can exist alongside her, he can live with her, and care for her, and eat with her, and watch her for a while when Meg is busy, but he cannot quite love her as his own. Not quite.

So Meg does two things. First, she teaches Margaret to count. She teaches her, as Hal had taught her all those years ago in the smoky Harwich kitchen, how to draw lines of income and expenditure, how to draw the sign for a pound, and how to make the sloping S for a shilling. She sits for painstaking hours showing her how to add and subtract figures so that they balance. So that if she marries a man who doesn't know how to manage it, she can do it herself. So that she knows her financial worth, and what it can buy her.

Margaret sits at the table, her round, brown head bowed low over the quill, her feet dangling.

"I don't know why you're bothering with this nonsense." Samuel, watching, wipes the ale from his lips with the back of his hand, sets his tankard down.

"She must manage her money, Sam. She will always have it."

"Her money will buy her the right not to think about it."

"No one has the right not to think about it."

He says nothing in reply. She has never told him how she fought, tooth and nail, for that money. How she would have killed herself for it. How could he understand?

The second thing she will do is call to her daughter. She will say, Margaret, come and sit with me, and I will tell you your story. I will tell you who you are, and who you're going to be. And Margaret will climb up onto the rocking chair with her, and curl her small warm body against her mother's, and Meg will whisper soft stories that no one else can hear.

"It is best forgotten," Samuel says at night, as she lies with her cold legs wrapped around his. "No good can come of her thinking herself better than she is. Keep her humble, for God's sake, Meg, and let the story end here."

But when Sam is busy, his attention elsewhere, she will lean down and whisper again. You are not an ordinary girl, she will say. You have royal blood in your veins, the blood of princes and the blood of dukes, and your children will carry it. And you will make something from it. Never forget it. Never let your children forget it. There is something in your blood that sets you apart.

And Margaret will listen carefully, small fingers gripping the little gold box with its ornate *F*, absorbing every word, her small, pale face pressed against her mother's chest.

PEGGY

Lost

Molly stands at the window in her blue silk, looking out. She always dresses in her old finery, although it is decades from the current fashion, as we both are, and somewhat faded and stained about the hem. She looks at me through the glass, and I raise a hand, reassuring, in the way I always do. And sometimes she raises hers, and sometimes she does not. Then I come in and open her door, and, once she has recovered herself and been cleaned, I make tea and soothe her. She always shakes when I come back to her. She does not like being locked away alone, although I make sure she has everything she needs.

"Moll," I say. "Molly. I need to talk to you."

She is bent low over her pebbles, which she likes to arrange in patterns on her table.

"Get away."

"Molly, it is important. I need to talk to you."

"Get away from my jewels."

"Molly." I place my hand gently, carefully, on her arm, over the thin silvery trails where she has scratched herself. "I have been to see the doctor in London."

"No, no, no," she says, "no, no, no. I do not want doctors."

"Not for you, Moll. For me."

"I don't want to talk to you." She picks up a pebble and moves it to a different place.

"You must listen," I say. "It's important."

"I would rather not." She stands up, petulant, and starts to pace the room. "I am due at Windsor, and must have everything ready."

"I am unwell, Molly," I say. It seems to halt her.

"What?"

I stand, and go to her, and put my hands on her shoulders. "I have a sort of sickness, a stomach sickness," I say. "A mass, they think."

"You told me you were better."

"I thought I was."

"Wrong again."

"Yes, wrong again. They think it might not be much longer, you see. Perhaps six months, perhaps less."

She begins to wail, a low, long sound.

"Moll," I say warningly. "Molly."

The wail builds. "You told me you were better," she says, turning this way and that, "you told me. You said you wouldn't leave me."

"I have made arrangements for you," I say. "You do not have to worry. I told you I would keep you safe, and I will."

"You promised me."

"It is a place where you will be cared for."

"It is a madhouse."

"It is not a madhouse, Molly—that is not the word at all."

"It is Bedlam from the pictures. It is Bedlam. I saw you looking at them, oh, I saw you."

"It is not—"

"Hiding behind the door, waiting to jump out, dirty—"

"Molly, it is not." I shake her hard, for it is the only way to stop her screaming out, but she twists from my grasp and begins to moan.

"You promised me."

"I have done everything I can. Molly, please."

In one swift movement, she turns the table over, sending the pebbles ricocheting across the floor. Then she falls to her knees and curls herself into a steel-blue ball at my skirts, moaning softly. "Don't leave me," she says. "Don't leave me," and I comfort her like a little girl, whispering into her ear that all will be well, that her cut will heal, that her cat will not die, that we will find her lost doll in the morning.

All will be well. It has been my life's work to make it well. And I have made arrangements that will keep it so, when I am in the ground. A small asylum in Chelsea, with good care. My mother did not teach me her skills with money, for she raised me not to need them. But I have found my own way, putting a little aside here and there. Selling the last of the paintings. Our mother's ring. The marbled green necklace. The little gold box with its *F* on the lid. I have kept the notes sewn into the mattress until the time came. They will be all I have to speak for me. For though I have prided myself on my protection, on the fierceness of my love, in the end it burns out like all the rest, and in spite of everything, my promises will not hold.

In December, when the fields all around the cottage are frozen over, they put Molly into the locked carriage. I have imagined it since I was a little girl, scared out of my wits, tying my big sister to me in the night so that they could not reach her.

332

I pull the covers over me, too weak to stand, and put my hands over my ears so I do not hear her calling. They have promised me. Only minimal restraint. But the sound is there, whether I imagine it or not, finding its way through my hands, pushing its way into my head. And as I lie there, breathing into the darkness, waiting for the house to fall into silence, I wonder if perhaps Fischer was right after all. To suggest that we can keep our promises, to suggest we can ever truly save each other by keeping each other close, is naivety, the naivety of a young girl in a gilt frame, in her best hat, a haughty look in her eye, thinking that she has the answer.

Epilogue

Sudbury, 1750

The room is low-ceilinged. Rustic. Not the sort of place he frequents much, now, but which feels, somehow, comforting.

He leans over the cot, casting a shadow over the tightly folded sheets. The room has that distinctive smell he remembers from visiting his own newborn children in the cloistered warmth of their mother's lying-in. Powder and new skin and something almost sweet, like wheat.

"I have brought you a present," he says to the baby. "Although it is a little too big still." He places the necklace of marbled green beads gently beside her. The baby turns her small, fat face from left to right and looks up at him. Her eyes are a dark blue, almost black in the dim light. Unusual, he thinks, for a baby. He likes children. He and his wife have eight, and he dotes on them and frets over them until even she has had enough of it. He feeds them soft sweetmeats from a silver bowl when they are ill. "You're worse than a woman," she always says, shaking her dainty head. "Worrying all the time. Fussing." They are pale, regal little things, the lot of them, all silks and satins and curls. As he had been. No wonder he worries.

This one is hardly the same, of course. He rarely sees the mother, visiting in secret once every few years when she was an infant, no more. Bringing a pincushion, a doll. But he has not forgotten Meg Grey. The way her face always seemed somehow transparent, as if one were reading the book of her thoughts. The dips and ridges of her body. Its bruises. The way she stood, determined, filthy, in the shade of the tent, prepared to bargain her way to freedom instead of simply marrying that boy from the inn as any other woman would have done. A refugee of sorts. Dislodged, like him. Their encounter in the inn has been buried under the weight of time, but still, here is proof of it, pushing its way into the future with all the forceful insistence of nature. Pink balled fists; a tiny pulse beating hard and quick on the soft head.

"A name?" he says, looking up at his daughter. There is an accent there, only the faintest hint of it, rubbed away by the years.

"Mary," she says. "But we shall call her Molly."

"Your mother was hoping for a Margaret, like the two of you, I should think."

"Perhaps next time."

He laughs. "Already thinking of a next time, and the baby not a week old?"

The mother laughs too, and nods her small round head.

"Ah, you are like your mother," he says. "Made of strong stuff." He leans down and kisses the baby lightly on the forehead. "May you be made of strong stuff too, little Molly. May you be often laughing." He straightens up, brushing the crease from his velvet jacket. "And the young Beaufort keeps up the payments, in spite of his father's death?"

"You would hear from my mother if he did not."

He laughs again. "I have no doubt of it. What is it that your young husband does?"

"He is a painter. Of likenesses."

"A painter? Then you are most certainly in need of the

money." He turns and looks at the two men who stand behind him near the door, and nods, then kisses the thin fabric of her house cap. "Goodbye, Margaret. It is good to see you well."

She nods, but as he bows his head to pass through the narrow doorway, she is already looking back at the baby. He is an interloper in her life, and that is natural. His own life is not here.

Back out in the night air, he is flanked by men who hide him from passing glances, but there is no one on the Sudbury street on this freezing February evening. He steps up into his unmarked carriage and is borne away into the dark. The clatter of the hooves fades into silence, and the road stands as it did an hour before, as if he was never there at all.

He will be dead by the time the next summer comes, this man, gasping between embroidered sheets behind palace walls, as Molly takes her first wobbly steps over the sun-warmed paving stones of the little house in Sudbury. Two lives that will not touch. But he has left something with her, her grandfather. It is something that began with a look in the room of an inn, or with the crush of bone under steel in a flat, gray land across the sea. It is something in the blood, something that has passed through the generations, surfacing when it chooses, then disappearing again, weaving its way undetected down the years. He has left it with all his children, all his grandchildren. He himself has inherited it, and will carry it silently inside him through the last year of his life to his grave.

The baby Molly wriggles in her cot, opening and closing her fingers, looking up at the shadows dancing on the sloping ceiling, kicking her legs against the stiff folds of her blanket. She lets out a cry, a sudden complaint that pierces the sleepiness of the room. Her mother, resting in a chair nearby, places a hand on her small, warm chest beneath the covers, and says softly, "Shh. Shh, Molly. There, stop it now. Crying won't help you at all, now, will it? No, no. Crying won't help you at all."

Notes

I have moved the year of the cricket match at Kew from 1731 to 1729 to enable Meg Grey to find Frederick again there before giving birth. I have also condensed the timeline of Molly and Fischer's romance. In reality, they married slightly later, in 1780, when Molly was thirty, and Peggy twenty-nine. The pictures of the girls with a cat and of Peggy fixing Molly's hair were probably painted in the very early days of the family's time in Bath, around 1760, rather than in Ipswich just beforehand. There is no evidence that Gainsborough had an affair with Ann Ford; I have drawn together the noted sexuality of Ann Ford's portrait and his reputation as a philanderer.

Ann and Thicknesse traveled Europe after their marriage, and were on their way to Italy in 1792 during the Reign of Terror in the French Revolution, when Thicknesse was taken ill and died at Boulogne. Ann was arrested and imprisoned as a foreigner. She was only released in 1794 when, after the execution of Robespierre, she was included in a general pardon for all prisoners who could earn their own living. Her profession stood her in good stead.

Very little is known about Meg Burr, the mother of Gainsborough's wife. All that is recorded is the birth of her daughter

337

Margaret, the illegitimate daughter of the Duke of Beaufort, in London. The idea that the Duke of Beaufort had taken paternal responsibility for the baby Margaret in order to help his newly arrived friend Frederick out of a tricky situation was tucked away in only one article in all the research material I found on Gainsborough's life. The evidence to support the theory was based on the possibility of Molly's illness as a case of hereditary porphyria, which travels recessively and resurfaces apparently at random. Frederick's eldest son, George, would inherit the throne as George III, the "mad" king. One much-speculated cause for this madness was porphyria. I was also intrigued by the Duke of Beaufort's interest in supporting unmarried mothers. In later life he became one of the founders and major beneficiaries of the Foundling Hospital in London.

There is one more curious detail: Margaret Gainsborough being overheard directly referring to herself as "the daughter of a prince." Susan Sloman suggests that this might simply be a byword for duke, but as we will never know, I found myself inspired to write Meg Burr's story as a what-if, which, like all stories, says more about the teller than the tale.

Thanks and Acknowledgments

My extraordinary, sharp, thoughtful editor, Francesca Main. Your lightness of touch and editorial brilliance have transformed the book. Thank you also to Carina Guiterman, my editor at Simon & Schuster US, who has been a voice of such support from the beginning.

Sue Armstrong, my agent at C&W. You are everything I hoped I'd find in an agent—a cheerleader, a calming influence, a hugely experienced pair of hands, and a lovely person to boot. Your faith in me and in my writing is like a warm glow that keeps me going when I'm in the middle of a writing day, or a particularly tricky bit, and it makes all the difference.

Thank you also to Andrianna Yeatts, my agent at CAA in New York, for taking the book on with such enthusiasm, and to Sophie Wilson, for a fantastic early edit. All at C&W, Phoenix Books, and Simon & Schuster US. Caroline Raphael, who said that the story should be a novel when I first approached her with it. Augusta Annesley, without whose kind words about my writing it probably wouldn't be. Jo Fletcher and Lisa Baker, for early advice on what to do next.

Thanks and Acknowledgments

The amount of research material to which I am indebted is too vast to list. I am particularly thankful to James Hamilton for his fantastically thorough and entertaining biography of Thomas Gainsborough, and to Susan Sloman for her excellent series of books on the Gainsborough paintings. Thanks also to Ian Mortimer for his *Time Traveller's Guide to Regency England* and Lucy Inglis for *Georgian London: Into the Streets*, both of which superlatively capture the drama of the era and were formative in helping me understand Meg's London.

To all at Mslexia, for the opportunities you create, the sense of community you engender, and the way you demystify and democratize the process of writing. Jo Unwin, Marianne Tatepo, and, of course, Hilary Mantel, whose generosity toward new writers was legendary. I still feel shaky when I think about the fact that she not only read the book but liked it.

Charlotte Mendelson, all at Curtis Brown Creative, and my wonderful group of fellow writers. I honestly don't think I would have had the confidence to finish the book without all of your constant camaraderie, humor, ideas, and encouragement. Particular thanks to Ally Zetterberg, Becky Alexander, Fabian Foley, Abi Graham, Jenni Lieberman, and Roisin O'Donnell for early full reads.

Rachel Widdowson, who told me so matter-of-factly that I should write a novel, Hannah Ruthven, Debbie Martin, Rosamond Martin, Cressida Johnson, Jade Townsend, Paul Melody, Noelle Woosley. It sometimes feels as though writing is a constant battle with the voice in your head that tells you that you have nothing worthwhile to say. You all consistently help me to silence that voice with your steadfastness and loyalty. I hope I do the same for you.

My family, in particular my mother, who put herself aside, as she so often does, to help me pay for the novel-writing course when I couldn't afford it.

Thanks and Acknowledgments

Thanks to Toddy, always ready for a research trip, umbrella in hand, for your unwavering belief in me through all the ups and downs in writing this book.

To Kit and Rose, who make me laugh every single day, and who are, in the end, the most important thing of all. And to Ernest the dog, who has been no help whatsoever.

About the Author

Emily Howes has worked as a storyteller, theater maker, performer, writer, and director in stage, television, and radio. Her short stories have been short-listed for the Bridport Prize, the Bath Short Story Award, and the New Scottish Writing Award, and she won the Mslexia Novel Award 2021. In addition to writing fiction, Emily has a master's in existential psycho-therapy and works as a psychotherapist in private practice. She lives in London with her children. *The Painter's Daughters* is her first novel.